BLOOD IN THE EYES

RIFET BAHTIJARAGIC

PublishAmerica
Baltimore

First printing

All characters in this book are fictitious, and any resemblance to real persons, living or dead, is coincidental.

PublishAmerica has allowed this work to remain exactly as the author intended, verbatim, without editorial input.

Edited by George PAYERLE.

Translated from the Bosnian by Dennis DEHLIC.

The picture on the Front Cover: Bosnian emigrant in Canada, Prof. Milivoje Bato Jeftic, pacifist and firm fighter for multiculturalism and nonkilling on Balkans and on entire our planet.

Softcover 9781462676194
PUBLISHED BY PUBLISHAMERICA, LLLP
www.publishamerica.com
Baltimore

Printed in the United States of America

To my grandchildren:
Una, Sandi, Adrian, Dylan and Denis,
And to all children of the human race,
Today and in the future,
With my wish that they and their parents
Are doing whatever they can do
To create societies on the basis of nonviolence
And nonkilling.

OTHER BOOKS
By
Rifet Bahtijaragic

Skice za cikluse (Sketches for Cycles), poetry, "Oslobodjenje", Sarajevo, former Yugoslavia, 1972

Urija (Barren), poetry, "Zapis", Belgrade, former Yugoslavia, 1982

Krv u ocima (Blood in the Eyes), novel, "Bosanska Rijec", Wuppertal, Germany, 1996

Bosanski bumerang (Bosnian Boomerang), novel, "Bosanska Rijec", Tuzla, Bosnia-Herzegovina, 2001

Oci u hladnom nebu / Eyes to the Cold Sky, poetry, bilingual edition, "Bosanska Rijec", Tuzla, Bosnia-Herzegovina, 2004

Tragovi (Footprints), poetry and prose, "Bosanska Rijec", Tuzla, Bosnia-Herzegovina, 2008

Footprints, poetry and prose, "Traford", Victoria, British Columbia, Canada, 2008

Chernovs' Toil and Peace, novel, "Publish America", Baltimore, MD, USA, 2010

U oluji vremena (In the Storm of Time), novel, "Bosanska Rijec", Tuzla, Bosnia-Herzegovina, 2010

I am impressed by the interconnectedness of main characters of this book, the two brothers of mixed culture, Yudja and Osman, and yet their complex disconnect that the Author beautifully depict. A nice story telling device of father narrating his past to his illegitimate son made invalid by the war and at the same time seeking reconciliation with him. The novel has some great lines on the futility of violence. A good anti-war and anti-killing novel.

Bill Bhaneja, Ottawa, Canada

CONTENTS

PREFACE...11

INTRODUCTION......................................15

CHAPTER I..21

CHAPTER II...29

CHAPTER III..40

CHAPTER IV..63

CHAPTER V..93

CHAPTER VI...127

CHAPTER VII..160

CHAPTER VIII...192

CHAPTER IX...204

CHAPTER X...218

CHAPTER XI..245

CHAPTER XII..273

ENDNOTES...289

PREFACE

The horrible aftermath of Yugoslavia's break-up some twenty years ago has still not been fully digested by the international community. The International Criminal Tribunal for the Former Yugoslavia continues its work in The Hague. The siege of Sarajevo began in April 1992 and was so monstrous an event that it has been compared to some of the worst atrocities of World War II. It is still difficult for outsiders to understand why the Serbs unleashed a hatred of other ethnic and religious groups in the Balkans, a hatred which surely must have been latent for very many years. How was it that they had so much blood in their eyes?

Very many people who followed the Balkan atrocities of the 1990s perhaps do not know is that there may have be a link to the outbreak of the second World War, and if not a link, then at least a similarity. When the German army entered Bosnia Herzegovina, thereby upsetting a *modus vivendi* of the Bosnians, Croats and Serbs, similar terrible events—much killing, rape, mutilation, and people displacement—occurred. Rifet Bahtijaragic's epic novel, *Blood in the Eyes*, casts light on the dreadful Balkan scene at that time.

The novel opens as the Serbs' ethnic cleansing is starting up in Bosnia in 1992. The main character, Yudja, a peace-loving elderly man, a Bosnian, is amongst those forced into a camp by the Serbs. He is separated from his wife and daughter. As a refugee, he eventually finds himself living alone in a tiny apartment in North Vancouver waiting for the day when he will be reunited with his immediate family. He spends his time carving figurines out of linden wood. It is not long, however, before his illegitimate son, Fehrat, the product of a secret love affair with a woman Yudja loved dearly but with whom he has never had contact, arrives at his doorstep. Fehrat, also a refugee, is missing a hand and a foot, both hacked off by a Serb during the latest Balkan conflict. Fehrat's terrible disfigurement was perpetrated by someone with whom he once attended the same school.

Fehrat moves in with his father. The old man and the young man do not know each other, but they begin to talk and to exchange stories of the atrocities they have witnessed and experienced. Yudja in particular begins to tell his life story to his son. This is how we learn what he went through at the outbreak of the Second World War. We learn of life in the village before the Germans marched in. He talks about his father and his mother and their lives, about the multi-ethnic nature of the village's goings-on. In much detail he describes his relationship with his brother, Osman, who is a human being quite different to Yudja. In contrast to Yudja, Osman also has blood in his eyes.

This is how the reader is introduced to Yudja's philosophy of nonkilling. It is also the reason why Bahtijaragic's novel is a major contribution to the literature which agitates for nonkilling societies and a nonkilling world. In the earliest pages of the novel, Bahtijaragic, through Yudja, summarizes an important tradition in Bosnian multi-ethnic harmony—*Whatever you are doing to other human beings, you are doing to yourself.*—which is one of the underpinnings of the philosophy of nonkilling. In contrast to this, it turns out to be Yudja's fate in life to have had to witness over half a century two appalling episodes of neighbours setting off to kill their neighbours. In his old age as he carves his figurines, it is this separation between his society's underpinning principle and the century's realities that his reflections turn to.

The novel has many powerful and unsettling descriptions of butchery and killing carried out for the sake of political objectives. Aghast at what he sees, Yudja struggles intellectually with the problem of the individual sensing that he is becoming a criminal in the battle against other criminals. Some of the most moving dialogues take place in the period after the Germans have entered the region of Bosnia when Yudja is on the move in the forests and has fallen in with freedom fighters who are setting themselves up as the Partisan movement. The dialogues are between Yudja and Emina, a beautiful competent young woman who is convinced that in their circumstances only killing can lead to political victory. At one stage Yudja exclaims, "You think you will succeed by defeating the butchers É Do you really think this will be the last of the butchery if you win? If you think there will be no more killing then you are blind!" Yudja foresees in the 1940s the events of the 1990s. Later on he muses, "Each army measures its men by the numbers they have killed."

The novel's denouement is deeply ironic. At the end the reader, that is, the English language reader, is left with a deep understanding of what the Balkan conflicts half a century apart did to ordinary people at the village level. Bosnian readers no doubt know this already. What both Bosnians and Canadians, and readers of any other nationality, will take away from this sweeping piece of fiction, however, is that all killing, including killing for political and religious purposes, is a terrible, terrible waste.

Adrian de Hoog
Author of **Natalia's Peace**

INTRODUCTION

"Blood in the Eyes" is a novel about the harsh fate of the Bosniaks, an indigenous nation in Bosnia & Herzegovina, who accepted Islam from past conquerors, and who, in this century, their fellow southern-Slav neighbors, Serb and Croat, have either claimed as their own or tried to banish and exterminate. The novel portrays the whirlwind relations in one ethnically and religiously mixed Bosnian family who at the end of the twentieth century are seeing the tragic events of the last war repeat themselves in their homeland and who are unable to free themselves of the ghosts which haunt them in their exile on the Pacific coast of Canada.

At the beginning of the war in the Bosnian town of Pset in 1992 we find the main protagonist, seventy-year-old Yudja, leading a hermit-like, misanthropic existence, spending his days carving figurines out of linden wood. To his shock and dismay, he learns that his well-armed Serb neighbours have been struck blind by nationalism and are terrorizing the town's relatively small number of Bosniaks, eventually banishing them out into the world. Among those banished are Yudja and his family. While his wife and daughter are placed in a women's refugee camp in Croatia, Yudja goes to Vancouver, Canada—as far from Bosnia as possible.

Now living in North Vancouver, in a bachelor's suite in a three storey apartment building overlooking the city harbour, Yudja is surprised by the arrival at his doorstep of his illegitimate son Fehrat, with whom he has had practically no prior contact. While imprisoned in a Serb concentration camp in Bosnia, Fehrat's captors had severed his left hand and lower leg as punishment for defeating the main guard in a karate fight. Thus crippled, he was released out into the world. The father and son get to know one another through the mediation of Yudja's wooden figurines, which at times show signs of having metaphysical powers.

Yudja is tormented by the realisation that he cannot correct the wrongs which he caused Fehrat by leaving him, since birth, to make his way through life without a father; but he decides that this is the last opportunity for him to pass down the family history to the only other male remaining in his family. Thus he begins his remembrances.

Yudja and his twin brother Osman were still children when their mother, Marija, died. The brothers, though as different as Cain and Abel, remain dependent on one another for a long time, so that in Yudja's memory the fine line between the two is often lost. Yudja grows up to be a man of slow action and great sensitivity while Osman evolves into an energetic proponent of political adventurism and radical change. Yudja first begins to discover mystical qualities in his brother in the days leading up to the second world war.

The eighteen-year-old twins are mobilised into the Yugoslav army as it tries to resist the onslaught of the German military machine. In the tragicomic scenes prior to and during their encounter with the enemy, Yudja discovers that his brother is a murderer but even in a situation where he witnesses the sentencing and execution of an innocent soldier he lacks the strength to confront Osman. The terror of the new Fascist regime against the Serb population definitively severs the brothers' ties: Yudja is repulsed and flees while Osman looks for a way to meet up with local insurgents hiding in the woods.

In Yudja's apartment in North Vancouver, during a pause between the old man's remembrances, Fehrat talks of how at the very beginning of the Bosnian war the Serbs in their town had butchered the entire family of one his relatives. The shocking revelation sends the trembling Yudja under his blanket whispering: "Why are events repeating themselves?...What damnation is this that reappears with such alarming regularity from the very depths of darkness?...How long must this butchery in Bosnia continue?"

Continuing with his story, the old man recounts how the new government in Pset accused Osman of having participated in the murder of one of their policemen. Sent to prison, Osman comes into contact with the communist agitator Vavan and in a surreal set of events kills the guards and frees all of the prisoners.

For their safety, the twins are secretly sent by their father to stay with their Serb mother's relatives up in the mountains. Yudja discovers first-hand the blood in the eyes of the Serb guerrillas who take their revenge for the terror of the new regime against ethnic Serbs by slaughtering the innocent Bosniak Muslim population in the Una River valley. While in the mountains the brothers take part in a search for a Serb woman who has gone mad after her husband is killed.

In his struggle to understand the logic behind the frequent genocides and expulsions which have plagued Bosnia's inhabitants, Yudja learns of the existence of a "mad magnetism", a crack in the earth's crust which spreads from the substrates underlying Denmark, across the Balkan triangle, ending in the deserts of Yemen, and which is claimed to be a key cause in the exacerbation of the destructive mentality in human beings.

During a journey across the mountains with Osman and some Serb relatives to buy salt, Yudja makes new discoveries about his brother and about the Serb mentality under extreme situations. The existence of such a dark side in him also is made painfully clear to him when he kills a Serb guerrilla in self-defence.

The torrent of the Serb uprising causes the occupational forces to withdraw from Pset, along with the town's Bosniak population. The Bosniaks fear the vengeance of the Serb guerrillas, who accuse them of collaboration with the enemy. Osman joins the guerrillas in the woods while Yudja, after the killing of the guerrilla in the forest, secretly returns home sick and falls into a long coma. It is in this comatose state that his father takes him and joins the refugee caravan which makes its way to town of Bihac. During his occasional moments of consciousness Yudja remembers grotesque scenes of the people's suffering.

In the well-fortified German stronghold of Bihac Yudja finds work at the military warehouse. There he meets the black marketeer and partisan sympathizer Omer, who introduces him to a young woman, Emina. Yudja falls in love with her as she takes advantage of her charms, flirting with him enough to get him to participate in a sabotage mission for the partisans. While she is using him, Yudja talks of his disgust with all forms of violence and manipulation of the masses.

Amidst these stories of the conflicts in their homeland, the crippled Fehrat inquires, to Yudja's surprise, about a nearby sports centre where the local karate club trains. Continuing with his story, Yudja talks of the tragedy of the women in wartime Bihac, who during each such bloody confrontation between men become the victims of rape and, often, the murderers of children conceived under such circumstances. Emina, Yudja and a co-worker of his from the warehouse, mine the railroad tracks in order to prevent the enemy from bringing in reinforcements during the partisans' attack on the town. In the scenes of the battle for Bihac, Yudja initially reacts with bravery, followed by fear, and ends with a renewed emergence of the beast within during a surprise encounter with partisan soldiers. He is reunited with his brother, who is accompanied by Emina, leading him to conclude that his satanic twin will forever meddle in his fate.

Concurrent to the culmination of the events in Yudja's remembrances a more complete story emerges concerning Fehrat and the deepest reason for his arrival to Canada and Vancouver. The head guard at the camp where Fehrat's limbs were severed was a distant Serb relative of his, Damjan, who soon after the closing of the camps emigrated to Canada. Fehrat learned of his whereabouts while in Germany.

Yudja ends his story with him joining the partisans towards the end of the war only to find among their ranks a large number of former Chetniks (Serb Fascists) who upon realising the imminent outcome of the war conveniently change sides. This discovery dilutes his faith in the future of a new unified Slav state in the Balkans.

Osman quickly advances on the social ladder in the early years following the war, but during Tito's rift with Stalin makes a mistake in declaring himself for closer ties with the Soviets. He is condemned and sent to the infamous "re-education camp" for political deviants on Goli Otok (Barren Island). There he comes across two former Chetniks who are now prison guards, kills them and is brutally tortured. He is saved by his uncle's artist daughter with whom he begins a secret love affair, out of which Damjan is born. Soon after his release from prison, Osman dies from the aftereffects of the harsh prison ordeal.

Not long after Osman's death, his father (and Yudja's) also passes away.

Fehrat goes to the sports centre and finds Damjan working there as a trainer. As he is looking on at his former camp tormentor, Damjan also notices him. In the ensuing unequal fight, both men die.

The police come for Yudja so that he may identify the dead man lacking a hand and leg. As he is looking at Fehrat's immobile body, Yudja notices that the young man has a number of birthmarks in identical spots as Osman had and again realizes that even long after death his brother continues to meddle in his life. He then discovers that the dead karate trainer is his nephew Damjan, and in his face also notices an unmistakable resemblance to Osman. Concluding that he has led his entire life in his brother's shadow, he becomes despondent and crawls into bed determined to wait for death to come and take him away.

Trapped in a state somewhere between life and death, Yudja is awakened by the arrival of a letter from his wife and daughter, who are now in America. He learns that his daughter is engaged to be married.

The news rejuvenates the old man, giving him the ephemeral hope of being reunited with his family and with life. He decides to immediately rejoin them, but even in the moment of decision, his body fails him.

CHAPTER I

Mig fighters of the Yugoslav Air Force thundered as they went supersonic, but through the opened window Yudja noted the exotic scent of the pear trees in bloom. They bloomed regularly each year in the middle of May but more often than not the late mountain frosts would rob them of their fruit.

"These jets are driving me mad," the-seventy-year-old Yudja complained to himself. "They fly too low and destroy everything running through my mind." His keen-edged knife slipped against the linden figure he had been carving. "And I lose control of my hands."

Placing knife and half-finished carving on the heavy wooden table, he walked over to close the window, but changed direction when a knock sounded on his workroom door. His daughter, Alma, stood before him, of sky-blue violets in her dark hair. An instant smile played across his face.

"Forgive me father for disturbing you. I've been waiting since morning to tell you but you haven't come out. I'm working the afternoon shift at the factory and I don't think that what I have to say can wait until I return from work," the young woman awkwardly began.

"The flowers in your hair make you seem even more secretive," her father said to help her along, "Come on in so can see who has the stronger fragrance—your violets or my pear trees."

She came in and sat next to the window. From her body language Yudja realised that it was something serious. The first thought that raced through his mind was that she had come to tell him that she was getting married, but her next words convinced him otherwise.

"Father, you haven't set foot outside this room for months now… Frightening things are happening. The Serbs in town have put on uniforms. They are flying some strange flags and watching us Bosniaks with…menace. More and more every day. It's not just me. Everyone is beginning to fear…for their safety." She spoke quietly, as though in confidence.

Yudja stared questioningly into her large green eyes, seeing only fear and alarm staring back at him. Lately, he had been hearing this alarm often in the voices of people passing by outside his window, along with increasing sounds of automatic gunfire coming from various parts of town. He knew well that every man could tire even of the greatest good and make mistakes in his search for change, but he failed to take his daughter's words quite seriously.

"We're so inter-mixed here in Pset, and everywhere else in Bosnia for that matter, that it's difficult to tell whose blood runs in whose veins," he commented, a touch of uncertainty in his voice. "So you say only the Serbs have put on uniforms?" he asked, his left eyebrow rising into a question mark.

"There are a few Bosniaks in this army also…but, in fact, it is not anymore a Yugoslav army. It's a Serb army."

Yudja looked out the window, toward the town's main street, which wound itself down the hill and deep into the barren mountain fields. He ran his hand over Alma's hair, trying to reassure her, not looking back into the room:

"Go to your factory. I don't believe that anything will come of this. Times have changed. People have changed a great deal, man has walked on the moon…What could happen in this sleepy, insignificant little town?…"

Alma left, while Yudja's attention returned to his carving knife and the block of wood.

The very next day at twilight, his daughter again knocked at the workroom door. This time she brought along his old friend and godfather to his daughter, Dane. At first, Yudja was both surprised and delighted to see him, but Dane's words quickly changed his mood.

"I can't do it any longer," Dane whispered to him. "I cannot follow orders from those who only the week before were the town's coachmen and bartenders…They want to take control of my Military Department, disarm all the Bosniaks, take away even their hunting rifles and fire all non-Serbs from the civil service…They expect me to turn my back on yesterday's friends and neighbours…This I cannot do, nor do I want to do it!" Dane's voice rose alarmingly, causing Yudja to get up and close the window.

"I don't understand, my friend…"

"What is there not to understand, foolish old man! Either you are blind, or you are pretending to be. But of course, you've been holed up in this house and haven't seen a thing…I'll make it brief, and you decide for yourself: The Serbs have decided to create a Greater Serbia upon the remains of Tito's Yugoslavia before the other nations get an opportunity to run off with pieces of it. They now have the kind of power that they have never had before…"

"So, what does this have to do with me?" Yudja inquired stupidly.

"The Bosniaks stand in the way of the Serbian nationalists' ambitions," Dane responded, his eyes moving away to examine horrible possibilities.

"What kind of an obstacle can the Bosniaks be?" Yudja was still amazed by the very idea of it all.

Dane then proceeded, with obvious pain, to explain to him what had been going on recently, not just in Pset but throughout Yugoslavia.

"New leaders have emerged and they do not talk of unity among the Southern Slav nations or any ties between them. Instead, they are stoking their fires with hatred toward everything that was once held in common. They are sowing fear into the minds of their people, fear of being threatened by one another and even exterminated."

Yudja suggested that perhaps Dane was exaggerating the normal appearance of nationalism in the transition from a one-party state to a multi-party democracy. Dane looked at him with sorrow. Lines appeared on his forehead and his voice struck like thunder, seemingly originating from somewhere far away:

"Just a short time ago, two Bosniaks were butchered in the lower part of town, and I mean butchered. Their throats were slit. I can tell you for a fact that the people who committed this savagery thoroughly enjoyed themselves while they did it. They smiled as the blood sprayed from the slit throats. Do you believe me? Afterwards, they murdered old Havaz and Mashukic's son-in-law in front of their doorsteps. They tied Gashin's son Elvedin to a military jeep and dragged him through town on his belly until all of his ribs were broken."

Yudja looked at Dane's face, not believing the words that were coming out of his thick lips. He realised that he had isolated himself for too long in this little room and that his friend had pictured a scenario for him which he couldn't have imagined in his wildest dreams.

"The Serbian Crisis Headquarters will, on account of one-time friendships and family ties, allow Bosniaks to leave and go out into the world, but before that I have to send the wealthiest and most influential ones to special camps, where all trace of them will disappear. Why, Yudja? Because of the insane wishes of madmen! I cannot do it..." Dane had reverted to whispering.

"If that's the way things are, then you will have to... You have no other choice, my friend..." Yudja whispered back, observing the twitching of the veins in Dane's neck. His old friend from Serb's nation had done well to alter Yudja's view of the new situation in Pset. The lindenwood carver's eyes were opened in fear to the violent storm rolling down from the mountain peaks onto the highlands where their town stood.

Dane turned toward the door. "Maybe," he said, little more than a growl. "But it's late now. I must go...

Yudja grabbed his friend, the commander of Pset's Military Department, by the arm and muttered intensely, as if all life depended on what he was saying. "Dane, brother...How come?...It looks like our rulers have become stupidly obstinate nationalists. It looks like they are blind and have forgotten the most important message of our tradition: *Whatever you are doing to other human beings, you are doing to yourself.*"

Afterward, events unfolded at a fast pace. The next day, as he was finishing the recalcitrant leg on the lindenwood figurine of a man-like character, he overheard a group of women in the street excitedly talking about something. As his attention focused upon the panic-stricken group, he learnt that his friend Dane had committed suicide that fateful night and had left a letter saying he refused to take part in the butchery of the Bosniaks.

Three months later, two and a half thousand Psetian Bosniaks, mostly Muslims, were rounded up in the natural park by the lake in the middle of their city, loaded onto flatbed trucks and transferred to the Komar Mountain plateau in Central Bosnia. In this refugee caravan were Yudja, his wife, Delveta, and their daughter. From the woods by the roads through which the caravan passed, Chetniks*, until yesterday their neighbours, would occasionally fire upon the defenceless human mass. Some Serb women and children stood by the side of the road and threw rocks at the passing ranks of their ethnically mixed relatives, friends and schoolmates, who were now becoming former countrymen. Twenty-seven Bosniaks were killed, and seventy-five wounded. The majority managed to reach the first mountain pass alive. There they were told to get off the trucks. Thirty kilometres of no-man's-land lay before them. The people formed a kilometre-long column and headed along the asphalt road toward the old town of Travnik, where the French General Consul had spent two terms during the reign of Napoleon.

In the column were many elderly people, children and the sick. The wounded who couldn't walk on their own were carried. Everyone dreaded the thought of being taken by one of the Chetnik patrols roaming the countryside. These were men—and women—wild with the passions of rebellion, totally unpredictable. Some had fired from a distance. Some, whom they regularly came across at forks in the road and in forest clearings, were no worse than surly and arrogant. As time passed, the asphalt became harder; the legs, the suitcases and plastic bags heavier; and the suffering of the wounded more painful.

Yudja walked upright, rebelling against his misfortune. His thoughts evaporated into the scorching heat of the sun, from where he expected some kind of explanation to come. Instead, shots rang out from the woods with alarming regularity, slicing into the hapless column. Men carried the mortally wounded until their arms grew numb and the whites of their own eyes took on a death-like gleam.

When the increasingly heavy and sluggish caravan of Bosnian refugees reached yet another mountain pass, below them appeared a deep canyon, dangerous cliffs leaning out over dark gorges. In the depths below, the string-like river was obscured by mist.

People began to stir in the group ahead of Yudja; a dull moaning sound was followed by a woman's shriek which reverberated down into the canyon. Everyone ran to the source of the shriek. Yudja, also, ran to see what had happened. Out of the group at the edge of the road ran a woman, staggering down the slope toward the canyon gorge, hands wrapped around her stomach. After she plunged deeper down the slope, two women ran after her.

A heavy-set, blond young man stepped forward. "It's my sister," he said. "Since she returned from the camp, she hasn't been the same. She goes for days without saying a word, always looking for some corner to crawl into, and at night, all of a sudden and for no apparent reason, she screams out loud at the top of her lungs, scaring everyone else half to death."

The two women led the struggling sister behind a large rock, trying to comfort her.

"Who knows what they didn't do to her in that Chetnik camp, those bastards!" a hoarse woman's voice rose above the crowd.

"Come on, the column is leaving us behind!" a diminutive, middle-aged man began to shout, constantly switching his bag from one shoulder to the other. "She will reach us later! Those animals up in the hills are just itching to let loose a rain of bullets onto us. Any second now!" Having tried to reactivate the stalled portion of the column, he hurried off.

Some followed him while the others were again stopped in their tracks by two new female shrieks. A few moments later, one of the women who had gone to care for the distraught girl ran out from behind the rock, full of fear, and addressed her brother:

"Omer! Lejla aborted and cannot go any further..."

"What do you mean *aborted*?...What did she abort?" retorted the youth in shock.

"A child..." groaned the woman.

"What child, damn it!?" Omer demanded, quickly losing control.

The woman stood there, uncertain as to what she should say or do next. Yudja walked toward Omer and just as he was about to tell him to go and get his sister loud sobbing sounds came from behind the rock, followed by an ear-splitting scream. While everyone stood paralysed the second woman appeared, approached the crowd, helplessly shrugging her shoulders. In a barely audible voice, she murmured:

"Lejla has killed herself…Threw herself into the gorge. Said she could never live down the shame and threw herself down the cliff."

Omer broke free of the crowd and bounded over the rocks to the very edge of the cliff. Yudja and two others ran after him. Climbing onto a promontory, Omer tried to find sight of his sister down in the depths. Suddenly, somewhere out of the canyon, a burst of machine-gun fire thundered down. The young man staggered, his white shirt immediately blossoming dark red. He swayed back and forth briefly before disappearing head-first into the gorge.

"Dogs!" shouted Yudja in the direction the shots had come from, the gorge twisting the sound of his voice and carrying it down to the river below.

The two men with him grabbed his hands and pulled him back to the column, to his wife and daughter, as far away from the gorge as possible. As he was being hauled back, he heard the protests of bewildered, frightened people and someone's explanation of Lejla's tragedy:

"We all knew that she had been raped in the camp. When she realised that she was pregnant, she went mad. She hid it and thought about nothing else but how to get rid of it. She couldn't bear the idea of giving birth to a Chetnik's child."

These last words tore Yudja away from Alma and Delvete's hands. He stood upright, straight as an arrow, and stubbornly walked on, leaving them to follow.

When the caravan of Psetian refugees arrived at the foot of the mountain, two mortar shells fell a hundred metres away from them. The caravan heaved like an ocean wave during a storm. Thinking that their only chance lay in speed, the mass of people rushed toward the town which stood visible in the plain below. Yudja was among the last to reach it because he could not allow any of the sick and wounded to remain behind him.

"I could have sworn that those two shells came from the direction of the town," Yudja commented to one of the limping men in the column walking with him, loud enough for some of the soldiers at the reception point to hear him.

"You should thank your God, Boshnyo*, that they missed you," came the bitter comment from one of the soldiers, a sneering smile on his scarred face. "You've burnt all your flags and now you're here to recline on our tired backs," he added sarcastically, looking toward the red and white checker-board of the Croatian flag which hung from the church tower.

From Travnik, the greater part of the Psetian refugees were sent out into the world. Yudja and his family were transported to Zadar in Croatia, where they were quickly separated: the two women to a woman's camp near Pula, while he was sent to a camp for old people outside Zagreb. The "final solution" for all three was to come later.

Eventually at the Zagreb camp he was given the choice of where he wanted to go.

"As far away from here as possible," he answered pensively. "If I could have my wish, please send the three of us together as far away in the world from our borders as you can. Thus he was dropped one morning at the end of 1992 on the Canadian coast of the Pacific, in Vancouver. Before leaving Zagreb he was given a piece of paper certifying that his wife and daughter were in Pula, as if they were two bales of cotton left behind for storage. He was assured that they would be sent to him as soon as the opportunity presented itself. A year later, that opportunity had yet to present itself and he was beginning to doubt if it ever would, especially after receiving a letter from the Refugee Bureau in Zagreb which stated that Alma, as a Bosnian of conscription age, would not be allowed to leave Croatia until further notice.

Delveta, of course, remained with her daughter.

CHAPTER II

Yudja's solitude in the tiny studio apartment in the Lonsdale area of North Vancouver was entering its second year. He had begun this period of his life with the hope that here, on the other side of the world, he would succeed in finding peace in the waning years of his life and finally have time to solve the riddle left to him by his father, Fehrat. For days on end, he would sit in front of the fireplace, trying to catch the tufts of smoke which he was beginning to consider a part of his being, an integral part of his echo and his aura in this bewildering world. The better he grew to understand Fehrat's riddle, the more enchanted he became with it, and the role it suggested he himself now take in life, which he increasingly saw as a vaudeville hall in which you couldn't tell the actors from the audience. Yudja determined to become one of the musicians of the orchestra ranged at the edge of the disharmonious auditorium, musicians whose breathing, fingers and voices were being guided by the unpredictable movements of someone else's magic wand.

He spent that first refugee year in his North Vancouver bachelor apartment, continuing to carve his memories into ten wooden figurines, each representing a turning point in his life. These figurines were his response to all the human contact he had experienced. Eventually, he came to be convinced that he had unmasked the riddle of his father, which he had found engraved on the stem of the long pipe which old Fehrat had carried between his lips for more than half a century, without once emitting the slightest puff of smoke or even the thinnest whiff of burning tobacco. The engraving read: >*From mountain to mountain, there are both desolate wildernesses and sunny pastures.* Only after distancing himself thirty years from his father's death, and with all trace of the pipe lost, did he realise that this motto was both his beginning and his destiny, like the conductor's wand along whose arabesques in air man crawls through life.

He first received a taste of this conductor's wand when, by the grace of Allah, Yusuf Kahric beat his ears bloody with a willow whip. Just a boy, Yudja ran crying to the beardless Imam Selman, seeking justice. The Imam wiped the blood from Yudja's ears with warm water, smeared some butter upon the wounds, sat him down on a bench before him and said something that would turn over in Yudja's head throughout the coming years and decades—That man's fate is in the hands of God and everything man does during his lifetime will one day be weighed on the scales of truth and divine justice. From that day on, he began to feel that his life was in someone else's hands, though these hands couldn't possibly be God's. In the following years, whenever he tried to figure out in advance the final reading of the balance of his life, his vision of the scale's needle was always obstructed by two nagging questions: why he was born in the first place, without being allowed any input to the process; and what kind of machinery was it that took people away from this world, again without bothering to consult with them about the time or method. On one occasion some years after the whipping incident, as they were returning from a funeral, he told Imam Selman of these doubts of his. Frowning at the impudence of such ideas, the Imam quickened his step enough to join the group walking in front of them, but not before snorting a warning to Yudja about the dangers of interfering in God's business.

Years had passed since the incident with Yusuf's willow whip, Imam Selman's life had been weighed on the scales of justice long ago. Yudja had grudgingly come to accept the fact that his entire life— or the ungainly shell which remained of it—was contained under the roof of a box-like three-storey apartment building on the North Shore of Vancouver, where evil winds had unceremoniously blown it. Whenever he managed to close all of the stubborn windows facing out into the world, his mind would inevitably wander off and once again reflect upon himself and his family. With the same reliability, he would hear the voice of his father whispering to himself as he ran his hand over his moustache:

"This Yudja of mine: he will either become a great mind, or the devil will take him down the false path, ahead of his time. With him, there will be no middle road."

The devil had taken his father before him and it dawned on him, some thirty years after having lowered the old man into the grave on a rainy afternoon, without so much as a tear in his eye, that old Fehrat's passage through life had not left a single imprint on him, not even a trace. Except, of course, for the fact that he existed, doubting son of a dubious father. And yet now, unfathomably far from home and all the grotesque pictures of his recent experience, he began to fearfully see that he had missed the main current of his mixed-blood life at its source, its powerful subterranean force—missed the earth-shaking tremor of the groundwaters now tearing his homeland apart.

His mother, Maria, had also left few traits to him. Perhaps, others would say, he had her green eyes and the same sluggish walk. But his manner, height and scrawniness were unique among the Psetian Bosnians. It was as if nature had decided to play a particularly harsh trick on Yudja, singling him out from all his kith scattered over the slopes of the western mountains and the valleys surrounding the rivers between them.

In vain did Yudja wait for time to distance him from the images which continued to suffocate him. They would surface despite all his efforts to keep them submerged, sucking him in as an active participant Eventually he could no longer distinguish between his nightmares and the daytime flashbacks which came and went as they pleased. It sometimes seemed to him that the actors from his subconscious life were quicker in accepting his new one-room surroundings, and the view outside of the city's grey skyline which complemented the metallic colour of Burrard Inlet more fully, than he ever could himself.

As his thoughts grew heavier, the realisation that nothing in this world should be taken too seriously nor too lightly made life somewhat more bearable. In fact, it was all just a house of laughter, glued together with misery, and all one had to do was to begin laughing or weeping—for the entire structure would surely come crashing down into the mud upon which it was built. He kicked his slippers around the room in an effort to convince himself that he still existed and all of this had not been just a bad dream. Then he would laugh so loudly and uncontrollably that the tenants below his room on Lonsdale Avenue called the building manager to complain that he had gone insane. This would occur with alarming regularity. It became clear to him that this strange laughter had been with him ever since, as a young man, he was forced by his peers to run in a district marathon. They wanted to have a good laugh at his expense, but in the end it was Yudja who had laughed last and longest when he won the race by a good distance over his nearest competitor. Laughter had always burnt within him but it wasn't the ordinary, spontaneous and good-natured type. It was a unique laughter; a strange combination of ha-ha-ha, quivering lips and weeping.

Yudja's dramas in the small North Vancouver room became increasingly realistic, the characters of his imagination and the wooden figurines more lifelike. Voices would often burst out through closed doors, descend the stairs—and people were amazed.

One day, as the rain mercilessly battered the entire city, a man soaked to the bone and walking with the aid of crutches rang at the building manager's door. As soon as the blonde, middle-aged woman took a good look at the figure standing before her, without wasting a word, speaking slowly and using her hands as if talking to a deaf and dumb child, she pointed him up the stairs, to the last door on the right. The man in that suite was surely the one he was looking for, she thought to herself with certainty, it was obvious.

That is how Fehrat, Esma's illegitimate son, who everyone in Pset knew was the result of Yudja and Esma's forbidden love, arrived at Yudja's doorstep.

Fehrat resembled an apparition from a nightmare. Yudja was startled when he opened the door, thinking at first that his imagination was up to its old tricks. He was about to ask the person standing in front of him whom he was looking for but, at the last second, as the stranger was wiping the wet hair from his forehead, Yudja recognised that it was Fehrat, the high school teacher in Pset, his illegitimate son, who on the one occasion when he tried to call him "My son" in public promptly spat on him. Yudja relived the embarrassing incident as he stared at the man at his doorstep. It had happened in the town's square, in front of a group of his schoolmates, when Fehrat was just a young man. Yudja had long since forgiven him for the insult because he knew that Fehrat wasn't to blame for his poorly coordinated entry into this world, nor for the fact that fate had assigned him the role of the unwanted egg.

During the ten seconds spent standing at the doorstep, Yudja changed colour several times and tried to detach himself from the recurring memory of Esma holding the dark-haired baby in her arms. When Fehrat was still a child, Yudja would find times when no one would know, and go to see his son, simply to run his fingers through the thick black hair on his little head. As the boy grew, he would watch him from afar, all the while cursing fate for not allowing them to walk together through the same doorway. When Fehrat went off to university in Sarajevo, Yudja left town and wandered through the forests and fields for three days, cursing the nation to which birth had sentenced him, the primitivism which shackled it and the codes of conduct which bound it.

Fehrat's mother was proud of her son, working day and night to put him through school. When, by chance, the mother and grown son came across Yudja, she would jealously cling to Fehrat's arm, defiantly puff out her chest and carefully observe out of the corner of her eye the reaction on the young man's face. Yudja never could understand why she had decided to name the child after his own father. Though she was often courted by the town's widowers, she never married.

Yudja realised that standing before him was an invalid. He slid his arm around Fehrat's hips and helped him to sit down in the shabby old armchair near the radiator. He also helped him to free himself of the rain-soaked jacket, shoe and wet sock and brought him a towel with which to wipe his face and hair before sitting himself across from Fehrat on the heavy, wooden bed. They stared at one another unblinkingly, as if neither the father nor the son knew how it should all begin. The only thing about Fehrat that seemed fresh were his fiery red lips. Everything else about him spoke of the misery that he had recently lived through: the murky, sunken green eyes; the unshaven face; the elongated, thin ears, hairy at the top. Instead of a foot, at the end of his filthy left pant-leg, there protruded a wooden shaft. Now that Fehrat was without the coat, Yudja could see that his left hand had been severed, just below the wrist.

"Somehow, I found you," Fehrat eventually said, shrugging his shoulders as if to excuse himself for arriving unannounced, for even existing, "and managed to hobble over...somehow", he continued as his eyes softly followed the length of the left leg and stopped once they reached the wide part of the wooden prosthesis.

"But, how?...From where?..." uttered Yudja, unable to take his eyes off Fehrat's missing extremities. "How did you manage to find me here?"

"They told me at the Refugee Centre in Zagreb that you were here in Canada and so they sent me after you."

"Are you here alone?..." Yudja summoned all his courage for this question. Fehrat immediately understood what was meant and answered:

"Mother was killed immediately after you left Pset. She knew that I was still in the camp and refused to leave with your caravan without me...Perhaps you didn't hear about her death? Well, I somehow managed to stay alive or, at least, most parts of me did..." He spoke quietly as his eyes wandered around the room.

As Fehrat spoke, Yudja had the impression that something was stuck in his throat. These first moments lasted for what must have seemed like an eternity for both of them. Fehrat began to second-guess the wisdom of having come at all, thinking that perhaps it would have been better for both of them to have remained strangers. Yudja's thoughts were not much different. His whole life, from Fehrat's birth, he'd planned ways to make reconciliation with his estranged illegitimate son. Now this strange destiny had brought them together; he felt astonishment, awkwardness and confusion. Nevertheless, he quickly decided to welcome his new guest.

"It's a good thing that you've come. My situation here isn't the greatest but it's still a good thing that you are here…"

"I didn't have anywhere else to go. In Bosnia, they crippled me. In Croatia, they couldn't wait to get rid of me. They said that there are organisations which could help me get the necessary prostheses. When I found out that you were in Canada, I asked to be sent here also… Anyway, I no longer have anyone else." Fehrat's voice was beginning to relax, slowly opening up to the old man.

"What happened to your mother?" Yudja asked, emboldened. "I knew that she wouldn't leave without you and was hiding when the rest of us left in the caravan."

"They murdered her…I heard that it was Topina, along with his butchers…It's difficult to believe that it was him. We went to school together. We used to be friends…"

"I believe it!" the old man virtually shouted, "He was a thug even during peacetime. He comes from a throat-cutting family. He'd even kill his own mother if he had the slightest suspicion that there might be something in it for him. We were blind. So blind!" Yudja was swept with anger.

"It is possible…Only now, since this war, have I realised that everything is possible. The human brain becomes sick during war. People start to act like dogs when you try to take meat from their jaws. Some more, others less. Some hide behind the excuse of collective insanity, seeking to justify their crimes by citing national interests, as if that was all the justification they needed to rape, pillage and butcher. As soon as they say that the goal justifies the means, everything becomes clear. Morality, dignity, friendship, blood-ties—all are thrown out the window and conveniently forgotten. Everything is turned upside down. The abnormal becomes normal when guns are readily handed out to all criminals and psychotics. These are the new heroes." Fehrat made this statement slowly and calmly, stroking with his right hand the place where the left one had been severed.

Both men fell into a lengthy silence. Outside, the rain showed no signs of intending to let up.

Increasingly, Yudja was beginning to feel the onset of a fever attacking his insides, particularly the brain and the nervous system. For years, there was nothing he had wished more than to finally give life to the frozen seed which had always paralysed relations with his son, but not under these conditions. Ever since Fehrat's birth, under someone else's roof, all of Yudja's contact with people had been tainted by the ever-present shadow of this sin of his. He often found himself on the verge of deciding to abandon his father's house and Delveta and to move in with Esma and Fehrat, the only true-blood successor who could carry on the family name. When he told Esma of his plans, expecting to hear her support, she took a few steps back, looked him over and replied:

"Stay where you are because you cannot do otherwise! Did you think that I gave birth to your son just so that I could have you? How can you be so certain that he is your son? When he asks, I will tell him about his father but I will never force him upon you!"

Fehrat's eyes became fixed on the old shelves where the wooden figurines were lined up. These works of art Yudja had created amid the constant trembling of pain.

He had begun carving figurines out of linden wood at a very young age, shortly after his mother's death. He returned to this childhood hobby after having decided upon the self-imposed punishment of shutting himself up to await death in the solitude of his father's old house. At night, he recounted to himself old stories drawn from segments of his memory, while during the day he would carve out the figure of the previous night's most significant character, the one who carried with him the main idea and message. He managed to pack some of them into his overstuffed linen suitcase when he was forced to leave on the refugee-caravan journey which had lost him Delveta and Alma and landed him in Canada.

"There was talk in town about how you were carving some goblins out of wood," commented Fehrat with an enigmatic smile, looking back and forth between the figurines and Yudja's thinning grey hair. "Is this all the wealth you managed to bring with you?"

At once, with a sudden jerk, Fehrat bit down on his lower lip, as if discovering that the source of his aggravation lay among Yudja's grotesque figurines. His eyes devoured them one by one. When he was through with the figurines, his eyes moved down toward his own disfigured limbs and from there his laser-like intensity found shelter in the darkness of the night outside the window.

"Nothing special..." Yudja shrugged his shoulders, pretending not to have noticed the bloody flame in Fehrat's eyes, as if he were far removed from the old man's intentions. "Their only use is in that they replace the outside world for me. Sometimes, they speak to me. Sometimes, in fear of them, I bury my head under the blanket. We laugh together, cry together. Where they are wounded, so am I. They have prolonged my life while I, without their permission, am making cuts to their bodies like a parent trying to show his child...Here, look at this Kokic! This freebooter against his own people!..." Yudja realized with amazement that he was confiding his secrets to Fehrat. Taking into his hands an ungainly, human-like figurine of about thirty centimetres, he continued as if criticising some little monster:

"This one here gave us more grief than the Chetniks in the last war. To think we were once kin. But no, it was war and people were going insane, so he too, perhaps, lost his mind...And I, look here, cut out his heart and put in its place a viper."

Yudja returned the figurine to the shelf, walked over to the fridge and returned with a bottle of juice, a can of beer and two glasses.

"Refresh yourself a little. Their beer is stronger than ours and the juice is freshly squeezed." He waited to see which one Fehrat would choose.

"I haven't the strength for alcohol," Fehrat answered, his glance returning to the figurines on the shelf. He felt an easing of the pain in his lungs and a lessening of the cramps tormenting the corners of his mouth.

"This old man has created his own world and no outside reality can destroy it. He has carved his personal complexes into these linden figurines and is now free to continue his life, like a sinner after confession," he thought to himself as he observed his father at his artistic creations.

"Who is this beauty with the horns and the apple in his hand?" Fehrat asked before taking a sip of the juice.

Yudja took the wooden athlete from the shelf and placed him between them. Staring directly into Fehrat's eyes, unable to hide the nervous twitch of his bottom lip, he gave a short explanation:

"It was supposed to be my brother Osman, but something came over me as I was working on it and this is the result."

"Mother spoke of Osman a number of times…As a child, I remember her saying that he was a hero and how they killed him on Goli Otok*."

"O, no! He wasn't killed over ther…"

Yudja made no more comments. Fehrat's eyes returned to the shelf.

"Who is the one with the long pipe in his mouth?"

Yudja got up again, walked to the shelf and returned with the figurine Fehrat had inquired about. The long pipe in its mouth resembled a musical instrument more than it did an instrument for smoking. Placing him next to the figurine of Osman, he gave Fehrat an enigmatic look and answered:

"This is my father, your grandfather and namesake. Whenever he talked about our ancestors, he would take the pipe out of his mouth and rap it on his knee, as if by doing this he was opening up the secrets of our family tree."

Fehrat looked at Yudja and the two figurines, his silence an indication of his desire for the old man to continue.

"Often, when he spoke my father would ask himself what sin had our ancestor carried with him, and could it be that our recurring periods of exile are just a part of the family's atonement," whispered Yudja, all the while staring intensely at the figurine.

"I don't understand?…What atonement?…" asked Fehrat, but the old man continued, as if not hearing him.

"Our seed was planted during a period of collision in the Balkans between the great empires of the Middle Ages…And it all occurred amazingly, unbelievably, contrary to all norms and laws of human interaction; in a manner, it seems, that could occur on this globe only in Bosnia. It began when my grandfather's great-great-grandfather, a self-willed and intensely energetic man, detached himself from his father's shop on the Adriatic coast and made his way, bloody-backed after some altercation, by horse to the first Turkish watchtower in Klis. Before Beg* Pintorovic, he took the oath to serve the Turkish Sultan till death, as long as they never sent him to war against his own people or mentioned who he was and where he came from. He put on a turban, around his waist he wore a Damascus sabre which he had received as a gift from the Beg, and after a few years, he became the assistant to the merchant Novakovic in Pset. Seeing that he was a better merchant than soldier, they allowed him to choose which path he would take through life. The Psetian Bosnians, fortunately, never inquired where he came from, nor who he was, and Master Iliya only once commented that his face was more like that of a Vlach* than of a Turk*, but after seeing the burning-charcoal look in his eyes, he never again repeated the comment."

Yudja's eyes slowly made their way from the figurine with the pipe in its mouth to Fehrat's eyes and he finished as abruptly as he had started:

"The story goes that he had eyes as blue as the Adriatic. Yet, we all have green eyes. Perhaps, over generations, the eyes adapted to the greenery of our forests."

Yudja lowered his head but out of the corner of his eye he observed the tormented face of his son.

"It is easier to retell these stories to myself than to you…But, I must pass down to you all of these things which have piled up in my head all the years of my life."

Fehrat said nothing. He was listening to what was going on outside, and all he could hear was the monotonous rain, drumming as it came down the drainpipes, returning to the earth from which it had originally started on its adventure up to the clouds from which it had fallen back down into the dust it now turned to mud.

CHAPTER III

The night descended silently, freed of the intrusive sounds which would have signaled the end of day in each and every sleepy little Bosnian town. No sheep bleated as they ran to the water trough upon their return from the pastures. No cows moaned at the courtyard gates. Nor could be heard the dwindling human voices which would have convinced even a blind man of the coming darkness. On this other side of the world, in Yudja's room the one and only window looked out toward a lamplit row of grain elevators at the harbour's edge, and mounds of potash waiting to be loaded on ships. The window was adequate only for the entry of fresh air and the occasional screeching of automobile brakes. It made little difference to Yudja if outside these four walls it was day or night.

During supper, he inquired where Fehrat had spent the period following the first shots aimed at human flesh in this war which was still raging across the mountains and valleys of Bosnia and Herzegovina. The two men had quickly overcome the shock of their initial human contact, and after a few hours of uninterrupted conversation reached the point of being acquaintances. Though Yudja's voice could barely hide his desire to avoid at all costs offending his guest, the conversation increasingly infringed upon terrain usually reserved for old friends.

"Do you remember Yanya's son Zoran, the one who operated the crane at the sawmill?" asked Fehrat. Without waiting for an answer, he continued:

"He came to the high school one day. By coincidence, all of us, the schoolmasters, were in the staff-room at the time. Zoran whispered something to the Principal, Gasha, and then, full of self-importance, he turned to us. He said that he had been appointed Coordinator of Schools and that the time had come to free the schools of communist ideology. Marxism was to be dropped from the syllabus because Marx was, according to Zoran and his leaders, just a Jewish dreamer and disbeliever. In its place would be Religion. He also recommended to us that it would be wise if all of the masters joined the new, modern political organization, the Serbian Democratic Party, because in the future it would be leading the nation. I remember how Milan Tomic angrily interrupted him and provocatively asked if that meant that he had come to baptise the Muslims and if he had erased from his demography of 'the nation' the two Croat teachers, the math teacher from Montenegro and the Slovenian physical education teacher. He was gruffly told that they could all go where they wanted because democracy was knocking at the door. Since then evil, not democracy, has been knocking at our door, as you can see from what has happened to the two of us."

"So, for you it started with that fathead, Zoran. He's a relative of ours. Your mother was related to his family." Fehrat started to say something, but Yudja continued: "No, no…It's not important. But I suddenly remembered when you mentioned his name…My mother was a good soul but he's a filthy savage."

"I want to tell you how it started for me…Zoran angrily stormed out of the staff-room, down the stairs and, as we all looked on from the window, he took a can of black spray paint out of his briefcase and wrote THIS IS SERBIA! on the front wall of the school building. The next day, we found that someone had written underneath: NO, STUPID, THIS IS HIGH SCHOOL! I was accused of having written it and they even claimed that the writing on the wall matched my handwriting. Ha…Before they could fire me, I packed up and went to Travnik. A friend of mine is the principal at a high school over there and helped me find a way to make a living."

"Strange," Yudja shook his head pensively, "as soon as evil winds begin to blow, we are always the first ones they hit. It's been that way with our forefathers for as long as we've existed. Nothing but refugees. As if we were cursed. You had to flee as soon as they wrote *This is Serbia*. For me, at the very beginning of the Second World War, someone wrote on the Sports Hall *This is the Independent State of*

Croatia! And so it has been with each generation. Just when you've finished building a roof above your head, it happens: either they burn it down or they throw you a carry bag and ship you off into the wide world. Sometimes hunger and famine, other times sabres and bullets... Since we've existed. How can such an unfavourable fate be known in the world? Only now is it becoming clear to me. It is as if we are the dust on a unlucky road over which various armies have trodden. It doesn't matter which army passes by, we are always walked over and scattered in all directions. Somehow, we always return to that road, to be walked over and scattered again. It is as if we've come to embrace our miserable fate."

Fehrat listened to Yudja, gratified at having finally met him and finding him to be a man of greater intelligence than he had expected. For the longest time, he had always made a great effort to quickly forget everything that he heard of his father. As this realization flowed through Fehrat, he began to feel a stabbing pain in his amputated leg. He felt pain in the fingers of his left hand, but as soon as he remembered that he no longer had those fingers or that hand, the pain shot up through his neck and directly into his left temple. Extending the hand he still had toward a hideous figurine, he asked Yudja to hand it to him. Yudja looked toward the figures lined up in the wall-unit, and instead of handing his son the one he had asked for, gave him one from the next row—a moustachioed old man holding in each hand half of a torn book.

"This is Vavan. It is better if I begin by telling you about my experience with him instead of with Ipic."

"Vavan?" inquired Fehrat, trying to remember, "I don't know of any Vavan from our area."

Yudja sighed deeply, and began.

THE STORY OF VAVAN

He was killed during World War II. He was smarter than anyone in our district. It was said, for a long time after, that he was liquidated by the political commissar of his battalion, who didn't want anyone in the unit who was smarter than he," Yudja explained, without any intent to delve into further details. He then pulled up a small table between them and placed on it two bottles of dark beer and a bowl of pretzels to munch on. He extended himself on the bed and began again, slowly, quietly, as if trying to think back to the beginning of time, not merely to his youth:

It was war. The same stupid, senseless war as all the others have been throughout history. It was the great world war which began in Bosnia, in Sarajevo, when under the patronage of the Greater Serbian Colonel Apis a group of misguided young men assassinated the Habsburg Crown Prince Ferdinand. And, where? In Bosnia! In Sarajevo! Why could it not have occurred in Poland, or in Prague? Why did it have to begin in Bosnia when neither the Greater Serbians nor the Crown Prince intended anything good to happen to Bosnia? There was much blood, killings, and injustice; and tears, and despair. Far too much pain!

My mother was running from a group of starving Gypsy children, with her bundle of clothes and a loaf of bread. Just as their bony hands began to bring her down, she heard someone's iron voice and the little Gypsies scattered. And so she met my father, your grandfather, Fehrat, and agreed to be his wife. Most of this I learned later, when my mother would rock me back and forth in her lap and tell me how my father was a warrior and her saviour. She also told these stories to my twin brother, Osman, who in turn would retell them to all the other children—but not before adding many interesting and clever details.

Before me and Osman, she'd had five children, two sons and three daughters, but they all died early in childhood, three of them during the large smallpox epidemic of the thirties. Soon after that, my mother, Maria, also moved on to the next world. Thinking back, I have a more vivid memory of her being lowered into the grave, just behind the church fence, than of her life and what she looked like. Later, because my father didn't want to remarry, his sister Habibe moved in with us. Aunt Habibe's husband was killed during the Great War, somewhere in south-east Bosnia. She didn't have children of her own so for the longest time she took the place of our mother.

Following my mother's death, father changed and became a different man. There wasn't a trace to be found in him of the heroic character from my mother's stories.

My brother Osman and I grew up on two different planets; from the very beginning we felt ourselves to be completely unlike but still in need of one another. As I grew up, I felt a large heart growing within me while Osman was turning completely into a huge head. From the very beginning, he showed incredible cleverness which at times threatened to break away and disappear into searching for some otherworld of wisdom. It seems to me that no one was as confused by the life and the inventions of men as I, and at the same time no one had alongside them a more clever person to explain the world to them.

When we stood above a puddle and watched races between fantastic creatures which were made up of just head and tail, Osman calmly explained to me that these were tadpoles and their heads were so big because with smaller brains they wouldn't be clever enough to evade their enemies, and in this world there wasn't a greater miracle than the transformation of a tadpole into a frog. He told me, and the other children gathered around, what even our teacher Mitar had neglected to point out—that the frog is the best evidence that life on Earth first developed in water, and then on land. Whoever heard my brother Osman was amazed by his intelligence.

But our aunt, Habibe, in great secrecy, knowing that my father would never approve, visited Imam Kahriman, a well-respected old man, to tell him all about her fears and worries. And her greatest worry was Osman's blasphemy, ideas which could never have come from the stack of father's books. She told him how I was a normal and dear boy, full of emotion and love. I had always thought that she and my father were more proud of Osman than they were of me. I even heard my mother one time say that Osman would become a more admired doctor even than Saka's Milovan. The Imam listened to Habibe's fears and wonderment, all the while running his tiny red eyes over her breasts and across her ample hips—which she had impudently encased in pleated Turkish trousers—as if trying to imagine what exactly these clothes were concealing. He spoke in a manner which caught her off guard and which even she had never used when attacking my father:

"I knew what would happen. Fehrat ran after a Serb, as if there were no women for him in our holy faith. She gave birth to Yudja, giving him our heart and soul, but also gave birth to Osman, that clever one with the Muslim name. Fehrat and the Serb have mixed so thoroughly that not even God can untie them now. It will be as Allah dictates, but no good can come of it."

Habibe did not expect such a reaction from Imam Kahriman and the only thing that she could think of doing was to move back a few steps from him and allow him to take in a fuller view of her beauty. Some years later, she visited his grave and spat on the still-fresh earth.

My father was a merchant who did business in a region spanning a hundred kilometres in each direction from our town. He dreamed of one day returning to the old glory of his father, Becir, and grandfather, Salim, both wealthy merchants. Osman knew all the details of our family history, beginning with our forefather who came to Pset from Dalmatia, converted to Islam, accepted service to the Turkish Sultan and began our line. I mentioned him earlier. He adapted very quickly to Bosnian customs and dress but forever retained his Dalmatian accent, even when using Turkish and Greek words. They sometimes noticed him up on Skender's hill standing under the cherry tree and looking toward the sun in the west and swallowing his sorrow for something completely unknown to the people of our town. I remember Osman saying how two worlds met in our forefather, two ways of life—one eastern and the other western—and the fault line between them ran down his back, a split life suspended between birth and death while the rift was filled with a torrent rushing down a twisted and winding course between its banks. Only later did it occur to me that Osman and I had inherited this polarity from our distant Dalmatian ancestor— Osman got the intelligence and brilliancy of the West while I had the passion and heart of the East.

I grew quickly as a child and from the moment I began to speak I brought all of my heartfelt emotions of love and hate into my relations with people around me. I remember placing my ear against the grass and hearing the melodies created by the winds upon their delicate blades. I remember watching a flock of crows and imitating with my hands the movement of their wings, secretly hoping that someday, if only in a dream, I could take off on a long, long flight. When I was ten years old, I fell in love with the beautiful Sara who was not only five or six years older than I, but was being wooed by a number of young men who had completed their military duty long ago. For days on end I ran through the fields, with a constant vision of her before my eyes, and lifted countless stones in order to strengthen my muscles for the inevitable day when I would be forced to challenge the strongest of her suitors to a fight.

When I was in my third year of high school, all indications were pointing to a new war catastrophe. That which I could feel by instinct, Osman explained away by pointing to various competing socio-economic blocs in the world. With greater frequency, he mentioned our mother and her foreboding and fears that just like her we would find ourselves caught up in a horrific war. I remember how shortly before her death she had often whispered something to father. Osman later told me that she could feel the coming of a new war among our people and, remembering the war she had survived, for the longest time she shook uncontrollably under her quilt. For days she followed every move Osman and I made, followed my father around and cleaned the courtyard and the walls of the house. She managed to talk father into painting the house a light blue and the wooden fence white, suggesting Serb culture. At night she was tormented by nightmares and visions. Images of the last war kept returning to her and she could not shed the fear she felt for her sons and husband.

She felt no fear when her father, mother, brother and sisters, even uncle Yandriya, turned her out of their house on account of her marrying my father. She courageously faced the uncertainty; only rarely did she quietly stutter, because in those first years she believed in her husband and his rough, dignified face. When the children began to arrive, she began to change. When they began to die, at first she was in shock for months but, with time, she unobtrusively accepted the existence of sin and damnation. Before dying, she attempted to transfer all of her identity to Osman and me. Both of us were much more attached to our mother than to our father.

My father was far too practical for Osman's liking, with little desire to be clever. He never stopped to analyse the social situation but was known to rage against some imagined or real injustice out of the blue, like a torrent breaking through a floodgate. He used to say that it was an honour and a great human duty to help the unfortunate, not through charity but by allowing them to work and earn. To this, Osman would usually say that it is every honest man's duty to take from the rich and to give to the poor. Father would argue that such thinking could lead only to lawlessness, anarchy, and wouldn't do much good for the rich or the poor, but he didn't elaborate on this. When he spoke of people in authority, he spoke of them with respect and fear, without a flicker of the discontent or protest that could always be felt with Osman. He didn't forbid Osman to go and visit Vavan, though on a number of occasions he commented that it would take a lot of brainpower to understand what was going on in Vavan's mind, and that when heads started to roll in the town square, those of Vavan and his group would most definitely be the first. He warned Osman that the authorities knew all about what was said down in Marta's Cellar and that it would be better if he didn't go there.

My father didn't like to talk about himself and his family. When Osman once asked about our only uncle, he said that his brother knew how to carve a man and a horse like no other in our corner of the world and that, perhaps, he would return when he tired of wandering the globe. He disliked talking about this brother of his and whenever someone asked about him a spasm would pass across Father's forehead and end in his piercing eyes. I remember, once, while Mother was still alive, he said that Osman reminded him of his brother and Mother's uncle, Yandriya.

I was a spirited boy. Above all, I loved the plum trees during autumn, when their branches hung down wearily from the weight of the dark-blue fruit. During springtime, my eyes would devour the yellow and crimson colours of the flowers and I would buzz around them like a bee. For hours on end I would smell the newly opened buds of the older trees in our orchard and feel their odour make its way to each cell in my body. Out in nature, all around me, I saw the harmony for which man should strive; in its spring joy I saw the basis for my approach toward other people. Even Osman was known to say that I was as pleasant and naive as spring, as the wind played with my long black hair while I was running across scented shadows of almond trees in the back alleys.

Father instilled in us a love for reading and always remembered to bring back books from his trips to Banja Luka and Split. My favourites were *One Thousand and One Nights* and Homer's epic poems, and as a young boy I learnt to sing many Bosnian folk songs accompanied by the wailing sonority of the gusle*. Osman began to read the philosophers and the politicians at an early age. The only two books to which we both regularly returned were the Bible and the Koran.

Now, when neither my father nor Osman is around any more, it seems to me that my brother and I had the most contact on account of my little wooden figurines. I began carving them out of linden wood soon after Mother's death. The first figures that I did were all connected to her. With time, as I got better, in addition to the breath of life (which reminded me of her), I tried to impart into my figurines a touch of mysticism. I stopped carving for a time after one of our neighbours, a good-for-nothing by the name of Dzafo, stole all of them and traded them away to some merchant at the market for two water melons. The melon man in turn sold them for two dinars a piece and made a hefty profit. That's how all my creations were sold off without the slightest benefit to me.

I returned to the blocks of linden soon after retreating to my father's old house following the death of Tito. I started carving one night after hearing Mother's voice, for what must have been the umpteenth time. This time, however, it sounded different—heavy and cold, like never before. She told me that she was leaving for the unknown, that she had had enough of me and this world, and that there would be nothing left of her grave and those of father and Osman because a bulldozer would be coming to cover them up and make way for a soccer field. The idea came to me that perhaps Mother's spirit had gone mad. Osman was very much alive—and why a soccer field? Afterward, I waited for days to hear from her again but there was nothing; it seemed that she had left for good.

With Osman it was different. We truly were polar opposites. Just before the Second World War, he even began to look like a brain. He read constantly, avoiding both wind and rain. He would burst through the front doors of the high school and go and visit Vavan to enjoy his stories. He wasn't satisfied with himself, nor with the people around him. Toward others, he was always more likely to show civility than love and respect. Scenes of nature brought forth in him a desire for contemplation, and even the sight of the pale moon inspired him to think of the bottomless well of knowledge and intellect, of the great brain whose sole duty it was to banish the darkness of ignorance from the minds of others.

He realised early on that our mother's love and father's pride weren't enough to make him happy and looked on in amazement at how the simplest things satisfied me. His inquisitive mind instinctively wanted to deconstruct every object and idea, and Vavan's ideas provided perfect exercises for his constantly developing mind. At that early age he came to a number of conclusions concerning his childhood, foremost that happiness is by nature treacherous because unhappiness always follows close behind. When mother once asked him why he had to take apart everything he came into contact with, his response was that her smiling face wasn't enough to satisfy his curiosity. He realised that there is very little harmony in relations between humans, and through nature's example of the battle between opposites found what he believed to be the only way toward this harmony. As a bare-chinned boy he made his break with religion and even Vavan was surprised when he took to heart only the wisdom of past generations while rejecting their dogmas and laws whose main purpose was to maintain control over the body and soul of the ordinary man. When I complained to him over his seeming dependence on Vavan, he answered, calmly, that the bearded old man, his forehead covered with lines of wisdom from too much thinking, was exposing him to an analytical mode of thought. Through him Osman hoped to discover the truth at the core of existence.

"Yudja", Osman would say, "your happiness is false and you will never learn the truth because you see the world through your eyes and heart and not through your brain."

"I don't see any point in your knowledge if all of its paths make you unhappy," I would often answer.

"You should accept the wisdom of other people just as an apprentice must accept the teachings of his master, but you shouldn't leave it at that because you must strive to become a better master than your teacher," commented Osman one cold day, and suggested that I go with him that night to Marta's Cellar.

I accepted his invitation even though neither the cellar nor Osman's wiseman held much interest for me. That same afternoon, father arrived with news from the town square that the gendarmes had beaten senseless a group of young men who had been posting signs against the government and fascism. He also said that the railroad workers in Bihac had gone on strike and there was talk of German troops having entered Czechoslovakia. Osman was visibly disturbed. For me, both Bihac and Czechoslovakia were far away and I only felt sorry for the young men beaten by the gendarmes. As I entered the hay barn at twilight to fetch the cattle their evening meal, there, under the dark, fragrant planks, Mother's voice was more convincing than father's news and Osman's worried forehead. She spoke softly, as if in fear that someone might overhear us, saying that the gates of hell were opened wide and evil forces had marched out in force, determined to paint the world black. Until then, Mother's spirit had mainly concerned itself with mundane things but her ominous warning frightened me.

At dusk, the southern winds grew stronger and dark clouds full of rain brought with them the taste of salt and fish from the sea. There was a story going around that some fellow by the name of Yovandeka Zelic bragged about how he could see ships sailing in the sea from the very top of Kameniti Peak. Before and after, no one else claimed to have seen the ships, but the story remained. The entire tale was probably made up by Jovandeka and the people only to quench their thirst for water because our highland was known to go for months during the summer without a single drop of rainfall.

Osman and I marched in measured steps along the long street descending in a curve toward the graveyard, which was overlooked by two pairs of poplar trees aspiring to the skies. The street along which we walked was typical of our rural surroundings, where everyone built wherever they wanted, whatever they wanted. Houses bunched like shirts drying on the line among small log cabins covered with thatch and almost engulfed in their own gardens, the odd stone building immediately standing out due to its sheer size and shape. At the very mouth of the street which led to the hills, above other objects rose a white three-storey house with a mud-brick roof. Twenty years before, immediately after the First World War, it was built by Beg* Kulen, but he never managed to sleep in it a single night. After it had been plastered with mortar and painted white, one morning they found the beg's bulky body at the bottom of a creek. Witnesses claimed that the beg had stayed longer than usual at the house of the judge, Srdic, that the most skilled hunter in our region, the watchmaker Efraim, Jew from Sefard Kavezon family, was with them, and that they drank, ate and, as always, talked about their hunting exploits. In the morning, shepherds found his body in the creek and, they say, Gendarme Mile had great trouble removing the steel hook normally used for pulling hay from the stack, that had impaled his chest.

"I feel uncomfortable every time I pass by this house," I mentioned to Osman, "I'm certain that there are no such things as vampires or werewolves, but whenever I walk by it at night, it's as if someone is watching me. Once, I thought I heard a crying noise coming from up in the attic. It was probably just some cats."

"Your imagination! Frightened people create the very things they fear!" Osman angrily interrupted me, "As if the vampire Kulen would be waiting just for you!"

At first, I was struck by the tone of Osman's words but as soon as we were a little further from the house, I quickly forgot the conversation. Osman began talking about how everything had to be destroyed, and replaced by a new order in the way things were built and in the way people interacted. In front of her little wooden house, which was constantly in danger of being blown away by a yet stronger wind, stood the old woman called Chastara, leaning against the fence, mutely staring into the wind. She was mute, but her eyes and ears were fine. She made herself heard with screeching noises, always during drastic changes in the weather. It was said that she instinctively began to mumble and shriek inarticulate sounds just before the arrival of some misfortune.

"Of what use is this Chastara?! Our town, unfortunately, is full of people like her. Look at her wretched house—ugly, bizarre!" Osman declared. I didn't want to argue with my brother, but my opinion of Chastara ran more toward pity than Osman's conclusion that she was expendable. She wasn't to blame for the way she was born. She had wronged no one. I was slightly revolted by my brother's uncompromising attitude but didn't worry about it a great deal. When he spoke of how in the new society all houses would be the same and all granaries full, I suspected that my brother was also a dreamer who had accepted some strange aesthetic and ideology of revolution. Vavan and the books had confused his perception of dreams and reality. I, however, dared do no more than comment that it would be a shame to destroy all of the houses and courtyards, and then build new ones, all exactly the same. There was a place for new ones, but the ones that were now standing should be allowed to remain for as long as they serve their purpose. And furthermore, I went on, it is impossible to expect everyone to have the same. Even if everyone were locked up in a prison, some would create things in their cells while others would sleep throughout their sentence.

As we walked down toward the town centre, Osman became increasingly talkative, as if making an introduction to what I was about to hear in Marta's Cellar. Most of the things around us he denied and dismissed, almost fantastically trying to convince me that our whole human construct was a lie or an illusion, that there existed an entirely different view of life. Houses reminded him of the differences in wealth, courtyards of the pathetic state of human taste, orchards of lack of discipline and ignorance. In the graveyard he discovered inequality because some graves were more opulent than others. Men of religion were magnets for the dim-witted; merchants and bankers were bloodsuckers; politicians, parasites on the gullible…The whole world around us was, for Osman, one big incarnation of lies, a sign of the rotting state of our society's affairs and our own spiritual depravity, while human joy was no more than proof of self-deception.

As I listened to his words, I regretted coming along. For the first time since I had begun to seriously consider things, Osman seemed far from my heart, like a stranger. Even in his eyes I saw a colour I had never noticed before, the colour of blood.

In the lower part of the town we noticed increased activity among the local gendarmes. Three patrols passed by, moving quickly, rifles slung on their shoulders, suspiciously scrutinising all passers-by. From the third patrol, we were greeted by Gendarme Hase, but we didn't say a word in return. When we were out of their hearing, Osman muttered:

"Aunt Habibe said that Father warns us to be careful tonight because the authorities expect a group of agitators to pass through town. There's word that they are locking up anyone suspicious or unemployed, and they came for Medo and Jukan at the high school and took them away. Yesterday at the soccer game, two gendarmes beat the hell out of Yakov Sajdzic. Strange things are happening. Vavan probably knows more…"

We dawdled as Osman was becoming talkative again, but three schoolmates from the Sports Hall caught us up, interrupting his discourse. They cautioned us not to be late, then quickly went on their way.

Marta's Cellar was in a two-storey, well-appointed house built of carved stone, a building material plentiful in our region. During the last war, only the roof, windows and doors had been destroyed, and Vavan and his brother Milenko had restored the building soon after they returned to Pset. They were the sons of wealthy parents, both educated in Prague and Vienna, who had completed their studies and spent the entire war in the bloody trenches of the Habsburg army. With them followed the story that both had been married, that their families had fallen victim to civilian massacres and that they returned to their home town in order to get as far away as possible from the gentlemen who invent such wars. Milenko found employment with a forestry company, while Vavan renovated his father's tavern and named it Marta's Cellar and let himself go—growing a beard and parting his long, grey hair to the left side.

A few years later, Milenko died unexpectedly and the only thing that remained of him was the debate in town over where he would be buried. The priest, Simo Jovanovic, wouldn't permit his interment in the Orthodox cemetery because Milenko hadn't belonged to the church's congregation, nor had anyone seen him crossing himself. Someone suggested that they bury him between the church and the Muslim graveyard, in a no-man's-land where occasionally you would see Didovic's sheep. Not long after his burial, at various gatherings and meetings, the story began to emerge that the deceased Milenko had turned into a werewolf because he hadn't been baptised and because he wasn't sent into the next world in a manner which befitted a baptised soul. The story eventually faded, only to be replaced by other werewolf tales when several new graves joined his in the land between the two religions' burial grounds, and as the leaders of the two religious communities began to prosper materially.

"Did they ever learn who started the stories about two exceptional Pset's Serbs, Vavan and Milenko; about their war exploits and the massacre of their families? Why did Vavan name the tavern Marta's Cellar? Who was Marta?" I asked Osman as we neared the largest house in that part of town.

Osman was caught off guard by my questioning. He looked at me inquisitively and then answered:

"I don't know who started all of the stories, nor how the tavern got its name. Vavan never talks about it. And why would you pick this moment to ask me these questions?" enquired my brother and in his voice I heard an unusual jumpiness and discomfort. It seemed to me that he was cursing himself for having taken me along.

Inside the dark tavern, at a corner table beyond the bar, sat four men. The waitress, Hanka—a young, compact, woman with a wide smile and overexposed breasts, who, it was said, came from eastern

Bosnia—quickly approached us and told Osman that "they" were waiting for us down in the basement. Osman greeted her by touching her lips with two of his fingers and, without a word, we went down into the basement. Even though we were already young men, and many of our age were already marrying, Osman's contact with Hanka surprised me because I believed that women still didn't interest him—or at least, that's how it seemed to me and others from our circle.

Down in the basement, two petrol lamps highlighted ten male heads seeming to float above shadowy tables set in a circle. At first, the only one I could recognise was the bearded Vavan. As my eyes grew accustomed to the dark, I began to recognise most of the others. Two of the faces were from out of town. Most of the rest I expected to find there though I never would have expected to see among that group the town simpleton, Ale Mlinar, more likely to be mocked than taken seriously by anyone in Pset. There in the darkness of the basement, however, even Ale's face seemed more serious and notable and while all the others welcomed us only with silence, Ale nodded his head to me in a sign of greeting. Vavan motioned with his hand for us to sit down. Immediately, the basement, its darkness and the silence which lent it assurance, invaded my brain. It was as if I had stepped out from the crowded humanity of everyday and entered the temple of the prophet Isaiah.

Vavan spoke precisely and knowingly. His baritone voice, creating a metallic echo, dominated the room as did the light emanating from the two lamps, which created larger-than-life shadows on the bare, stone walls. His impressive upper body, looming across the table, gave substance to his air of conviction and helped his words seem more brilliant than they might have been in the light of day. When, in the heat of his speech, he stood up and circled around us two or three times, dragging behind him his shorter leg, I noticed that from the waist up he in fact looked like Ferko, the town mascot, who lost his toes in the trenches of Galicia after they froze and had to be amputated. As a consequence of his shortened feet Ferko walked rocking back and forth and one always had the feeling that he would, at any moment, fall flat on his nose and crack his skull on the cobbled pavement. Stalking around the room, Vavan patted me on the back a number of times, probably with the hope of making an impression on me. The atmosphere in the basement of Marta's Cellar infused with Vavan's words affected me incredibly. My body grew cold and my sole preoccupation became, at first, to memorise the dark Isaiah's every word.

Vavan was explaining how nationalist movements were sweeping through Europe, how in Italy and Germany they had risen to the point where they had succeeded in impressing upon their populations the messianic role which their respective nations were preordained to carry out. Blinded by promises of a happier future, the masses, having lost their ability to recognise the blackness of these politics, offered up their blood and flesh to the insane goal of destroying all that was not of their alliance. He spoke of how the nationalist propaganda apparatus had succeeded in spreading this blindness to other, smaller, nations, with the aim of harnessing what destructive energy they possessed against future opponents and preventing a united front against the German and Italian powers.

"Nationalism is a terrible sickness of the human soul, able to attack all intellectual levels because it attacks a man's psyche where the intellect is powerless. It brings to the fore the satanic aspect of the human character which destroys until it is destroyed," Vavan pronounced, while we, sitting there like schoolchildren in a classroom, stared mesmerised at his dignified head, soaking up his every word. The two strangers, I noticed, every now and then exchanged knowing glances.

I didn't give any of this special significance. Only when he began to talk of the situation in our country, and the danger which was growing with each passing day, did my interest return. He spoke of how the Yugoslav government was preparing the stage for high treason and how the ghosts of the past were being awoken within our two largest nations, Serbian and Croatian, even though ghosts can never be anything other than ghosts.

"You must fight the battle against the evil which is approaching from afar, but an even worse evil is gathering momentum here, under our very noses, in our own courtyards," continued the old man, moving from one to the next, making direct eye-contact with each. "They will begin by herding you like sheep into separate pens. They will paint you in different colours and send you out to fight one another. And we…we always have, somewhere in our subconscious, enough barbarism to harm ourselves sufficiently that others are spared having to write our history in yet more blood. Just take a good look at our profanities! It doesn't take any great analysis. While others are more than satisfied with "merde" or "scheisse", we insist on raping and massacring the entire family. I remember our squabbles in the muddy trenches of Poland and Belarus. The others were amazed at how we cursed each other's mothers, sisters, wives, everything under the sun. They turned their backs on us, except to occasionally spit in our direction. Yet, it was almost always one of our men that risked his neck to go and bring back one of theirs when they were wounded and left to rot in no-man's-land. The best and the worst humanity has to offer. That's us. Now, it's the worst that is coming to the top," Vavan stared at the dark corner under the stairs, as if seeing images from his wartime experiences.

"People build history. The pages of history reflect how we are as people. If some nations could burn the pages of their history and erase it from the minds of their scientists and professors, they would have a brighter future. A history which burdens future generations is not worth preserving. And what, you may ask, is our history? Butchering and thievery!" Vavan clapped his hands against a post for added effect. "Whenever our 'wisemen' think back to our past, immediately they reach for their knives and head off into mutual destruction. Our graveyards have more who died at the hands of a brother than those who died a natural death. Always, from the beginning, because it is simpler to continue the way things have always been than to tear everything down and begin building anew.

"A new round of destruction is before us. They have already begun cleaning their rifles, filling their cannons, sharpening their knives, fattening the flesh for the butchers…We must warn the people not to fall victim to these mad hooligans, not to give allegiance to their blood-soaked symbols, because even the most holy totems of the past cannot serve as symbols for the future!" Vavan was on fire, his eyes radiating both determination and fear.

The two strangers followed Vavan's monologue with delight. Ale's forehead wrinkled up like that of a great thinker while Osman was constantly looking around and scratching his left ear. During Vavan's speech, Rasim Medin kept rising halfway out of his chair, as if wanting to say something, but after each pause the old man continued talking, not paying attention to him and he was forced to sit down again. The same phrases began to circle my brain like vultures: "butchery and thievery," "sharpening their knives and fattening the flesh," "burn down history"…

Hanka came quickly down the stairs and whispered something to Vavan. He threw back his head and hurriedly explained something to her. Hanka ran back up the stairs while the old man, with a quick step despite his uneven gait, went toward the opposite end of the basement, opened up a wooden closet to reveal a hidden door, and, gesturing with his hand, indicated for us all to clear out. In just a few seconds, all of us, except Vavan, were standing in the darkness outside the door leading to the plum orchard behind the house. I was excited to see what would happen and waited by the door, trying as best I could to follow the action in the tavern. Vavan had returned to the other side of the basement. From above, we could hear noise and activity. Hanka's half-crying voice could be heard, trying to convince someone that the basement was empty and that Vavan wasn't home. I could see one and then another gendarme descending carefully down the basement stairs, revolver in hand.

"Here I am," Vavan's voice could be heard, "Who needs me?"

"Police," answered a rough voice from the top of the stairs.

"Where are the rest of the agitators?", shouted a voice from the tavern.

"Search the basement," the rough one ordered the two standing next to Vavan "And you, old man, get upstairs!"

When I noticed one of them nearing the closet, I fled into the darkness. As I ran, I could hear Hanka's pleading behind me, men's voices and the heavy sound of boots running. The tense night was shattered by a shot fired from a revolver. The first shot was followed by a hail of others, then several rifle shots. I flew through the orchards and the gardens, jumping countless fences. I noticed a couple of silhouettes running in the same direction. As I was trying to find a way to get over the high gate into Semanic's courtyard, a hand gripped my shoulder and nearly startled me senseless. It was Osman. He pulled me in the opposite direction, toward Senukic's tall walnut grove.

"Climb to the top of the highest one," whispered Osman, "and I'll go down the creek."

As my brother silently vanished into the darkness, I looked around. The lamps in the town square had been turned off and from behind dark clouds the light of the moon was breaking through. From the direction that we had come, I could hear the sound of wooden fences breaking and someone's gruff commands. I hurtled toward the walnut trees before me and, noticing a particularly tall one with a clear view of the town, I shot up it to the very top, like a cat. The moon had freed itself of the clouds and was now illuminating the night. I could see a number of the pursuers running in the direction in which Osman had disappeared. Raising my head up at the inquisitive huge moon, I prayed for the clouds to smother Luna but, in pure vindictive fashion, she began to shine brighter than ever. From a small, shingled house, fifty meters from my walnut tree, a window squealed and through its narrow opening I recognised a fat-assed young fellow named Hasan crawling out. I remembered that Murat, the gendarme, and his wife lived in the little house and chuckled at the thought that for some people the entire meaning of life was realised in jumping in and out of other people's windows.

"There's one! Running behind Murat's house!" a voice shouted and immediately three of the pursuers bolted in that very direction.

Sitting up there on the highest branches, I smiled at the thought that this adventure through Murat's window could cost Hasan dearly. At that very moment, about a hundred meters down from me, from the direction of the creek, came the terrifying shriek of one, and then more people. As I looked on, the group of men in uniforms began dividing in all directions, like a drop of water scattering over a hot stove. Soon after, silence returned, and the moon disappeared again behind the clouds. From the houses of the wealthy came sudden barking sounds which were immediately answered from several directions by dogs in the lower part of town and then, again silence. I carefully came down the tree and, walking along the narrowest streets, headed for home. There was no trace or sound of Osman.

My brain was empty. The only activity in my body, apart from the legs, came from the area surrounding my heart. I could feel hot and cold flashes battling in an easy but persistent rhythm for power over my heart. Sudden shots of hot blood made their way from my chest to my brain. Like ocean waves, these flashes battered against me, each one of different strength yet relentless and constant.

As I walked softly and worried over my constantly changing body temperature, for a moment I forgot all about Vavan and the running and shooting down in the town square. In front of the grainshed of the taciturn woodcutter Yevrem, what seemed an article of clothing was hanging from a branch which drooped strangely, like a frozen hand. Walking toward the strange object, I noticed a ragged scarecrow nearby, watching with empty eyes. Something under it was convulsing, rolling around in quiet agony. Upon seeing me standing in front of it, this human lump stretched out its large, disheveled head and uttered a pleading cry:

"What else do you want? She belonged to both of us, you gendarme dog!"

From the voice and the large round eyes, I recognised fat-assed Hasan. Wanting to help him stand up I reached toward him but he, in sheer agony, pushed my hands away and wailed:

"Oh, it's you! Go and get my brother Yavor," he uttered painfully before collapsing like a sack of garbage to the ground and continuing his quiet groaning.

Realising that something horrific had happened to him, I ran toward his brother's street. As soon as I knocked on the front door a heavy male voice answered:

"What do you want? Is it you, Hasan?"

"Hasan is hurt. He's over by Senukic's scarecrow," I blurted out, "Hurry up and come with me!"

When Javor and I arrived, Hasan was no longer moving. He was dead. Later, thinking back, I was surprised by Yavor's coldness in approaching his dead brother.

As we carried him home, I could feel that his pants were soaked in blood. Once inside the house, under the light of the petrol lamp, we were horrified to find that his pants had been torn away around the crotch. When Javor took the pants off, we were faced with a gruesome sight—his penis hung by a thin strip of skin, the large open wound still dripping blood. Before leaving for home, Javor had me swear that I would tell no one of his family's great disgrace.

Upon questioning by Father and Aunt Habibe, I explained that I had been hiding in the orchards after hearing the shots being fired. Osman was already in his room.

In the morning, word quickly spread through town of how the previous night the gendarmes had broken up Vavan's illegal organisation and had shot fat-assed Hasan as he tried to escape. There was also a tale spreading of how five of the gendarmes had come face to face with a horned devil over by the creek and, despite being shot repeatedly from close range, it was unharmed. They were lucky to have survived the incident with their heads intact. In front of the mosque and nearby church, people were talking about the incident, and ascribed the characteristics of communists and the devil to Vavan's followers.

Hasan's funeral was in the afternoon. As the body was taken from the mosque to the graveyard, Javor and Murat the gendarme carried the two front handles of the stretcher. They wouldn't allow anyone to take their place.

That evening, leaning against the corner of our woodshed, I decided to carve out a figurine of fat-assed Hasan. While I was working on the eyebrows, for a brief moment, a brilliant blue light appeared from the figurine's large, round eyes. As soon as the light vanished, mother's voice resonated up from the shingles. She spoke slowly, stopping uncharacteristically often and changing rhythm:

"You were meant for the winds and the rains, the fields and the forests…" She seemed to be reprimanding me for the previous night. "Some people have been given thundering voices, while others leave scented tracks behind them…Follow your father in the days ahead and let the wind take Osman. Do not fear the human in man but beware of the devil in him…You must follow the sun…"

The next morning at breakfast, I caught the look in my brother's eyes. From that brief glance, I vividly remember his flushed eyes, the pale hands and the outstretched fingers. He said that everyone in town was praying for Hasan's soul.

The next time I saw Javor, he again begged me not to tell anyone our secret. As time passed, the memory of Hasan began to grow. At first, everyone was surprised how Hasan could have been involved in Vavan's illegal group but then, over time, Hasan's significance grew and, eventually, even surpassed that of Vavan. I waited for one of the ten people who were down in the basement that night to come out and say that Hasan was never at any of their meetings but none of them did. I expected, also, to hear one morning of how Murat's wife was found hanging from the tree next to Senukic's woodshed, next to the scarecrow, but this also never happened. The next spring, Murat had his little house painted brilliant white. At night, this house had an unreal glow about it and could be seen from every small hill that surrounded our town.

CHAPTER IV

That whole night Fehrat twisted around on the couch next to the stove. >From time to time, the rhythm of his breathing changed. At times it was so slow and silent that Yudja would get out of bed and carefully approach to see if his son was still breathing at all. At other times, Fehrat's respirations would become so loud that Yudja would be startled from half-sleep and softly call out, fearful lest he alarm the young man.

"Who knows what he didn't go through in that Bosnian hell," Yudja whispered to himself as he watched the tormented face before him, all the while feeling his connection to the man grow stronger. Fehrat was obviously racked by nightmares. He lay there shrivelled, biting down on his lip as if trying to hold in a scream, eyes half open, sockets showing only the whites. He was enduring all these nightmares, teeth clenched, without a word uttered in despair or protest.

Yudja had his own ghosts to haunt him, but he was awake. As he lay there watching his new-found son wrestle with his demons, before his eyes emerged various encounters with people from the past. Even his figurines came alive, waving their hands and stamping their feet, twinkling eyes dancing in the near-darkness of the room. This strange dance of the figurines was dominated by fat-assed Hasan, holding his crotch with one hand and waving the severed penis as a torch high above his head, looking not unlike the French Statue of Liberty at the entrance to New York Harbour. Whenever faced with the lives of his figurines, Yudja's lips began to tremble and his fists clenched in protest against the fact that everything about these wooden heroes of his had to be so exact, to the life. His anger further increased when he noticed tears in the eyes of his creations and a look of reproach for having made them such as they were. In desperation, he would lift his head up towards the heavens and, in a metallic voice, cry out:

"None of us is free to choose our destiny. When one of us discovers and creates something, You whisper from above that it has already been written down in Your program. Who gave You the right to make robots out of us, to shape us and our destinies?!"

Afterward, lowering his head toward the floor, he had the feeling that he had done wrong by having the gall to condemn that which he could not reach. While Fehrat wrestled with his demons, Yudja felt sickness in his stomach, clenched his teeth and stared aimlessly toward the attic. When he briefly glanced toward his figurines, Irena held out her hand as she shook her ripe hips. Yudja moved his head: Fehrat's face appeared, bright red, foam gathered around his mouth as though he were a tired horse after a race.

In the morning, Yudja quietly dressed and, while Fehrat still slept, went to buy fresh bread and milk. Outside, the rain continued to fall with no end in sight. Olson's Bakery on Lonsdale…the smell of fresh bread and buns was everywhere. When he returned, he found Fehrat standing next to the window.

"It seems that only your body is here while your soul is still in Bosnia," Yudja commented with an easy smile. "You spent the whole night fighting some battle. I couldn't sleep so I stood behind you, guarding your back so no one would surprise you."

"How do you get information from Bosnia around here? Do you get any of our newspapers?" Fehrat inquired as he looked at the plastic bag with the bread and the milk.

"There are some Serbian and Croatian newspapers but you're better off not reading them. All lies and disinformation. You'd think that Tudjman and Milosevic were writing it themselves. Sometimes, the odd Bosnian newspaper makes its way here from Germany but even those are largely under the thumb of Izetbegovic.* I know so little English that the local newspapers are worthless to me. At the immigration centre they gave me a list of our clubs in this area but I didn't contact any of them. It's better this way. Anyway, I have my informants," Yudja pointed at the figurines standing lifeless on the shelf.

"I saw..." Fehrat tried to smile. "It seems they were arranged differently last night."

After they finished breakfast, Yudja's son suggested that they continue with the stories.

"There is something that I have yet to fully understand. When I listen objectively, believing only that which I can see with my eyes and hear with my ears, it seems that the reality you describe is often overtaken by a dream-like quality. But, it is too early for commentary..." Fehrat temporised.

"Do you think that outside the human logic which is based solely upon primitive materialism and which accepts only what the eyes, ears and nose tell it, there doesn't exist any other world? If that were so, then this already miserable life would be even more wretched and depraved. Some people are given the ability to rise above that which only the fingertips can reach and to enter a world with more complex relations between its creatures. It is up to you what you choose to believe, but I would ask you to respect my beliefs as well. So, if you don't mind, I will continue with the story in my own way," proposed Yudja, while Fehrat spread out on the couch next to the window.

THE FIRST STAMPEDE OF WAR

"After that night at Marta's Cellar only Vavan was imprisoned. They tortured him in order to find out the names of other members of the group but he didn't say a word. Hanka, the waitress, disappeared from town as quickly as she had entered it. From the outside world, alarming news filtered into town. That outside world eventually reached us also and there was a massive mobilisation. The people all knew this meant war and though no one was particularly fond of war, many were accustomed to it, almost indifferent. Osman and I were mobilised, as were our friends from the third year of Gymnasium.* Also mobilised were the healthy horses from Pset and the surrounding area, along with a large number of bulls, cows and sheep, all meant, like us, for the use of the army. It happened very quickly. On the faces of the officers, who were increasingly to be seen running around town, and the gendarmes, one could see tension which would soon turn to panic. With us, events followed a scenario carefully prepared for the benefit of recruits by taskmasters immemorial. First we were housed at the town's Sport Hall They gave us uniforms which smelled of gasoline and then for two days they lectured us on the strength of our army. Major Sredoyevic, a tall, bulky man from somewhere around Niksic's Mountains in Montenegro, would often repeat how even at the mere thought of our army, Hitler's little moustache would shake and his left eye would twitch uncontrollably for hours. Next, we spent three days at the shooting range in Lazo's field, where we were familiarised with the long Kraguyevac-made rifles. After the target practice, we were given one day's leave to say our farewells and goodbyes to our loved ones before we prepared to head off and meet the enemy, who, it was being whispered, had already levelled Belgrade to the ground.

It was a Sunday when all of the Psetian units gathered out in the field below the town. I was surprised to see what a military force had been hibernating in our peaceful valley. I was even more surprised when the mass of horses, cows, bulls and sheep began to sway, moo and bleat behind our units. On the faces of the officers, all strangers to me, I noticed harshness and discipline, and pride in the force under their command. The formations were lined up, guns raised high and aimed westward, and upon command the entire valley detonated as if in a delirium. The young and the old, everyone came out to see us off, even aunt Habibe, but father wasn't there. The most excited were the children, and the bravest of them followed us all the way to the first slopes of the ridge up which our road led.

By night we were deep in the mountains and when we reached a hamlet the order came to prepare for supper and sleep. From the nearby church came the odour of cooked food, but that was only for the senior officers. The rest of us dived into our backpacks for rations and then looked for room under the trees where we slept on our uniform overcoats.

Our people are used to seeing armies. That is why it had felt normal not to see a single tear on the faces of the mothers saying goodbye to their sons. Yet, everyone knew that not all of those leaving would return to their homes. Some mothers spent the rest of their lives waiting for their sons to return from the battlefields of the long-silent front. My mother didn't see me off to war. The day and night before we marched away, I spent hiding around the barn and sty, expecting to hear her voice. But it never came.

I was wakened before sunrise by the dew and a faraway thud. It sounded like a distant thunderstorm. While we were eating breakfast from the food we had brought with us, just when the first light came, we were brought to our feet by aeroplanes which appeared from behind the peak of Drenova Head, the steep-sided hill which stood like a sentinel down the valley in the direction of Bihac. About a dozen of them flew over us, only to turn back in a wide arc. Not until we heard the sound of the machine-guns being fired from the aeroplanes' wings did we receive the command to dive to the ground. The planes deposited on us a part of their bomb load and them headed west. As they disappeared behind the mountains, Stevan, our machine-gunner, jumped to his feet and showered a long burst into the now-empty sky.

Just then, as the clouds of dust which the German bombs had caused began to settle, the entire herd of horses, cattle and sheep, which up to now had been rigid with fear and confusion, turned and stormed back toward Pset as if on command. There was no mooing, bleating or huffing to be heard, just the thud of hundreds of hoofs, the snapping of branches and breaking of the stunted trees as they tore through a grove near the hamlet.

After the aeroplanes' attack, and having heard the gunfire and bombs, the people of Pset ran out of their houses and instinctively headed toward the parkland by the lake. The gendarmes tried to calm them down but when they heard the thundering sound rolling toward town, not even the attempts of Mayor Semanic had any effect. The people, again instinctively, headed back to their houses and grabbed whatever they had—rifles, pistols, axes, pitchforks—and ran in the direction of the thunder. The closer it drew, the more mysterious the rumble of the stampeding herd became because after seeing and hearing the aeroplanes, the people expected motorised units to follow. Those who moved deep into the field and spread out behind the thorns and junipers were the first to sight the enormous cloud of dust which was nearing. Mayor Semanic, rifle in hand and accompanied by a group of gendarmes, ventured out the furthest to get a better look at just what was charging toward them. >From behind one of the thorn-bushes, three men with hunting rifles suddenly jumped out and shouted:

"Horses! Horses are coming!"

Everyone on the first line of defence sighed in relief. Hundreds of men and women stood up and looked westward. They saw the herd of horses emerge from behind the large boulders known as Lynx Rocks and head straight toward their town. When the leaders of the herd were only a few hundred metres away, the town's defenders frantically began to wave whatever they happened to have in their hands in an effort to stop the panicked animals. The horses extended their heads and opened their eyes wide to see more clearly what was blocking their path, but behind them the cattle were relentlessly advancing, their horns lowered and sharp. Trying to avoid the human barrier in front of them, the horses spread out. The majority of them succeeded in avoiding full-frontal collision with the people but the cattle behind, blinded in the semi-darkness of the horses' dust, bunched up and became a true stampede. The first shots from the town's defenders were aimed to the sky, an effort to frighten the cattle, but seeing that these had little effect, they directed their next ragged volley at the animals themselves.

The cattle at the head of the stampede were brought rolling and convulsing down. Those following were tripped up but managed to continue moving forward, pressed on by the hell-bent herd behind. They tore the ground with their hoofs and heads as they struggled to halt. Some managed to change direction, to either side of the first defence line, but the majority became entangled with the mass of humanity and a brutal crush ensued. The first to find themselves under the hoofs were the mayor and his gendarmes. They were followed by the rest of the front-line defenders.

When the dust settled, the landscape that remained for hundreds of metres around was a wasteland. It resembled a battlefield after the battle but without the greys and greens of the uniforms and helmets strewn all around. The final cost of the first engagement of the Second World War in the Psetian field was twelve dead, over a hundred injured and a mountain of cattle meat. The sheep never arrived at the field. Realising early on the stupidity of following the horses and the cattle, they headed instead for calmer pastures.

News of the tragedy back home reached us by way of army scouts sent to retrieve the escaped animals.

The aeroplanes and the cattle stampede had flustered the soldiers. The recruits were confused most of all, those for whom the mobilisation was their first encounter with military weapons and discipline. The anxiety among the officers was also obvious. The panic increased when we began to receive contradictory orders: first, to fall into formation on the fields behind the village plum orchards; then to stand at ease. At first, we all remained silent, expecting to hear the order to move forward, toward the Una canyon, but instead whispering began, from soldier to soldier down the lines. Word spread that the animal stampede had killed and wounded many people. The murmuring became louder when Ahmet and Vasva Redzic were rumoured to be among the dead, as well as old Asim Kartal and the mother of Savo Petrovic. Both of the Redzic brothers, Ahmet's sons, stepped out from my unit and approached Captain Skundric. A heated exchange ensued. From those standing near enough to hear the conversation, we learnt that the Redzics were asking to be allowed to return home so they could bury their parents, after which they promised to rejoin the unit. The Captain at first merely shook his head but then, as the Redzic boys persisted, his voice grew louder and he motioned abruptly with his hands for them to go back to their places with us.

Panic grew in all the units. Increasingly, officers could be seen running toward the regimental headquarters located in the priest's house. Soon, the military police went among the units and took away those they deemed the loudest and most threatening. Twenty men were taken toward the small house next to the village store. Suddenly, while they moved through the large orchard, revolver shots rang out. As we looked on, a number of the detained men stepped out of line and ran toward the forest which was about a hundred metres away, beyond the orchard. The first shots had been merely a warning for them to stop, but then a volley of rifle fire rang out and two of the escapees collapsed to the ground before our eyes. The three others made it to the first trees in the forest and disappeared. A few seconds after the shots the whole regiment still looked on in disbelief. Then, with tension growing ever higher, as if an order had been given soldiers started rushing toward their fallen comrades. Captain Skundric stood before our unit, hands outstretched, but the first soldiers heading toward him managed to side-step him while the ones who followed brought him down and soon our Captain was lying on the ground, unmoving.

When we reached the two who had been shot, we saw Savo Petrovic and Enes Druzic lying mortally wounded on the ground. Savo was already dead, the bullet having hit him below the left shoulder-blade. Enes was screaming, spurts of blood shooting out at short intervals below his right breast. Then he was silent, gripping with both hands the place where the bullet had entered, jerking a few times. After that, his arms relaxed and his legs began to stretch easily. The soldiers crowded around, each wanting to be as close as possible.

I looked around for Osman. Not seeing him, I shoved my way back out of the crowd. From there I could see the military police pushing men aside in order to make way for senior officers trying to get to the scene of the incident. I felt a pain in my stomach and throbbing emptiness in my head. I began to tighten my grip on my rifle, as if intending to break it into pieces. There was no trace of Osman, yet I felt a need to be near him. Leaning against a tree trunk, my back to the crowd which was now overcome by a deadly silence, I let my eyes wander toward the spot where we had left our Captain lying. Numbly,

I watched as a soldier repeatedly hit the Captain over the head with something resembling a large rod. I realised what I had just seen only after the soldier, walking in sure, short steps, returned to the orchard and re-entered the mass which surrounded the two dead bodies. Looking in the area where the soldier had entered the crowd, between two trees I glimpsed my brother Osman. Paralysed by shock, I numbly looked on as Osman again disappeared into the crowd. I came to only when a pair of soldiers grabbed me by the arms and shouted in unison:

"Did you see who killed the Captain?"

"No…Which captain?!" I answered, once my brain regained its composure.

At that moment, a shout came from below the orchard:

"There's Tale!…It's him!…"

The two soldiers next to me let go of my arms and ran toward the field. I ran after them. Down from the spot where the Captain's body lay, next to a hazel bush stood Tale Harambasha, pulling up his pants. When he realised that they were all headed toward him, he threw off his cap and fell into the bush.

I stood there looking at the growing crowd which had come over from the other side of the orchard, trying to spot my brother.

Soon, all movement stopped. Out of the hazel bushes, three men pulled Tale, his trousers still askew. One of them was furiously beating him about the head, the legs and in the ribs. They brought him before a captain who also took the time to deliver a few punches and kicks. The higher-ranking officers approached. On their faces one could see a combination of shock and rage. A tall, thin one with a pencil moustache and a large round mole above his right eyebrow ordered Tale Harambasha to stand up. We could see Tale's battered and bruised face, blood running out of numerous wounds. He tried to stand straight before the senior officers but his knees would not hold him. As he was about to collapse, he was caught by the two soldiers next to him and held upright by the armpits.

"Why did you kill the Captain, you worthless nothing?!" shouted the pencil-moustached officer, his eyes piercing into helpless Tale.

"What captain?…It wasn't me!…I have diarrhea…," stuttered Tale, his eyes jumping between the Captain's lifeless body and the very much alive officers standing around him.

One of the other officers approached Tale, lifted his head by the chin to have a better look, turned to the pencil-moustached officer and said:

"Traitor! This is the one who was constantly whispering during the march how the German Army is invincible and how he had to leave his blind mother alone at home. Coward!"

Tale's fate was thus sealed. Perhaps the sentence was meted out so quickly because of the explosion of fear and discontent which began with the appearance of the aeroplanes and worsened after the animals stampeded. They took Tale to the house which served as headquarters while the bodies of the Captain, Savo and Enes were taken to the church. The order came to line up according to individual units and our lieutenant, Tavcar, was named company commander.

Osman was walking toward me, together with Milan, our friend from school. I looked into my brother's eyes, expecting to find in them an explanation of what I had seen, but they were completely at peace. He asked me how I had managed to lose myself in this crowd. I didn't answer.

While our new commander told us how we would soon be on the move again and tried to convince us of the falseness of the news being spread about the tragedy which befell our fellow Psetians, a courier arrived with the order for all units to form up according to battalions in the field below the village. Soon there arrived before us those same officers we had seen earlier. The senior officer was Colonel Rajic, commander of the regiment. He of the pencil moustache. They were followed by Tale Harambasha, who was being escorted by four soldiers. It all took place very quickly. The colonel briefly informed the soldiers that things had happened today which were unheard of for the powerful Yugoslav Army, that traitors had infiltrated our ranks whose aim was to weaken us before our conflict with the fascist forces—and that Tale Harambasha was one of them. The military court martial had sentenced him to death for the murder of the Captain and for traitorous actions.

The four soldiers took Tale and stood him before a large, blossoming wild-cherry tree which had been left standing when the villagers cleared the land. He turned toward our unit and shouted:

"I didn't kill him!" after which the four seized Tale and pushed him hard against the cherry tree. Tale again turned toward us and shouted once more, this time even louder, so that the echo reverberated above the village several times:

"Kahrics, tell my mother that I ran away across the border!"

I could no longer bear to look at Tale. Something seized me by the throat, around the Adam's apple, and began choking me. I looked at Osman, who calmly watched Tale and the firing line. When the burst of gunfire rang out, I could see the twitching muscles below Osman's eye. Otherwise, he showed no emotion. The soldiers looked on in disbelief, not fully understanding what was going on. When Tale's body stopped moving, a large sigh of relief could be heard from all directions and the tension began to subside.

The "at ease" order came again, along with the command not to stray far from our units. I sat down next to a large ash tree, looking toward the forest. I turned off my listening senses and began to stare blankly at the heaving bosom of the mountain. My mind frantically jumped from topic to topic, from picture to picture, but each time I returned to a vivid vision of Osman murderously hitting the fallen Captain over the head. This repeating vision was faithfully followed by one of the peaceful face of my brother. This vision led to one of Tale Harambasha and my brother, together, listening to rifle shots being fired and only one of them falling to the ground, the wrong one, the innocent one. The entire cycle of events which had taken place that morning in the fields and orchards below the village kept repeating themselves in my head. My imagination added and subtracted from what I had seen and what I gathered that I had seen. Faces changed shape and colour. In the end, the image which stood before me, stubbornly refusing to leave, was one of Tale's sheepish head, and a horned Osman looking on from above. In the background, I could hear music, marching songs mixed with old folk songs from our village. Grotesque madness overcame me, worsening the grotesque reality around me. I heard the sound of my mother's screams, like a tocsin echo from the depths of the mountain ravines. It had a strangely calming effect on me.

I was jolted back to reality by Milan's hand on my shoulder. He shook me and then I heard his unmistakable, screeching voice:

"What are you all alone for!? Don't you know that we'll see much worse than this! That's how it is. Anyway...Come on, they are seeing who can throw the rock furthest, let's have a try at it."

Turning toward the other soldiers, I could see small groups standing around eagerly watching the rock throwing contest. I stood up and followed Milan. They were measuring their strength against one another in what is a traditional competition in our parts. There were two groups; Milan and I joined the one which included Osman and Lieutenant Tavcar. The blond, fair-skinned Tavcar was only of medium build, but athletically proportioned. Spinning a mid-sized rock, feeling out the best grip for throwing, the Lieutenant mumbled something to the rock. Someone close enough to hear repeated it as "If only you were a shot for me to put." From this, and the practised maneuvering of his body, it was evident to all who were watching that he had done this before and was not without technique.

With his right hand, he lifted the rock above his head, slowly placed it alongside his ear, bent his knees into a half-squat, and then, in a flash, extended himself upright, like a catapult, and the rock flew past all the markings made by the previous throwers. Everyone looked at the Lieutenant in amazement. He looked at the place where the rock made first contact with the grass, then at the rock, and then he repeated his throwing motion, moved his shoulder left and right, as if to re-evaluate the effectiveness of his motion and positioning.

Milan threw further than the rest but fifteen centimetres less than Tavcar. I matched Milan's throw. A few more soldiers threw and, finally, it was Osman's turn. We knew that Osman didn't think much of brute strength. I normally would have been surprised to see him show any interest in the contest but, now, everything had changed. Osman was no longer the Osman of old.

Taking off his soldier's jacket, he picked up a rock as though it was something that needed to be gotten rid of as quickly as possible. Walking toward the grub hoe which marked the foul line, he took a last look at the distances made by those before him. Placing the rock in his palm, then on his shoulder, he turned his back to the marking and, like a snake jumping out of the grass, shot forth with his upper body, twisting in a semi-circle. The rock unglued itself from his palm and passed all of the markers before settling directly on top of the Lieutenant's.

We all ran to the place where the rock had landed. Osman also approached, his face the picture of peace and tranquility. Either something truly momentous had happened to him or he was just a great actor. The Lieutenant picked up the rock, motioned as if he was going to return to the throwing line, stopped, looked at Osman, then at us, threw the rock into the grass and held out his hand.

"It's better that we leave things as they are. If you agree?"

Osman accepted the outstretched hand, but below his right temple, and across to his nose, I noticed him twitch several times. At that moment, from the forest which hugged the road leading to Bihac, came the sounds of motors. We all turned in the direction from which the noise was coming, when out from under some low-lying trees emerged a soldier on a motorcycle. He was followed by two more three-wheelers. They stopped by the first soldiers they encountered, asked something and then rode on towards the regimental headquarters.

"They are bringing orders from the high command," commented the old soldiers, Djuro and Yakov. A few minutes passed when, from the direction of Bihac, at equal intervals, came the sounds of five or six cannons firing. Seconds after that, the shells landed, one after the other, on a hill not far from our unit. We gathered around Lieutenant Tavcar like chickens around a hen when an eagle circles in the sky above, waiting for him to explain to us what was going on. The Slovenian looked toward the small clouds of smoke left by the cannon shells and said:

"Heavy Mörsers![1] They can fire from fifty kilometres away. The Germans are in Bihac."

That is how the Second World War really began for us. We all understood Tavcar's explanation to be a warning of the formidable force we faced, and knew that our mountain artillery would be no match for their Mörsers I was shocked by the Lieutenant's explanation and, especially, the thought of being destroyed by an army without ever seeing any of their soldiers.

From there on, everything proceeded at an accelerated pace: when dusk settled, from the direction of the Una canyon came the murmuring sound of machinery; the colour and intensity of this sound remained the same for quite a while but it gradually began to increase. Again, the old soldiers talked about the enemy's approaching mechanised force. I could feel the fear overcoming our soldiers' will to face the enemy. When the officers relayed the regimental command's order to head toward the road and take up positions in the nearby forest, sporadic protests could be heard. Nevertheless, as if we already had the feeling that the darkness quickly overtaking the villages and mountains would soon settle matters on its own, we went without further complaint and followed the order.

Since the incident with our Captain, my brain and my heart were waging a tug of war. I had discovered so many new things about my brother in such a short space of time that my entire notion of who and what he was, which I had been piecing together since we were infants, began to unravel. The emotions, the blood, the memories from childhood and youth…everything became uncertain. >From the time when I first made contact with my mother following her death, I had accepted as true the notion that life couldn't be confined to what the eye could see. But this matter with Osman…

And then, as we marched toward the road, Osman and I, shoulder to shoulder, I asked myself if this was my brother marching next to me, the same person with whom I had played in the fields until exhaustion, or was it someone else? Why didn't I ask him for an explanation? Just as I decided to provoke a conversation on the subject, I was struck by the fear that we wouldn't understand one another and a chasm would separate us from that moment on. Rather than lose him forever, I remained silent. I needed Osman. Somewhere in the back of my head another gnawing thought began to rear its head diligently—perhaps Osman is Osman, while all of these incredible events of late are some inexplicable nightmare produced by my over-active imagination. What else had I imagined? At first, it had seemed completely normal for me to communicate with my mother, even after her body was buried with the whole town watching, but now?…My brain was too weak to answer such questions.

"What's wrong? Did someone cut out your tongue?" said Osman in a loud whisper. "Are you frightened of war and combat? Don't worry! Tomorrow night you'll be sleeping back in Father's house."

I shook as he spoke but didn't answer. I waited for him to continue. I tried to see him out of the corner of my eye but darkness reigned and his face could not be seen. Like a flash, my mind's eye returned to the sight of the Captain's head, one eye open and the tongue hanging out. I stopped, and the soldier walking behind me gave me a shove in the back. Osman grabbed me by the arm, tightly squeezing my triceps.

"They murdered Tale and he was innocent," I blurted out uncontrollably.

"Executed," Osman's voice returned at me like an echo, whispering into my ear, "and after the Captain had dishonoured Tale's sister, Zemka."

I wanted to scream, grab Osman and all those around me and throw them into the charcoal black sky, far from the face of the earth. I'd had my eye on Zemka for the past few years and we thought we had been careful that no one in town find out about us. I took Osman in turn by the upper arm and began insisting that he apologise for what he had just said. The soldiers behind us pushed forward while those in front of us stopped. The white road was in front of us.

Our company was given the task of positioning ourselves along the lower Vrdjevic Forest road. Lieutenant Tavcar skillfully organised the platoons. Our platoon was the furthest west. Osman and I, along with four other pairs, were given the task of scouting the territory in the direction from which we expected the enemy's troops to come.

"The enemy also sends out its reconnaissance ahead of the regular army. Be doubly careful," warned the commander of the scouts,

Second-Lieutenant Kosovic, the same one who was among the first to run over the helpless Captain Skundric. "The enemy's reconnaissance needs to be taken out." He further demonstrated the gist of this statement by running his index finger along his throat. "But the most important thing is to keep your own head in one piece."

The darkness was visible, though the moon had just begun to light up the sky in the surrounding Grmec Mountains and toward the north-east. The southern winds had grown silent; the autumn leaves had already rotted; the first blades of grass were coming out from under the dried grass of last year, so that there was no sound being made while walking among the trees and the bushes.

My brother and I walked toward a second road, which led from the west to Pset. We reached the first fences by the ploughed fields. From the smoke, we knew that village houses were near but there were no lights or signs of life to be seen. The dogs barked in the courtyards as we lay down next to the furthest fence. Someone ran toward us and we prepared our rifles and bayonets. There were three men rushing in our direction. Lying next to the fence, we prepared to shoot. Twenty paces from us, they reached the same fence and dexterously jumped over it. One of them, in our language, muttered "Over there, by the brushwood" and the three of them sat down next to a shrub next to the fence. We could hear the sound of knives being withdrawn from their scabbards. The dogs in the courtyard had unsettled the other dogs in the village; barking could be heard all around but nothing moved toward us. The three men nearby waited in silence until they realised that no danger threatened them from the village. The striking of matches could be heard, followed by the firefly glow of tiny embers.

"Zvonko, give me your cigarettes. Mine are flattened," a rough voice could be heard. By its accent and colour, the speaker was obviously not from our parts. I could sense Osman, too, gripping his rifle firmly.

"This village is like a graveyard," a second voice murmured. "They must have shit their pants at the thought of Hitler".

The third one waited a while before loudly commenting: "They're Serb villages here. Our fellows who served in the Austrian regiments say that the Bosnian Serbs are like vultures—heroes when fighting corpses. But…St. Joseph help me, the army following us is no corpse."

"Quiet, womaniser! The Yugo army also has its lookouts. Finish your cigarette and lets go have a look around."

"What Yugo army? Around Karlovac, entire divisions surrendered without firing a single bullet. When they saw the tanks and heard the Mörsers they knew they were in shit up to their shoulders." The "womaniser" had grown conversational, perhaps thinking that he was at some village meeting.

They stood up, threw their butts into the grass and headed in a direction away from the village. Osman whispered to me that they were Croats in Hitler's service and that we would have more problems with them than with Hitler. I was surprised that he'd mention such foul hearsay because I knew that we had never had any problems with the Croatians. I remembered that there was no two better men in our town than Yakov and his father Jozo, and they were Croatians. But I didn't contradict Osman.

We stayed down on the icy ground by the fence for a while before agreeing to go through the village to the road. The moon had already come out over the flat top of the nearest mountain and its pale light illuminated the entire ravine. As we walked around the fence I was suddenly struck by the thought that of late Osman had developed into something of a wise and intelligent type while I lagged far behind him and thus his attitude toward me had become similar to what one would have towards a much younger and less competent underling. Revolted by such a thought, I made up my mind to start a serious conversation with him in which I would confront him and demand a number of explanations for his recent behaviour, but I quickly abandoned such an idea. It was as if something in my brain whispered to me that now was not the time for such clarifications, especially with my brother Osman. In fact, I began to fear him a little. I was embarrassed by the realisation that since we had both put on uniforms, whenever I was around him I would instinctively keep one hand free and within quick reaching distance of my dagger.

Walking around a grove of unusually tall trees we came upon a large brick house. Through the narrow window which looked toward the fence shone a weak light. As if by agreement, both of us crouched close to the ground and observed everything in our field of vision. Not a soul could be seen anywhere. Believing that some courageous peasant had lit the candle to spite both the advancing German forces and his own fear, we approached the window in our crouched positions. Two or three steps from the house was a cornel-wood bush whose yellow flowers were visible under the milky moonlit sky. We crouched by the bush, trying to get a better look through the window and into the house. We were both tense. Our skinny Colonel, with his pencil moustache, was sitting by a wooden table across from a large headed, dark-bearded man wearing a black leather coat. They were drinking out of a green bottle, taking turns, each making a toast before taking the next swig. They were discussing something serious. If it wasn't for the fact that one of the two men inside was our skinny Colonel, we probably would have moved on from the house and its inhabitants. However, our curiosity, like a magnet, would not allow us to leave before we found out the nature of the conversation taking place inside.

"Well! They have…They ordered us to halt the enemy advance here and hold them down until reinforcements arrived from Banjaluka. And what do you think became of those very people who gave me these orders? They have already fled over the border with their luggage bags full of gold and American dollars. We have been betrayed, Mr. Karan," expounded the Colonel, sitting rigidly upright in the chair, visibly pleased with himself.

The other one sat there nodding his head and rolling his eyes, letting it be known with his grimace that none of this surprised him and, in fact, was all to be expected.

"I knew they would eventually overrun you, but I didn't think it would all end so quickly." Karan brought his hairy head closer to the Colonel's. "I knew the Slovenians and Croats would betray us, but our own people quickly gave up in Voyvodina, and in Lika. Draza Mihajlovic has let it be known that everyone needs to get their hands on as many weapons as possible, otherwise Black Friday* will soon be at our doorstep."

"That's why we're here," smiled the Colonel. Lifting the bottle toward the attic, in a voice full of pathos, as if delivering one of Shakespeare's soliloquies, he continued: "Perhaps the hour has struck for us to unite our long-suffering Serbian nation. The German and Italian armies will pass through the Balkans like a storm, but after each storm life goes on. You, Mr. Karan, must lead our people here in resistance to the occupier and be one of the brightest stars of our final victory. I am here to help you as much as I am able."

The bearded collocutor took the bottle from the officer after that worthy had swallowed a few more gulps, and looked directly into his skinny, shaven face with the ridiculous little moustache.

"You, Colonel Rajic, are a military specialist. The kind of man that we will need to lead our nation. Heart and will are not going to be enough. Especially now that Hitler has attached Bosnia to Pavelic's* Independent State of Croatia. Pavelic has sworn that he will kill all the Serbs who don't flee across the Drina..."

"Yes, sir!...That is true. But, whether he knows it or not, Pavelic is doing us a great service. How else will we unite the nation quickly? Serbia will reach as far as Karlobag in the Adriatic, and beyond Karlobag it will be Italy. Djuic* has already taken over the Lika hinterlands, with the blessing of the Italians. Our flag will fly over the Adriatic before anyone expected. Bosnia is not a problem..."

The dogs again began barking throughout the village. We tried to listen for any other sounds but, apart from the barking, there was nothing to hear.

The bearded one changed the direction of the conversation. "You say that you can hand over five hundred rifles, along with ammunition?"

"Along with anything that you manage to get your hands on at the crack of dawn after the soldiers begin to abandon their positions..." That's news, I thought. "There will be plenty of weapons to be had," added the Colonel. "As far as compensation is concerned, it's like we already agreed: your people with their wagons at the munitions dump, where I'll be waiting after midnight. Naturally, you will remember to bring the money and the gold, everything that you Chetniks have taken from the bank and from the rich Psetian merchants and landlords. It is all for the generals and their ladies who surround them. Nothing for me. I am doing all this purely for patriotic reasons. I will need to disappear for a while but I will rejoin you when the time is right. First, I need to return to my people in Southern Serbia. Send my regards to our friend, Juicy, when you see him…"

From the direction of the German positions, a series of flares shot up into the sky. Both these noble fellows jumped toward the window while Osman and I dove to the ground, flat on our stomachs. Typical of many rural homes, a stable extended under the house. Its doors creaked open and two soldiers, rifles in hand, rushed out. They headed toward the front of the house. Osman murmured to me: "The Colonel's escorts."

In soft steps, we retreated to the surrounding bushes, and then on to the grove.

"Tonight is the biggest turning point of our lives," whispered Osman as we quickly and silently ran through the grove. By their rough bark, which kept skinning my knuckles as I ran between the trees, it was easy to recognise them as oaks.

"We will have to take sides with these that are coming: for them or against them. There will be no middle road. If you decide to serve the fascist enemy, you will become the fascist enemy. If you decide to resist him, then you will have to go through hell. Those who manage to come out of hell alive will be able to continue."

My brother's words were spoken so softly that not even the light wind which cleverly managed to enter even the most remote corners of the grove could catch them and take them any further. But, in my head, they resonated like the heavy blows which Lalo the Gypsy's Herculean hammer delivered to his anvil. I realised, to my surprise, that we were at the onset of a great tempest and, if it were up to me, I'd prefer to have it all blow over, to allow the accumulated electricity to spend itself so that I could lift my head up again, the way an ostrich takes his head out of the sand when he senses the danger has passed.

Osman's ultimatum of choosing between two extremes was the most difficult decision that I had faced in my young life.

The breeze turned into a gust, while small, elongated clouds began arriving from the southern chaplet of the mountains and along toward the ravine. The moon lifted itself high above our heads, as if wanting to distance itself from our troubled earth.

The flares again shot up into the sky. These seemed to be much closer than the first ones. Bending low, we made our way to the foot of the dense spruce forest and sat there for quite some time, our backs to one another. We were silent, drowsy, just listening to the nightlife of the woods. The dark clouds began to collide with the moon, and slowly drown it. Having failed at that, they settled on pushing it to the background and turning off all of the lights in the sky. Soon, you couldn't even see the hand before your eyes and we decided to stay put until the first light of dawn. It was growing colder, so we leaned back and remained quiet. Half-asleep, we were abruptly brought to our senses by the sounds of German war machinery. The growing roar of their engines told us that they were on the move and could come into contact, and combat, with our troops at any moment.

In no time, the sound of the engines drew level with us and passed on, yet there was still no sound of weapons being fired. From the direction where our units should have been positioned, there was nothing to be heard. The various coloured flares, rising high above our heads, were now becoming more frequent. The time for staying put seemed to be ending. I suggested that we head toward town. Haphazardly, we blundered up through the woods and across fields, the direction of our movement decided for us by the noise of machinery behind. There was no trace of our troops anywhere.

When we reached the flat peak of Lipa Hill, below which lay the broad field leading to Pset, dawn was beginning to replace the night. The enemy machinery was moving roughly at the same pace as our walking. Sitting under the cover of the wide hazel grove at the very top of the hill, we were in position to see a good deal of the road, toward the east and the west.

On the east side, morning fog covered the roadside trees which wound their way through town, so that the only objects visible were the church tower and the minaret of the mosque. Seen from such a distance, they appeared to be leaning against one another. The broad field below us was peaceful, seemingly carved out of stone. If one were not to turn around, he'd be left with a memory of eternal peace, a deeply religious impression. But, from the west, martial life was arriving and its roar could not only be heard, it could be felt in the ground beneath us. It entered our bodies, from the toes right up into the brain. It was constantly moving, pausing briefly in the heart to change its beat. Looking down at the German machinery, I felt like a young man upon seeing the one he loves in the arms of another. A choking feeling in my throat further provoked my fear and desire to weep uncontrollably. The sight, which memory and the passing of time can never erase, of the seemingly never-ending column of war machines winding their way along the macadam road which passed through fields and clearings, became lost to the eye only when it reached the western chaplet of the mountains. Before the German column and to its sides, only a hundred or so metres away, were the remains of our scattered troops. The ones in front were walking quickly, as if trying to reach the town before the enemy, while the ones to the sides seemed to be guarding their flanks from an non-existent surprise attack. No one touched anyone. Both armies accepted this strange game and unceremoniously moved together along the approaches to Pset.

The two of us also played our roles. As yet, we could do nothing but watch, half-expecting something to happen down below which would turn the smoothly running situation into a living hell.

Our troops had already reached the level surface of the broad field, several kilometres outside the town, and still nothing had changed. At the head of the enemy army were ten tanks; following them was the endless mass of trucks carrying troops and pulling cannons. Such a military force had surely never before set foot in these parts, not even the mighty Austro-Hungarian army which passed through on their way toward Sarajevo, carrying out the annexation of Bosnia and Herzegovina decided at the Congress of Vienna. The old people remembered them by the trail of manure left behind, since all their cannons, supplies and troops were being drawn and carried by thousands of horses. Since then, along this path from Bihac to Sarajevo, there has evolved a race of bulky brown horses with yellow manes, much different from the diminutive horses which had long roamed the mountainous Bosnian terrain. After the Austro-Hungarian march, most of the native mares died during foaling, probably because the western stallions were twice as large and heavy as the local ones.

Things began to go wrong when the first tanks emerged out of the low-lying oak and hornbeam forest and continued along the road now leading through the grazing lands. The road went by Herendic Moat, actually an abyss which carried surface water into an underground mountain stream. The first tank negotiated the curve around the moat while the second and third tanks were at the sharpest portion of the turn when, under the weight of the iron, the road caved in and both of the tanks collapsed into the immense rift. Those behind them immediately interpreted this to be an attack upon the Aryan force, came to a halt, turned their cannons toward our closest units and the field began to quake. The tanks had as targets the mass of defenceless human flesh before them. The easiest marks were on the exposed left wing of the column, where with each new explosion, along with the uprooted soil and rocks, arms and legs could also be seen flying into the air. The blood of Psetian soldiers fell to the earth like red rain.

After the initial confusion which paralysed our soldiers, they soon responded in two separate ways. One group began, as if on command, to flee as far as possible from the iron that was sowing death all around them. Seen from above where the two of us looked on, the orderly picture was immediately shattered, as though a heavy rock had fallen into still water. The other group, much smaller, fell to the ground and began firing back at the armoured leviathans. The tanks then turned off the road and roared onto the fields on both sides, where they sprayed machine-gun fire upon anything and everything that moved…The military confrontation provoked by the poor foundation of the road around Herendic Moat once again changed the rhythm of events. Those parts of our defeated army that were closest to town fled toward the nearby orchards, while those closer to the forest quickly disappeared among the trees. The tanks had divided into several groups, depending upon which particular group they decided to fire upon. Out of the German trucks which were beginning to flood on to the clearing, no soldiers came. It was as if they realised that the fighting had nothing to do with them.

The final part of this bloody drama came when the tanks decided to stop pursuing our scattered troops and began returning to the road. Frightened by the explosions and gunfire, out of the narrow gorge carved across the field by the underground stream emerged about twenty horses, who most likely had been there since yesterday's stampede. They galloped across the field and toward the hill where Osman and I were lying. Between them and their intended destination stood the column of tanks. At first, I thought that when they saw the iron obstacle before them they would turn away. But, their eyes perhaps clouded by fear, they headed straight for the tanks. The machines stopped and at any moment I expected to hear the loud and sustained sound of machine-gun fire. Like an ocean wave, or a living grey carpet, the horses surged forward, past the tanks and toward the hills and valleys. From their extended muzzles could be seen little clouds of steam; the hair of their manes stood as upright as that on a frightened cat and their tails streamed level with their hindquarters. The man-holes on the tanks opened up and out of each one emerged a head in a leather cap. Soldiers jumped out of the trucks and fixed their eyes upon the maddened horses. Soon, all I could hear was the thud of hoofs. When the horses were some fifty metres away from us, I saw their abnormally wide-open eyes, the foam gushing from their mouths and tufts of grass flying in all directions.

When the noise settled, from the direction of the town could be heard the clamour of the inhabitants. The people were well accustomed to ill-fortune and knew what the thundering of the cannons and the shrieking of the machine-guns meant. Everyone had someone in the army whom they had sent off mere days before.

Once again the tanks lined up on the road and began to move. The two of us headed off also, unsure whether or not to throw our rifles, ammunition and overcoats into the hazel-bushes or if we should take them with us. In the end, we decided to take them with us. We could see about a hundred of our soldiers, in a group, marching along the right flank of the column, and behind them followed enemy soldiers in three-wheelers. An entire unit must have surrendered to the enemy. We moved parallel to the German troops but with enough distance between us to feel relatively safe.

Already, in the nearer parts of town, changes were to be seen: from the highest trees along the road flew the German flags with the crooked cross, and in some places could be seen unfamiliar flags with a red and white chess-board in the middle. At home, my father explained that this flag with the chess-board was the flag of the state to which we now belonged—the Independent State of Croatia. I was confused to find that we now belonged to some Croatian state when it was the German army that had defeated us.

The two of us hid in the house. Father would from time to time bring us news from the town square and market. The first news was encouraging—the German army commander read out in the town square a declaration granting amnesty to all of our soldiers because not a single German had died in the capture of the town. And so, the war of the Psetian troops against the mighty German Army which took place in April of 1941 lasted only two days. The defenders were easily defeated and, of the twenty-seven dead, most fell victim under the hoofs of their own cattle. The people of Pset had changed rulers and flags often in their four-hundred-year history. However, this was the first time that on the church tower and on the mosque's minaret hung two flags next to each other, tied together at the ends, which led limping Dzakota, glass of wine in hand, to comment in Hucina's Tavern:

"Flags were meant to fly in the wind. These two, tied together like that, seem to have passed their own sentence on the future."

Someone from his usual crowd of the perpetually inebriated remembered Dzakota's prognosis and repeated it at home to his wife. She in return confided it to someone else, and so on. Eventually, it reached the ears of short Yuray, the new mayor. Yuray, in turn, could not let this pass and needed to make an example of someone quickly, thereby discouraging such irresponsible talk in the future. Two men in long black overcoats found Dzakota in the tavern and took him to the police station. He returned home late that night, when the town was covered in darkness, his tongue split open, and dragging behind him a leg that been healthy up until that day. It would be a long time before he could speak again, not even to explain what had happened to him at the station, but he would never again stand on his left foot.

The incident with Dzakota was the clearest example for the Psetians of the type of masters they were now dealing with. That first night in our new country my brother and I spent in the stable. When darkness fell, my father came to get us, bringing with him the latest news from town:

"Some other fool got drunk and told everyone at the Old Hotel how they already know who attacked the German column." Father spoke quietly as we passed through our orchard to the house, "According to him, some Serb major from Grmec Mountain took two units with him to battle. That's why the new authorities will tomorrow *reward the bandits' bravery. Not a puppy will be left standing, nor a kitten living, in the bandits' lair. Or so he says.*"

"Do the Serbs up on the Grmec know about this?" I asked Father, pulling him by the arm.

"I don't think so. There are checkpoints everywhere, and no one is permitted to come and go between here and there," responded Father, stopping at the last fence post. "They should be notified tonight. If only I could get word to your mother's uncle, Dmitar. He could warn the others."

"We'll go," Osman and I volunteered in unison.

"No, never. They would shoot you on the spot if they noticed you. You two keep quiet and stay here. I'll go and see Dmitar."

We knew that there was no use in trying to argue with Father. He had decided to go and warn the Grmecians of the fate that awaited them. Later that night, he left. The two of us were in the attic while Aunt Habibe was in the kitchen, wrapped in her shawl, prayer beads in her hands. She didn't know where Father had gone off to but she suspected the worst and prayed for the good of her brother who was all that was left to her in this world. When Father woke us up in the morning, all tired and pale, he gave us more bad news.

As soon as he'd told Dmitar what was going to happen to the village, Dmitar went to warn the people to flee to the woods, while Father returned. He circled the town so that it would not look like he had come from the direction of Grmec. Dawn was glowing in the eastern half of the sky, but he decided to wait until daybreak, so that he could enter the town without arousing any suspicion. None of the many guards at the outskirts asked him where he was coming from. When he reached Copo's house, a number of people were gathered around the doorway. Upon seeing him, Copo motioned with his hand for Father to join them.

"They hanged two peasants over by the Gymnasium!" he eagerly confided. "Naked, so it's hard to recognise them, but they say that they're from Karanic, over in Ogumaca."

Hearing this, we decided to go into town with Father, despite Aunt Habibe's attempts to convince us that the best thing would be for us to stay where we were.

Even though it was still early morning, the town square was alive with people standing around and whispering in small groups. There was no sight of soldiers or policemen. It was as if they had decided to leave the people alone and let them reach their own conclusions about the warnings which the town's new rulers had left on the Gymnasium's poplar trees. The crowd approached to within fifty metres of the hanged men and observed from there, as if the two were infected with cholera. Two completely nude bodies hung from two tall poplar trees. From far off, you could tell that they were older men. One was skinny and tall, with an abnormally long neck, while the other was shorter and had large fists and feet.

As I looked at the hanged men, my stomach began to turn. Who would think that they used to be men?! A naked man, hanging from a tree branch, looks more like a butchered sheep. It would be better to say "skinned sheep" because the little hair that they had was on their heads and crotches.

Just then I realised what a sorry creation man is, how ugly is his body, and awkward, and how insignificant and pathetic he is once dead. Who would think that this creature rules the planet? Who would think that such bodies managed to create everything that civilisation has produced? Looking at the people around me, they seemed somehow different, more acceptable. The idea came to me that the secret of man's success lies in clothing, that man's brain was able to begin developing only once he began to first feel shame and began covering up, one by one, parts of his body. Yes, this covering up gave him significance and gravity. It separated him from the other living creatures on Earth and made both king and clown of him. Clothes were important, unlike the hulking bodies hanging from the graceful poplar branches.

"You're right," said Osman, as if all my thoughts had been spoken aloud, "The human body is insignificant. Not just human…If it was important, the worms wouldn't eventually have their way with it. These are no longer the same people as yesterday."

Father didn't hear our conversation, while I was baffled at how completely Osman had read my thoughts. I moved away from him the way one would move away from a burning fire. In his upper lip I detected an unmistakable smirk.

"We're leaving," Father said abruptly and pulled me by the hand. We turned and walked toward the hotel. Just then we noticed the handbills posted on the trees along the street. In large letters, the announcement read:

PEOPLE OF BOSNIA! YOU HAVE BEEN LIBERATED FROM THE SERBIAN TYRANNY THAT WAS YUGOSLAVIA! FROM THIS DAY FORWARD, YOU ARE THE CITIZENS…

"What tyranny?" I turned to Osman, more to comment than to question. "See what kind of fortune they bring with them," answered Osman turning toward the announcements.

Passing by some women, one of whom was Hankiya, the town whore, we overheard her explain to the others how the testicles on the shorter one were hanging down to his knees while that other "thing" had shrivelled up like a cigarette butt. Father stopped, turned toward them and gave them a piercing look which immediately caused the other women to lower their heads and distance themselves from Hankiya.

The people were now speaking little. Most were simply sighing. Their eyes avoided focusing on concrete objects, preferring to look at nothing in particular, wandering along the space between houses and trees, fearing the uncertainty which could be felt in the air even before the German troops had come into Pset, and which had not left since their arrival.

I, also, felt undefined, like a block of wood before the sculptor has begun to shape it with his knife and chisel. In all this there was uncertainty, and helplessness, and fear, and even a little indifference which reached apathy. I was startled by the sight in front of Solak's kebab-stand: three men in long military overcoats wearing little circular red badges on their epaulettes and lapels. Though I instinctively turned my eyes away, an ineluctable curiosity returned me to their faces. Once again forcing myself to turn away, and while looking for something else to put my sights on, I realised that one of the three faces was familiar. One part of me pushed my eyes toward the overcoats while the other pulled them away fearfully. The first part was stronger and my eyes attached themselves to the face of Maho Hasedin. I stared into his face but, as hard as I tried, I couldn't reconcile his face with the long overcoat and the horned hat on his head. One tuft of blond hair hung down to his eyebrow. He was now returning my stare. When our sights locked onto one another, he opened his eyes wide, flared his nose like a bull threatening a calf, stuck his chest forward and straightened his back. He was visibly pleased by the surprise I had shown at his appearance, and through his posture he attempted to show me the importance of his new status in town. Until yesterday, he was picking up cigarette butts and waiting for hours in front of Huca's hash-house, hoping that someone would call on him to do some small job or run an errand, anything to earn a piece of bread. And now, Maho had suddenly become "someone" and was trying to demonstrate that very fact to me.

"These are the ones who will be chopping off our heads," whispered Osman.

"Evil days have arrived, my sons," observed Father, not looking at us. "If Maho has become the law, nothing good can come of it."

At first, I had expected the foreigner's army to leave just as it had arrived, and our small town to return to the way it used to be. I was now struck with the fear that the foreigner would depart but in his stead he'd leave the town's scoundrels, good-for-nothings and spineless weasels. Those who until yesterday were shouting "Long live King Peter" loudest were the same ones now shouting "Heil Hitler". A heavy feeling came from my stomach so I told Father and Osman that I was going home.

Going around the hotel and down the hill, I passed the Stublic well, where women were doing their washing and which was the source of a creek frozen like an icicle during winter, boisterous during spring and autumn, and too slow-running to quench the thirst of a cow during summer. In a flash, I had a feeling that 'Mother's voice was calling me to the Stublic well. I stood over the well, looking down, eyes and ears peering, but there was nothing to be seen or heard apart from water. "If only Mother would help me," I thought, instantly feeling ashamed because the time had come for me to take my life into my own hands. Before I could complete the thought, from behind my eyeballs something whispered that my life was beyond my control and it was foolish to even consider trying to become its master.

"Just keep your hands and feet moving. That is all you can do because your destiny will always be too far from your grasp," came the whisper from behind my eyeballs. Revolted by the whispers and wanting to pull the voice out from behind my eyes, I was brought back to reality by Lazo's barking dog, which ran past me and disappeared behind the wooden fence.

CHAPTER V

The rain stopped falling in the afternoon and soon the sun's weak rays scribbled over the wallpaper in Yudja's room. Outside, it was somewhat more alive. Ambulance sirens could be heard, and off in the distance, toward the cold Pacific ocean, the horns of ships sounded in the approaches to the port. For the first time since he entered Yudja's room, Fehrat could feel around him everyday life which was completely unrelated to the butchery of Bosnia. Yudja removed from the stove a pan in which lettuce and potatoes had been stewing. Placing his hand on Fehrat's shoulder, the old man sat down next to him.

"It's a good thing you managed to get out alive. Bosnia can survive without the two of us," said Yudja, all the while watching the sun's track trace shadows in the dusk of the room. Sensing that his comment was ill-chosen and inappropriate, especially considering his guest's experiences, he hastened a clarification:

"We're no warriors. Or, at least we're not the kind of barbarians it would take to defend ourselves from these monsters. Barbarity has to be answered with barbarity, yet I never even had the stomach to kill a chicken. After all, in our region, we had no chance. What could a few of us do against an army of madmen? We're more useful with our heads still attached to our shoulders...," Yudja mumbled, but seeing the spasm which crossed Fehrat's face from chin to temple, he again regretted mentioning the subject.

As he spoke, Yudja had the opportunity to observe Fehrat better than ever before. During their earlier sporadic encounters, each of them had kept his eyes firmly lowered. Only now did he discover that the upper lip on Fehrat's handsome face was wider than the lower, and slightly crooked, just like Osman's. The brows above his son's charcoal black eyes were long and thick. He had shoulders like his own—wide, upright, so that the neck seemed short and somewhat sunken. Hands also like his; wide palms, short yet agile fingers of which the thumb, with its wide nail and unmistakable whiteness around the roots, stood out.: He was only ten centimetres taller than Osman and himself, and there was a swing in his walk which immediately made one think of a sailor stepping on shore after a long period at sea.

"They butchered Nefko's entire family," Fehrat suddenly blurted out. "It happened after they suffered their first casualties at the Kupres front."[2]

"Butchered Nefko's family?!"—Yudja's voice was full of fear and incredulity, bitterness and questions. "What did Nefko's family ever do to them, Fehrat?"

"Yes! Niko's Chetniks butchered them like animals. And Nefko, too…All of them…We had already heard about the kinds of things Ostoyic and his White Eagles had done in Foca and Arkan and his Tigers in Biyelyina…But, Foca and Biyelyina are far away. Then again, we all thought that we were so mixed and interrelated that there was no chance of anything similar to eastern Bosnia happening to us… What they did to Nefko they would never think of doing to cattle. They forced the entire family out into the courtyard to watch as they tortured Nefko. First, they beat him with the pikes used to load logs on to the sawmill table and shouted: "Give us all your deutschmarks and dollars, you old dog, and then we'll let you all go." He could only manage to groan under the countless blows from the pikes. Black Niko then brought his adze down on Nefko's right hand, just above the fist, so hard that spurts of blood sprayed all over Niko and his butchers. Nefko made a futile scream up to the sky, while his wife, son, daughter, and granddaughter huddled into a horrified knot by the macadam path leading from the house to the family sawmill, their heads together as if trying to sink into the ground in unison. They made not a sound. Only the little granddaughter, Eldina, was screaming, all the while fumbling at her mother's and grandmother's bodies, searching for something safe to hold on to.

Several Chetniks, decked out in uniforms complete with insignia and crosses on their caps, turned their eyes away from Nefko and his family, while Niko grew emboldened, madness overflowing. Charging at them like a bear, he began to slap them around as though they were *all* children. When he'd finished giving them this barbaric lesson, he ran to the gang mill, turned it on and shouted: *Bring me the Baleya.**

Two of them grabbed Nefko, who immediately began to struggle frantically, knowing full well what was in store for him. His family, still gathered in a muddle, began to scream. The blood from Nefko's butchered hand had gushed along the path and all over the Chetniks. When they brought him before the gang mill and the waiting Niko, Niko grabbed him around the waist while another Chetnik held him by the head and the two of them forced Nefko onto the track which pulls the logs toward the saw. They tied him to the trolley and then pushed it toward the spinning teeth of the saw. Blood sprayed all over the gang saw and the Chetniks looking on while Nefko's head fell to the sawdust-covered ground. The rest of the body remained on the trolley, the legs still making spastic attempts to reach toward the wall and away from the saw, the hands holding the neck from which blood continued to gush, and the chest inflated trying to break free of the ropes which bound it.

Still unsatisfied, Niko shouted maniacally to his accomplices: *Kill the bastards!* His bloody hand pointed toward Nefko's family, helplessly bunched together in the middle of the courtyard.

A fog suddenly came over Yudja's eyes. Something became stuck in his throat and he couldn't even swallow his spit. He had heard about the tragedy of Nefko's family, but he had not known that they had suffered such horror. They were relatives…But, even if they hadn't been…Nefko was a man worthy of respect. He worked day and night, never turning down a request for help. For those very Chetniks who had ended his life in such a bestial manner, and for their fathers, Nefko had cut logs at his sawmill without charge, whenever they wanted. Even they, now monsters, had valued his friendship, often inviting him to their celebrations. Niko had been Nefko's neighbour. He had eaten more often at Nefko's than at his very own mother's kitchen.

"What's happened?" Yudja asked himself for the umpteenth time, his throat still blocked, unable to make words. What damnation was this that reappeared with such alarming regularity from the very depths of darkness? During the last war, the Chetniks had butchered, but so had the Ustashe,* and the Germans, and even the Italians. Tito's Partisans were also known to have put the odd bullet into an innocent head. But this, now...Our people did nothing to deserve this.

As Yudja listened to Fehrat's accounts of the crimes which their Serbian neighbours had committed upon the family of Nefko Zeynilov, he remembered the story Solak had told him about the death of Uncle Nuhan. The Chetniks from Radyenica had ambushed Nuhan and twenty other Muslims as they were returning in a merchant caravan from Sanski Most sometime in the middle of the Second World War. Their bodies, mutilated with knives, were found on the forest road. Solak was later sentenced to two years in prison for telling the story because those same Chetniks had come over to the Partisan side in 1943. Now numbered among the victors, they were protected by law against defamation. To whose side will they cross over this time and for how long will this slaughter repeat itself in Bosnia? Yudja wondered, focused on Fehrat's deeply cleft chin. Noticing the stare, Fehrat was shaken as if from a dream and continued talking.

The bloodied Chetniks, spurred on by Nefko's death, had pulled his wife, Mina, out of the group and began dragging her toward Niko. Her family tried to pull her back into the group. They were all screaming now. Seeing the struggle going on, Niko rushed in and grabbed Mina, lifting her above the group, throwing her on to the macadam path, bending down toward her and pressing his knee against her chest. Her children froze in fear when they saw Niko's bloody hand reach for his knife. In a split second, they all rushed the butcher.

Alarmed by the screaming, Nefko's big flock of pigeons burst into flight, fluttering chaotically through all the air over the yard.

Niko swung the knife. The group scattered across the courtyard. Grabbing Mina by the hair, with a single practised movement Niko slashed her throat, nearly severing her head. Mina's children once again rushed at Niko but upon seeing their mother's sundered head and body, her blood running freely from arteries and veins, her arms and legs thrashing in the air like the limbs of a badly slaughtered beast, they ran to the logs and scrap wood, looking for the nearest hole or corner in which to hide.

Kill the bastards! Niko screamed again at his accomplices as he wiped the blood from his face and wiped the knife on Mina's skirt."

As Fehrat described the incident, waving with both his healthy and mutilated hands, from the colour of his face and the powerful heaving of his chest it was easy to see that painful emotions had overcome him.

"Wait, slow down a little…" cried out Yudja, wiping the sweat from his own brow. The yellow patches on his pale face made it obvious that his nerves had reached their end and could no longer bear to listen. He stood up, taking a glass of water and splashing some on his face before drinking the rest, and let out a deep breath, as if someone had forcibly held him under water. Fehrat took a glass and did the same. After a lengthy period of silence, Fehrat completed his story, but with less detail:

They hunted the rest of the family down and murdered them like animals. Three of them raped Nefko's daughter, Semira, all the while howling like dogs. When they were done, they hacked her to death. Grabbing her bloody corpse, Niko carried it with him, looking for Adnan, her brother, and imitating a woman's wailing: *Cursed are you forever for leaving us so young.*

When his thugs finally did drag Adnan before him, Niko threw Semira's corpse into the sawdust next to Nefko's headless body, sat down on a log and ordered: *This one we will castrate!* Three Chetniks, who had all managed to lose their black woollen caps in the courtyard, began tearing away at Adnan's clothes. Adnan in turn straightened out, threw his hand toward Niko and pleaded: *Don't, Niko, for the love of God! Have you forgotten that it was your mother who breast-fed me when my mother was sick?*

Castrate! shouted Niko, and the other Chetniks continued to pull the clothing off Adnan. Frantic, he began punching at his attackers' heads but Niko walked behind him and buried his entire knife into Adnan's back. Collapsing to the ground like an empty sack, Adnan arched backward, trying to staunch the outrush of blood with his hands. After a while, he curled forward and completely stopped moving.

Where is the little one? Niko looked around. When they brought him the limp body of Semira's little Eldina, who had fainted at the butchering of her grandmother, he turned away to the side, as if trying to think of what he should do next."

Fehrat's voice slowed to a crawl, eyes glued to the window.

"They killed her also?" Yudja whispered.

"Yes…" Fehrat whispered back. "Niko killed her with a single blow to the temple so that she didn't even feel it."

The sun's rays were angling up to the ceiling as the two refugees sat together, heads lowered toward the floor. The silence was broken by the sound of an ambulance racing down the street outside, siren screaming. Fehrat lifted his head, sighed and completed the story:

"The entire event was witnessed by the miller, Stevan, who was looking on from the roof of his house. He ran through his garden to town and found the chief of police and the commander of the local garrison in front of the hotel. With a number of local SDS leaders present also, he told them what he had just witnessed. They sent the military police to arrest Niko and his group but Niko simply slapped them all around, giving them a kick in the pants and screaming at them for obeying an officer who had the nerve to protect the Baleyas.

That night, both of the mosques in Pset were destroyed and the next morning, when the district commission entered Nefko's courtyard to make a record of the crime, they did not find a single body. News of this quickly spread all over town, and Niko was soon boasting in front of the old hotel how Nefko's family had moved to Croatia and how they had left all of their property to him. A mass of people, soldiers and police among them, began to murmur, but Niko waved a piece of paper above his head all the while, insisting, in an insane laugh, how his neighbour Nefko had made a gift to him of his house and lumber mill and should anyone doubt it he had it all down in black and white.

Only the odd word broke through the mute, cabbage-scented atmosphere of Yudja's room. During the intervals between words, both men fought back vivid and grotesque images, full of rage and rank emotions. Observing Yudja, all the while wrestling with a disgust which glued itself to him, at times even threatening to choke him, Fehrat was struck by the sight of the blood-red setting sun, something which looked more like a new-born infant fighting to return to his mother's womb than the natural departure of a man who had any reason to look behind him.

Yudja could feel his eyes becoming accustomed to the sight of the crippled Fehrat, the shortened arm and the severed leg. Yet, deep within, he was outraged at the evil which had engulfed this man in misery, depriving him of a name and origin, deforming both body and soul. He was enraged at all the people who had done evil to Fehrat. He was unexpectedly shaken to find himself at the head of this long line of inhumanity. Yudja knew well that Fehrat was the result of his sin, but he didn't know what Fehrat thought about all this and to what extent he placed his misfortune directly upon the father who had been absent for so long.

"What happened to Delveta and Alma?" unexpectedly enquired Fehrat. The question struck Yudja in the ribs before lodging itself somewhere in his lungs. He attempted, on the basis of the tone and colouring of Fehrat's voice, to ascertain if his son truly cared to know, or if it was mere courtesy. Suddenly, the reason why Fehrat had asked about his wife and daughter became very important to him. Then again, perhaps it was because it had taken him so long to ask.

"They remain in Pula, as the Women's Refugee Centre," replied Yudja.

Standing up and walking to the wooden figurines arrayed on their shelves, from a drawer at the bottom of the cupboard he took a stack of letters and put them in front of Fehrat. When he approached the sink to fill up the glass teapot, which was decorated with drawings from the ancient Finnish Kalevala,* he began to be troubled by uncertainty over what he had just done—or had he merely begun to open the well-hidden door behind which he hid things he had previously considered very personal?

His son's voice startled him from his musings. "I can't help you there!" Fehrat had raised his left hand; traces of colour began to appear on his pale face. The stack of letters lay scattered on the table.

That night Yudja fell asleep despite a dull pain below his ribs. During the night, through his half-sleeping state, he could feel the pain move into his shoulder blade. The whole left side of his body felt bruised, and from the depths of his eye sockets an ominous heat was spreading. In what seemed more like a nightmare than a dream, Fehrat's likeness constantly appeared before him; one moment with an innocent face, and the next like a donkey-headed beast. He was startled awake at dawn, eyes darting across the dark room, when, out of a dim corner, that very same donkey's head rushed toward him, and equally quickly returned to the darkness from which it had originated. Yudja jumped to his feet and bent over Fehrat, whose forehead was covered with large beads of sweat, his cheeks white as flour. He returned to his bed, closed his eyes but remained awake.

As soon as he opened his eyes on the light of the new day, Fehrat told him how it would please him if Yudja were to continue with his stories.

"Everything that is distant from us, even though it may be our own, seems preferable. It refreshes me. By exposing me to your past, you let me escape from my future—however briefly. As I am drawn into your destiny, I feel that I am escaping from mine."

"It is important for me too. I have had no one to whom I could pour out this mass which has been building up inside my head all these years," Yudja replied. "I thought that my figurines would release me but as soon as one was completed, it would distance itself from me, becoming something different from what I had originally wanted it to be, and always leaving me with the same worries and memories... But first, tea, then coffee, and there will be more than enough time for storytelling."

The host returned his teapot to the stove. And then he continued his confession to his crippled son about the events of the previous great conflict in Bosnia, which like all the others, past, present and future, before and since Osiris, Zeus, Jehovah, Christ, Mohammed and many other rulers both mythic and earthly, was more likely influenced by Satanic powers than anything Holy.

OF THE FIGURINE "OSMAN"

Only during the first days of the occupation of Pset and the surrounding region was there any semblance of rule and order, even though the mechanisms of those organising principles now came directly from the occupier. At the beginning, the people were merely curious, while the new rulers wore smiles on their faces. The German soldiers, whose numbers dwindled with each new day, passed out chocolates and candies in shiny golden wrapping to the children. The children fought over the wrapping more than they did over the sweets themselves. To the older folks, they offered cigarettes from gold and silver cases, while to the more available women, they gave out silk scarves with sewn hems. The trouble came later.

The first notable event in occupied Pset occurred when Hankiya and Solomon's Dragica, two loose women, as people used to call them, strolled, arm-in-arm with two blond German soldiers. Later, they boasted to their friends how the Germans had given them heaps of silk underwear hemmed with lace. This was probably a signal to the occupying soldiers that they could smile more openly, even around the veiled Muslim women. It all may have stopped at that, at Dragica, Hankiya and the smiles of the stiff Nazis and the black-coats, if the new rulers had not brought with them little Yuray from somewhere around Slunj in Central Croatia, and made him our new mayor.

One morning, accompanied by the toothy mountain sun after a night when petrifying lightning shook the Psetian highland, the most prominent Muslims were taken to the town's main administration building. The gaunt-looking Yuray delivered for their benefit a lecture about the newly declared Independent State of Croatia and German power. Afterward, he proposed that they work together. Conspicuous by their absence from those invited were my father and Niyaz Basic, two respected merchants who had married Orthodox women, and the Imam Selman. As if reading the minds of those present, the sly new mayor reminded them in a sharp and menacing tone that he fully expected them all to keep the new government informed of all suspicious activities of the Vlachs and the communists and their sympathisers, and to beware of evil tongues, no matter how holy the mouth which holds it. His meaning was clear to all and everyone remained silent. Everyone except for the obstinate and arrogant Adem, who got up, looked self-importantly toward his fellow townsmen, then bowed deeply before the picture of Hitler and the new Croatian ruler Pavelic shaking hands which hung on the wall behind Yuray.

"We thank Allah for your arrival in our town! For our part—" he again looked toward the men seated around him, whose faces betrayed their fear and uncertainty "—we will be loyal to the new government and protect it from scoundrels and traitors."

"Good. That is good to know," smiled the mayor, before offering his hand to everyone in the room.

That night, in the lower part of town, not far from Mara's Cellar, Maho Hasedin and two other long-coat gendarmes were badly beaten. Like a windstorm, word quickly spread through town that despite their masked faces Maho had recognised the attackers.

Father arrived at supper-time and didn't touch a bite of his food. He couldn't hide the worry which increasingly dominated his face. Normally, he was the picture of composure, but business was falling off and events were progressively getting worse.

Aunty observed him out of the corner of her eye and only by the occasional movement of her lips could you tell that she was saying prayers to herself.

Osman sat next to the narrow window, looking out into the endless darkness and listening to the scratching of the wind against the branches of the apple and pear trees in front of the house. In a short space of time he had quickly ripened, going from boy to man seemingly overnight. That very evening, with him sitting and facing the night, I noticed again how on his right temple something resembling a bean was constantly moving up and down. I had noticed this a number of times since our return. His face was taking on a darker colour. I had dreamt about it and now I was afraid.

During the dream, I could feel the sun's head coming down full-force around my neck. It was hot as hell and the entire town was like a drum upon which the sun's sticks were beating furiously.

Osman was shouting: "Rope! Give me rope!"

"Why rope?" I asked myself, though I had a feeling that he probably wanted to tie it around my neck. Fleeing down the field like a deer, I began to feel my legs growing shorter. The sun's heat went crazy. My bare foot stepped on a snake, spotted and cold. I could feel its head squishing like spit, yellow like the sun-beaten rocks. Turning around, I was startled to see Osman behind me, his hands bloody up to the elbows. In his right hand, I could see tufts of hair. Dark hair like the mane on a black stallion. In his left hand, a butcher's axe. Grabbing me, he indicated that he just wanted to readjust my larynx. Turning my head away toward a peach tree, all in bloom, its fragrance spreading all the way to the outskirts of town.

I suddenly awoke and the sight of the moon greeted me outside my bedroom window. The wind had opened the window and its frame was creating a rattle, tapping repeatedly against the wall. I was overcome by the need to hear my mother's voice. Concentrating, full of hope, for a brief moment I was certain that I heard something but, again, it was only the wind blowing against the rattling window frame. Moonlight played with tiny apple branches. Going to the room next to mine, I found Osman not there. His window was also open. I concluded that, as was his habit, he was probably in the orchard, up in his favourite apple tree, contemplating under the bright moonlight.

Till morning, I was suspended in a state between sleep and consciousness. Zemka's face was continually appearing before my eyes despite the intractable pride within me which stood opposed to any sort of contact with her. Ever since Osman had alluded to an affair between her and Captain Skundric, I had made an effort to evade her, even in dreams, fearing the truth. I could not bring myself to ask her directly for an explanation, and this fear was like an enormous log lying across the road, an impassable barricade. Since her brother's death, she had not been seen leaving the house.

I was abruptly woken in the morning by loud pounding at the courtyard doors. Someone was knocking and calling my father. After I heard the sound of doors opening, a robust voice asked for Osman. This was followed by the same voice, this time much quieter, explaining something to Father. I clearly heard him tell Father that they only wanted to talk to Osman and that he would soon be allowed to return home. Something struck me directly under the ribs. When I entered the kitchen, my aunt was there, hands crossed and shaking. Osman entered also, looked me directly in the eye, placed his hand on my shoulder and whispered so that Aunt couldn't hear:

"Seems like some fiend paid with his head." In a normal voice, he added "Don't worry, I'll be back," as he walked out the door. Father returned into the house, yellow as a hoopoe bird.

"Maho claims that he recognised Osman among those who attacked the Ustashas[3] patrol," Father explained, visibly concerned. "This morning leaflets appeared all over the town square denouncing the occupier and the Ustashas' government. Anything could happen."

Osman was a head taller than both of the policemen. When they passed by the Stublic well I could just see the idea come to him that the best thing to do would be to push both of them in. He could then use the large rock against which the women beat their washing to hold the well's metal cover shut.

His dilemma was ended by Yusuf Zokic, the photographer who always wore an ironic look on his face. Rising from behind the rock, showing his sparse, large yellow teeth for all to see, he turned toward the policemen, winking:

"Fehrat's Osman! Him, him…He's the ringleader. He's hated Maho since he was little. He hates you also…and me. It's him…it's him," shouted Yusuf, not bothering to hide his repulsive, crowing smile.

>From the lower town's mosque, the southern wind carried Imam Selman announcing in his call to prayer that somebody had died.

"The dog is dead," thought Osman, and hurried toward the town square. The policemen had a difficult time keeping up with him.

On the wall of the old hotel, large whitewash letters read: BETTER WAR THAN THE PACT, BETTER THE GRAVE THAN BEING A SLAVE, and on Aron's house the large white NDH letters had been crossed out with black paint.

By the time they arrived at the jailhouse the weather had changed: the southern winds had dragged dark clouds with them over the mountain peaks to the plateau and soon the entire town was covered by a dark kerchief. The wind, singing its arias and spreading the coniferous aroma of the mountain forest, was in turn descending to the valley tree tops, which resembled naked beggars. From the forest glistened a road, once used by Diocletian's phalanxes on their way into the belly of the Balkans, winding down to the widest side of the plateau and then cutting directly to the centre of town.

"What was here before?" thought Osman as he looked out the barred cell window, "and who, and for what reason, decided to call this mountain village Pset, when he could have chosen any of a number of other, more fitting, names? Why call a village 'Dog'?" Perhaps the secret would have been plain to succeeding generations if someone had bothered to leave them a Patarenian or Bogumil* dictionary from the Middle Ages. As things stood, the only thing known for certain was that Diocletian's troops had made this path before the arrival of Slavic tribes fleeing the onslaught of Asian barbarians. What had happened before, what had been built here, road and settlement, no one knew for sure.

Osman's eyes stared blankly into the emptiness on the other side of the prison bars. One ear strained to hear sounds from outside his cell's damp walls, while the other was pressed against the door, trying to catch, despite the howling of the wind—anything. If the window had been glazed instead of barred, it would have reflected two wrinkled green circles bordering two black pupils with shining dots in their centre. A mound of sand was like a shout of calm in the midst of the darkened background of the setting which reflected in the glass of the pupils. The forehead above these lizard eyes was cut across by two train-track lines, and the puffiness of the cheeks was perfectly round.

I was certain that Osman had nothing to do with the previous night's ambush. I couldn't understand why Maho would mention his name just before leaving this world. I thought that it must all be connected to the campaign against potential enemies of the new state, but I still didn't see how my brother's name could find itself on such a list...

First, they hadn't invited Father to hear the mayor's speech, and now they had locked Osman up after the first attack upon the defenders of the new government. What was to follow? A strange and heavy feeling overcame me as I observed myself in the window's reflection, but I had no clue as to what I should do. I tried to see Osman's face on the other side and to look upon him with someone else's guarded eyes. I tried to look from the very depths at him in the hope that I could see something in his face that would free him of all suspicion. But, without success. My brother's image fled from my eyes like a guilty man hiding from the truth.

The moat where the gendarmes where attacked held no clues as to the identity of the attackers. Either they were attacked by skilled masters of the highwayman's trade or the attackers had wings and had no need to walk in the mud which surrounded the moat. Or, the strange thought struck me at once, could it be that the other two gendarmes attacked Maho and then fabricated the story about Osman and his accomplices? I knew that each version was possible; all acts come innately because of the nature of the human mind. You can change the characteristics of a horse by breeding. If you prefer a black mane, on a blond horse, match your bay with a yellow one; if you dislike fickleness and speed, you match him with one with obedient and sluggish genes. But with us? Like water, we change hair, colour and tongue, but never nature. The murderous instinct comes to us not only when we begin thinking about food.

I returned to my seat by the window and my gaze wandered among the branches of the trees. Father returned from town and said that the mayor did not wish to get mixed up in the affairs of the gendarmes. He didn't have the time for a conversation.

"What will we do now, Father?" I asked, the words seemingly coming out of someone else's mouth.

"Things don't look good, my Yudja," Father answered, placing his hand upon my shoulder. "Things that I've already had to live through are repeating themselves. When the blood heats up, the eyes become lost in fog and the mind contracts a strange illness for which there is no medicine. People start to group everyone according to their descent, flags, by the way they pray or don't pray to God. I'll manage somehow but what will become of you and Osman? Whoever isn't firmly grounded on one side will not have a chance of choosing later on. People are on the brink of having their blood shoot up into their eyes, and when that happens the first to pay will be those who see the most clearly, those without blood in their eyes. We'll wait a while and then decide where our heads belong." Father ran his fingers through my hair. A sudden gust of wind struck the window, leaving an imprint in the foggy dew on the glass which resembled a snake with a flower on its nose. Father immediately wiped it off with his palm and through the humid glass I tried to find the old pear tree in the orchard. My view was obstructed by the bare, intertwined branches of the plum trees which screeched and danced madly in the wind. A loud thud came from a rotting board at the edge of the roof, and behind a frowning beak appeared two sharp, authoritative eyes and black streaks running toward the rounded part of the head. The woodpecker was hunting for worms under the boards while they, knowing full well the meaning of the pecking sounds and the destiny which awaited them if found, contorted themselves into the minuscule holes of the wood.

"Face him like a man!" I addressed my thoughts to the prospective victims. "Why should he have a natural right upon your flesh?! Leave him a landmine, and blow his beak to smithereens or, better yet, wait for him to dig deeper, and then, while he is still preoccupied, enter through his nostril and make your way to the depths of his intestines where you can begin chewing away to your own melody. You have shrivelled up into your holes waiting for him to swallow you because that is how it has always been: woodpeckers eating worms. Well, what Fate has the right to bequeath your life to another!?"

Realising that my thoughts applied more to humans than woodpeckers and worms, I turned red and bit my tongue.

They took Osman from the solitary cell to see the officer heading the investigation. When they closed the door behind him, he found himself face to face with our neighbor Hasib, wearing his new brown uniform. Osman was surprised, unsure if he should offer his hand, but Hasib's suspicious glance immediately settled all uncertainties. Blood rushed to Osman's head.

"Sit down!" Hasib's voice was stern.

"It's me, Has." Osman walked toward him, thinking that perhaps Hasib hadn't recognised him.

"I know, I know…I see that it is you. Now, sit down, you son of Maria," the voice gravely commanded.

Everything became clear as day to Osman, struck by the realisation that he was here partly because of his mother, that as her child he was stamped and easily recognisable to people such as his former schoolmate, the formerly introverted Hasib. He realised that something significant had occurred, that a new world was being created, which Vavan had tried to explain to them. He was further convinced of this by the large-headed, moustached man standing behind Hasib, a notebook open in his hand.

"So, you murdered our gendarme because he cursed your Serb mother, or because he had seen you with your bearded prophet?" questioned the stranger, running his dirty fingers over his opulent, grey moustaches. Osman's mind could not detach itself from the sudden, overpowering desire to sink his teeth into the throat of the parasite before him who had obviously prepared all of the questions and answers. But thoughts of Father and me must have stopped him from carrying out his wish. He remained silent, thinking how things had already been decided for him here because the moustachioed one had stopped writing and closed his notebook. Squinty-eyed Yusuf had spread the word throughout town, and the town was loath to believe otherwise once it had accepted the deadly slander as truth.

Osman was transferred the next day to Kula, a prison where men had been rotting away since Austro-Hungarian times. He wasn't formally convicted but he was sent with those who had been. Father began taking gold and other valuables to the mayor, the moustachioed investigator, and even to Maho's mother, Haseda, and uncle, Murat. On one occasion, the investigator told him that perhaps something could be arranged but that it would be a good idea for both him and me to volunteer for either the Ustashas or for the newly-formed German SS unit. This was when a further misfortune paid our highland a visit: the so-called voluntary mobilisation into the German and Croat armies. Tragedy was barely averted when the merchant Nikica's son Koyo went to apply for the civil service and Yuray, the mayor, threw him out of his office with the explanation that they didn't need Serbs.

Kula had an eerily depressing air about it. The windows were like gun-holes, so small that what little light did penetrate rarely had the strength to reach the sooty walls. The greater part of the place, the narrow hallways and the damp rooms, had never seen any form of natural light.

Osman had the dubious fortune to be thrown into a larger room. The first thing that he felt after they closed the doors behind him for the first time was the intense glares of five pairs of eyes coming at him from the depths of the darkness. It took a while for his eyes to adjust to the darkness but when they did the first thing he recognised was the bearded face of Vavan, who was sitting underneath the one paltry window, and, to his left, an equal distance from the weak shaft of daylight which ventured into the cell and served as a reminder that life still existed, was the town's best known musician, Merho, who had sung more songs and played his accordion at more weddings than anyone in Pset. The other three didn't have the privilege of being touched by the feeble light coming from outside, and it wasn't until much later that Osman was able to recognise them. Startled by the fact that Vavan's only reaction was to silently look at him, Osman's dilemma was eventually broken by the old man:

"You don't expect me to be glad to see you? I wouldn't choose such a fate even for a dog."

The very silence in the jail cell was tainted with darkness. It smelled, or better yet, stank, of dampness. The silence was far from being one of tranquil peace, for it was full of heavy thoughts and confused emotions. It choked the throat, pushed against the chest and, in its worst moments, drummed ceaselessly against the back of the prisoners' skulls. Osman was quiet. The others, without any notable interest, also remained silent. A while later, the dry, somewhat coarse voice of Vavan again called out:

"It's a good thing that scum such as Maho are leaving life, but it's just as bad that ones such as you are joining us here." He spoke softly, often pausing between words, as if he had difficulty speaking. "Do they have any proof that it was you that killed him?"

"Hmm..." Osman responded, and old Vavan immediately understood.

"Who needs proof nowadays? Power creates its own version of the truth. Until it's blown out," Vavan reasoned, "but this one has just started to suck in air. Power takes different forms, often hiding like a storm in the clouds, waiting for the right moment and then beginning with murmuring, grumbling, lightning, thundering, pouring, taking with it everything in its path. Each drop destroys, murders, removes borders…When it reaches its peak, when it runs out of evil creativity, it settles down, bowing to the cleared sky and disappearing, leaving behind it pandemonium, unearthed graves and painful memories. It is the same way with men. The history of human civilisation is a constant game of roulette: when you spin it and throw the dice, the force of your movement beckons the dice, or the metal ball, no matter. And everything is up in the air, uncertain. This is like a state of chaos— as long as the roulette wheel is turning. But, when the wheel stops, you find out the colour of the field and the number and who the winner is. This winner rules until the next spin of the wheel. The more you wager on a spin, the greater the anxiety."

After this peroration, the old man fell silent once more. The others kept one eye on his beard and the other on the ray of light which brought with it a breath of fresh air from the river. >From somewhere above their heads Osman heard a short, dull moan, which was soon followed by a longer, more painful one. Vavan lifted his head toward the dark attic, while two of the other four ground their teeth loudly enough for Osman to hear, a sound which sent a chill down his spine. Through the window, which faced the paved courtyard, entered the ringing sounds of army boots, while from up above, in the same rhythm, came the continuing howls.

"Today is May the First. They've brought in some merry-makers who decided to organise a workers' picnic. They are now holding a lecture," commented the saccharine voice of Merho the Musician.

"They are worse than Satan," came the voice of a curly-headed young man who stood up and approached Osman. "Eventually, they will outlaw breathing," he tried to joke.

Osman had seen him somewhere before but couldn't remember the name. Handing Osman a deck of cards, he motioned for him to cut the deck. Osman knew his face was betraying both surprise and distrust.

"I was the first resident of this jail. Before any of you," the young man explained. "The previous government sentenced me for writing. Sometimes I write something, not often…When I'm alone…They searched my room, read my things and told me that I was an evil prophet. They locked me up in Kula and now I truly am a prophet. I told the old man that they are going to burn him alive, and now I will tell you your fate."

Osman coldly transferred his focus from the "Prophet" to Vavan and returned it by way of Merho the Musician. He felt an emptiness in his stomach and a pain in his kidneys. He did not fear Kula, nor its dark cells, even though this was his first visit to the infamous house of moaning and screaming, which he had imagined from the outside to be completely different. He could feel a shapeless mass spreading through his mind, going past his eyes and ears and drowning him in a world of dripping grey colours and foul old smells. Above his left temple came a knock which seemed to originate in the very centre of his brain. He heard a whisper, followed by howling like that of monkeys in the jungle. His hands uncontrollably made their way toward the throat of the gaunt "Prophet," but Vavan's metallic voice commanded:

"Stop! Look! He's your brother in misfortune…We aren't the owners even of our own deaths…"

The Prophet jumped back, the cards fell out of his hands and scattered to the dark floor. Bending down like a snake, he reached for the nearest card and brought it up to his eyes.

"No, that's not the one!" he whined fearfully, throwing the card into the darkest corner of the cell. Bending again, he lifted another card to his eyes but this one too he threw into the corner, as if he had discovered that he was holding a scorpion in his hands. Reaching for a third time, he changed his mind at the last second and stretched out his head toward the newcomer:

"I will not tell you your fortune!…Your star has disappeared. Each card that I lift is empty," he concluded, walking away backwards.

Merho the Musician began to pick the cards off the floor, looking at each new one in his hands. After grabbing a few more, eyes wide open, he handed them to Vavan.

"They are all empty, sir. There is nothing on any of them." He spoke to the old man in confidence, a questioning tone in his voice. The two from the far end of the cell jumped forward, picked up some more cards, held them up to the window, moving about spasmodically while staring into them, and their faces showed the unmistakable look of fear.

"Those cards are the handwork of the devil," Merho's voice appraised.

"Man-made, my friend Merho! There is no greater devil than man," commented Vavan pithily, stretching his hand toward Osman, who had been standing in the same place all the while and observing the scene. Osman accepted the outstretched hand and sat next to the old man. The others, also, returned to their places. A voice in the courtyard was cursing an unspecified prisoner's mother and pulling something across the cobbled pavement.

"This is a house of horror," Vavan essayed, as if he needed to explain. "Who manages to walk out of here will be stronger than steel.

Most don't survive the fear nor the prescriptions of Imam Selman… Anyway, have you seen Milan recently?"

"He's hiding somewhere in the Grmec mountains," answered Osman. "As soon as the army fell apart, he fled for the village. Uncle Dmitar told me that he then fled to the woods because the Ustashas were near. They have word that the Party is planning an uprising."

The old man was looking for additional information in the expression on Osman's face. Vavan's beard seemed darker than before, perhaps due to the lack of light in the cell, and his moustache was curled steeply toward his ears. Osman noticed a bruise below the old man's left lip. His eyes were fresh, round and full of youthful glitter, like a deer when it tries to see what its ears have just discovered. His forehead had reached high, nearly to the top of his head, cut by intersecting lines which smoothed away toward the temples.

"Evil arrived under our skies long ago," the sage Vavan began again, his voice full of pathos, while in the obscure corner of the cell all whispering ceased. The screams and moans from the upper cells began to resemble the far off sounds of cattle.

"The evil began when they pushed us from the other side of the Carpathian Mountains toward this god-forsaken corner of the globe. That's when our forefathers committed the crime of destroying the local inhabitants, either by exterminating them or by assimilating them into the Slavic tribes. Entire nations were destroyed here, leaving various curses behind them. We've been cursed ever since we arrived here. Fighting among ourselves, conquered by others who then sent us to once again fight one another; we were always more willing to embrace the foreigner than to protect our own. We traded our gods for foreign ones and the foreign ones divided us into three camps, placed in our hands three different symbols and buried their sabres in our blood. The Satan himself placed in our subconscious the cursed habit of having always to reach for the sabres as soon as we dig a little deeper into our history. We begin cutting each other down. The devil's servants have again woken up, taken out their dark flags and begun waving their daggers above their heads. The foreigner is again pushing us against one another so that he may have less blood on his own hands while the curse from our subconscious has just about begun to boil up."

Complete silence surrounded the stone building above the river. The last rays of light seeping through the narrow window were pale, without life or strength. Outside the Kula, night had already entered the villages and valleys. The smoky smell of burning branches and rotting leaves from someone's garden entered the cell. Life outside announced itself through the smoke which brought with it images of farmers in their fields. Low in the social order, at one with the soil, these folk could live a little above the evil dragged through here for millennia by human egotism and hate.

Merho the accordion player took several deep breaths, as if trying to store somewhere deep in his lungs a hoard of this wholesome spring burning, while at the same time mumbling incomprehensibly to the others.

With the full darkness of sunset, the guard came and handed out aluminum bowls. Each prisoner received a ladle of bean porridge and a piece of hard barley bread. Before leaving, the guard reminded them to lick the bowls clean so that less water would be spent on washing dishes. Soon after they finished, the same guard returned, stood at the doorway and officially notified them that it was toilet time. They all got up, walked toward the swaying light coming from the lantern in the guard's hand and, one after the other, filed down the hallway toward the latrines.

When he returned and stretched out on the floor next to Vavan, Osman felt the old man's hand reaching for his:

The Prophet spoke up from his corner: "You must not think about anything here. You must free yourself of all wants. Everything is forbidden. Even the barest necessities are out of your control. Instead, they have strictly scheduled everything: five times a day for the first one and once for the big one. If you aren't able to discipline yourself to that extent, then you will end up walking around with shit in your pants." The Prophet spoke as if reading a rule-book on rights and freedoms to a new member of the cell.

Merho added, "Everything is all right as long as you are together with the rest of the group. If you are the unfortunate one whose name the guard calls out, then you have nothing good to expect. Everything can change here: government, guards and seasons of the year, but the basic rules remain: lick the plates, go to the toilet when told to and when the guard calls out a name, someone will never be the same."

The night was heavy. Only when the world outside Kula's walls fell under the complete rule of darkness did Osman come to realise the true nature of his predicament. Kula separated man from life, freezing within him all playfulness and clarity, concentrating instead on squeezing from him every possible ounce of sorrow and despair. Only then did Osman come to feel a connection to the heavy stones which made up the cell, and thus make the plunge into acceptance of this world in which life manifested itself only through the blood-pulse of automation. In fact, for the first time in his life, this young man found he was alone with himself, in a situation where all his feelings had to be directed inward, where he could roam only within himself, where he could force his mind to concentrate its entire composition on itself and discover all its own hidden corners, corners he had never even imagined. Only then, surrounded by heavy, suffocating walls and darkness, was he able to pull his own, unique identity out from the mass of others and be alone with himself. He wasn't surprised to find that his main preceptors were useless outside of nature and were, in fact, created to keep him in child-like dependence. Thus bared, he realised that he was only a fragment in a complicated machinery of whose reason or shape he knew nothing.

"Only when swallowed up by darkness do we begin to long for light," old Vavan quietly insinuated himself into Osman's thoughts, as if he had a special hearing device for reading the most intimate confessions of his brain. "And when your jailors cut off all the paths along which it can enter, then you will rediscover it in a different state. This is a cocoon in which pupae, ugly even by human standards of beauty, are glued to the floor and then the crawlers inside metamorphose into butterflies, the most beautiful and free of all the creatures known to us.

This Kula is like a cocoon, and if we don't succeed in going from larvae to butterflies then it's a pity that we were ever born."

The Kula is like a cocoon. The slogan rang out in Osman's head and it didn't take great creativity to understand the old mentor's message. For a moment, Osman had the feeling that he, the old man and all the others in the corners of this and all the other cells had managed to free themselves from the narrow confines which bound them to the ground and held them in slavery, and these hundreds of liberated souls lit up the darkness of the prison like fireflies on a clear spring night.

This brief moment of hope was shocked from him by sudden awareness of the freezing stone floor whereon he lay, which sucked him back into the mass of flesh, bone, hair and saliva he was, and surrounded him with the unnerving sounds coming from neighbouring cells. Someone was beating their fist against the wall in the rhythms of the Morse code. He quickly realised that this was the prisoners' means of communication between cells—the most sophisticated information system of human beings far removed from freedom and protection. As soon as the pounding on the other side of the wall ended, Vavan's whispering voice explained that prisoners in the cells with windows facing north from Kula had noticed burning villages below the mountain peaks.

This was followed by someone in the opposite corner passing on the message to the next cell.

Tiny Yuray had kept his word—the government had punished the mountain villages for the attack upon its fascist forces when they entered this highland. The fascist marionettes were aiming their terror against those parts of the territory which looked to harbour the greatest potential danger. That was logical. Hmpf. If the hanging of two peasants from poplars in front of the school had been meant as a warning, the new rulers now showed the full face of their malevolence.

"The doors to the Bosnian butcher shop are once again being opened," whispered Vavan into the darkness of the cell. "Once again they will split us into different groups and send us to fight one another. But, we must not let them! We must hit back at those who are stirring up this bad blood. We must set out on the path from larva to butterfly. No one knows how painful this metamorphosis will be but we cannot allow ourselves to forever remain damned larvae."

Osman fully understood the old man and when the pounding on the prison's walls had died down, he felt a shivering coldness in his chest. Can there be a heavier sentence than the knowledge that you are eternally damned, doomed to continually spill the blood of those closest to you? To allow the burning and looting of our Bosnian corpses and souls by everyone, whenever and wherever they wish to? Osman questioned mutely. He felt aversion overcoming his hands and jaw. Reflexively, he grabbed the old man by the leg, shook him and stuttered: "The fires may burn Bosnia down but in this ash, one day we will plant strawberry fields."

Much later in the night, the pounding on the walls returned. Vavan again deciphered the message for him: a mobilisation of Muslims for the German and Croatian armies has begun...those who refuse will be sent to labour in Germany...while trying to escape from a transport truck, both of the Karayic brothers were killed...the new government is unhappy with the turnout of volunteers...

This news was much more worrying to Osman. "What will happen to Father and me, and all the others?" he asked himself.

We could have no contact with Osman. Thus, my brother didn't know that the occupational government had already selected me for a mobilisation check-up on the following Thursday. I had, therefore, only five more days. Father and I were united in the decision that I had to avoid the army at all costs, but we waited for Osman's release. We believed that he would be cleared of all suspicion in a few days.

At the very break of day, when the nearby rushing of the river could still be heard, Vavan crawled up to Osman's head and whispered in his ear that he immediately had to disappear from the cell and make contact with Milan and Zdravko Tchelar.

As soon as the morning lights in the hallway came gloomily on, a different, heavier and more dismal guard opened the door of the cell and formally called out Vavan's name. When the guard also looked him in the eye, standing there at the door, Osman was convinced that his name would be called too. However, it was the old man's turn and his turn alone.

As though Vavan had known by the clanging sound of the keys at the door that he would be moving on, he rose without comment and stepped forward. He was ready. As Osman watched him walking out the door, he observed how Vavan's imposing figure was folded almost in half in the prison; he had quickly hunched down before striking his head on the cell's stone ceiling, and his arms were unnaturally extended. As he reached the door, the wise old one suddenly turned toward his cellmates and extended a hand in farewell. From the cell, silence and raised hands returned his final gesture.

In our parts, the peoples' rebellion against the occupying rulers who had quickly demonstrated their true intentions began with the case of the sage Vavan. I don't remember who gave him this epithet. I think his enemies, those who feared him, because the word *sage*—wise man, or philosopher—had a negative connotation among the ordinary people.

As soon as Vavan descended the creaky wooden stairs of Kula, everything came to life in the heart of the prison and in the cobbled courtyard. Osman and the other four from Vavan's cell jumped to the tiny window to try to see what was going on. Around Kula, an unusually high number of uniformed men, prison guards and soldiers, were to be seen. In a far corner of the courtyard, a continually growing number of prisoners were being assembled. From the other side of the prison, from the direction of the church, came the motoring sound of trucks.

"They are transporting them somewhere." Merho the Musician whispered.

"The old man is there," the Prophet pointed out in a voice strained by nervous tension.

Vavan walked in front of two guards along a tiled path toward the centre of the courtyard. As he was passing a group of guards, one of them stepped in front of the tall old man, grabbed him by the beard and pulled him toward his cronies, shouting as if trying to be heard above the grinding of a watermill:

"Look at this bearded one! A real Bosnian Vlach…How about if we shave him?" he shouted, reaching for his knife.

The sage Vavan stood there and looked above his tormentor's head as if he, and his words, did not concern him. One of the two guards who had marched him out explained, in a lower tone of voice: "This is the famous communist agitator, the red philosopher. He wants to burn down our Independent State of Croatia…"

Upon hearing these words, the group of guards closed in around Vavan, who continued to look high above their heads. His disinterested attitude further infuriated them: one pulled him by the ear, then another pulled him to the ground by the hair. The old man continued to say nothing. He did not resist. At that moment, the one who had originally tormented him reached for the canteen at the back of his belt and declared, his voice carrying far outside the prison walls: "Hold out your hands!"

Vavan obeyed, as the other poured some liquid and again, even louder this time, commanded:

"Rub it in your beard! You haven't had a bath since Easter, and you can't go before God with a filthy beard…"

Vavan obeyed. The thug took a match out of his pocket, lit it and quickly tossed it at the old man's face. The beard exploded into flames. The guards and soldiers standing around him jumped up and down, shouting like children gathered around a monkey at the zoo. Vavan stood there paralysed, stoically silent.

Merho and the other three began to "oooh" and "aaah," shocked by the barbarity of the soldiers' game. The same noises of shock could be heard coming from all the cells which faced the courtyard, and then from the ones facing out over the river. Word had been passed somehow without the pounding of Morse. Some of the guards and soldiers also turned away when the fire began to die down and the burnt face of the old man became clear for all to see. Five or six more guards ran out into the courtyard from the bowels of Kula and stood before the old man, looking at him as if he were some miraculous apparition. The prisoners, from their narrow windows, mutely looked on the scene below. The first to react was the thug who had struck the match. This one stepped behind Vavan and forcefully shoved him toward the group of prisoners standing frozen as Rodin's *Burghers of Calais*. Vavan stumbled at first, then stood upright and took a few steps forward. The prisoners rushed toward him, held him up and took him with them to the corner of the courtyard.

Petrified to the depths of his soul, Osman mumbled to himself:

"That man is a medical phenomenon!"

"What medical phenomenon?! What medicine, my Osman!...That man is far above all those walking piles of manure who caused him such pain. You schoolboys don't know anything else, only medicine. They hang a man, his eyes go to the back of his head and his tongue hangs down to his chin, and you—you want a doctor of medicine to confirm it. The bare eye can see that he's dead, while you demand proof...This man, Osman, is both martyr and hero!" came Merho the Musician's strident whispering protest in Osman's right ear.

Many years later, Osman admitted to me that the scene which he observed at that moment through that narrow window of his jail cell moved him toward the world of mysticism, far from the pain of the world's reality, which man has proven capable of disfiguring to such an extent that it becomes repulsive. If you hold your eyes shut, even if you just turn away, as did Harkan when he turned his back on his mother when he discovered her in the clover with Dzafer the shoemaker, you see a better world. Watching Vavan's suffering, Osman concluded definitively that people will find millions of reasons to condemn you if they wish you ill. They would burn our sage for being intelligent, and they did, and if he wasn't intelligent, they would burn him for advocating a society in which all men would be equal. If he didn't even say that much, they would burn him just for being a Serb, or for looking like one.

That night, information began circulating early through the prison walls. The first pounding brought news that three truck-loads of prisoners, among them Vavan, were transferred to Bezdan—that huge and deep hole in the forest with a *noce* of underground water somewhere in the dark deep—where all had been shot. Some of them jumped into the Bezdan before than soldiers shot them. Since the old man's departure, the Prophet was now the only one who knew how to decipher the knocking on the walls. Who brought the information into Kula from the outside world, and from what sources, were mysteries which no one tried to solve, but the informant had proven in the past to be a reliable fountainhead of fresh news for the prisoners. Word reached them later that after the burning of the Grmec villages and the mass executions of prisoners an uprising had taken place among the Serbs living along the edges of the highland and at the foot of the mountain chain. At that news, something in Osman finally cracked. His whole body was overcome by a preternatural heat. Throughout his nervous system and into each and every cell of his flesh came the command for the entire organism to stand to for a momentous event, a cataclysm. Realising that he was entering a state over which he would have little control—the awakening of a force he had only rarely suspected within his own body—he began to fear himself.

Shortly before the clanking of the guard's key in the heavy door lock, came the news that hostile groups of people had descended upon the village of Kremusha, inhabited by Croatians. A bloodbath was underway between people who had lived side by side but prayed to different gods, who spoke the same language but gave it different names. When the light of the guard's lantern shone upon Osman's face, the tall, moustached man startled backward and barked: "Quickly, to the toilet, one by one!…" It did him little good.

Not many minutes later, that same guard was hanging from a wooden beam in the dark hallway and all the cell doors in Kula stood wide open. Next day, the story goes, the authorities found two guards under the heavy wooden stairs, both run through with a metal rod that had come from the front gates. The fat guard, Ivo, had hidden in the Catholic church and in response to all of the priest's questions could only manage to roll his eyes and press himself tight against the wall below Jesus' cross.

Fehrat remembered folks version of the story about Vavan and his suffering, which was generally confirmed by Yudja's tale, but Osman's role in these events was something completely new to him. With numinous fascination, his interest in Osman grew the more he learnt about him, while Yudja's attributing surreal qualities to his brother's personality he understood as a desire to reincarnate a being who meant so much to him and whom dreadful reality had taken away. Though isolated within his crippled body, sometimes he found the strength to crawl into the skeletal husk of his former spirit, which could take him from the life he was now leading and afford him wanderings along surreal paths where he could rediscover people and nature, and take the opportunity to make forbidden inquiries into taboo subjects. Only thus was he able to quiet the nightmares connected to his mother's explanations of how he came into this world. Yudja's remembrances of Osman again pushed him beyond the cover of reality and for the first time in his life he was glad to be a blood relative of that fiery man.

"Did you succeed in finding out the details about the uprising at Kula and Osman's role in it?" inquired Fehrat when he started to feel Yudja's lengthy pause scratching at his curiosity. "How did he carry it off, if he was the one who started it all? How did he manage to win the confidence of the other prisoners so that every single one of them followed him?" Yudja's stare fixated upon the shelf holding the wooden figurines, as if trying to find the answer among these strange creations of his intimate memory. Standing up, he grabbed the figure of a finely shaped young man with two grotesque holes in the upper corners of his forehead. Turning him around, as if looking for something, he ran his thumb along the figurine's brows and in the area between the eyes and the ears before handing him to Fehrat.

"I both loved and hated my brother." Yudja sounded as if he were giving away a deep secret. "I hated his ability to build new worlds, to occasionally enter them alone and walk among his buildings. The only way that I could compete with him I found in the wood and chisel. The first thing I did was to place the devil's horns close to his brain.

Then, one night, after meeting my brother in a dream, I cut the horns off and dug out two holes in their place as a symbol of my inability to understand him, my protest against his being stronger than me and managing to scale the wall ahead while I remained behind, pounding my fists in futility." Yudja opened up his private bitterness in a tone of sad relief.

Fehrat turned the work of art in his hand round and round. If it wasn't for the maker's provocative explanations, he would have graded the end result as a success, perhaps better than that, especially the striking tension of the leg muscles and the strange look beneath the icy brows. Now, however, when Yudja's worm had managed to crawl into his soul also, he hurried to return the figurine to its creator in the hope that he could free himself of the strange power which had suddenly begun to emanate from the piece of linden wood.

"Osman never spoke about the details with me," Yudja answered his son's question, then added: "He went out of his way to confuse me with his arrogant evading of questions, never clearing anything up. Where he only touched on matters, he left behind blinking lights which I could never turn off. He left me and the lights together to make each other suffer so that he could depart in triumph. I never learnt the absolute truth about what happened at Kula, but it did happen, and shocked both the people and the authorities. Of all the prisoners who escaped from jail that night, they managed to catch only two men who had been inside less than a week and departed for the other world without ever understanding their guilt. After a while, someone allegedly discovered the secret of the Kula uprising: Vavan. Ustasha investigators of this rumour found a hole through which the old sage had crawled out of the mass grave and, like a vampire, returned to the prison. The fascist NDH authorities gladly embraced this version because it served as an excuse for their inability to learn the truth, and as fuel for their campaign against the outlawed Communist Party. In that, of course, the Communists were condemned for their godlessness and service to the devil."

Father and son looked at one another questioningly. Fehrat discovered curiosity in Yudja's eyes, while Yudja saw a lack of faith and many unanswered questions in Fehrat's. The silence brought them back to the realisation that they were here, under the roof of an old building on the Canadian coast of the Pacific, distant and cut off from events in Bosnia, left to fend for themselves with the near dark of their souls between the wallpapered walls.

Yudja returned the Osman figurine to the shelf with the others, stood by the window and explained how that night his father had received two visits. First came a pair of the mayor's toadies, who expressed a desire that he spread the word among the people that the new government was favourably inclined toward the Muslim population because the Bosnian Muslims were in fact nothing more than Islamic Croatians and the time had come for them to return to their nation.

Yudja leaned against the flimsy wooden drawer and remembered the bleak conversation held in Father's room. Old Fehrat's courageous answer was engraved in his memory. He opened his mind to young Fehrat again.

"Father told the visitors, whom he obviously had never cared for, that he may have been an Islamic Croatian until that night but he no longer felt this to be the case. He then suggested to the new government that it embrace all of the nationalities if it wished to be around much longer. The two men left the house commenting how they had expected such an answer and that the only ones worse than the Serbs were those who married them.

Later, a soft knock came from the window of my room. From the other side of the wall, out of the darkness, I could hear my brother's voice. I immediately knew that the devil had dug his claws deep into our lives.

Osman jumped into the room. Father appeared at the door. All three of us stood there looking at each other. Father spoke first:

"By God, where did you come from at this time of night?!"

"Things aren't good, Father. If I wasn't here now, I'd be in front of the firing squad tomorrow. Those who didn't escape from Kula tonight will never leave it alive."

"But, they will find you. This town is not an abyss where you can hide. That fat gendarme promised me that you would soon be released. He only had to complete some formalities and you would have been freed."

"I know, Father…I might have been released from Kula…But, what then? Join the German army or the Ustashas? You know that I don't belong there."

"Where then, Osman?"

"To the forest, for now. Later, I'll see. All three of us must flee to the forest. We have no chance if we remain here. Being without a chance here means certain death."

"You think that we have a chance in the forest? That we belong there, is that it?"

"From what's going on in Pset, Father, it's clear there is no room for us here. The villages below the Grmec mountains have been burnt to the ground. These new rulers are brutal and blind; the brutality will leave like a surprise storm but the blindness will create further destruction and misery. I think that only in the forest will we have the chance to survive."

"My Osman, my son! It seems to me that there is no room for us here or there. This evil has caused people to be placed in separate pens. Unfortunately, we don't belong in any one of the pens. If we were to escape, we would have to flee far away, which is something I am unable to do. I have thought about this night for some time now. I knew that it would come. You two must go to Dmitar tonight. He will watch over you. I will stay here. I am too old for the forest and you will need someone to help you from town. Habibe and I will stay. Then again, Nuhan and his family will also be here."

These words decided everything. We both knew that there was no use trying to argue with Father. So much had happened recently that it was no longer difficult to flee into such uncertainty so quickly. The most difficult part for me was the comprehension that there was no pen that would accept me in the midst of all this misery, that fleeing to the forest wouldn't guarantee my safety because even there they would accept us only as long as they needed us, and then…The worm was nibbling away at my soul. It was only that night that I learnt that the same worm had been eating away at Father, and he came from somewhere in the past, a time when none of us could act. As soon as they tell you what you are, but that you belong somewhere else, despite the fact that you don't belong there either, everything becomes clear as day. Everything must be clear because if it isn't, then you will be lost. Being lost at such times is fatal.

That night, Osman and I walked through the groves and orchards to the part of town called Red Pits, from where we reached the woods and made our way to our uncle's house. He awaited us like the true brother of our mother, as if he had expected us long ago.

CHAPTER VI

Late into the night, Yudja was still carving away at a sizable chunk of linden wood though the shapes in his mind were very slow to take form before his eyes. It was obvious that he was struggling, troubled by an unformulated idea, wandering aimlessly, searching for a style. He took long breaks to stare at something only he could see, moving his lips as if to consult with a confidante, furrowing his brows. And then, staring at the tip of his carving knife, he reached for the whetstone and slowly began to sharpen, not because the blade was dull but because his concentration needed to be honed. He exchanged only a few words with Fehrat, who quickly realised that Yudja needed solitude, that he had probably become accustomed to it, as a man can sometimes become accustomed to things in life totally opposed to what he would normally consider common sense.

Ever since the day he lost all contact with his mother or, to be precise, since she stopped communicating with him, Yudja had not come across anyone to whom he could open up his soul and to whom he could tell the story of his life and of his ancestors, ending in this exile which had been forced upon him without any opportunity to come face to face with his accusers and judges. He believed that this misfortune was truly the final one and that he would never return to Bosnia. Instead, he was destined to roam strange and unfamiliar places. Even here, in this pale Canadian existence, he felt he was merely at another transit station, from which he was sure to be evicted yet again. His homeland had grown increasingly distant and faded; it even seemed to have become cold to him—this idea kept inching closer to him, like a slimy snail—what kind of place is it that forces upon its inhabitants nothing but eternal fear of exile and uncertainty? He wrestled with these inexorable thoughts, and as his knife once more made its aimless way over the linden wood, he began to identify with the defenceless object before him, itself being shaped and carved without any opportunity for input into its destiny.

Looking toward his son, he caught Fehrat staring at his hands as they worked the wood. He was immediately overcome by intense discomfort. Hadn't he, Yudja, been largely responsible for this man, or what remained of him, being condemned to a life of eternal uncertainty, shame and pain? Hadn't he created him in his imagination, so that he could pass on his own damnation, thereby prolonging his life, even beyond death? He certainly had much to prolong, he reflected cynically, and he had much to pass on...Nevertheless, his need to confess to someone was out of his control, exceeded his strength. It seemed to him to be the will of someone else, decided elsewhere, to resurrect the past, even though he knew that there is no greater madness than the return to life of someone or something already dead, because after death only fear and discomfort remain.

"You're struggling tonight...It seems the carving knife just won't listen," Fehrat threw into the silence. "Better to stop and wait for inspiration to arrive."

"It happens. Sometimes I have the will but not much else. But, something will surely come...A little cut here, a cut there, and just as I begin to fear the worst, the right shapes begin to appear. Often, not in the dimensions that I had imagined, but they appear. And then, everything goes quicker and the struggle ends."

"Alma writes there is the possibility all of the women in their camp will be transferred to America. Didn't you say that they promised to send the two of them here?"

"They really did...But, that was more than a year ago. It seems the Canadian government is also content to provide us with lip-service. We're simply not worth the effort. Why should any of them care whether or not my family and I are ever reunited? Now this talk about transferring them to America. Perhaps things will be better there..." Yudja spoke in a tone which was a mixture of sorrow and disgust. As he spoke, his head dropped as if it wished to crawl into the block of wood in his hands and become the creation which he intended for it.

He sighed, and Fehrat immediately placed the sigh somewhere in the mountainous terrain above the town centre of Pset. Fehrat noticed two enormous tear-drops in Yudja's eyes, which like pearls were created by that part of the body which offers a window to the soul, revealing moods and emotions.

The old man held the linden wood tightly in his hand, as if it was all that remained for him, fearing that it too might be taken away. The carving knife, which he had received as a child from his mother one day at the fairground, had become the instrument with which he could best express himself, reveal his most intimate secrets, pour out his soul.

"I will have to contact the social worker over in downtown Vancouver…" With this, Fehrat changed the direction of the conversation, while Yudja looked at him in surprise. "The people from the Canadian embassy in Vienna told me in Karlovac, and later in Zagreb, that they would be sending me here specifically to get help for my hand. They said there are specialists here who could make me an artificial fist and fingers. I could eventually regain many of my hand functions. That's what saved me. Anything that will take me further away from the evil which suffocated me and which I was powerless to fight."

"And all this time I thought that you had come to be with me," Yudja smiled ironically, reflecting that his son had said *fist* before he said *hand*, "when in fact they sent you here for rehabilitation…Eh, my Fehrat! Somehow, you will surely rehabilitate your hand, but never your soul. I would rather be without a hand than without a soul."

Just as Fehrat spread his classically shaped lips to return the smile, from the floor below them came the scream of a child, followed by sounds of people running. The child screamed in waves.

"Olaf's daughter—beautiful as a daisy, bright, light complexion. Born with a chronically nervous stomach. She can't eat sweets or even fruit. When the illness hits, she starts to scream as if running from ghouls. As soon as she begins to cry out, they have to bathe her. She doesn't stop until she feels the water. I think Olaf is not far from screaming himself. His wife has lost more weight than the poor child…

There is nothing worse than evil within man. Wherever he goes, he carries it with him." Yudja spoke softly, listening for the inevitable sound of running water to come from the apartment below.

"That is very true. When it is next to you, you can change a hundred Bosnias, but when it is eating away at you from within…I don't think we Bosniaks will ever have peace. Even if they were to take us all and move us to some Canadian prairie or Australian desert, some Chetniks and Ustashas would be there to hold a knife to our throats. Even a nervous stomach is easier to bear than the constant expectation of some knife coming for your throat. It makes no difference whether it comes from the left side, or the right."

"Whatever became of your teacher friend?" Yudja wondered, thinking of the woman who had been Fehrat's love for a long time and, as everyone in town knew, would have become his wife had it not been for this latest ethnic butchery.

"Snezana also caught the collective sickness…She listened to the propaganda of the Serb media and conceived that the entire world was against her people, especially the Bosnian Muslims and the Albanians. There was no use in pointing out to her that the Muslims were unarmed and posed absolutely no threat to the Serbs. She remained at the school, to teach the children about the fateful battles of the Serbian people.

"Even after the bloodbath which went on day and night in town during those first days of madness, and the banishment of the entire Bosniak' population from the highlands, her final words to me were: "The mind of my nation has finally opened up Pandora's Box, regardless how much this determination of ours may cost." Imagine hearing that, after the three years we had been together. Shocked by the extent to which she had been poisoned by the nationalist toxin, my only comment was that somebody probably foisted Pandora's Box on them instead of the Paschal Lamb and they were waging war with the wrong enemy and in the wrong place.

"After that, I left her with her Pandora's Box and the winds of war blew me toward a unit of the Bosnian army which was trying to break through the Grmec hills toward the Una Valley. We were ambushed up in the hills, some were captured…That's how I ended up in the death camp near Priyedor." Fehrat spoke wistfully as he concluded this story of innermost pain to his father.

Yudja understood the meaning of these words and agreed with the theory of 'the wrong war' but, at the same time, there flashed through his imagination hundreds of horrific images which had befallen their ill-fated Balkan nation and which would surely continue to curse future generations. The idea struck him to carve out a Pandora's Box resting in one hand of his wooden work-in-progress, while the other hand would be holding a battered and scarred globe, and he described this idea to his son.

"You can, if you want…But, your Titan, with his heavy symbols in his hands, cannot come alive. There are just too many of them on this planet, each with the same characteristics and outlooks toward life in our cosmos," Fehrat critiqued.

Nonetheless, Yudja returned to his carving. The main activity of his knife centered upon the left hand of his creation, while Fehrat moved from one corner of the couch to the other. He coughed violently. Yudja glanced toward him and gave him a look, as if to reassure him that he knew the meaning behind the coughing. Both concluded that it wasn't too late in the night to continue with the stories since neither of them had to rise early in the morning. They could go and see the social worker responsible for the refugees after lunch.

Yudja began:

The two of us, Osman and I, were physically men, but our experience was limited, just as it is with young eagles who have the look, the coloured feathers and the cold-blooded piercing eyes, but can fly only short distances, uncertain, hopping from one foot to the other before throwing themselves into the abyss of life outside the nest.

The next day, when we reached the top of the hill above our uncle's house, I could sense Osman's heart contracting and the apple anxiously pushing the nervousness through his throat. Our plans had been to sign up for studies in Sarajevo after completing secondary school, but…

On the eastern slopes of the Psetian highland before us, our town looked like a bird's nest. Behind us was the Grmec mountain range and all the uncertainty which emanated from that direction. For the first time, I found myself standing on the fault line between two worlds. The world below me was a materialistic civilisation where you must be a slave if you wish to be held in its lap, where, like high tide and low tide, periods of happiness and prosperity were followed by times of fear and uncertainty. On the other side was a provocative world of wildness, full of life's juices and suprahuman laws, which each battle against the world of the valleys and chimneys inexorably brought nearer to final defeat. All around, there rose columns of smoke from unextinguished fires. Scenes of arson, homes put to the torch.

Days passed as we waited. Our only activity was getting acquainted with Uncle's horses, who were much quicker to accept me than Osman. At night, the most common sounds were human voices, the rustling of the horses and the rattling of weapons, while Uncle's eyes increasingly became redder and more swollen. His third wife, Savka, was usually silent. If we hadn't known her from before, we would have thought that she was bothered by our presence in her house. She had been suffering for some time from a stomach ailment and lately most of her thoughts were on her own health, to say nothing of the war which at any time might boil up out of the valley.

Our father did not come to visit us and we heard nothing from him.

As we were getting ready to go to bed one night, we heard the sound of voices from outside the front doors. Soon after, Uncle and two other men entered. Uncle immediately pointed to us and commented:

"There they are, still awake. These are my nephews. I owe it to my late sister to look out for them in these evil times. And Fehro has also earned it."

He then explained to us that the two men were relatives from Tavani, at the very crest of the mountain, and that for the sake of safety we would be better off with them. I was speechless, because things were tolerable at Uncle Dmitar's but up there in Tavani... Dmitar immediately read my reaction and tried to clarify the gravity of situation. The Occupiers' forces were preparing large operations to suppress dissent in the territories where the people had risen, and a large number of villages close to the highland were being evacuated this very night in order to escape what would most probably be brutal death at the hands of the fascists.

"Everyone is heading for the forest. The best thing for the two of you would be to avoid joining any group until we see where all this misery is heading," Uncle tried to convince us.

We both knew that it would be better to keep our distance from any place where the Occupiers' forces would pass, but we still feared for our father and other family and friends who remained in town. Nonetheless, in the middle of the night, bags on our backs, we headed out behind the two relatives into the thick darkness and up the mountain. Sometimes we heard the noises of people and cattle moving in the same direction, but as yet saw no one. When we reached the first mountain spurs, we were stopped by sentries. We hadn't seen them when a couple of voices shouted in unison:

"Stop! Who goes there?"

Our two companions answered: "It's us, locals!…Stevo and Rade! Dmitar's nephews are with us…"

They allowed us to pass, and as we climbed by the sentries' post we saw a large number of bonfires at the very edge of the field beyond. Only then, as if awaking from a dream, we heard the barking of dogs and bellowing of cattle from below the ridge of the mountain and it was clear to us that the enemy's operation had begun.

"They are burning everything in their path but fortunately the people have already fled to the mountain," said Rade as he proposed that we rest. Only when we sat down were we able to catch the full manifestation of the chaos taking place down below: the burning villages and the noise of people fleeing with their animals and bundles of food. Sounds of gunfire came from the direction of Dobroselo's Bends. The initial gunfire transpired into a real battle when, from deep in the plateau, came the roar of cannon fire. The barrage was initially directed at the foot of the mountain. Soon, though, they raised their barrels and fiery mushrooms began to tear away at the mountain's bosom.

"The bloodsuckers have realised that the people are making their way up here so they are now aiming above the villages," whispered Stevo, standing up and urging us on before one of the cannon blasts reached us.

Stevo and Rade were brothers, both in their forties—Stevo, by the look of his less tense face and hairier ears, was a year or two the elder. From the first day we realised that he was second to the feeble Uncle Milos, who despite suffering from asthma and kidney stones, was the head of the family and the one who decided the outcome of all disagreements.

Milos received us as Dmitar's relatives, and Dmitar was obviously viewed with great respect by the entire family. However, after supper, as his eyes followed the trail of smoke coming from his pipe while he gave us a short explanation of who his family were and what their ties to our uncle were, I noticed that Milos never called us by our first names, and though he mentioned our mother several times, he alluded to our father only once, calling him only "Dmitar's in-law". From this man, despite the sickness which tormented him and had reduced him to a bundle of skin, bone and hair, sprang an impression of hidden force guised in an air which was more habitual hospitality than warmth and confidence. Perhaps I was mistaken, perhaps it was some inexplicable jealousy which used my distaste for our host as an excuse to convince me that this was not the place for me, but I was disturbed to find that during the entire course of our conversation old Milos looked mainly at Osman, turning toward him when he expected an answer, as if I wasn't even present. Perhaps he was one of those who in each new contact with others instinctually chooses a favourite, and from that point on tries continually to convince himself that his first choice was the right one.

Their very house, from my anxious outsider's perspective, lacked warmth. It was all alien and claustrophobic, very different from what I had imagined to be the free life far removed from urban surroundings.

Stevo and Rade's mother accepted Milos as the head of the family, even though both of her sons seemed to be healthy and capable men. The same applied for the two men's wives, as well as their children. To make things even more awkward for me, I was tormented by the fact that I knew that this was something over which I had no right to judge.

As if in compensation, from the first day Rade had decided to favour me. He quickly realised that I was feeling uncomfortable and, while Milos and Osman entered into the reasons for the misfortune which the Occupiers' rule had brought with it, he took me out and showed me around their place.

"Don't worry about Uncle," Rade said as we walked behind the hay-loft, after which he turned around several times to make certain that no one had followed us. "He loves and respects your uncle. Milos is the oldest in our family, and raised us together with our mother. Our father disappeared when we were still children. Ever since, Uncle has taken over responsibility for us. He also had a wife and three children and they had half of our house. There came one particularly hard year: the wheat burnt from the heat, the potatoes dried up, and the cattle came down with dysentery and all died. The people also became sick from the dysentery and little good came of the charms of the old woman Persa, or the one-eyed Muslim from town. All three of Uncle's children died within a week and after she had buried them, his wife threw herself into the well. And so he was left with us."

Even though all this held little interest for me because I had already begun to think seriously of how to get out of there—fear and uncertainty preoccupying me, and the desire to be with my father staying with me like a nightmare—surprisingly I asked:

"And what happened to your father?"

Rade shook as if hit by an icy wind. Standing up, his sight set on the southern peaks of the mountain chain, he began to speak in a tone full of melancholy and condemnation:

"My father disappeared that same year. The famine had taken everything that the people had and the dysentery had filled up the graveyards. Only the landlords were better off. Some people from far away came to town, from somewhere in Istria. People say they spoke more Italian than our language. These Istrians offered good wages to those willing to go and work for them. They immediately gave a sack of wheat to anyone who signed on. Mother says that my father was a very proud man and was particularly devastated by the poverty which had overtaken everyone. He signed on, slapped us two on the ears, gave mother a serious, dark look, and told her that he would return sooner or later. Uncle saw him off as far as the town square. Afterwards, Father sent us money several times through some merchants. Two or three years later, the money stopped arriving. We heard stories about a group of our people leaving on boats for work in America. It seems that our father was among them. Since then, no trace of him, no word. All that was left of him was the family nickname, 'Karizan'".

"Why that?" I asked, "You and your brother seem like peaceful people. *Karizan* sounds like something dark and bitter. Perhaps your uncle, but you two?…"

"That's what they call us, after our grandfather. He was as mean as a serpent on St. George's Day. Short, stout, moustached and as wicked as the devil. There was no one meaner up here on Tavani. Always had his ancient pistol at his waist and a pipe in his mouth. He carved out the likeness of his Milunka in an old cornel tree—Grandmother had died early, while delivering a stillborn child. Only sentimental thing Grandfather ever did. He enjoyed sitting in front of the hearth, smoking his pipe and talking about the uprisings of our people against every ruler in this part of the world. They say he always complained that each government tried to enslave the honest man while declaring a holiday for all good-for-nothings. Once, as he was sitting in front of the hearth, talking in harmony with the corn gruel bubbling in the copper pot over the fire and pushing fresh tobacco into his pipe, pulling out the small knots which didn't belong, just as he decided to take into his calloused hand a small lump of fire from the hearth, a snot of gruel shot out of the pot and landed directly in his pipe. They say he jumped up, opened his eyes wide in fury at the copper pot and the corn gruel in it, reached for his pistol and emptied it into the bubbling mess. The bullets left three holes in the pot and it would never be used again to cook corn gruel. Since this type of copper is called *karizan* in our parts, the people began to refer to Grandfather by that name. After he passed away, the nickname remained and is still with us to this day."

As he spoke, Rade looked off into the distance, while in the depths of his sight, where imagination and the pictures transmitted by the eyes meet, images of his father and grandfather emerged from the fog and turned into the words he spoke to me. When he was done, he looked into my eyes, as if trying to read my mind. All the while, I'd been struggled with my own emotions and when I caught sight of Rade's eyes, my mind shot back in time, as if into someone else's head, and I declared aloud: "We were made for misery. Never good! One good year is sure to be followed by five evil ones. When you mentioned how much grief one year brought you, I remembered what some monk wrote down two and a half centuries ago:

1689. Epidemics and fires came down upon Bosnia. That same year, snow and frost ruined the wheat and there was hunger the likes of which no one had seen before...Many people died of hunger and began fleeing from the River Sava...They started eating the catkins from hazels, the bark from trees, vine leaves, dogs, cats. In Sarajevo, children ate their dead mother. In Banja Luka, men hanged on the gallows would be ripped apart overnight for their edible flesh...The other regions also faced similar misery and the message arrived: the famine will last seven years. It spread to the Posavina and around Pljevlja. The hunger spread to all corners of the land. Five kilos of grain sold for three gold ducats. People everywhere died of hunger.

"Our entire class had to memorise this passage, so that we'd remember it for the rest of our lives. Whoever didn't know it had to face the history professor, Dayo." I tried to explain to Rade the why and where of the quotation from some old Bosnian book stored in the back of my head.

We sat under the sheltering branches of the wild beech-tree and observed the wind which was making its way from the plateau below us. An experienced nose could detect a burning smell in the air, accompanied occasionally by resonating sounds coming from the bosom of the mountain above, the thick sounds of striking axes and mallets. The fleeing masses were improvising shelter, feeling somewhat more secure in the greater distance from town. The offensive was at an ebb. The sounds of gunfire coming from the villages closest to town had ceased to be heard. In the group of houses hidden by fir-trees just below us, men were transporting something on horses.

"Zorka came by in the morning to ask Uncle if we had seen her Milan down at the base of the mountain. He had loaded up his mule with grain and was taking it down to Pecanac's mill when the offensive caught him by surprise. She's worried because he's still not back." Rade pointed toward a woman who was chasing some sheep away from a house.

From behind us, Rade and Stevo's children came racing up on their makeshift hobby horses.

"Grandma's calling you to go and eat lunch!" they shouted all at once. After taking a quick second look at me they turned around and ran back in the direction from which they had come.

Before dark, the four of us chopped wood in the grove. While we gathered together the axes and mallets and wedges to go back to the house, we noticed a group of armed men coming toward us from the direction of Zorka's house. By their movement and dress, it was immediately obvious that they were not a regular military formation. Stevo and Rade, as if wanting to protect us, walked a dozen steps forward and awaited them. They greeted each other with: "God help us, people!". The bearded one who marched at the head of the group wore a black leather jacket and held a double-barrelled shotgun in his hands. Not waiting till he reached us, he began to verbally attack Stevo and Rade for not being a part of their first victory over the Ustashas. He ordered them to go get their weapons and join the guerrillas. His attention was distracted several times as he suspiciously looked us over. When Stevo told him who we were, he quickly turned away and headed toward the Karizans' house.

Stevo briefly explained to us how they were the main shock troops from Karan's group and the bearded one used to be the village thug and layabout who was now the leader and had already demonstrated his courage. Stevo suggested that perhaps it would be better if he and

Rade followed them to the house while Osman and I took the tools and returned them behind the shed.

The two of them hadn't even disappeared behind the hay-loft when, from behind us, came another loud group, led by Uncle Dmitar, hunting rifle in hand. The others were similarly armed. Embracing us and asking how we were, he didn't wait to hear our answer before running off after Stevo and Rade, only whispering that they had an important meeting and that he would see us later.

"Inquire about Zdravko," Osman shouted after him. Uncle stopped in his tracks, made his thinking face, walked back a few steps as if he was going to explain something, but swung his hand and turned back toward his group, not before mumbling:

"OK, OK!…I'll ask…"

It all seemed to me like some nightmare. Some of their faces frightened me, while the bonfires and smoke which had been following us ever since father left us with Uncle Dmitar seemed like something out of Dante's *Inferno*. I realised that war didn't only mean the arrival of foreign armies and the establishment of new administrations, it also mean countless changes in people, those whom I had known since I was a child and of whom I had developed convincing images which I believed would never change. Now everything had suddenly changed. In such a short period of time, so many enigmas had developed in my brain that I was constantly pinching myself to make sure that this world was real. I tried to separate the reality from the nightmare which was without explanation.

Why would Osman ask about some Zdravko? My thoughts spun like a merry-go-round. As I rummaged through my memory, trying to return to the roots of truth in From's systems of destiny, I became tripped up even more. I tried to find the Freudian schema of my predicament, the boundary between the conscious and the subconscious, but found all of the doors closed shut. I felt a bolt-like pain hit me as I carried the axes toward the shed: my stomach cramped up; my head seemed bursting like a volcano, brain cells spilling forth like lava; full of anxiety, fear, blindness and an overwhelming desire to bite down hard, to shout…Osman tormented me especially. I felt a strange energy radiating from him, yet didn't know how to respond.

He knew everything. It was as if I had already confessed everything to him. He read my thoughts and knew my state. He leaned against the mallet that he had been carrying and stung me with a deadly glare, like a poisonous snake trying to paralyse its victim with a look.

"You still don't understand, Yudja," he said in a tone of voice which I had only suspected him of having. "Why must you be the one who has to make sense of what I am doing?! What use would it be to you even if you could understand? I know you are confused by this nonsense within us and surrounding us. Nonsense, I tell you, because there is no use in trying to understand it, none. We are always trying to find some logic in events, as if that is all that exists in this world of ours. Logic is something that we have brought upon ourselves, so why shouldn't we free ourselves of it? Be reasonable, Yudja! Don't hesitate! You must decide what you will do in these times, because new ones won't come for quite a while."

I stared emptily at my brother, then at the wooden door behind which the group of men had disappeared, and then down toward town, which couldn't be seen behind the hook in the mountain. The sensation of vertigo overcame me. Before my eyes, everything distorted, now thick, now straitened, now round, but increasingly resembling shapes seen before only in dreams. The lines of objects before me came alive in an endless whiteness distinguished only by bland differences in shading. Crowds of people appeared, relationships were established, leaders and followers chosen, smiling at banquets, clapping at meetings before turning inward and devouring one another. My eyes became watery as they began to flutter, becoming a shapeless mass and flopping around like dying fish in a plastic bag.

As I returned to my senses, the first thing I saw was Osman's concerned face. He held me with one arm while with his other hand he wiped the cold beads of sweat from my forehead.

That night at the Karizans' house, an insurrectionary military committee was formed. Zdravko Tchelar was chosen to be the commander. The man after whom Osman had mysteriously asked.

The first signs of tension between the two main factions of the insurrectionists were already evident. Later this tension would explode into full-blown hostility when one group attached itself to Tito's Partisans while the other joined the Nationalist/Royalist Chetniks. Rade later spoke of how on that first night Zdravko suggested that the committee accept into its units all Muslim volunteers from the plateau. The mouthpiece of the Royalist faction, the bearded ruffian Karan, responded to Zdravko's proposition by declaring that he didn't trust anyone who wasn't a Serb and of Serb birth. He also claimed that in the previous night's government offensive on the surrounding villages a large number of Psetian Muslims took part. As he spoke, Karan's eyes burned bright, his teeth were grinding and his head was constantly turning to face Uncle Dmitar.

At night, the wind changed direction and a cold dampness descended upon the mountain. Osman and I were lying on a bed of hay alongside Rade and his little son. I couldn't fall asleep for the longest time. When I finally did, I dreamt that Mother's voice was calling after me as I rode through a foggy landscape on an enormous red rooster. Dawn arrived just as I became comfortable in my sleep. Though I was asleep, something told me that morning would soon be upon us. Beyond the closed shutters tentacles of fog were converging, slithering over and around the cold wet bark of trees, crawling under the rafter-ends of the roof and even into the foul outhouse holes, unwinding, grasping and merging into the growing white mass. In between the coils of fog, for a brief moment there appeared an icy pale smear in the sky, a circular shape. From the attic, the cat could he heard scraping along the ceiling rafters.

The old, worm-holed bedroom doors unexpectedly flew open and with a sharp thwack found themselves flat against the wall. I saw Rade also startled awake, sitting upright under the quilt. Old Karizan stood at the door, looking upon us with uncertainty. A thick strand of grey hair cut across his forehead. His white night-shirt reached all the way to the floor.

"Get up, Rade! Milan's Zorka has gone mad!...Some time last night, they brought back Milan's dead body on a gelding. She started weeping, then howling like a bitch before running off into the rain. Stevo is already up..." The old man spoke in a wild, alarmed tone. "She ran off with the child and still hasn't returned."

I dressed and followed Rade outside. On the table the grandmother had set out milk, cream and gruel and was putting something into two bags. Stevo and Osman were already sitting at the table. Stevo commented that the two of us from away needn't go because the fog was so thick. My brother and I simultaneously refused to hear of any such idea. Rade suggested that I go with him, that we take his dog Teri with us and head toward the Byelay hollow. It was agreed. Osman went with Stevo.

I felt a pressure building up in my head, a desire to walk firmly, each step premeditated. Rain was drizzling through the fog. My brain formed images of our town square, of Father, aeroplanes, tanks, burning houses and Zorka with her child held tightly in her arms, both of them naked, wet and freezing. Rade unhitched the dog's chain and passed its loose end to me, motioning for me to lead him along. The dog followed me without enthusiasm, lagging slightly behind, hopping from one foot to the other with apprehension, as if stepping among countless puddles of water.

We turned along the hook of the mountain while the other pair headed toward the Black Ridge. We passed by a grove of large-limbed wild pear trees and following a sodden path between hawthorn and sloe-bushes, quickened our pace toward the incline which fell away before us. The Grmec heights were wrapped in clouds: grey, heavy and full of freezing rain.

Rade led us through a shortcut made, he said, because the people below the mountain had settled along the terraces just behind the first peak, now overgrown with dense coniferous trees. Suddenly before us in the fog stood the ruins of what once must have been a house, a reminder that in these ravines times of peace and building alternated with periods of war and destruction. In the glen a large wild beech tree spread itself. Rade motioned with his hand for the dog and me to go through the glen while he checked out the brush above us.

As I descended the gradual slope, I unchained Teri. He immediately ran toward the foot of the large tree. Several tufts of fog extended themselves upward to its highest branches, while a few meters lower, on a thick limb which favoured to the right, squatted two grey ravens, completely disinterested in the floating fog and branches, or us, below them. One of the ravens was significantly larger while the other had several tail feathers which resembled those of a turkey-cock when demonstrating his manliness and strength.

Teri floundered around under low-hanging branches, letting loose several unusual howls, soon after which a third raven materialised from the white miasma like a hedge-hopping aircraft, startled by the dog and finding his wits at the last moment, in time to pass dangerously close before finding safety in the pear tree's higher limbs. He had been plucking away at the carcass of some other, deceased dog before being disturbed in his task by the ranging Teri. Rade's dog burst into a frenzy. Perhaps he couldn't stand the idea of his relative's remains being mutilated by a carrion crow. When I called him over to continue our search, he began to howl and dig around the carcass. Only the sound of Rade's quiet whistle managed to detach him from the scene. From the direction of a group of houses to our left came the sound of geese.

The higher we ascended, the more the fog remained below us. We found ourselves with an unforgettable sight: the Psetian plateau resembled a grey sea—tempestuous, frozen, full of rocky, greyish-dark waves and vortexes. From this roiling mass there rose the slender blackiron chimney of a sawmill, connecting the fog below with the clouds above. It seemed unreal, like a geometric gene among a host of ungeometric forms; like a reed of civilisation in an inhospitable mass of fields, hills and clouds. And off in the distance, toward the usually foggy Una basin, like and old man thinking, sat the rocky peak of Mount Osjecenica.

Just one move on the part of nature and our entire plateau completely changes in appearance. Instead of the hard life which everyone has come to accept...Instead of the fear in the eyes of the powerless people and the bloody appetites of the uniformed slime...Instead of the roar of tanks and pecking of machine-guns, this rocky surface from a dreamlike landscape seems to be suspended on some far-away body in the cosmos. If some force could drop its magic micro-organisms through this greyness and alter our terrestrial genetics so that we could build a world in which the food chain did not dictate that the strong devour the weak...

Such were the thoughts that drifted through my mind as we stood atop the narrow peak of Kosijer.

Perhaps that's what raced through Teri's mind when he discovered the raven mutilating his fellow dog's carcass? Perhaps some mind, completely the opposite of the human one, could arrange relations in which there would be no butchering and devouring, my mind continued wandering as I watched the dog run around the evergreen trees.

"It chills my heart when I see the fog down below me," commented Rade as he looked over the terrain. "And it almost freezes it completely when the fog is at my feet and the grey clouds hang above. I shall have enough of the grave after I'm dead, closed in from above and below," he added before lifting his head toward the sky hidden by a grey sheet of clouds from which thin, steady rain came down on us. "After all the burning and the masses of people forced from their homes, this rain is inevitable. That's usually the way it is. The same thing happens when men go into the army. The old people say that it has always been that way," he concluded as he rose to his feet and slung the bag over his shoulder.

"Did they take the people away?" I asked.

"The villagers of Rakic, Samardzija and Novic weren't all able to flee to the woods in time. They gathered together some fifty people, including women and children, and marched them into town. Karan claims that they will be sent to camps. Perhaps they will all be shot. He said that new Ustas have arrived, along with one Italian unit," Rade recounted to me what he had heard at the previous night's meeting. What he didn't tell me was that Zdravko wanted to organise the insurgents into partisan units under the leadership of the Regional Command communists in Drvar, while Karan, along with some of his cronies, were dead set against any such idea, saying that this was a communist faction whose sole aim was to betray God and the Serbs.

We headed together toward the spring at Straziste. Around the spring, several cows were grazing, while from the canyon could be heard the sound of cowbells and someone calling. Rade told me to head on along the left path up the mountain and to wait for him at the first clearing I came upon. The dog followed me.

The first peaks of Grmec were behind us. The forest was increasingly taller and thicker. Evergreens mixed with oak and beech trees.

A bird landed on a branch just above my head, bouncing it enough to shower me with raindrops. Shaking the water off, I looked up in time to see a jay fly away, flaunting its tail feathers at me. Teri also watched its flight.

I had to follow the path because it was more probable that Zorka was taking the well-traveled trail. About a hundred metres ahead of me, I noticed some people. By their movements, I realised that they were a part of a different search party. Attaching Teri to the chain I still carried, I took him along a different path which brought us a little further to the right, so as not to distance ourselves too far from Rade. The incline increased, the wet leaves and moss on the hard ground making the path even more difficult so that Teri often found himself having trouble digging his nails into the terrain and staying on his feet. Whenever he slipped and fell, he would look toward me with an apologetic expression on his face.

The forest was becoming sparse, the trees yet thicker and taller. The beeches had sunk deep roots, while above ground they branched off into many thick, curved limbs. At the crowns of these trees, strange shapes had been waging a folk-fable struggle for ages.

Holding the chain firmly, I tried to look ahead between the trees. The pleading sounds of a woman and the mewling of a child reverberated in my ears; the branches seemed to come alive, began to move, shake, sway, creep up toward me, only to freeze still half-way. Teri was snarling. My view became distorted, unclear, and when a low-lying branch brushed against my hair, I began to snarl also. Teri's voice suddenly distorted eerily, as if someone had grabbed him by the throat and slowly begun to strangle him. A jay shrieked and flew toward a tall fir.

In the trunk of a tree, I noticed someone's engraved initials S.R. With my axe, I chopped away a good deal of the bark where the initials had been carved, leaving a white scar in the tree. A drop of sweat ran from my temple toward my ear. His tail between his legs, Teri stared at the tree with the fresh scar.

When I discovered in the mud the trail of sandals and children's gum-boots, there was no sign of the other search party. The imprint left by Zorka's right foot was deeper and more distinct, the steps ever shorter, stoppings more frequent. The path joined a road which emerged from the woods onto rocky ground. The tracks were lost. Teri sniffed around but without result. At the end of the rocky ground, there were no tracks to be found. The day was passing by quickly.

Under the low-lying branches of a huge spruce, Teri and I stopped to rest. As we ate, we exchanged quick glances. Our ears, dog's and man's, were turned in the direction we had been moving, trying to catch some sound which would locate our target. I could feel that Zorka and the child were somewhere near, so I decided not to stray from the area. While the dog stretched, I sat on a bed of moss next to the tree. When I got up, Teri came and sat by the tree, his head leaning against the trunk, as if waiting for sounds to emerge from the earth. My thoughts raced back to unfortunate Tale and Zemka and I felt guilty for not having called on her before I left.

Perhaps she didn't do anything? What if Osman made everything up, all lies? The idea hit me for the first time, making matters even worse. I pressed on, summoning the dog, in the direction we had been going. There was still no sign of their tracks on the hard surface of the mountain side.

Some hundred metres further on, under a hollowed out rock, Zorka and her son lay huddled. Drops of rain fell from a long maple branch directly onto the youngster's head and shoulders. His knit cap was soaked, but the blue windbreaker continued to defend him from the rain His gumboots were covered in mud. He shook, more from fear and the uncertainty of the situation in which they found themselves, than from the cold. He looked toward his mother, eyes glued to the right side of her face, which was disfigured by spasms rippling at intervals down from her temple to her unnaturally curled upper lip. His little face was smeared with mud: tears which must have begun running down his face 'way back when his mother dragged him with her into the night had by now created two waterfalls which spread out at the red cheeks and disappeared into several small backwaters.

A small stone loosened and fell into the deep, narrow hole in the hollowed rock below the boy's feet.

"Damn them! Even here, they won't leave us in peace!" growled Zorka through clenched teeth, looking toward the boy's feet and the hole below them. "My Zoran, how are we going to manage through this winter?"

"Mummy…" the boy whimpered, "When are we going back home? I'm not scared, but it's cold…"

Not far from them, the dog began to bark but soon stopped, as if he had been caused pain by the effort. The fog again descended down the trees. The rain continued to drizzle, now mixed with snow. The boy held on to his mother's overcoat. They shook at the same time.

"We're not going back down there and fall into their hands," she whispered to him, her tears competing to see which eye was more abundant. "I didn't know much about life; I was up there minding the sheep when it happened with that Jela, the whore. She cried to me that he had been with her since last Christmas. Eh, and I hung the bell around his head that time. My curse is on him. Damn him wherever he is now…Oh, if only I had enough water to pour over myself. I too am damned. Burn!"

"I'm cold!" shrilled Zoran.

"Now, now, son. Soon we'll be with your grandfather. Mummy knows where we're going. They didn't hang him on Lynx's spar. That's just another one of that liar Yandriya's tales! You'll be a good man just like your grandpa, my son!"

She caught sight of a bare tree branch, pressed the child against her body and made facial gestures as if she were listening in on something and wondering whether she should go further up the mountain, toward the place where her long-since deceased father's house should have been located. She froze. Her thoughts seemed to be returning. She didn't understand why she had taken off with the child, but something egged her on. As the fever in her head increased, she increasingly began to shake from an inexplicable fear. This return of reason was short lived, however, and Zorka again began to descend into a sweet world full of fog, distorted images and the sticky undulation of air under her nose and before her eyes.

The dog began to bark again. She interpreted this barking as the roar of a mad creature, long and incoherent, whose echo became ever more dull due to the darkness which fell over her consciousness.

The dog and I headed further up the mountain. Every ten or so steps, we stopped to listen for some sound of them. Apart from the falling rain and the odd grain of hail, there was nothing to hear. Legs spread apart, Teri dug himself into the wet ground as if trying to get hold of the earth so that some torrent of wind wouldn't take him away. The hair on his neck stood straight. He held himself erect and shook his coat thoroughly, sending water flying in all directions, including mine. My face and hair soaked, I stepped aside to adjust the bag on my back and headed in the direction in which Zorka and the child had been going. Teri hesitated a while, turning toward me as if to protest any further useless wandering on the mountain, but when he saw me disappear behind some trees, he trotted after.

We soon found their path again. Zorka's right footprint was deeper and wider than before, as if she felt more sure of that foot and used it to push herself along. Both of us quickened our steps. Then suddenly, a series of howls coming from above stopped us in our tracks.

"Wolves," I thought, and the dog also was visibly shaken by the sounds. His hair stood up again and his ears pointed in the direction from which the howling came. The howling of beasts soon came from the opposite direction as well. Both of us were certain that it was wolves. Teri moved closer to my legs, and looked me directly in the eyes. I was trying to think of what to do. Apart from the small axe, I had no weapon. Certain that the woman and child were in our vicinity and needed our help, I decided against turning back.

We hesitatingly headed on. A few hundred metres below us, the sounds of a shotgun firing could be heard, followed by incomprehensible calling. A handful of water spilled from a hanging beech-tree branch directly onto my face. The dog coughed, as if laughing at my drenching, and then brought his head down and followed the tracks.

We caught up to them under the rocky peak of Kosijer. When she sensed someone behind her, Zorka grabbed her son, pressed him to her breasts, shot forth her head and hissed like a snake:

"Don't come near me, you bastard! I curse the woman who gave birth to you! I will devour you! Kill you! He's mine, not some bastard! I'll devour you!"

She shivered in confusion. Her eyes flashed toward the dog in particular, only to gradually ease back into their sockets. The wolves again howled, but now they were closer.

"Zorka, it's me...Rade's friend...don't be afraid," I pleaded and realised that there was no return for her to the world of sanity.

On hearing my words, her eye glistened even more, and when the child began to scream at the sight of the dog nearing them, she slowly put him down, hollered rabidly and attacked Teri as though she were an animal herself.

Everything happened so quickly that there was no time to think. The dog, seeing that the woman was attacking him, leapt on her, barking and yelping in rage, while she struck at him with hands and feet, foam coming out of her mouth. I jumped toward them when a shot rang out from behind me. It was followed by a woman's death cry and the death-rattle of the dog. Even in the grasp of death she scratched with her hands, trying to distance herself from the dog, while Teri rasped with his collapsing hind legs, keeping his head aimed at her. They struggled for some time before expiring, each thinking that they had delivered the fatal blow to the other. One bullet had pierced them both. The child continued to scream, louder and louder, its terrified glances jumping between his mother, the dog and me.

I remained still, frozen in the same position ever since the sound of the shot, looking in the direction from which it had originated and seeing the second search party. The most prominent among them still held the barrel of the gun pointed at us.

From between the beech trees, Rade ran toward us but, upon seeing the scene, he too froze in horror. When the little boy noticed his neighbour, he jumped into his arms, wrapping his arms around Rade's neck.

Zorka's house was sealed up with hawthorn rope; Milan and Zorka were buried together while little Zoran remained with Rade and his children.

Old Karizan called me to his room afterward, far from anyone else's sight, and told me, in a tone akin to that of a judge ruling in favour of the accused, that I shouldn't feel any guilt over what had happened up in the mountain. Because, he said, her insane eyes had provoked the dog. Djurekan had the best of intentions to hit only the dog but the devil must have given his trigger finger a push and both, the woman and the dog, were sent to the other world. Perhaps the old man saw something in my face which he supposed was a feeling of guilt, so he added that little Zoran had me to thank for his still being alive. Without me, he continued, the wolves surely would have torn them apart. I hadn't expect to hear this from the old man who had looked upon me with suspicion from the beginning.

Days passed, and nothing notable happened to solve our situation. I could feel Osman growing restless and I felt like a mouse among cats. Despite old Karizan's gesture, apart from Rade no one showed me any sign of friendship. Even the children, it seemed, would stop talking and playing when I walked by. My nerves were on edge, full of anxious anticipation, even though I didn't know of what. It might indeed be necessary to hide in a safe place until things settled down in Pset, but I felt no safer up here than I had down there. If we were supposed to go somewhere further away, somewhere far from this nightmare, we were waiting too long in the risky haven of Karizan's farm. When I confided this to my brother, he said that he too had had enough, up to his throat, but that he wouldn't return to town, alive or dead.

"If only we could make contact with Zdravko," he would often say.

"Why Zdravko?" I would ask.

"The only solution for us is to join Zdravko's fighters. I am certain that he is fighting the right fight, for all of us…You saw that Karan fellow. Stevo says he's organising Chetnik units. His kind would love to twist our necks as though we were nothing but chickens…Zdravko is the only answer!"

"What will happen to Father? I fear for him," I said.

"I also worry, Yudja. But, I can't help him. He will be glad to hear that we are safe."

"What do you mean safe, Osman?! Do you really think we are safe? It seems to me that we are more unwanted here than we were in town. I can feel the hatred growing. They are all the same, even Rade…When he mentioned that new Ustashas were arriving in town, he gave me a suspicious second look."

"They are hesitant. The plateau has been sealed shut by the powerful Axis forces at the puppet government's command. They are pushing the Muslim to join their army, by hook or crook. All this in order to set us off against one another, have us at each other's throats. The only answer is a unified struggle by all our peoples against the foreigner."

"But, Osman…We both saw Karan and his men. Who knows how many more there are? Down there, in town, there are some Muslims—Mujos and Suljos—who could barely wait to put on the foreigner's uniform. Hatred grows but hatred is a bad adviser. It has no other goal but to spill as much blood as possible."

"That is exactly it! Only the Party is fighting for all of us. Only among its ranks will Mujo, Jovo and Ivan, Muslims, Serbs and Croats, stand tall, shoulder to shoulder. And when they defeat the oppressor and his lackeys, when they shake hands, no one will divide them again, no God and no foreigner."

"What luck, Osman..." I took up this opening my brother offered to continue the debate because it seemed the right moment to settle some things between us. He seemed to have absolved himself of all the suspicions which I had built up against him recently and which had increasingly separated us. But the sound of horses' hoofs coming from the behind the grove interrupted us. Ten seconds didn't pass before the first rider appeared in the field by the orchards. He was followed by others. There were about thirty men on horses and all were all heading toward Karizan's house. The two of us hid in the shed. I felt much worse than unwanted and desperate to get away from there as soon as possible.

The horsemen came to a stop in the courtyard and one of them shouted:

"Karizans! Stevo, Rade!..."

I recognised the voice of the bearded Karan. Osman stood up and moved to the side of the shed which faced the house. Between the logs, one could see the events transpiring outside. I joined Osman.

The horsemen were armed with hunting rifles and the odd carbine. Karan held a machine-gun in his hands and across his chest were two cartridge belts for it. When Stevo appeared at the door, Karan lifted the machine-gun above his head in a gesture of greeting and shouted so loud that his voice carried far along the mountain woods:

"If you wish to join us in avenging the dead, the burned and the banished Serbian people, come with your weapons and horses after noon to Lakic's field!"

Thereafter, not waiting for a response, he kicked his horse in the belly and rode off. The rest of his party followed him.

Osman couldn't hide his anxiety. Even though he had long been secretive and distant from me, in the moments before the horsemen arrived at Karizan's house he had spoken openly, and now, having heard Karan, he could not hide his concern. He said that what he wanted to do most was go before that evil warlord and spit in his beard, but he couldn't because he feared what would happen to me. After that he was silent, lost in thought. Walking to the wide open doors, he followed the horses and their riders with his eyes as they made their way down the mountain. He asked then if I had noticed anything familiar about the bearded Karan, as he at last had. When I answered that my mind had been trying to figure out where I had seen him before, Osman smiled and made an expression as if he had discovered something great.

"He's the one who was buying all those weapons that night when we were looking through the window. The one who made the deal with the skinny colonel for the weapons and munitions from the arms dump."

Yes, it was the same man. Too much had happened too quickly in the last weeks for me to have a clear memory of events.

Osman had read my thoughts. He came up to me and ran his hand over my head, like a teacher petting a confused student while delivering a lecture.

"Our brains have been strained in the past month or two more than they have been in all the years combined up to now. Who knows what we might learn from this. Have you noticed how you startle awake when you dream of something completely new, strange, something you had never previously thought about? Characters appear in your dreams whom you have never met. As if you had jumped into a life outside the one you have been conscious of. It's been happening to me quite often lately. It convinces me that we aren't just what we think we are. We aren't only the images we see before us in the mirror. There is another life going on which we aren't usually aware of except for glimpses which we catch briefly in the moments of waking from our dreams. If there was a way to photograph those dreams, I'm certain that we'd discover another self living within us, in a different world. This wouldn't be a world running parallel to this one. I think it would be completely different."

My mind recoiled. "Don't frighten me any more than I already am," I thought. "I've had about enough of all this fear which surrounds me, and now you want to spread it to my innards. I often pray to God to help me fall asleep, to escape to the security of the dreamland, and now you want me to fear that also. To think that everything I had dreamed about this summer has been eating away at my soul. You don't expect me to believe that even mother's voice was a thing of my imagination; that I had dreamt your story about Kula, about those hung and butchered. You are trying to take me somewhere I don't want to go. You are no longer my old Osman, you are a devil." I bit my tongue and realised that I hadn't said what had just been on my mind. I was relieved not to have done so.

As far as Karan was concerned, I was certain that he had been the one who had made the deal with the colonel. And it's just as well that he did, I'd thought back then, better than to have the dump fall into enemy hands. Now I knew that as far as my fate was concerned it made no difference whose hands the weapons from the dump fell into. Every faction in this madness was the enemy.

After lunch, we helped Stevo and Rade prepare their horses for the ride to Lakic's field. After they'd mounted their horses, Rade bent down and whispered to me, as if apologising in advance:

"Uncle Milos says that Karan will be passing out weapons. Today, weapons are more important than anything else. What we have now isn't even enough to go rabbit hunting!"

Stevo and Rade didn't return. Night had descended already among the mountain peaks. We were dining on cooked potatoes with cheese, the chimney on the lamp was already blackened, and they still had not returned. Their old mother had gone outside several times to look westward, but in her face I couldn't find any trace of worry. Karizan didn't leave his room. Before setting supper for us, Stevo's wife, Radmila, had taken some meat, bread and raw garlic to his room, and later a bottle of plum brandy. The children who earlier had raced around the house eating slices of bread covered with clotted cream, were now soundly asleep.

Rade's wife looked out the window often, as if she expected her husband to arrive at any moment. We hadn't even finished supper when she jumped toward the window and cried:

"The sky is ablaze above the plains!"

We all ran outside. Far toward the west, on the other side of Osjecenica, the sky was red in the places where it met mountain slopes. The sun didn't go down so far north at this time of year, so we concluded that the redness could have nothing to do with the sunset.

"There must be some great fire under Otchijevo," the grandmother noted. "It was just as red in thirty-three, but on the other side of the mountain, when the forests caught fire during the summer. But that over there is no forest fire, my children. I'm afraid those are villages burning toward Lika."

The two young women could only cough and whisper to each other, something which resembled a prayer in which the only audible words were the names of their husbands.

Fear grew within me. Something in my brain kept on telling me that I should get as far away from this evil as possible, while reason answered that even though I wanted to there was nowhere to run. My internal state couldn't yet be called panic, but it was certainly the foundation for the beginning of it.

Even though the night was clear, the plateau below us resembled the darkest of ocean depths, where life exists but the very thought of it sends shivers down men's spines. Above the darkness the fire was swallowing something on the other side of the mountain. Above it all the icy, silent sky was full of stars.

"If only there was some way up there. If only the sky would provide a single entrance, a door leading out of this butchery," I thought, vainly waiting for a signal of hope.

With these thoughts still in my mind, I finally went with my brother to our room and fell asleep. I don't remember what time of night I was awakened by the feeling of someone else's presence. By deep, one-dimensional breathing, I concluded that Osman was sleeping. Complete darkness reigned in the room, but between the wooden boards of the door a few rays of light managed to find their way from the main room. Voices also came from that direction, quiet, secretive, but in the general silence they were loud enough for me to hear and understand them. I grew rigid on my bed of straw, trying to understand the conversation, because I immediately recognised the colour of Stevo and Rade's voices.

I had probably woken up after the most significant part of their conversation was completed. From the first sentences I gleaned that Stevo was informing Karizan and his mother of how they had attacked the Ustashas who were defending Muslim villages along the upper part of the river Una and how they caused them great losses and captured significant amounts of weapons and ammunition. Rade said not a word. Stevo explained that Karan had led the guerrillas and demonstrated great knowledge of military strategy. As soon as the main part of the plan was accomplished, he'd ordered a withdrawal and in the course of returning managed to win over to the cause of the Resistance all of the Serbian villages situated along the western slopes of the plateau.

Before the enemy units from Bihac and Pset could cut off their escape route, Karan continued the withdrawal toward Grmec and ended up with only three dead and six wounded.

"We've shown that they cannot kill us at will without suffering similar consequences," concluded Stevo, after which an extended period of silence followed.

"What kind of fires are those on the other side of Osjecenica?" asked his mother.

"Fires, like fires," Karizan tried to dismiss her question.

"I know, Milos…But I'm asking if the Ustashas didn't try to get revenge against our villages above the river."

She probably expected an answer from Stevo or Rade, but they kept silent. Their mother sensed that something was wrong and began insisting that they tell her what kind of fires those were that she saw in the distance.

"There were some of our men whose houses were burnt down in the enemy's offensive two days ago. There were some who lost family members. Rakics, Rokvics…And they burned some houses down over there," prevaricated Stevo.

And then, Rade finally spoke. His voice betrayed his disagreement and protest.

"It wasn't that some of our men burned down some of their houses. What they did was burn down all Muslim villages from Vakuf to

Cukovi. They burned down everything they came across, along with the people in the houses and the cattle in the barns..." As he spoke, bitter reproach of Stevo could be heard in his voice.

By what I could gather from the noise in the room, Stevo jumped up with the intention of going outside but the old man stopped him and said that Rade also had to be heard out, though it seemed to him that Rade was only feeling needless pity for people who had already shown whose side they were on in this conflict.

"What did they show?! Did our people in the villages around Dmitar's property show anything? Yet the cutthroats burned and butchered them anyway. If Karan had stuck to just fighting the Ustashas, everything would be all right. But, he gave the order to go into the plains and kill and burn. The people fled down the river, while we obediently torched buildings and fired upon women and children. From the burning houses could be heard the screams of those trapped inside. We didn't stop until we had burnt down everything as far as Ljutotch Mountain and heard the buzzing of the trucks coming along the Ripacki Pass. Only then did the order come to pull back and head home. Such a bloodbath I could never have imagined. I can't even talk about it. I'm still shaking from it all while you, Stevo, are trying to glorify and justify it."

Stevo defended himself by pleading that such things shouldn't be talked about in front of their mother and pointing out that Rade had a soft heart while war was war. Rade asked him why Karan didn't lead the men against the enemy's army in town instead of unarmed civilians in the unprotected villages.

"The people from those villages didn't do anything to us. Maybe the odd one joined the Ustashas, but why then kill them all? Some five or six thousand people managed to escape toward Bihac, but at least a thousand were butchered and burnt. Tonight you saw a red sky over there, and in a few days we won't be able to breathe in the stench which will spread from the masses of corpses," concluded Rade.

"And it won't end at that, my children," his old mother added in a strong, fatalistic tone. "Perhaps Hitler and Pavelic won't seek revenge for what you did to those in Vakuf and Orasac, because it seems to me that their goal is to have us butcher one another until we exterminate each other. I fear for us all."

The incomprehensible mumbling of old Karizan could be heard. It seemed that at first he wasn't certain what his judgement about all this should be, but soon enough his mumblings strengthened to a heavy baritone which didn't equate at all with his emaciated frame:

"This is war. It is our holy duty to go to battle against the fiends. They drove several truckloads of our people away to a camp. There will be truckloads and truckloads more. They will burn and they will kill…But, we are defending our own. Each rooster is stronger on his own ground. Our people have risen all over Bosnia, in Lika, in Kordun and Banija. You heard Karan, and even Zdravko spoke similarly. If the Turks, I mean Bosnian Muslims, Bosniaks, aren't with us, then they are against us…Anyway, see with Dmitar about what we're going to do with those two striplings of his. They may be our relatives but I don't trust them and they could bring suspicion down on our house. They don't seem like bad boys, but…"

The old man stopped, while the others remained silent. From somewhere far away, a burst of gunfire reached my ears. I stiffened in my bed. For the first time since we arrived, I was excited. This meant that something would be happening. They would be taking us somewhere and I much preferred uncertainty to this stress and fear, this feeling of being an undesirable, that they hated you and were only waiting for the right moment to say it to your face.

"You can't be that way, Uncle," Rade calmly spoke up at last. "Those two are Dmitar's nephews and our relatives through the late Maria. They are still boys. Leave things alone some more and then we'll see what Dmitar decides."

Karizan justified himself by saying that he wasn't thinking anything bad but that the feeling in the village was increasingly negative. He pointed out that it would also benefit us to know where we would be going—back to town or somewhere else.

"We're still safe up here. The Ustashas and the Germans won't be bold enough to come into our mountains. In the morning someone has to go to Palanka and get salt for us and the refugees in Bunara. Karan suggested that you four should go, you two and the striplings. We have the horses, so go. The day is more clever than the night, we'll see better tomorrow what needs to be done." With this pronouncement, the old man concluded the night's discussion.

When Rade entered our room, I pretended to be asleep and it looked as if Osman really was. Many years later, I learned that he had also heard everything but was playing his game, or perhaps he had decided to free me of his suggestions so that I could follow my own path. Perhaps I really was in his way. He, it seems, still held all his hopes in joining up with Zdravko, while I knew only that I had to leave this place as soon as possible. If only I could make it to Father and have a talk with him. If only I could be alone and hear Mother's voice. "Perhaps they have risen above all this and can see better and further," I thought, praying for some dream to overcome me.

CHAPTER VII

Fehrat walked slowly, barely able to endure the pain in his left leg. Even his right leg wasn't as firm as it had been in the days when he practised athletics and karate. The prosthesis on his left leg was taken from some old man who had been blown apart by a shell. They had been saving it for someone who managed to stay alive but lost a leg. Even when they were cutting off his leg, they did it so that later on the old man's wooden leg would be a perfect fit. What a joke.

Stopping every few meters to catch his breath, and for the pain in his leg to subside, Fehrat tried to hide his weakness by making small talk, asking questions like any naïve tourist—Why don't their churches have bells? How do I recognise Indians? He was slow and uncertain. The walk to the bus stop was only about a kilometre but for Fehrat it seemed an eternity. In high school, he ran the 800 metres for his school. His best time was just five seconds more than the European women's record for the same distance. In karate, his left leg had had a special duty; he used it for all of his favourite kicks because of its speed and power.

Yudja didn't ask him how it all happened. There would be time enough for such painful memories later, he thought. Even though the two of them had never been on friendly terms in the true sense of the word, the son had always been present somewhere in the father's deep feelings. Despite being largely unrealised, Yudja's paternal instincts found in Fehrat a compelling enigma whose solution forever eluded him. Lingering feelings of guilt prevented him even now from risking any brave steps toward closeness with the man whom he recognised as his natural son.

That afternoon, they had to go to the Immigration because of Fehrat. Fehrat didn't, or couldn't, confide to Yudja how crucially he felt the need to get quality prostheses, especially an artificial hand. He himself didn't know why he couldn't bring himself to confide such things to Yudja. Simply put, he was greedy with words and emotions, always preferring to listen. As a child, he laid down the foundations for what would be his attitude toward his natural father. As he matured, these foundations grew in their pride and intransigence. However, the elementary starting point of these feelings was the permanent nightmare between seeking acceptance and fearing rejection. At the same time, he had grown up with his own problems of betrayal and rejection in general, which played the dominant role in the development of his personality, the constant need to be at least a little better, faster and stronger than the rest.

At the corner their street joined Lonsdale, the wide avenue which led from the waterfront far up the mountain. Yudja stopped to buy the local newspaper. When he asked Fehrat if there was any print that interested him, the head-shaking refusal came quickly:

"If there was anything in French, maybe I'd read it. The newspapers from the Balkans don't interest me and I don't know enough English to be able make out what their newspapers say."

"I don't care for the media war between our tribal nations either. They are like mushrooms in the forest after a rainfall. We are rich in arguments and disagreements. I can imagine what it must all look like to people observing us from a distance. Just further proof that we're different from everyone else," Yudja elaborated on his son's remark as they waited at the crosswalk for the signal light to change.

Fehrat welcomed the brief pause in their walk because there was still some way to go down Lonsdale to the bus stop.

"When we began to free ourselves from state socialism, the new breed of politicians claimed that we had been forced to embrace our unity. But, why then, when this pressure no longer exists, do they have to choose a path of hatred and disunity? Probably to demonstrate how far we have come on the road to democracy. Celebrating and glorifying the differences between ethnic communities at a time when even the most powerful nations are coming together—nations who have nothing in common except a desire for a more prosperous future.

There, look…" Fehrat pointed his healthy right hand toward the flags of the world's industrialised countries flying from poles in front of the new, glass-enclosed conference centre across the harbour. "The industrialised countries of the world are talking about free trade while our fools are trying to pull us back into the Middle Ages. They are destroying everything that we built together and taking hate to our front doors…I agree with you. It's better to stay away from reading any of our self-appointed prophets of doom." As he spoke, his hand remained pointed toward the row of flag poles.

Yudja looked at him, focusing primarily upon the truncated left arm, which spoke better than any words could of the misfortune which the flame of southern Slav nationalisms had brought to this man at the end of the twentieth century. For the first time, the idea came to him that it would be meet and just to make a gift of his own left hand to his son. He could say that he no longer needed it because he used only his right one to carve. Today's doctors can transplant everything, even hands…Bringing the transplantable hand before his eyes to take a closer look, then extending it alongside the other one to compare, Yudja turned his gaze to Fehrat. He wondered how his old hand would serve his son. As he was about to articulate this proposal, he noticed that Fehrat's attention was taken up with a group of children on the other side of the street.

The inside of the bus was clean and quiet. Most of the heads in the seats were pale and fair-haired. There were a couple of dark ones also, just as in a flight of swans there is the odd black one. A swan is a swan, regardless of the colour of its feathers. The white swans never drive the black ones away. Naturally, the opposite has also never happened, if we are to believe the American Society for the Prevention of Racial Discrimination. Just as the swans try to present a dignified picture of themselves for all the onlookers at a lake, it seemed to Fehrat that his fellow passengers on the bus were trying to do the same. Even the three dark heads on the bus didn't disrupt the general atmosphere. The same scene repeated itself at the next bus stop: people got on while others got off, there was no pushing or rushing, no one feared being without a seat or being left behind. No one feared being shot. Even though Fehrat felt an urge to shove his way to the bus doors, the peace and order worked in favour of his wooden left leg.

A particular text in the newspaper visibly irritated Yudja. By the number of lines forming on his forehead, it was obvious that he was trying his best to understand what was written. Whispering to Fehrat, he explained that NATO experts studying the earth's crust had discovered strange magnetic fields in a two-hundred-kilometre-wide crack which extended across the lower part of the surface layer, from the Skagerrak at the very top of Denmark all the way down to the deserts of Yemen. The newest research into the phenomenon had shown larger than average deposits of this aberrant magnetism in the Brandenburg region, in the Balkans, and deep below the holy shrines of Palestine. The article ended with a commentary by a specialist in psychopathology and ethnography which was enough to disturb even the most optimistic reader: this mad magnetism was a magnetic neurosis, which developed in areas of damaged equilibrium between Earth's gravitational force and its centrifugal thrust, dramatically influencing the development of destructive mentalities.

"Perhaps it's true. There is so much that we don't know but I'm surprised that they would allow such findings out into the open," Fehrat casually commented.

At the immigration centre, both men were unnerved by the arrogant airs of the interpreter. The woman was thin, in her fifties, untidy, hair destroyed by decades of various chemical treatments. She was visibly nervous, despite initial efforts to charm them with a motherly smile. Their irritation grew when in response to many of the official's question to them she answered without bothering to listen to what they had to say. She would simply translate the question for them and immediately answer it, as if she was acquainted to the smallest detail with their grief and wishes.

Yudja was the first to speak up, commenting that they were there with the aim of helping Fehrat obtain the much-needed prostheses. Only then did the interpreter notice that Fehrat was missing a hand and part of a leg. She mumbled something to them about this first meeting being only a formality. Her deformed Serbian dialect suddenly began to mix with those from Bosnia, and even the odd one from the Croatian hinterlands.

"But, Madame, please tell the man that I have come from one of the Serb concentration camps in Bosnia where they severed my hand and leg before handing me over to the International Red Cross. The Canadian consul in Zagreb gave me this letter of reference," said Fehrat, passing it to her as they all sat there in the official's office.

She took the letter and read it. The others looked at each other, and watched. As she was reading, the expression on her face became one of obscene disgust. She handed the letter to the official, whose face took on a similar look of disapproval as he read. The interpreter turned to Fehrat and said:

"Please accept my condolences. What happened to you is horrible but nowhere in that document does it say that you lost your limbs in a Serb camp."

She looked directly into Fehrat's eyes as if wanting to provoke him. Yudja could feel Fehrat's blood begin to boil with his desire to give her what she was asking for. He knew that it would be senseless, that they must not fall into her trap, because the question of whether or not Fehrat would get his prostheses depended on the official, and the official was depending on the interpreter.

"This man is an invalid. Can't you see that he is no Bosnian soldier, just a man asking for medical help? I beg you, please make that clear," Yudja pleaded with the woman, in the calmest tone he could muster.

She looked straight ahead of her, and the anxious movement of her throat made it clear she was disinclined to be of any real help to them. Finally, the official broke the heavy silence. He said that he would pass the consul's letter on to the responsible health officials and that Fehrat would be informed of their decision by letter in a few weeks. Remembering Fehrat's special refugee status, the official mentioned that he would drop by and see him at Yudja's apartment to see what further help he would need during his stay in Vancouver.

As they were returning, Yudja could feel Fehrat's confusion and discomfort. He was also dissatisfied with the meeting at the

Immigration office, but he tried to be positive about the eventual outcome. He tried to change the topic by mentioning the child who lived on the floor below them; commenting on the cold, grey look of the Pacific in Vancouver, so unlike the deep blue Adriatic; and speaking of the completely different mentality of the Canadians. Nevertheless, the after-effects of the meeting would not leave them in peace. Yudja couldn't get it out of his mind that Fehrat hadn't told him before today's meeting that he had lost his hand and leg in the camps. Why?

Fehrat was growing frustrated with the situation in which he found himself. Increasingly, he regretted his decision to come to Canada with the hope of getting fitted for the proper prostheses when he could have gone to Germany for the same purpose. Perhaps both of them would have been spared these added troubles had his disfiguring injuries not given birth to his wish to get to know Yudja and find out once and for all the mystery of his place in Yudja's family. This desire had been eating away at him for quite some time, especially since the conversation with his mother, when out of spite she had told him that even though he was mentioning Yudja's name in his sleep, if he took a closer look at the mirror he would see a much greater resemblance to Osman. At the time, he didn't take the gist of his mother's remark seriously, but as the years passed he became increasingly preoccupied with this provocation his mother had thrown at him. Some internal pride hadn't allowed him to confront her again in order to arrive at the truth, but ever since the night when he noticed a long hawthorn stake in his mother's hands, only to hear the next day how everyone in town was talking about the wooden cross pushed deep into the still-fresh earth which covered Osman's grave, the truth about the triangular relationship of his mother, Osman and Yudja had gnawed at him like a constant sickness.

After the bus ride, Yudja went to pick up some groceries at the market where he usually shopped. Waiting outside, Fehrat leaned against a postbox, trying to rest his left leg. As they walked up the incline toward Yudja's apartment, the pain in Fehrat's leg became unbearable. The wooden prosthesis rubbing against the stump of his amputated leg shot bolts of pain directly to his brain. The wound in his lower thigh had opened up again. He could feel blood running down to the wooden prosthesis. The stairs were the last, and most difficult, hurdle standing in his way. Everything would be so much simpler, he thought to himself ironically, if only he had a flying machine strapped to his back and no longer needed legs. Even though Yudja had an easier time navigating the steep flight of stairs leading to the top floor, Fehrat noticed that he too was expending an unusually high amount of energy. The grocery bags he was carrying turned the walk up the stairs into an alpine expedition for them both.

"The same country can be a good mother to one man, while a wicked step-mother to another," Yudja continued with his reminisces after supper, to Fehrat's great satisfaction. As if by agreement, they had spoken no more of their visit to Immigration.

The four of us rode on horses. We had linen bags covering us, trying to keep out the rain. Each of us carried a rucksack with food and a water bottle. Stevo and Rade had army rifles while us two had jackknives, the kind that Karizan made in his blacksmith shop. We were going toward Sana, where a merchant known as Rich Marko lived in a nearby village, Stevo told us.

Grmec was before us. The rain swooped down along its wooded slopes. The horses, adept at navigating their way up the forest paths, stoically put up with both us on their backs and the rain from the clouds just over our heads. We took the wide way around the flat mountain highlands so as not to come upon any of the dugouts where families who had fled from the foot of the mountain were now seeking shelter. The horses trod softly, we didn't talk and the mountain silence was interrupted only by the odd jay warning us not to move about in its vicinity.

At about noon, we reached the northern slopes of the mountain, which overlooked a wide basin cut through by a river. Avoiding a cluster of houses which were nestled among tall beech trees, we stopped to rest the horses only when we were certain there was no chance of being spotted by anyone from the village. As the horses chewed on the leaves of low-hanging branches, we also took out our food. All of a sudden, coming from between us and the group of houses could be heard the sound of a woman wailing. The woman was shouting at the rainy mountain. There was something harrowing in the way she called out:

"O Milun! Mi-lu-n, oh my Milun! If only God had turned you into a grain of wheat, by tomorrow you'd be growing up toward the sky. By God, if only we had been taken with you instead of being left to starve till summer. O-o-oh, forest, o-o-oh, take me with you!" the woman howled. After pausing briefly, she went on but this time her voice wasn't as loud and we had to prick up our ears to be able to hear. „I will find you, my wound, in Grmec. No matter if you are hiding in some dugout, I'll still find you. If only I could catch me a grey horse and on his back flee down this field and over to the other side…They cut you up in wretchedness, destroyed your fields, and all because of me. O-o-oh, bury me. Go ahead, sweep me away in a snowstorm. O-o-oy!"

„That's Milun's Jeka going over to Medvedije," commented Stevo, while we turned our ears in that direction, listening for any further sounds.

„She returned to the village. After they took away her Milun to a camp, she lost her mind," added Rade, „Maybe she's been over to the pool. She'll catch her death in this rain."

Osman and I didn't say anything. I prayed to God that this trip be over as soon as possible so that I could see what I would do next. This forest, these voices, everything here was so foreign and terrifying to me. I was listening to Jeka, but my mind wandered off to town and Zemka. I imagined her long, dark hair blowing in the wind and becoming entangled in the branches of these beech trees in front of me. Looking toward Osman, I found him standing next to his horse, straight as a cliff. His eyes were bright and calm. I felt restless. I felt as naked as a wild animal, like leaning against a fence which someone suddenly knocks over, leaving your stomach turning as you are temporarily suspended in mid-air, looking for support. I was a slave to my situation because, without a word of protest, I had accepted the decisions of others and now found myself in a spiritual hell. Maybe this is the way it has been with man in general, throughout the ages…I'm not one of those who will rip out your throat if you kick over the fence I've been leaning against. Or, those who only write into the soil that they will rip it out as soon as they get the opportunity. A thought, slow as spit, crawled around in my head—that the hunger to control your own destiny is greater than that for bread, greater than the hunger for lost youth, more all-encompassing than blood-red moonlight before full moon.

We soon found ourselves in the fields below the forest. Between us and the fields around the city of Sana stood one more hill. We had to go over it because going around would have taken too much time. The rain stopped and the clouds began to move off, one by one, creating a growing blue rift. Stevo warned us to be careful because a road ran through the middle of the valley and the enemy was especially vigilant in keeping all the roads open and safe.

The horses preferred travelling through the forest. They feared roads and open fields. Even though exhausted, they quickened their step, held their heads up, eyes wide open, and became restless at the sound of all strange noises.

The hill was covered in low trees and bushes. As we came to its crest, we turned and looked toward Grmec. The fog had cleared and the sun's rays were steadily breaking through. Passing across the flatland, we had left such obvious tracks that I wanted to mention it to Stevo and Rade but I didn't say anything.

From the hill's peak we could observe the terrain all around. There spread the seemingly endless, richly fertile Sana plains. Into the distance, the colour of the stream below us matched the green of the grass so that were it not for its glass-like surface, it would be indistinguishable. On the other side was the road.

„There it is," Stevo pointed with his hand. „That group of houses. That's where Rich Marko lives. His store is also there. We don't have to cross the road. We'll cross that creek below and follow the willow patch. If the Ustashas or Germans spot us, head straight back for Grmec."

When we reached the small river, shallow enough for the horses to cross, they wouldn't go into the water until they first took a long drink. They stopped again when belly deep. Handy for us. Bending down from our saddles, we also took the time to quench our thirst.

Business was soon finished at the village merchant's. He did his best to free himself of us as quickly as possible, as if he were waiting for someone much more important to come any time soon. The store was barren but it was obvious that he had hidden most of his goods in the warehouse behind. There he would keep, among other things, the flour and salt, and sell only to trusted buyers. At Rich Marko's, all currencies which circulated in these regions were accepted—Yugoslav dinars, Croatian kunas, German marks and Italian liras, but he told Stevo to warn Karizan that this was the last time he would let him have the salt for his dinars. From now, only German and Italian money would do, or gold and silver. This village was well guarded, and from Marko's behaviour toward the armed men, it was obvious that they were his private army.

The salt was in goatskin bags. Stevo managed to buy eight of them. Each horse would carry two. Before we left, the merchant took him aside and quietly talked to him about something.

As soon as we'd left the compound, Stevo told us that Marko had warned him not return the same way that we'd come because the Lusicani had risen up and by nightfall would probably be at the very edge of the plains. So we headed along a roundabout route through Sanica and Bravsko.

We rode parallel to the river, a few hundred meters from it, up into the hills toward its source. The steeper the terrain was, the louder the noise made by the river. The day was passing, clouds were appearing and descending. Soon, a light rain returned. It became evident that we would have to find a place to spend the night. Stevo and Rade talked it over, trying to decide where we should stop to await darkness.

I realised that Osman and I were a liability on this trip and that it would have been better had we not come along. Those two never called us by our names when someone else was around. We knew what this meant and both of us felt more comfortable trekking through the rainy mountain forest.

They concluded that it would be best for us to continue on toward the eastern highlands, where the territory held by the guerrillas from their villages began.

„Why are you so afraid of meeting up with the insurgents? Doesn't everyone who rose up against the occupation have the same goal?" I asked unexpectedly. At first, it seemed to me that someone else had spoken because I had grown so accustomed to my own passivity.

All three of them were caught off guard. Osman looked straight at my eyes, as if searching for an explanation. Their looks provoked me. My earlier uncertainty and discomfort couldn't last forever. A spark of rebellion flickered, a scream from somewhere within me like the sound made by an eagle locked up in a steel cage.

„What are you two afraid of?" I screeched at Stevo and Rade. "I'm afraid of all these ravines and dark faces. I'm afraid of those sentries before whom you quicken your step. I fear Karan and Karizan," a different Yudja whistled out of me, „Return me to Father so that he and I can find some other way out."

The words came out so quickly that I didn't have a chance to filter them. It was as if they had been gathered behind some dam and the dam had now burst so that the words charged out into the air.

Rade sat scratching the horse's mane, his eyes wandering somewhere to the side. Stevo looked at Osman, as if waiting for his reaction. Osman was silent He looked through me somewhere into the distance where his torn feelings were taking him. None of them had expected such words from me, and especially not in the way I had said them. The long seconds ticked slowly away. Heavy, unpleasant feelings were filling up the silence when mother nature drew attention to herself. Far in front of us to the west, somewhere where there must have been mountain passes, the fog was growing bright, then took on an orange glow, as if on fire. Seeing my disbelieving stare, the others turned their heads toward the unusual light. Slowly it formed a broad disc, then the spread-out golden mass compacted into a reddish ball as large as a kitchen table before hungry mouths waiting to eat. We realised that just there the sun had succeeded in thinning out the blanket of clouds, thus reminding us that it still existed.

"It's not easy for you," Rade's words reverberated like a gunshot in my ears. „Down in the town, evil has reared its head. Up in the hills, it is just now appearing. It's not what you think but I fear for you two. Even in the forest there are all sorts of things. When a bad man and a weapon meet, it is better not to be anywhere near."

"Be patient a little longer," Stevo put in. "Dmitar will come and then we'll decide. It is hard to get to Zdravko. I don't know where he is. I heard that Karan said there wasn't enough room in Grmec for the two of them. Karan has guns, some money, wheat…" Stevo spoke calmly, all the while carefully following Osman's reactions.

The rain had gone right through my clothes and my back was soaked. I began feeling hungry. The feeling of hunger was so great that it seemed to sucking the vigour right out of my bones. Looking at the horses, I noticed that their bellies sagged almost to the ground. Thirst began to burn my throat like a hot projectile slowly making its way down to my stomach.

Just then, less than half a kilometre in front of us, several horsemen appeared, galloping along the edge of the tall forest. They were riding single file, equally spaced about two lengths apart, looking as disciplined as a cavalry formation. The horses' manes were extended along their necks and the tails were almost horizontally straight.

"With a horse, you can catch up or you can get away. Being without a horse is like being without a family, without a harvest," Rade betrayed his feelings. Looking at our own horses, he added in embarrassment: "We're riding them as if they were some logs. Dismount so they can rest."

The river distanced itself from us in the steep canyon running eastward. My thoughts wandered along its watery bed toward Kljuc, in fact, right up to the walls which surrounded the old-town part of Kljuc. I was always amazed that they had decided to build old fortress towns on such steep hillsides, inhospitable terrain even for mountain sheep let alone human beings. It then dawned on me that the people who first settled there were fleeing from others. I would also, the thought came to me, if I could, build a citadel without doors and windows. Even then, I wouldn't feel safe. There before me was the proof, for old-town Kljuc had been destroyed, even though it boasted the largest number of citadels and fortifications in all of Bosnia. They weren't destroyed by winds, thunder, rains or snowstorms. They were destroyed by inhuman people and left behind as scarecrows for the future. Across centuries.

On the other side of the rolling stretch of highland, below the forest edge where the horsemen had passed, we came across burnt out houses, barns and sheds. Out of caution, we gave them a wide berth. From the direction of the burnt houses, a large yellow dog ran toward us, frightening the horses. Rade jumped to the ground and chased the animal away with rocks. The dog was probably starving.

Along the edge of the dense forest, we were surprised by mounted sentries. They came out from behind the beech trees, fingers ready by their triggers and shouting to their horses:

"O-o-oy!"

They looked at us from behind their barrels, just as wet as we were.

"Who are you?" asked the shorter one with the thick moustache, his long, wet hair sticking to his neck.

We were slow to react and looked at them mutely. It wasn't difficult to answer who we were but we weren't sure who they were. They realised what we were thinking.

"Are you with us?" added the tall one, also moustachioed.

The shorter one had a leather cap and wore his furry vest inside-out so that the rain could strain down through the lambswool. The taller one wore a little hat with a pin on it which resembled clapping hands.

"No we aren't," Rade answered unhappily and twitched as if he had just bit his tongue.

"No we're not," the rest of us added, to make matters worse.

"You're not with us? You're not ours?" they both repeated, raising their guns.

"No, we're up from Tavani," Stevo explained.

"I didn't ask where you're from! I asked if are you with us!" the tall one barked, obviously growing impatient. They both took a step back, so as to get a better look, and better shot, at all four of us.

We quickly came to our collective senses and together shouted: "Yes, yes: who else would we be with?!"

"Eh, good health and peace to you all, boys," both of them said, but still didn't lower their guns.

For a moment, the sun showed itself again, from the direction of Bihac. Not actually the sun, but its rays, which were like a handful of shining rope-ends entangled with the falling rain. A gust of wind blew in from the direction of the rays. The horses were startled, extending their necks and shaking their manes, as if wanting to free themselves of the rain which had begun to crawl under their skin. Below the rays of light emerging from behind the clouds there appeared a rainbow with the colours of ripening spring. Another gust blew, taking with it the hat from the taller sentry's head, and we couldn't hear what he said. Another ray protruded through the grey clouds, cutting the coloured arch in half. Below it, mist began to rise as steam does from freshly baked bread. Both of the rainbow's ends leaned against the fir groves above us. The horses raised their heads, spreading their nostrils in an effort to take in the drenched sea of colours, then began to neigh loudly. I had had enough:

"Let us through, men! Can't you see that this humidity is suffocating us?"

They said nothing. Continuing with the interrogation of our nerves, they were obviously trying to decide what to do next. I thought to myself how nice it would be if it were true what the peasants said about a woman turning into a man if she walks under a rainbow. Or, the one that said that whoever walked under a rainbow would have all of his wishes fulfilled. If only there were some sort of dilemma about our situation, allowing me to hope. But this? Before us were the night and the mountain.

The sentries wouldn't let us through easily. They ordered us to dismount. Stevo and Rade had to lay their guns to one side on the grass while Osman and I had to return our jackknives to the saddlebags. We then had to open up each bag. They searched each piece of our clothing.

"Go on," shouted the tall one suddenly, waving his long sodden hands toward the mountain. "Behind that spur live the Mrdjas. Stop by and see Mrdja's Andja, and say hello to old Radovan. Maybe he'll sing to you the one about Lazar's supper, if Andja doesn't send you packing after supper and into the night."

We headed off, one after the other, like a column of forest horses. Rade moved to the side, so that Osman and I could go ahead, and followed close behind us. He was much different from Stevo. He was better natured and had a wider outlook. I was starting to distrust Stevo. There was always a cricket-like sound in my ears whenever he was near. It was the same as when you can't see anything but can still feel someone's eyes watching you.

My gloomy state was made worse by the fact that I was soaked to the bone. There was nothing on me that was dry. I could feel the icy water draining from my bag, from my knit jacket, the shirt on my back, and down my back to my buttocks, from there onto the saddle and the horse.

As opposed to us, the horses weren't freezing. Steam was rising from them the way it does from boiled potatoes. I could only envy the steam that was coming out of them.

We soon heard the moaning of sheep and the bleating of goats. There was life on Grmec. The mountain had come alive in this war. Something was constantly going on and the cattle bells were ringing loudly even now.

We caught sight of smoke. Its very smell reminded me of food and dry clothes. Among the group of buildings shingled with box-wood, the tallest one, only so tall that Hakibeg's lightning-fast horse could have stepped over it without difficulty, was distinguished by its two narrow windows. One was without glass, so the owner had filled the opening with a pillow which had weathered to a sickly blue.

Andja had a house, a private plot, a shed, and sheep, goats and a son in the Yugoslav reserves, whom she had been waiting for day and night ever since she heard that the capitulation had been signed. Above all, she had her daughter, Radmila, and daughter-in-law, Mileva. They were more trouble to her than the entire German occupation force that she had heard so much about but hadn't yet seen with her own eyes. Bitterly she fought to keep control over those two, but who could keep them safe when so many more valuable things had already been fouled? She also had her memories of her late husband, Gojko, somewhere in the Grmec abyss.

"Where are you cowards coming from?" the old woman greeted us in a suspicious tone. "I can't say who looks more cowardly: you or your horses."

"It's the rain. We are exhausted and famished. Allow us to spend the night here, doesn't matter where as long as the rain isn't running down our necks," pleaded Stevo.

The old woman evaluated us with her eyes, her sight eventually focusing on the bags of salt hanging below the horses' bellies.

"What's in those goatskins?" she questioned authoritatively.

"Salt for the guerrillas," Stevo answered bluntly.

"What guerrillas!" the old woman shouted ironically. "Why are you trying to scare me with some guerrillas!? Which ones are you thinking of: Karan's or those, God forgive me, soldiers of Satan who don't cross themselves and who run from the holy water?"

Stevo realised that under no circumstances could he be foolish enough to mention the latter ones. "We're taking it to our people up in Tavani. We bought it from Rich Marko," he added, hoping that the mention of the wealthy man's name might carry some weight with the crabby old thing.

"Go over there, to the coach-shed, while I think things over. You can light a fire if you want to."

While the old woman was in the house, I noticed someone's eyes watching us from behind the dirty glass window.

Presently, Andja came out and stood beside the fire. She looked at Rade, who was laying the fire, saying nothing. Suddenly, she began to speak, sounding like she was concluding an agreement which she had made with herself:

"I'll sell you one goat for ten cups of salt, for each of you a cup to stay the night, and for the horses two cups. That's sixteen cups in all."

"You want us to leave all of the guerrillas' salt to you!?" shouted Stevo, turning his head away from her and toward the fire, which was a sign that old Andja would probably have her way. We stayed, giving her the sixteen cups of salt, which she measured out with great care, fearing that the rain had ruined the salt.

She guarded her daughter-in-law more carefully than her daughter. It was Radmila who brought us a good chunk of cornbread and a pot of boiled milk. Mileva did not appear. As Rade reached for the cornbread, his hand touched Radmila's and, I could swear that I saw it, he winked at her. Instinctively taking a step back, she immediately turned red. The old woman noticed this also and Radmila did not come again.

Night had begun to rule over the mountain. Andja was always near and kept a watchful eye on us, especially vigilant after Rade mentioned to her that we were Karizan's nephews.

Hunger began to torture me even before I noticed the aroma of kid roasting on the spit. Andja was sitting on a stump across from us, while from the house the sound of young women singing could be heard. Radmila and Mileva sang softly at first, but then more and more loudly. Rade's leg began to vibrate, as if he were in a delirium. As soon as Andja noticed, her entire body quaked with anger and she stormed off into the house. The young women inside began to laugh.

We heard Andja yell: "Mares! Be damned! Your stallions are in the woods and may they rip you apart when they return!"

The darkness was absolute, like the darkness in the eyes of a blind man. Two or three times, we heard the tramping of horses, and then nothing. The dogs gave voice only after the rain stopped.

Sometime after midnight, Andja accommodated us right behind the tin stove. The house was still, the young women nowhere to be seen. She listed her conditions and seriously warned us not to gamble with our heads. Just as we were going under the damp covers, a black cat jumped down from the attic, brushing against the old woman's leg, checking each of us briefly. When her eyes met Osman's, she grimaced, tensed up and flashed him her fangs. Lifting her tail, the cat dashed up the wooden stairs back to the attic. Andja eyed the cat's flight, then approached Osman. Looking deeply into his eyes she began to sniff and snort, as if trying to rid her lungs of the air that she had just inhaled. She also sniffed me and then Stevo and Rade, but very briefly. Obviously, they didn't emit any unusual odour. Stepping back from us, she turned toward Stevo. Out of anger her eyeballs had disappeared behind her eyelids:

"Who are they?" she motioned sharply with her head toward Osman and me.

We were all surprised. The cat's actions we could have somehow forgotten, but the old woman's...I wasn't sure if I was dreaming or not, whether all this was actually happening or some nightmare. Stevo and Rade also turned their noses toward us and then, with meek smiles which were probably meant as a kind of apology, they also sniffed. Looking at each other, they shook their heads, the joint conclusion being: "We don't notice anything strange".

"They stink of the town. That's where all of this evil has been coming from," Andja commented. But her voice had softened let it be known that she didn't mean anything bad, attempting to smooth over the initial negative effect.

"You didn't even ask us. They are our uncle Dmitar's nephews. They are from Pset," smiled Rade, giving away that a great load had just been taken from his shoulders.

Andja left and settled herself in the anteroom between us and the women. A one-headed Kerberos. I felt awful. I don't know how to describe my state. Perhaps the most memorable thing is the thought which kept needling at me—that I would have been better off in some dungeon. At least the cell doors would protect me and I'd know the reason why I had been locked up. But as things were, I hadn't done anything to anyone, yet still, everyone meant me harm. They could even smell me out.

My poor state was a spiritual problem, while the body looked after itself. Falling asleep, my brain pulled me along sun-drenched streets, and then, I don't know what time exactly, I recoiled as if I had just seen a snake. Something was scratching against the window. The first thing that fell to mind was the idea that Karan and his bearded henchmen had come for us, to take our salt—and because of the salt, they would also have our heads. It was as dark as in a vat. As I pushed the slightly open window pane wide, the night's darkness struck me like a blow. I don't remember what force made me decide to go through that window and into the night but I did. Pressing my hands against the logs, I slowly made my way behind the corner of the house. From inside the log wall, through the unlatched window, someone's whispering could be heard. The women were talking. They were lamenting to one another and cursing old Andja.

"I can't take this any longer. Since Bozo left, the old woman has been trying to keep me bottled up. Just now, I feel the need for a man more then ever before, I can't rid myself of the idea. It won't leave me. While Bozo was around, even the thought of 'that' disgusted me. He may be your brother but he wasn't meant for women. For him, other than 'that', a woman is like a cow: feed it, give it water, milk it and then give it a kick in the behind. But now, I want some tenderness," confided one. It was obvious that the two sisters-in-law were very close.

"I'm afraid, Radmi. Brane promised me that we'd wed as soon as the corn was picked…but now, see what has happened. He was here the other day, you saw him. He has changed: the beard, all hairy. His eyes have taken on a horrible red colour. I don't know if I still love him. The blood has overtaken his eyes and he no longer looks human."

"Eh, don't talk like that," Radmila's provocative voice interrupted. "I saw how you could barely wait until you two could slip away into the woods. You returned teary eyed, with your clothes all wrinkled. There must have been something that went on, huh?"

"There was. But he's become cold. He's touched me before but this last time it was by force. I felt like a bitch. He even slapped me."

"But you? You, like this? So firm all over, like I used to be, dear God, before Bozo. Why?! You're beautiful. Look, touch me, I'm quivering next to you."

A long silence followed. I felt as if I could see through the night and the wooden wall as Radmila slithered next to Mileva, while the other one, still without any real amorous experience, clenched her hands and legs together and became rigid, not knowing if she should respond in the same fashion or jump out of the bed. Listening to their tumid conversation, I could feel my manhood growing, swelling and trembling. Suddenly, all of the evil that had been burdening me became distant and dim. I wanted to find my way between the two, twist myself between their warm bodies, entangled as if in a cobweb, and shaking from the uninhibited heat.

From the other side of the wall could be heard sounds of increasing motion: the women had obviously freed themselves of Bozo and Brane and were finding enjoyment despite the old woman's iron fist.

My skin had become so sensitive I could feel the rustling of sheep and goats in their fold. A previously unknown force pushed me into the darkness, urging me to get my hands on a sheep's body at least, or a goat's, it no longer mattered.

I froze in my tracks as a hand landed on my shoulder. Whipping around like a snake that has just been stepped on, I was equally prepared to strike or to flee into the night.

"Where are you off to?" I immediately recognised Osman's voice. "The old woman has woken up and is cursing at someone in the anteroom. Let's get back to the house."

We returned and crawled under the covers. We had barely lain down when Andja pounded on the door, entered the room and screeched:

"Get up! Up! You thieving thieves! Up!"

We all four jumped from our pallets and saw her standing before us, kerosene lamp in one hand and a large club in the other. Her hair was scattered in all directions, as if she had just been wrestling with the devil.

"Get out of this house. Damned be your Tavanian father! Isn't it enough that you've been farting and snoring like expecting horses but you also have to rile up my sheep. Get out!"

We had no other choice but to leave. Stevo and Rade began to curse and threaten but it didn't change a thing. In front of the house, a man with an axe was waiting. Looking toward us as if we were old familiars, he murmured:

"Let's go. If we hurry, we can gather them up before dawn."

Stevo and Rade returned to the house for their guns.

"Who's he?" I thought to myself while Osman stared into the darkness behind him. "This fellow must have come to visit one of the two women but because of us couldn't get near her. Probably turned the sheep and goats loose just to create a ruckus and wake up the old woman. Who knows what he didn't tell her before she ran into the room where we were sleeping."

The Karizan brothers returned with their guns and Andja, who was jabbering instructions. They were all trying to decide who would go where with whom in pursuit of the missing animals. Andja had obviously changed her tune.

I was to go with the man carrying the axe, whom Andja addressed as Veka., the old woman finally decided. I followed him down the edge of the field. He was mumbling, cursing sheep and goats and occasionally striking his axe against branches and rocks that we passed. A strange character right out of some Grmec folktale. Little did I know I was soon to meet an even stranger one.

The false dawn had opened up the night, and greyness replaced the charcoal black.

It would always happen to me when I was awake to see the changing of the guard between night and day, that I would hear sounds whose source and significance were a mystery to me. They awoke within me the feeling that the obscure world around me was trying to detach itself from the magnetic force of night, as young birds test their weak wings to see if they can leave the nest, while the safety of the nest pulls them back.

The creek had grown from the recent rains and we concluded that the sheep and goats couldn't have gone across the water. As we returned along the hill, we were startled by a sudden roar from behind our backs:

"E-e-e...a-yo-o-oy! The eagles have risen! Let the dawn shoot up into the sky!"

His head glowed in the near-darkness of the early morning. It was as if he had shaved his head and smeared it with linseed oil. Not a hair, or a whisker. Only a grey beard around a mouthful of widely scattered teeth. He was twisting around on one leg and shouting:

"E-e-e...a-yo-o-oy! Rise up, brother Yugovics! War lances forward! Take St. George with you!..."

"Old Radovan!" commented Veka, "Where is that blind bat going at this time of night? Could he be the Evil One? God help us."

Frightened by the bald man with the bulging eyes, I wanted to flee the light which was coming over the mountain peaks from the east, like water overflowing a dam. Frightened of the old man, and the noise of the creek, and the Evil One...Radovan's words fell heavily upon me. Visions of horsemen, some with lances ready, others brandishing their sabres, their heads naked skulls with bulging eyeballs, suddenly began to fly past my eyes. I imagined that we had revisited a scene of carnage from the distant past, in which only dampness and rotting flesh kept the brain going.

I moved my hand back to grab Veka's arm, but my hand caught emptiness. I turned around, but he was not there. I turned my head to the other side. The bald head was lost across the water. My fear crammed itself into desperate flight toward the farmhouse, which by now existed only like a scene from a less terrifying nightmare. Running along the hill, my legs grew shorter as my panic grew, and soon I was running in one place, not moving at all. I was saved by the sight of Rade returning with the sheep and goats.

The day that came was nothing like the previous one: sun quickly progressing above the mountain peaks and all of nature suddenly growing gentler under its warmth. The change was like a move from

Arctic igloo to desert oasis. Everything had come alive. Even the old woman's lips showed traces of a smile when we tacked up the horses and tied the goatskin bags to their saddles. It was evident that they had grown lighter during the course of the night. Perhaps the salt had dried, but by the look on Stevo's face it was clear that there was no way to return what was lost. Which suggested theft by something other than dehydration.

Even Radmila and Mileva were around to see us off and, arm in arm with the old woman, stood next to the sheep and goat fold. It seemed that Radmila was trying to convey a message with her eyes to Rade, while Mileva, arm half-extended, waved to Osman. I say that it seemed to me because I had begun to question the accuracy of my eyes and memory as a result of the scenes I remembered seeing the previous night.

Just as we arrived at the edge of the first clearing away from the farm, we saw a large group of horsemen riding at a steady gallop toward the heart of the vast mountain. They were undoubtedly guerrillas, probably moving from Grmec's southeastern peak. As we descended the still-slippery terrain, overgrown with oak and hornbeam trees, and succeeded in finding a favourable spot to cross the creek, the sun appeared above our heads and began to sweat upon us and the horses. Ahead lay a wide hillside overgrown with underbrush, so that we had to get off our horses and move slowly along the side. Often, we would have to search around for animal tracks because there was no other path.

"Maybe it would have been better to have gone around the hill," commented Rade as we stood in front of an impassable patch of rocky ground, trying to decide where to continue our ascent.

He had yet to complete his thought when our mounts suddenly startled, as if they had smelled rotting horseflesh, opening their eyes wide and flicking their heads toward the thick underbrush which surrounded the rocky incline. At that very same moment, from behind the rocks appeared a dozen men with their guns aimed directly at us:

"The first one to move gets his head blown off!" a heavy voice bellowed from the side while a short, stocky, moustached type emerged from behind a low-hanging hornbeam branch. His chest was decorated with an imposing bandolier while from between his hands the hungry barrel of his machine-gun coldly observed us.

"Move away from the horses and put your hands above your heads!" fell the next command.

While half of them were busy tying our hands, the others checked over what the horses were carrying. Stevo began to shout how we were also Serbs and that the salt was meant for the army in the mountains, when the short one, obviously the unit leader, came forward, looked him directly in the eyes, laughed and mockingly replied:

"Yes, yes, of course you are…Nowadays, everyone who enters the mountain wants to be a Serb, just as everyone who remains in town wants to be an Ustasha or Turk. Only, my hero," his head was directly below Stevo's eyes, "not all Serbs are the same."

He then walked over and whispered something to a squinting man, who by the look of him might have been his brother, or cousin. The other one looked toward us and nodded his head in affirmation. They took away our horses, along with the salt, bags and guns that we were carrying. Their leader once again approached us and said that they knew full well who we were and where we were going. As he spoke, his hand reached for the sheath holding his dagger at his waist. All the while, he was looking to the side, as if he couldn't bear to meet our eyes.

Without a word, the whole group of them disappeared into the forest growth above. Stevo whispered that they were strangers to these parts. By the way they talked he figured that they came from somewhere around Glamoc, a city beyond the mountain range to the south. Saying that he would again try to reason with their leader, he warned Osman and me under no circumstances to say who we really were.

It never occurred to me that anything might happen to us apart from being robbed of the horses, salt and guns. When they disappeared into the forest, I thought that they wouldn't be returning. Nevertheless, something kept on telling me to try to loosen the bonds around my wrists as quickly as possible. The rope was too thick to properly knot. I noticed the others also trying to free themselves.

A scorching heat radiated through the shrubby growth we were in, while the rocky area gave off an unbearable white glow. The sun was moving westward, shining directly into our faces. Keeping my eyes shut, I felt its heat beat directly into my brain, bright yellow and hot as hell. Above the slope hung the still breath of the torrid air. High above, an eagle circled the eternally blue sky, his wings like a unfurled flag. But, this flag was of the kind which brings only misfortune, torn around the edges, the bird's head and beak like the threatening blade of a sharpened spear about to impale its prey. We heard the sound of voices coming from the higher growth and knew that our captors had gone into the shade to discuss what they would do to us. Just then, I realised that we were being tried, without being present to defend ourselves. Suddenly, in the midst of the infernal heat, a cold sweat began to run down my back.

From behind us, someone could be heard making his way toward us through the thick hanging branches. None of us turned his head. The stranger appeared within my field of vision and struck Rade across the shoulders.

"You are Karizan's Rade, from Tavani?! I've heard that you're a real lion, especially around the ladies." As the man spoke, from the look in his dancing eyes it was obvious he was trying his best to be ironic.

His seemingly permanent smile was that of a man who had been pursuing someone for years and suddenly one day comes across his prey by pure accident. He disappeared behind us, just as he had appeared, the sound of his steps quickly fading. Stevo hissed toward his brother:

"That was Radmila's husband! I knew that you would pay dearly for trifling with her affections, but I didn't think that I would be with you when it happened."

"They are going to kill us," answered Rade, his heart visibly beating like an old-fashioned alarm clock, "We have to run for it, Stevo."

I looked toward Osman. His hands were behind his back but they were untied. In one, he held the jackknife that each of us was given before we set off to buy the salt. Looking up at his face, I saw a shadow from the night. He whispered to me in a tone I had not heard since the night when he escaped from Kula:

"Tell Father not to worry about me. Take care of our old man..."

Stevo whispered to us that it would be for the best if each of us ran in a different direction. As we freed ourselves, each took a good look at the route along which he would try to escape.

While I finished loosening my bonds, the sun glued itself to my eyes, burning through the lids and burying itself deep in the sockets. My chest was burning as I tried to take as many deep breaths as I could, with little success. Sweat poured down my face. Images of my father and mother floated before me. Father was leaning against an invisible wall and looking off into the distance while Mother had her arms outstretched toward me, trying to reach me. Quickly, they became lost in the yellow heat.

The excited trampling of horses could be heard some hundred meters above us. The snapping of twigs from the direction where the guerillas from Glamoc had decided our fate was the indication that they were rushing for their mounts. We also, as if on command, dashed toward the surrounding growth, each in a different direction. The sound of guns firing and machine-guns yelping motivated me on as bullets flew by just like in a real battle. Someone screamed, branches were thrashing and snapping in all directions, shouting and running could he heard coming from everywhere. After the initial mad rush, all I heard was someone shouting into my ear: Run, run, run...

I plunged through the brush, trying to protect my face, but quickly felt the pain on my cheeks, forehead, hands and legs as blood freely began oozing from the countless cuts and scratches. I could feel someone running behind me. His feet and the jagged branches beat in my tracks like wooden mallets, briefly severing all contact between my brain and limbs. I ran directly toward the sun, its circle branded into my eyes. I ran, bent down like a slithering snake, determined to go forward at all costs. The trampling behind was gaining on me. I could now almost touch the sun. Stumbling on a protruding root, I fell, the inertia flinging me backward into a cornelberry bush. I had no time to get up and continue running. My pursuer was standing before me.

He had stopped some two or three metres away, his face all bloody and clothes torn. He was breathing heavily, like a goose hissing at children or a dog. He held a dagger in his hand, its tip shining in the sun. I had nowhere to run: the bush behind me, his dagger before me. His mouth spread open in a victorious smile. Seeing that I was defeated, he stopped to savour my hopeless situation. Slowly edging forward, he bent down so that his dagger would be level with my throat. Realising that death stood before me, waiting, I shot forward like a wounded lizard fighting for its life, making a bridge of its body and driving its tail into the soil to launch its head like a ram.

For the first time in my life, I became aware of the processes in my viscera. My heart had been stunned to a stop. There was no beating; an icy liquid spread from it to all corners of my body; the muscles were rigid and began to swell; the brain…The brain was going through a real metamorphosis which can only be described as a head-first dive into death. In fact, years later, when I tried to think back to what really went on in my head in those critical moments, I came to the conclusion that my fall into the cornelberry bush led to the brief death of all my faculties for reason.

What I do remember is that I surged up like a possessed beast, jumped to my feet, grabbed my would-be butcher by the arms and flung him into a deep limestone pit behind the cornelberry bush. After that, everything went dark, a sharp pain cut off all communication between my eyes and brain. Drumming from the brush entered my ears, the branches reached for the sky and covered the sun's bright yellow sphere.

I was woken by the chill which fell together with the approach of night. I managed to make my way down to the level highlands, and from there to the first outskirts of town. As I struggled over the fences which separated the various orchards and gardens, I felt a burning in my stomach and lungs. Thinking that these were only the after-effects of the heat and fear and desperate exertion I had been through, I had no idea that in fact it was my health leaving me.

How long it took I don't know, but when I reached my father's house it was still dark, and through the window I caught sight of the old man pacing the room, prayer beads in hand.

His first words were to say how glad he was that I had returned. My aunt fed me bread and cream, and I drank rosewater. Both of them stayed up the little more time until dawn, waiting for Osman's knock on the window. Exhausted though I was, I couldn't sleep either. My intestines were broiling and my throat was parched. It felt like all the fluids had left my body.

At dawn, I told them two things: that Osman wouldn't be returning and that sickness had got the better of me, I couldn't get to my feet. My father also had a surprise for me: a large-scale attack on the town from the mountains was being planned. All our people would surely soon have to flee.

"I gather this is where you plan to stop or am I wrong?" said Fehrat, to his father, both of them surprised at the sound of his voice. Up to then, he had been an impassive listener. At least, that is how it seemed to Yudja. At times, this unresponsiveness of Fehrat's annoyed and angered him because he would begin to feel like a guilty man confessing his sins to a disinterested stranger.

"For a while there, I thought you might have fallen asleep even though your eyes were open," Yudja complained, although with a smile. "If you are tired, I can stop. Anyway, it's been an eventful day. It was enough to come upon that scorpion at the Immigration Centre…"

Though Yudja seemed fatigued and couldn't hide the shaking of his left hand, he had been speaking fluently, building his constructions without pause for thought. To Fehrat it seemed at times that he was watching an actor who has recreated his role so many times that by now he knows the text, down to the smallest nuance, inside and out.

"You and Osman were by then so different that you could no longer be together. But, your individuality exists in the denotation of these differences. Yet you don't want to explain them, while I don't want to come to my own conclusions." In this, Fehrat made an observation which Yudja would have preferred not to hear. He knew that this would be his last opportunity to speak, sensing that he and everything attached to him would soon be lost in time. He was aware that he was covering the dreadful period during which he and his brother irreparably grew apart. Then again, he realised, why should he hide from Fehrat the things that had been tormenting him all these years? Why should he hold secret that which only Fehrat needed to know?

"For the longest time, I thought that Mother's Christian legacy was stronger in him than in me. Probably because I didn't know our mother very well. Then, there were the tenuous relations with her relatives. We didn't have any great contact with them because most of them disowned her after she married our father. When we were staying with the Karizans, I had the constant feeling that there was nothing that they would rather do than to cut out our father's portion of us and feed it to their cats. The idea was wedged in my brain that we were all one nation, and that is how I found myself unprepared for what was to follow at the beginning of that war. They called us Turks just so that their future generations could hate us." Yudja sensed that he had hit upon a topic which was of great interest to Fehrat. He himself had escaped all such ideas of ethnic xenophobia until the fatal division among Yugoslavs led to bloodshed, until he saw the sky above Vakuf and Orasac on fire and heard from Rade what the guerillas, under Karan's command, done to the Muslim inhabitants of the Orasac plains.

"Or," Fehrat followed his train of thought, "those two peasants hanging from the poplars in front of the high school in Pset. They probably wouldn't have been hanging there had they not been Vlachs, as the other side liked to mockingly refer to them. The idea of each other as Turks and Vlachs has been a obstacle which both sides have been unable, or unwilling, to move past. Especially because Serbs have not been Vlachs and Bosniaks, or Bosnian Muslims have not been Turks. Foreigners have created wounds which our respective wooden wise-men and bloody-eyed warlords have resurrected with great regularity as a justification for the spilling of more fresh blood!"

Yudja turned to his son reluctantly. "I don't want to drag you into something that could disillusion you even more," he said in a gentle voice, "but, for me, the final answer to all this was the farce which took place over my mother's grave."

Fehrat winced in confusion. He knew that people always spoke in tones of mysticism about Yudja's mother, some portraying her as an unfortunate woman who committed a fatal error in the name of love, while others saw her as an evil seed who entered Yudja's family in order to return them to their true Bosnian origins. Even his own mother would repeat a passage from the Koran whenever Yudja's mother was mentioned.

"I heard things, but people fabricate stories to fit their own whims," commented Fehrat, not hiding his interest in hearing Yudja's version.

Yudja walked over to the cupboard and reached for the figurine of a woman. On each side of her, a dog had bitten into her leg. They were trying to pull her in opposite directions. She held her hands high above her head and was standing on the tips of her toes, reaching for something beyond her grasp. Or, she might be trying to climb free of the animals' jaws.

"As far as I have managed to learn, this is my mother. I have the feeling that she grew sick of the earthly world early in her life and wasn't sorry to leave it. Why should she have been sorry to leave a place that was trying to tear her in half or rip out her heart, whichever came first?" As Yudja spoke, he didn't take his eyes off the wooden figurine which he had carved out of linden.

"The dogs wouldn't even leave her grave in peace." He stroked the wooden kerchief on her head, a childlike sense of belonging evident in his eyes. "Not long after the burial at the Muslim cemetery, a dog's faeces were found on her grave, next to a gopher-like hole. Word spread throughout town that Imam Selman said in his sermon that she had turned into a werewolf and should be transferred to the Orthodox cemetery as soon as possible. When Father tried to strangle the Imam, he could be heard shouting how Heaven knew this wasn't true, that she was, in fact, a greater martyr than many who lay in marble Muslim tombs. I wept many nights, trying to reach her in my thoughts. Then, one night, her voice called out to me."

Lowering the figurine onto the small table, next to his cup of tea, Yudja sat. While clumsily adjusting his leg, he knocked the figurine over, causing his mother's wooden head to fall into the cup. He jumped to his feet immediately, wiped the figurine, and returned it to its previous spot on the cupboard shelf.

They remained quiet for a time after the embarrassing accident. Fehrat stole moments when Yudja was deep in thought to carefully study the features of his face.

"She remained there," continued Yudja at last, with the feeling that he needed to finish as quickly as possible. He knew that the accident hadn't been caused by mere clumsiness and wished to close his eyes. "How I used to love daydreaming about the fruit from my father's orchard and my mother picking up the fallen plums and taking them to the chickens." The thought hit him like a flash, and disappeared just as quickly.

"When the guerrillas entered our deserted town, the first thing they did was burn down the mosque and turn over the headstones in the cemetery. There was a priest with them and someone whispered to him that Maria's grave should be dug up from the "Turkish cemetery" and transferred among the baptised souls. They paid some idiot to dig up her bones, but he didn't find anything in her grave. It is true that there were some bones, but everyone who saw them swears that they were at least five or six generations older than what mother's bones would have looked like. To make everything go according to the ideas of some of the bearded creatures present, the bones were taken out and held overnight in the church, where the priest blessed them with holy water and, the next morning with all the pomp and circumstance necessary, they were buried in the town's Orthodox cemetery next to the rest of my mother's family."

Eyes closed, Fehrat turned his head toward the cupboard holding the various figurines. He looked like a man deep in thought who was storing away valuable information for later use.

"Is that why Osman had his Partisan unit crucify that priest above the Culumska cave?" he asked softly, in accordance with the atmosphere of piety and gloom which had suddenly come over the room.

"Probably…I never asked him but I believe that he had his revenge."

"Against whom?" Fehrat asked himself, "Against the wrong man. If the priest didn't dig up the right bones, who knows whose bones he blessed. Who really desecrated your mother's grave before the ill-fated priest?" Fehrat at the same time questioned and bitterly protested the injustice of it all, his exhausted eyes wandering along the remains of his hand and leg. "Horrific fallacy," a part of him added as the memory shifted to the millions of unfortunates strewn across Bosnia and Herzegovina's gorges and mass graves. "A land drowning in self-deceit…ruled and destroyed with the blood-stained weapons of madmen."

Both of them seemed to realise that this room looking over Vancouver's tranquil harbour was in many ways a continuing reminder of Bosnia's ill-fated existence. For, fleeing the blood and madness of their native land, they two and their countrymen had brought all their emotional baggage to this new world, their hearts colder and sights firmer—like plague-carrying survivors who have the potential to contaminate anyone coming into contact with them.

CHAPTER VIII

After yet another ample breakfast, Fehrat realised that this was Yudja's main meal of the day. It seemed unusual and illogical but he didn't say anything. He justified it to himself by rationalising that this practice was yet another product of insecurity: the wish to get your fill for the day as early as possible. Then, if you don't get another chance to eat that day, you will be able to endure. Bosnia, to go by this habit of Yudja's, had always been the kind of place where you could never be certain you would be going to sleep in the same place where you had woken up.

Tea was another one of Yudja's particularities. He was always drinking it, before meals and after, instead of water or coffee. He drank coffee also, but complained to Fehrat that it aggravated his acid stomach, especially the real, strong Turkish coffee that was such a focal part of Bosnian life and culture. If only he could find a place to buy some of that roasted barley coffee which he used to drink, he would sometimes say, things would be better. Fehrat did his best to adopt Yudja's fondness for tea, drinking it more often than he ordinarily would have wished. Each cup of the strange-tasting tea came unsweetened, with a slice of lemon in the cup.

As they were sipping the last drops of tea, Fehrat searched the newspaper's headlines for familiar, international, words.

"This game that Europe is playing with our heads is inhuman," Yudja offered, attempting to be of help with the translation process going on inside Fehrat's head. "While our people are being slaughtered by the Chetnik barbarians, the European powers are taking the time to study the roots of the problem. No, they've known the problem all along, they are simply pretending to be powerless, as if the Balkans were on another planet. I think it is in their interest to stand by and look on in feigned amazement, until the time comes that they can calculate their best advantage. It says here that Mitterrand and Kohl have agreed that the brutal Serbian aggression was the key cause of it all, but the Frenchman is still against suspending the weapons embargo for the Bosniaks, reasoning that if that happened then there would be even more casualties. What a perverse sense of humour! Whose casualties is he thinking about? As things stand, we cannot possibly suffer more than we are suffering right now. Don't we have a right to self-defence?! This reminds me of the young ruffians in town who would get their kicks watching cats fight. To make things more interesting, they would throw in a cat whose nails they had just clipped against one with long, sharp nails. You can imagine what happened next, since nails are a cat's preferred weapon. Well, what they are doing to us is pretty much the same as what happened to that unfortunate bare-pawed cat."

To Fehrat that game with cats was horribly ruthless. How much more so was the relentless replaying in his brain of the world's game with his land and people…Unfathomable, yet undeniable!. Yudja's reminiscences the night before had returned him to the beginning of the current game-playing with Bosnia, even though he knew full well that such games are as old as rain, that there isn't a foot of land on this planet which hasn't seen the like, or a single human individual who at one point or other hasn't taken part in some questionable act, at least from the aspect of human principles. Thus, he was glad to have his father continue the previous night's story, just as the sinner quickens his confession from the moment he admits his sin.

My sickness was serious and unusual. Actually, I didn't feel any great pain, but in my lungs there was less and less air. I guess you could say that I was like a fish from a clear mountain stream who during the spring runoff ends up in the muddy waters of a wide delta. In my stomach, a growing hypersensitivity to heat caused bewildering turgescence. At times, I felt as if I was going to burst from drink and gluttony, when in fact I was hungry and thirsty. After noon, my eyes began to shut, even though it seemed to me that I could see and hear everything around me.

"Where did you hide him up to now?" Dr. Simeta reproached my father and aunt as he examined my stomach and ribs. "You should have called me sooner. You shouldn't have worried, because in this state, nobody will ever try to put him into a uniform, or send him on work duty…It began with the stomach typhus, but I'm now worried by the murmur in his lungs, going parallel with his heartbeat. It is as if, God forgive me, some other creature has moved into his body."

The liquids which the doctor left them, with instructions to pour them down my throat, by force if necessary, didn't show any effect until nightfall. By then, my legs had begun to strain and contract, like those of a cow bloated from having just eaten fresh clover. I could now feel everything, but couldn't say a word. It was as if I had fallen asleep in a poppy field. An odour which I had never previously known began to enter through every single pore in my body. When the night achieved its total domination over all that could taste its sweetness and sense its stimulus for imagination, I began to feel a burning pain start in my lower back area and slowly spread in waves toward my head and toes. For three days, they tried to cure me with the liquids the doctor had left them. Then, there appeared above my head, first, Selman, and then the skinny, bug-eyed fortune-teller, Naza.

The Imam did his pre-prayer washing next to me and for a long time whispered prayers for health, all the while holding my eyes wide open with his fingers, probably so as to see the effect which his brand of medicine was having on me. Before he left, he placed a folded piece of yellow paper under my arm and told Aunt Habibe to stand above me and repeat some Arabic words, I think the call for God to free a dying man of fear, as often as possible.

When Naza came, her first action was to make her "healing potion," the main purpose of which was to free me of the fear she believed lay at the root of my illness. An interesting variation on the Imam's approach. With a wash-basin full of lukewarm water before her, she held in one hand a twisted figure, the result of contact between melting lead and water, and in the other a small mound of coal dust which she had skimmed off the surface of the water, all the while repeating her "magic" chants. When she was done with the chanting, she began to pinch and poke with her long, withered fingers all over my body. When she poked me in the lower part of my back, my legs tensed up. Noticing this, she again reached for the twisted lead, magically bringing it before her eyes before pushing it under my father's nose.

"Something bit him. Worse than a snake. Worse even than a scorpion. If you're willing to listen to me, you will first take that paper under his arm and bury it under a walnut tree. This water from the wash-basin, strain it onto his forehead and lips until he starts to speak. That is when he will tell you what ails him." She whispered all this most secretively, but I could hear everything as in a dream.

It all disgusted me but I could do nothing about it. I despised the fortune-tellers and their spells and potions, but could only lie there mutely on the settee. Naza disgusted me especially because I was convinced that she was filthy and had scabies. At the end of her healing ceremony, when she proceeded to lick my forehead four times and then spit in the four directions of the world, all of my thoughts concentrated on summoning the strength to raise my hands, but they remained unmoving. My legs remained tensed.

The fever held me in its grip for days. In fact, it came like a flood-tide, and with it I lost all rational contact with the world around me. My soul was running ahead of the tide, reaching for Mother's gaudily coloured dress and, as if on a flying carpet, flew over mountains crowded with sweet black cherry and mulberry trees and clear, gurgling brooks. On all sides, one could see butterflies with elaborately detailed wings and herds of deer, the large-eyed spotted fawns among them. And then Zemka appeared. When I'd go down on my knees and bring my lips to the rolling surface of a creek, her image would appear in the water. It swayed as if carried by the wind, now clear, now blurred by tiny drops. Instinctively, my hands reached into the water, only to have her disappear before the onslaught of the current which persistently pushed against Mother and me. With the current, my fever grew; faces lost their true dimensions, stretching and wobbling around like gelatin, only to disappear eventually in the thick scarlet fog.

The first thing that I heard after my lengthy absence from reality was my Aunt Habibe's voice. She was shouting, her voice coloured with joy and disbelief: "He's come back! He's come to his senses! Fehro, he's come to. The pupils in his eyes have returned."

I realised that I was riding in a horse-cart. All around me, the noise of many other iron-shod wheels on the macadam road mingled with the chaotic din of voices coming from the column of Psetian refugees, uprooted by the offensive of the guerrillas from the surrounding forests and headed toward Bihac.

Several thousand Muslims were again leaving the highlands. The uprising in the surrounding mountains had gathered such momentum that it was threatening to swallow up the entire town and the people in it. The Ustasha, the occupying forces command, had given the order to evacuate all territory as far as the Bihac basin. From the forests came the news that the Chetniks had vowed to punish each and every townsman who had collaborated. Since everyone knew that their concept of "collaboration" was very subjective, it was clear that justice wasn't to be expected. Not even the secretly sent assurances from Zdravko's partisans, that they were the people's army and the people had no reason to fear them, did much to change the general opinion. Fear of the guerrillas, which grew every time someone mentioned the word Chetnik, was further fuelled by the occupying Ustasha soldiers, who used every opportunity to remind everyone of the most recent massacres committed by Karan's butchers in the nearby Muslim villages up the Una River.

The refugees headed out under the escort of the local military forces, who were also, for the most part, withdrawing toward Bihac. I couldn't get up or stand on my feet, so I needed the assistance of my ears and imagination to piece together the look of the column. Tanks and other heavy equipment protected the front and the rear, while the infantry guarded the flanks. Adding to the sound-colour in the air were the masses of cattle which people were pulling along with them, and the squealing of the children. The guerrillas were allowing the column to pass in relative peace; only sporadic firing could be heard from the surrounding ridges.

Those thugs were too busy looting the deserted houses in town, I reasoned, to have the time to attack the column. I thought back to the scenes of the German army's entry into Pset; the horses and cattle stampeding, the town full of people. The same picture was now moving in the opposite direction, though everyone joined together: the soldiers, the people, and the horses and cattle. These last ones were also followed by the flies and breezes, so that they were bucking, shoving and foaming as if in a fit of frenzy, and we breathed their cloying smell. When a pack of German warplanes flew low overhead, the entire column began to sway; the heat, the people and the animals. I feared another stampede, but fortunately it didn't happen this time.

"Is Zemka among us here?" I asked my aunt.

"Which Zemka?" She opened her mouth wide, startled that I could speak.

Aunt Habibe said no more. Only then did I notice that she was walking alongside the cart and that only one horse, Vranac, was harnessed. Father was walking behind the cart with several other people.

"Didn't Osman come?" I asked.

My aunt bent over me and, as if discussing a forbidden topic, whispered into my ear: "Zemka went mad and ran off into the forest. A group of soldiers raped her and she lost her mind."

If only the fever hadn't let up; then I would have been free to jump and scream. It would have made this news less painful for me.

Aunt Habibe reached for a wet towel and wiped my forehead. She was probably still following Naza's instructions, though I didn't see the wash-basin anywhere near me in the cart.

Time had lost all meaning in my life. I could no longer feel it passing by. For me, there existed only the sweet running of my temperature and the occasional return to consciousness. I felt each new bout of fever originating at my toes, like entering a lukewarm river naked on a frozen winter day. I began insisting to my aunt that she tell me something about Osman, but each time her face disappeared from my view. I was running down a rugged cliff toward the dark green surface of the river and with each step I could feel my body shatter like a dropped egg. Once again, mother was there to pick up my pieces and a vision of Zemka could be seen in the river, as mysterious and unreachable as ever.

On the road to Bihac, my two worlds, the real world and delirium, took turns a number of times. Each time I regained consciousness, I knew that the next wave of fever would inevitably follow. Neither world arrived through my choosing, and at no time did I have the luxury of free thought or movement. My aunt kept me informed of events that had occurred while I was away. The surges in my consciousness soon became normal to her, though each time I saw her anew, she seemed increasingly pale and drained.

In one of these unusual encounters, she commented that things were awful. In some places the column had to wait for hours, while the nights were most difficult of all. First, there was the fear of those hiding up in the woods, and then there were more and more problems with the soldiers escorting us to Bihac. She whispered how they were becoming increasingly arrogant, lashing out at the refugees for the most trivial reasons. At night, they had begun to take away the young girls and women under the pretext that they needed someone to prepare supper for them, when in fact they would rape them. No one could say a word against these outrages. This was made painfully clear to everyone when Dzafer Sehic confronted the Home Guard officer, Teklic, to complain about the previous night's abduction of his wife by some of the soldiers. She returned to him the next day, bruised all over and no longer able to speak. Dzafer wasn't seen again, yet everyone knew what had happened to him. On our flight from one evil, we were accompanied by another, one which assumed complete control over our lives.

"May Allah forgive me for thinking it, but it would be better if this boy didn't wake up anymore by the time we reach Bihac," I overheard Father say to Aunt Habibe.

"Did they learn anything about what happened to Dzafer?" she inquired.

"It's not just Dzafer. Since last night, no one has seen the Semanic girls. Husein can only hide his face in his hands, he can't bear to look anyone in the eye. What a disgrace."

"It is better for him that they never return," commented Habibe painfully. "Knowing how proud he is, he could never bear to even look at them. May God repay their abductors," she sighed as she reapplied the damp towel to my forehead.

The piercing sound of a child's screaming again brought me back to consciousness. It was evident that the screams were the result of great pain. We were standing still. I couldn't see Father or Aunt Habibe anywhere near me. The child was screaming in waves. Occasionally, a woman's sobs could also be heard. After a second look, I realised that we were next to some village in a field surrounded by woods.

"Wretched people!" Habibe was all out of breath, "We're in Lipa now. That Serb woman's child was playing in a puddle while the pigs were sniffing around him in the mud. A sow bit off a piece of his manhood. Ibrahim, the barber, quickly ran over to try and stop the bleeding. Poor wretch," she repeated. From the tone of her voice and the redness of her eyes, one could see her deep compassion for the child and his mother.

I began to regain feeling in my legs prior to the next bout of fever. They cramped up painfully and stretched out rigidly as though in rigor mortis. Together with pins and needles in my soles came the high temperature. My aunt noticed the changes in my legs and ran to get Father. He arrived along with some other people and, after taking off the blanket covering my legs, they proceeded to poke my thighs and soles. I could feel them poking me, but they were lost from my sight. Aunt Habibe continually repeated the same observation: that I had lost a lot of weight but that the illness was obviously leaving me.

"If only he can rid himself of the fever. If only God could send some rain, or a few clouds. If the sun wasn't around, he'd have an easier time overcoming that internal fire," she said in motherly tones to Father.

"I think it has taken everything out of him. He has lost the will to live, that's why he has no strength left," an unknown voice commented.

"Considering what he's been through, it's a miracle that he's still alive at all," replied Father. "If half of what he said in his delirium is true, then he survived a real hell up in the forest."

"What happened to the other one?" a familiar voice asked, but I just couldn't match the voice to a face.

"I don't know," Father answered curtly. There was protest, anger and pain in his voice. "If he's alive, then he'll fend for himself better than Yudja would have. Osman is more clever and tougher." Father spoke as if trying to console himself.

"He is very thin," my aunt's voice could be heard again, "and there is no more of that sweat on his forehead and cheeks. He won't eat anything, and drinks only the odd sip of water. Says that the water falls to his stomach like on a hot iron," she tried to explain.

The fever brought with it a deafening murmur, drowning out their voices. Delirious visions circled my brain. After a while, one of a woman with a black kerchief stood out.

She held a child in her hands. They were both softly crying. I realised that it was the unfortunate boy deformed by the sow.

Walking by the cart, the woman looked at me and stopped. Coming toward me, she wrinkled her forehead. Her eyes jumped between me and some point off in the distance, as though she was trying to recall something. Aunt Habibe, suspicious, approached her.

"Thanks be to God and to that barber of yours. He saved my Dragan," she said to my aunt, her voice a mixture of soft stuttering and uncertain relief. "And this one," she pointed at me, "what's wrong with him? He's the spitting image of my brother Dujo, may God bless his soul."

After moving on, she held her head turned toward me for the longest time.

I was brought back to consciousness by chilly weather. After the daily heat, the return to cold weather by night seemed unreal. In the chill, one could almost feel the smell of water. I realised that a river was somewhere near and that we had descended to the foot of the mountain, into the Bihac basin. All around, fires could be seen burning and the sound of people and cattle was in the air. I tried to raise myself enough to be able to sit up but my body disregarded my wishes. Just across from me, I could hear people talking. >From among the tired and yawning voices, I picked out that of my father. They were discussing something that must have happened during my last feverish spell.

"If we can only manage to make it to Bihac," my uncle Nuhan's voice said. "Then we'd have the Chetniks off our backs. If only they hadn't attacked just after we got out of Lipa…And what did we do wrong for the Germans to blame us for their three dead soldiers?… Instead of going up into the villages and looking for revenge, they take away thirty of our people." He spoke quietly, often stopping to search for words which did justice to his feeling of helplessness.

"You didn't think that we are in the company of friends?" sarcastically inquired my father.

"I thought that at least they weren't our enemies. At least not the Home Guard and the Ustashas. At least not those who are ours, those Krlevics and the Drunics," an unknown voice entered the conversation.

"Now you see that we are the foreigners on these here mountains. Now I also see that we are nobody's. I thought otherwise before. The Chetniks attacked, and the Ustashas chose thirty of our people and handed them over to the Germans to shoot in reprisal. They say that afterward the Chetniks' leader sent word to the Germans that they had fired on them by mistake. They meant to shoot at the Ustashas and the Home Guard, he claimed, because they couldn't bear to see them escape from the plateau unpunished…So, the three dead Germans were an accident. By God, those thirty dead souls of ours were no accident. Whoever reaches for a knife always seems to prefer to stab it at our heads first. God only knows what is waiting for us in Bihac." The man spoke softly. By the sporadic sound of munching, I gathered that he was chewing on something.

Father spoke again. "And that long-legged, squinting fool Djevdo… Since he put on that Ustasha uniform, he's been slapping everyone around whenever he feels like it. He's been boasting to everyone how he will take Minka Smailova as his wife as soon as we reach Bihac. Smail doesn't know what to do, he's constantly whispering something to himself, while Minka…When I saw her standing at the bank of the

Una staring into the water she was probably looking for a place in the river's depths where she could hide."

I listened to them with a dull pain in my liver and kidneys. The heat was no longer shooting forth from my lungs. It had moved into my brain, moving from side to side in tiny waves.

Where were the roots of our people? The unasked question posed by my father and the other men began to burn also within me. Surely they must be scattered across the distant past. What arduous fate was it that distanced us from our roots? We are like the cuckoo's egg left in a strange nest. As soon as our feathers begin to grow and the birds of the nest discover that we are different from them, they immediately begin pecking at us until we are thrown head-first over the edge. And as soon as some outside power appears, they force themselves upon us, choose our flags and our uniforms. We are forever wearing other people's colours. When will these people walk on their own land and fly their own flags?!

The heat was twirling around in my brain, threatening to turn into hysterical sobbing or laughter, anything that would bring relief, just as the earth needs volcanoes to relieve itself of built-up pressure. When will my people be able to walk on their own land and fly their own flags? The question returned like an echo from my burning brain.

At the break of dawn, cries for help came from down the river. People rushed toward the water. Word came back that Minka Smailova had thrown herself into the cascading rapids and that no one had seen where the water had carried her. Not long after, Djevdo came storming past our cart but, noticing me trying to pull myself up into a sitting position, he stopped and walked toward me. Briefly looking me over, he lashed me across the face and howled:

"They want ones like you, Fehrat's seducer! Cowards and saboteurs! Pretending to be dying, aren't you?! You're only waiting for us to reach Bihac so you can make a miraculous recovery. You all want Djevdo to protect you from the Chetniks. Don't you worry, you will all remember Djevdo well!" Shooting out his boney chest, he spat upon me before running on ahead.

I could feel something waking within me. Strength was returning to my hands and legs. Jumping from the cart, I was stunned by the sudden change happening within me. Aunt Habibe was equally shocked and ran toward me, seizing me around the waist and pushing me back.

"Just you lie down! You only think you can. Eat, then rest and, God willing, you will be better," she said as she pushed me back onto the bed of straw and threw a blanket over me.

CHAPTER IX

In Yudja's small apartment in North Vancouver, from the first meeting with his father, Fehrat very quickly realized that their time together would be spent talking about the past and their Balkan spiritual heritage. His contact with Vancouver and its widely known beauties was limited to the permanent noise of the big city's life everywhere around the building, especially on the side behind Yudja's apartment. It looked as though the old man had a presentiment that this would be the last chance to transfer his own experience of life from his memories to his son's knowledge. Especially, his predominant memories about humans' mutual hatred and their killing of each other. Fehrat didn't wish to make any kind of protest against Yudja's choice of hospitality, realizing it to be the product of their physical realities and, yes, spiritual interests he now realized they shared.

Just before noon, Yudja hurried down the steep staircase, having left Fehrat behind in the apartment with the explanation that he needed to take care of some personal matters. Though at first he had thought that both would go, a sudden attack of suspicion made him decide otherwise. There were, after all, some dealings in which he shouldn't involve anyone else. Absolutely no one. The money that he put aside—fifty dollars from each monthly cheque that the Canadian Government handed out to every Bosnian refugee it sponsored—and then passed to some questionable character so that it could reach the hungry people in Bihac, that was his private matter. The sum was so paltry it could hardly help lessen the suffering of the people of the Una Valley, who were entering their second year of complete Chetnik encirclement in the Bosnian war. Nonetheless, he didn't want anyone to know that from his cheque, which was insufficient to maintain even his vegetating state, he was skipping four or five meals a month. Then again, he also couldn't be certain that any of the money he was handing to this slimy moneychanger, with increasingly meatier and softer palms, was actually finding its way behind Chetnik lines.

As he hurried on down the street, Yudja began to relax. He had a warm feeling in his chest at the thought that this morning he had managed to keep secret his monthly remittance. He had begun to feel jealous when he saw the satisfaction in Fehrat's eyes as the young man sat listening to his father's confessions. It was like two thirsty men stopping to gauge the size of one another's gulps. He preferred not to have anyone know that he was sending anything back to the land from which he had been banished and which was beginning to seem infinitely distant. It all made him think back to how, as a Psetian refugee, in the midst of the war-chaos of '42, he had declared his love to Emina Karabegovic next to the foamy small waterfall near the water-mill and she had responded with a slap and spat in his face, declaring that she'd sooner be seen with a Gypsy than with a refugee.

Even though fifty years had passed since Emina's hot-blooded gesture, Yudja instinctively passed his hand before his face to investigate if any trace of Emina's rebellion remained.

The wind lifted the dust from the large town square in the heart of Bihac and threw it into the dark-green river. That summer, along with the hellish heat, unexpected winds came to raise the dust of the town's unpaved streets and squares in choking clouds and spread the stench from the toilets and stables in all directions.

Thousands of refugees had found shelter in the Bihac Valley. The refugees arrived from all the surrounding areas where Serbian inhabitants dominated. The refugees, as a rule, were Muslims. Heading in the same direction could also be found the odd Catholic family, while some Serbs from larger urban areas headed the opposite way. For all of us, the places from which we had fled held about as much hope as cigarette smoke.

Bihac was overcrowded with refugees from Pset, Kulen-Vakuf and the Orasac Valley. When you examined this mass of humanity, you found individual tragic fates. But, when you looked upon us as a mass, you discovered immediately upon arrival a feeling of relief and joy at having managed to survive. Later, out of dreams in the increasingly longer and hungrier nights, came the nagging suspicion that while we had been forced to flee our homes, our new surroundings were no less unwilling to accept us. These second thoughts became louder and the feeling of rejection so great that we all began to say among ourselves that it would have been better to have stayed in our homes, come what may.

"The fury of the rebellion and the Chetnik terror blew us away," commented Father at my aunt's grumbling. "It would have been better if we had held tightly to our doorsteps. As things stand now, the authorities plant seeds of fear in us with tales of Serb burning and butchery and the Serb bastards also terrorise us, while we, like mice, simply look for deeper holes in which to hide. We leave our land and property as if it weren't even ours, as if it had all been lost in a game of dice. That is why in this bloody game we are only puny weights on the scales of the conflict. They are fighting over us in order to tip the scales against one another."

I shared Father's feelings. My conscience began to gnaw at me, telling me that I had betrayed my home, that I should have resisted both those who had led us to this so-called safety and those who were waving their sharpened daggers at us from up in the beech trees.

Old Zjakic gave us a small room in the basement of his house. At first, he claimed that he did not ask for anything in return but from the look on his face I was discouraged. He was measuring me from head to toe, from one shoulder to the other. Later, I learnt that two of his sons were with the Partisans and that his daughter had disappeared one night. His wife, hunched over with despair, face smooth and rosy like that of a much younger woman, sat next to the window and sighed.

I found work at the central warehouse, where I loaded and unloaded goods and kept track of the inventory. That is how I met Omer. He was short and jolly. Under his curly hair and unusually wide eyebrows was a spotted complexion. His black-market operation dealt with everything that was in short supply in and around town: soap, salt, underwear, shirts, blankets, flour, marmalade, cigarettes, cotton…He had contact with the Poles and Czechs in the German army and the Dalmatians in the Croatian forces, through whom he was able find the channels through which he could acquire goods which no one else could get their hands on. Among the refugees, he set up a supply chain which reached as far as the front lines and even past them to the rebels in the woods. People spoke about him in quiet tones during the war because even those who despised him often needed him. After the war, when the refugees returned along with the same wind which had brought them, countless actual and fictitious deeds and events were attributed to his name. He was a hero to some and a villain to others.

We first met when I was handing over a shipment of merchandise that had been signed for by the head of the military command, a Lieutenant-Colonel Seittler. As Omer stood next to me, he avoided looking in my direction, acting as if he didn't notice anyone was there. Apparently speaking to himself, he told me that he brought greetings from my brother, who was up in the hills. Without saying a word, I continued loading the boxes containing the merchandise.

"Tell your father that he is alive," he whispered, looking off to the side.

I was glad to hear that Osman was alive, but concerned by the way Omer had demonstrated that he knew about my family. Whenever the Germans and Ustashas shot people in revenge for sabotage, they went out of their way to select those they knew had relatives up in the hills with the Partisans. I could do nothing about it. Omer appeared in my life like a character in a dream whom you'd never seen before or known anything about.

As he put his professor-like signature on the release document, turning his head toward the warehouse sentry, Tusek, he added: "Emina proposed that you come with me. If you have nothing against it, we can go tomorrow night."

Omer disappeared out the huge entrance doors of the warehouse but his face was still frozen in my mind. I turned around several times, like a dog shaking his head while struggling to rip a chunk of flesh from an animal's body. All around me were warehouse workers busy with their specific tasks, and Tusek, leaning against his long carbine, with the obligatory straw hanging from his mouth.

In the afternoon, Tusek was standing guard at the transport entrance. The chubby, good-natured Zagorac* was obviously fond of Omer, or, at least, he had use for him. Omer would limp obsequiously around Tusek, lighting his cigarettes whenever the need arose, fetching Tusek's cap when the wind blew it off his head and constantly whispering to him, after which both would have a good laugh. Tusek was a skilled locksmith and made duplicates of every key he came into contact with. I saw him hide his collection of duplicates one day in the hollow behind a bulge in the wall. He would reach for them whenever goods arrived and if we didn't succeed in completely unloading a vehicle, make a note in the books and sort the discrepancy out in the warehouse.

That afternoon, trucks arrived carrying flour, rice and marmalade. Partisan attacks had rendered the railroad unsafe and the shipments increasingly arrived by truck from Karlovac. The warehouse became crowded with people and vehicles because the order had come down that this shipment be forwarded by horse cart to the unit depots located at the strategic points of the surrounding mountains.

Tusek was charged with organising the unloading and the subsequent transfer. He came across Omer, who in no time had arrived in front of the warehouse on a horse-drawn flat-bed cart. With Omer were two barefoot young men, their clothes all torn. They loaded up the flour and marmalade. Omer's pass permit to the Ripac garrison, ten kilometres away, was not recorded in the warehouse office register. Tusek was taking care of everything. Sitting on a heap of bags of flour, the black-marketeer winked at me as if I was one of his accomplices in this shady dealing. I later learned what happened after he left with his load.

Before the bridge, under which passed the shadowed river rapids, the two German military police sentries demanded Omer's documents.

"Military transport," responded Omer officiously, but when the sentries repeated their demands he did his best to keep from turning red. Taking turns poking him in the left breast with the barrels of their machine-guns, they were obviously suspicious. Slowly, he handed them his documents. The sentry looked them over and moved to return them when, at the last moment, his eye stumbled upon the signature on the document. Again, he scrutinised Omer. Taking out his ledger, he began scanning through it, looking for a signature similar to that of Tusek. He went through the ledger several times. Returning it slowly to his pocket, he stared tartly into Omer's eyes and ordered him to come down from the cart and follow him into the building by the bridge.

Once inside, they roughed him up a little and demanded to know who had signed the document for him. He replied that he didn't know the name but remembered the face well. In just a few moments, the entire German command in town was informed and all further transports were halted. Omer was escorted by two stern-looking German soldiers back to the warehouse. In the mess hall were lined up six of the warehouse sentries and managers. Among them was Tusek.

They ordered Omer to point out the person who had signed his pass permit. Without a second thought, Omer walked up to a heavy, blond German, who had often in the past arrogantly stalked around the warehouse, cursing Tusek and hissing under his breath, loud enough for them all to hear, that this riffraff should be sent to the camps. Omer pointed his finger at him. The German was surprised and smiled, not yet fully grasping the severity of the situation, before howling at Omer and delivering a direct kick to Omer's groin. A group of soldiers jumped in, brought down the fat man and, as he shouted "Pigs! Pigs!…Shit! Shit!" dragged him out of the warehouse. Tusek turned around and headed for the door without looking at Omer, who was burning from the heat and standing immobile on the spot where the German had just used his groin as a soccer ball.

The next night, I headed out with Omer to meet Emina. He had waited for me as I was returning from work and talked me into going with him.

By the market, a mass of people were crowding around something. Omer's curiosity pulled us in to see what the fuss was all about. The hunchbacked produce peddler, Noko, recognised Omer and shouted from ten metres away: "Rodjo killed a snake. That one had short, strong legs! It weighs at least forty pounds! Two legs, just like a man!"

Rodjo had nailed the snake onto a board and stood it up in the middle of the crowd. It was over two metres in length and as thick as a large fist. Its legs were short, thick and located half a metre from the end of its tail. Its feet were similar to that of a lizard but much larger and hairier.

"Where did you find this creature!?" shouted Omer from between several of Rodjo's fellow peddlers, who refused to allow him to get any closer to Rodjo and the snake.

"In Grabez," he answered self-importantly, "I'm picking strawberries between bigger bushes when, suddenly, this thing roars at me like a bear. Brother, I was startled. My brain ran off and I couldn't remember a single passage to pray to Allah."

"Shut up, you idiots!" snapped a yellow-bearded type to the chattering group around him, who must have already heard Rodjo's story a dozen times.

"It all took place so quickly, lightning speed," continued Rodjo, trying to convey with his eyes the fear he had felt in the strawberry field. "It stood erect on these little legs like a man. I turned around and ran. It made a cracking sound and slithered after me. Luckily, I came across a heavy stick, picked it up and began madly hitting everything around me. I got lucky and connected with its head. It backed off among the strawberries, shooting its tongue at me and hissing. Seeing that I had dazed it, I regained my courage, gripped that club and whacked it on the head, over and over again. Each time, I hit it on the head, and only on the head."

True enough, the creature's head was mangled. One eye dangled by a thread from its socket.

The crowd continued to grow, tongues loosened and a lively murmur could be heard from all sides.

"A monster sent by God," was the only response a woman behind me could come up with, over and over.

"What monster!?" snapped Omer, as if angered by the woman's superstition. "It's an aesculapian snake. That's all. They are big and rare but they are harmless. No monster."

I had heard of aesculapian snakes but I didn't know what they looked like, especially that this kind of snake could have two legs.

"Some of our people are so primitive and superstitious that it makes you sick when you hear them think. If I hadn't shut her up, she would have gone on about how this monster was surely a foreboding of greater evil yet to come and how this evil would come from the forest just like the snake. It would all gather steam from there and someone would figure out that all this meant that the lamb-skin-jacketed peasants and the Chetniks were going to attack the town…Yet, we all know well that such a thing cannot happen. The Partisans up there are weak and poorly armed. They wouldn't even think of attacking a force such as this."

As Omer spoke, under his eye he was looking for my reactions with interest. I remained as expressive as a rock. Ever since he had mentioned my brother, I had carefully weighed each and every word that I exchanged with him.

"You refugees don't have it easy either," he changed the course of the conversation. "Those up there threw you out, while these down here don't trust you. Those that stayed behind probably have it much easier."

I considered telling him to stop trying to test me, that I had had enough of all this insanity and wished that I could crawl into a mouse hole and hibernate until better times. I wanted to throw his way the thought that I sympathised with every person who has to suffer and be killed because of someone's politics. Especially those whose legs are tied, like that of a horse who is always trying to run away, and who are pushed forward against their will. Standing there next to him, I became unbearably sick of all the black-marketeers and profiteers who were so quick to lecture others on their morals and duties while, at the same time, never themselves missing an opportunity to rob those who had the least.

"I'm thirsty," I said, motioning with my head toward the water which was splashing from the water-wheel next to the wooden bridge. "More than anything, I need a drink of water."

Realising that I refused to enter into any compromising conversation, Omer spat into the dark-green river.

Emina wore a long, pleated skirt made from some light material and a yellow and green shirt with large white buttons. Her jet-black hair was slicked back and tied into a pony-tail. Her green eyes cut through me like a knife but the worst of it came when she bent over and handed me a three-legged stool to sit on. The sight of her glistening thighs and calves glistening through the translucent material became permanently etched in my memory. Years later, I struggled unsuccessfully to do justice to those thighs on one of my figurines.

Her skin was as dark as that of a beautiful Gypsy at the end of a long, hot summer. Her complexion was dark as twilight, like the color of an unripe plum when you touch the dawn's fog of its skin.

She seemed more beautiful than Zemka. Yet, there was something else which raised her above my memories of Zemka. Her entire person radiated intelligence, a delineated sharpness and energy. This was especially evident in the brows and forehead.

When she bent over to pick up the stool, she did it with such elegance of movement and so unhurriedly that I was certain that her aim was to keep my eyes glued on her for as long as possible; to arouse my feelings, my manly desires. The conclusion shot through me that she had sent Omer over to the mill where her father was so that we could be alone, so that she could toy further with my heartbroken refugee emotions.

What followed quickly brought me back to earth and reality. Emina put the stool down between us, placed her hand on my shoulder and just at the moment when I decided to pull her into my arms and cover her with kisses, she stepped back and ran her fingers in a motherly way through my hair.

"Only your hair is the same, and the surly expression of your mouth...I got to know your brother up in the woods. He is a hero.

Smart enough to choose the right side in this chaos." As she spoke my body grew cold and lost all of its passionate feelings more quickly than I thought possible. The sweat which had come out of me during my excitement turned so icy cold that I began to chatter. The sudden frost and the internal disappointment completely stopped my breathing and blood-flow.

"Again Osman!" the thought bubbled in me. I was unable to stanch my growing hatred toward my own brother. "My life is full of Osman. But why now, when this woman was about to draw me into something closer to hope and sanctuary?!"

I wasn't listening to what she was saying. My revulsion toward my brother brought my thoughts back to our childhood. In a few seconds, my mind fell upon numerous such incidents. I thought back to the many times when all I needed was one more step, one more second, to succeed, till victory, only to have him enter like a devil. It seemed like he was always standing behind me, waiting for the right moment to deny me my triumph. He knew all of my moves in advance, while I knew none of his. He had told me about Zemka and the Captain in order to justify his crime. He had placed the entire burden on my shoulders, and realised his own sick victory. I was his clown, his private refugee, whom he could deny happiness at will, constantly pushing me onward from the places where I wanted to stay. Was my transcendent relationship with our dead mother his doing, part of his plan to forever keep me wrapped up in uncertainty?

"You can't refuse this jelly* from roses," declared Emina, handing me a chunk of the sweet smelling stuff. "Up on the highland you don't have roses like ours. You people are cruder than us. When we met the first time, when you brought corn to grind at our mill, that wasn't a time to talk about love. My father was behind the fence, hoeing around the turnips in the garden. He could have overheard us. Around here, we don't talk about such things around our parents. But you stubborn, you went ahead anyway and decided to show me your love. Pardon the slap I gave you."

I told her, with a smile on my lips, that she was mistaken; it wasn't me that she had slapped but my brother Osman. She didn't understand what I meant by that. Tearing off some of the jelly, I gave the remainder back it to her, which she accepted without surprise. I didn't take my eyes off her. Her lips were even redder now.

"I didn't call you here to apologise for the slap. Between men and women, such things don't call for apologies. Anyway, a slap from a friendly hand is sweeter than jelly from an unfriendly one…I called you here because we need you. Osman said that we could count on you and that your faith is harder than a rock."

Questioning her about who exactly it was that had faith in me and needed me, even though I had known everything from the moment she mentioned that she had met my brother in the woods, maybe even as far back as when Omer suggested that he take me to see Emina, I refused to make things easy for her.

"We must win!" she told me, even though I didn't ask. "In this war, good must triumph. We are fighting for the people, for life and happiness. Not just the happiness of a few, but of everyone. We are not spreading hate, butchering or burning." Her voice had changed, as if she was speaking from a podium.

"From the very start of this war, I have seen completely the opposite: only hatred, butchering and burning. I was forced to leave my doorstep and come live among these strangers here. I also was up in the woods which you keep on praising, and nearly lost my head. The woods are also full of butchers and firebugs. Just like the towns. Only the uniforms are different. Daggers there, and daggers here… Fires here, and fires there…Very little is different.

"We must rise above this. The daggers will be defeated, the fires extinguished!" she retorted, her face taking on the colours of deep thought and melancholy.

"That much is true," I answered, conceding her the obvious.

"The Party is fighting for our future. For all our people. Your brother joined the Party long ago and we have decided that you should also join us. But here. It is worse here than in the woods."

We were both silent for quite some time. She was waiting for my reaction. Trying to hide my rage, I bit down on my lip. I had imagined our meeting would be completely different from the way it was turning out.

I wanted her as a woman but she stood before me as a soldier fighting the enemy, a member of the Party which I knew but didn't trust. I had ceased to believe in anyone from this land of ours. While I only wanted to sleep through this war, she was calling on me to take part in the fighting by joining the underground and placing myself in the direct path of the combined German and Ustasha forces. She was calling on me to join the Party which Osman had always refused to have me involved with. He didn't believe that I was capable. For the longest time, I had suspected that his satanic mind had staged the events of my visit to the meeting in Vavan's cellar, and the entire hellish night, only to demonstrate his dominance over me. Now, this woman was handing me membership in the Party on a platter and claiming that it was the only worthy side in this orgy of killing. Killing is destruction, regardless of who does what to whom and why. Is it more humane and justifiable to butcher in the name of a better tomorrow and some vague ideals?!

"Killing is killing! They are all butchers to me. There is no difference," I said, looking directly at her eyes.

"The fight against the criminals and enemies of our people must pass through a sea of blood," she declared, her eyes glittering and cheeks flushed red.

"So, you are suggesting that I murder for the sake of the future of humanity. That I become one more criminal in the battle against other criminals." I struck back at her this way even though I also knew that's how it had to be. Simply, I followed the logic she had introduced and by twisting it out of shape attempted to provoke her. I wanted to see at least a crack in her armour. I wanted to see her helpless, speechless... The wounded refugee within me had come to life: the homeless exile who instead of a moment of passionate ecstasy was being offered a bloody battle for a better tomorrow.

"You want our soldiers to take the bayonets from their rifles, to throw away the daggers and allow them to fall into the hands of the enemy. I tell you, a true humanist has come to lead us, offering a bloodless struggle! I am going to tell them in the Party that one true humanist is offering bloodless war...The New Messiah has appeared and he will lead the people to freedom and defeat the bloodthirsty enemy without shedding the blood of the weak and the innocent... without shedding the blood of anybody."

"No!" I jumped in. "You don't see who you are leading into the battle. You think that you will succeed by defeating the butchers in the woods and these in the towns. What you don't see is that the butchers will be victorious. One will defeat the other. It remains in us, pardon, in you! It remains in the people! We will forever be killing one another. Do you really think that this will be the last of the butchery, if you win? If you think that there will be no more killing, then you are blind!" I was becoming enraged. "These are stories for little children! These current graves won't even be grown over before a whole new patch of them is again planted. There is something inside us...If you win and if your Party manages to strain out the thirst for blood from our people, then you will truly be successful. It is easier to defeat someone else than yourself. If you turn these blood-thirsty vampires into people, then you will be victorious. But, vampires cannot do this to themselves." I was enjoying my temporary advantage, regardless of the fact that I had no idea where I was summoning these ideas from.

Emina was being Emina: beautiful, fragrant, amazed. She couldn't keep her nose from turning red, or the tears from accumulating on her lower eyelids, though she did manage to keep them from running down her cheeks.

"I know, Yudja," she admitted, now speaking as if to a friend. "My brother was among the first to join the Ustashas. We heard that he is somewhere in Herzegovina. Father thinks that he is somewhere up in these hills. If he really knew what his son was up to, he would die of shame."

I told her that I didn't know anything about her brother and hadn't intended to insult her but that I was not joining anyone's army. I would help them when my help was needed but I was dead-set against joining any army.

Our conversation remained unfinished because Omer appeared with Emina's father. However, it seemed to me that it didn't leave either of us indifferent. Emina remained convinced of my sympathy toward her and the Party while I was left feeling more confident and richer for having remained firm in my decision.

"If you are trying to save your family's honour and your father's pride, sacrificing yourself is the wrong way to go about it," I snatched a moment to whisper to her as the other two were busy discussing the details of starting up the flour mill to meet Omer's growing demands.

She understood the gist of my warning but remained firm in her convictions.

"Better the grave than being a slave!" she reminded me, the simple-minded slogan which the Party was using to urge the people to rise up.

"And life?" I asked, again trying to provoke her. "Maybe, I'll follow you into the Party if you will guarantee me that I will kill nobody and stay alive, and if we win, I'll be as free as a bird. And, that I'll be free to say which flock I belong to…And, that I'll be able to sing whatever song my heart desires…"

She amazed me with the sharpness of her mind: "Yes, exactly…You won't be forced to say that you are that which you are not. Finally, we will be able to say that we are Bosniaks, without the Serbs or Croats thinking it to be a threat."

"The young man is tired, Mina," her father interjected into our conversation. "Perhaps he thinks different. If we let you, you'd lecture us till dawn. It's too bad that the war cut short her schooling." He turned to me. "She was studying philosophy in Zagreb even though she had no need for it," he winked as if we had known each other since childhood and he was confiding to a close friend. "She has been a real philosopher ever since she could walk and talk. Sometimes when I listen to her, I mistake her for some coarse fellow from the café, instead of the beauty that she really is." As he spoke, his hand reflexively reached for her lush black hair.

CHAPTER X

Deep under the rocky shore, the ocean was unleashing its fury against the coast's successful resistance. It was using all its force to pound, shove and foam against the concrete quay of North Vancouver harbour. In the odd place, it managed to break through the barriers and make an insignificant cut, only to be driven off elsewhere. The steel grey colour of the water mingled with the dark sky as it tried to rush the paler coast. Various shades of grey fought for supremacy, the outcome never in doubt. Two men stood just above the furthest reach of the salt spray.

"It's nothing like the Adriatic," Yudja spoke out what had been in his mind countless times since his arrival. "Our sea is full of life. It has a clearer, softer colour…Waters differ just like people," he sighed as he followed the flight path of two seagulls who disinterestedly flew toward the port which was congested with shipping cranes and dark freighters.

Fehrat relaxed the wooden part of his leg against the slope they stood on, while his healthy leg stayed firmly grounded against the brown root of an evergreen tree. This was similar to ones found along the Adriatic coast, the only difference being in the latter's overpowering resin odour and the deafening sound of the crickets which were certain to be present around them.

"What do you mean 'our'?" questioned Fehrat, "You mean, the sea that once used to be ours? That was once, and it has all passed, Yudja."

Yudja understood what Fehrat was getting at. In fact, he had never considered that Adriatic to be his. He had gone there several times on summer holidays, but at night the heat and humidity of the coast would be suffocating. He would spend the days spread out asleep on the sandy beaches. While even up on the mountains the daily stifling summer heat was a normal occurrence, the nights that he was accustomed to were very different, cooler and without the constant sweat which the sea coast would strain out of every man the entire night.

"Do you believe in destiny?" Yudja unexpectedly asked. "Who would have thought that I would find myself here, on the other side of the world, at the end of my life," he answered his own question.

"I believe it," Fehrat nevertheless answered. His eyes followed a tanker as it headed off into the distance. "Perhaps that is one of the tankers built in our shipyards for the Norwegian oil company... Perhaps it's one of those that they called 'Istra-Berge'*. One of them split apart out on the open sea, while the other two are still afloat. For the one that sank, they initially blamed the builder. Later, it was proven that the blame lay with the ship's owners, who had tried to cheat the insurance company by transferring their own guilt."

Yudja tried to remember the incident that Fehrat had mentioned but his thoughts strayed along the grey water and toward the Atlantic, to some town in the vicinity of Miami from which the day before he had received a letter sent by Alma and Delveta. Those days, both he and Fehrat had been busy visiting various institutions, looking for one which would assist Fehrat in getting his prosthesis. Then, two surprises occurred in short order. First, the morning before, Fehrat had asked if Yudja could take him to a nearby karate club. After asking around, he found the name and location of the nearest one and took him there. Though he knew that Fehrat had practised karate previously, now with his crippling injuries he was surely no longer fit for the sport. He was satisfied by Fehrat's explanation that he simply wished to see how the locals trained.

Second, when he opened the letter and read that his wife and daughter were writing from America, the hairs on the back of his neck immediately stood upright. He wanted to beat on something and scream, to wish himself a pair of wings and fly to Bosnia and send down a rain of thunderbolts upon each and every one of the individuals whom he considered responsible for the misery which had befallen him and his family. Eventually, he calmed down, began to think clearly and came to the conclusion that it was certainly preferable to be an American than a Balkanian, or especially some unfortunate Bosnian. The only piece of unhappiness that he was unable to drive out of his heart related to the impossibility of his going to join them and spending the remainder of his life with them. He had his own belief in destiny and as soon as he concluded that something had occurred because fate had willed it so, he would retreat as if from something unfathomable yet demanding respect.

"Destiny," he sighed like a man who has just had a heavy load taken of his back.

Fehrat realised that the old man was waiting to hear his thoughts on the matter, his own feelings about destiny, but he hesitated after a worm in the back of his mind warned him to beware of the possibility that Yudja was trying to provoke him, to find out something which had up to now remained unexplained between the two of them. Nevertheless, he responded:

"Each of us has his own idea of what destiny is, but the only common thread is that everyone considers destiny to be that which is out of their control. That is their consolation when they begin to re-evaluate their lives. It allows everyone to flee the admission of personal failure."

All the while, Fehrat followed the movement of the tanker, which was heading toward Asia.

"In fact, destiny is a program which is out of our reach. We do not know the language of this program or have the code which activates it. We only find out when it is activated and the results change our lives." He was speaking as if to a group of students. "In the nucleus of each creature exists a program which directs its development, shape, metamorphosis, composition, level of intelligence."

"Therefore, you think that destiny exists within us but we don't know how to uncover it," countered Yudja, accepting Fehrat's method of debate. "I've never read anything relating to that."

"How could you?" Fehrat raised the tone of his voice. "You only read the books that were published during the Communist era, when the only ideas that were allowed to pass were those in line with official materialist teachings. Everything that went further than meat, skin and bones was rejected. Destiny is not related to this. In those books, there is a program which feeds on matter just as we need to eat to be able to live."

It seemed that this opportunity to theorize came as a blessing to Fehrat. Here, far from the world which had formed him but which continued to hold him firmly in its grip, he could now articulate his protest, even if his entire audience consisted of just the one old man before him who probably believed in their fateful bond.

"Darwin was mumbling when he spoke of the nucleus. He suspected that the program of development of human beings is mystical because one needs to look into extra-material and extraterrestrial relations. He had eyes and intellect only for that which Mother Earth had to offer. Who then is the Father who inseminates Mother Earth? Who dictates the program in matter? Who creates destiny? None of the scientists knew this because they were slaves to matter. They couldn't even allow themselves to wonder if matter was only energy meant for something more significant."

Yudja looked at him, unable to hide his feeling of satisfaction.

"You've surprised me," he responded in a congratulatory tone, "I thought that perhaps you would say that destiny doesn't exist because the Party said so. You know that you can't belong to the Party without thinking what that Party wants you to think. That is why I was in its proximity a long time but never its member. Simply said, I was a creek running parallel to a great river, always fearful of its main current."

"I was a member but that's a long story. I left the Party when one of the worst students that I ever had became the local president. He couldn't think, nor could he write. You must have heard of Bulic? Now he is one of the commanders in the defense of Bihac. He may be a good soldier but he was a pitiful student."

"I've been waiting for you to mention Bihac, so I could continue the story. I'm feeling an inexplicable pressure on my lungs and around my heart. I'm worried that I may not manage to finish it," he confided, all the while smiling, as if he didn't want Fehrat to believe his grievances.

"I'm not worried about you," came the quick reply. "You have more strength than the likes of five such as myself. You still have a lot of work ahead of you. There are many more figurines which have yet to be carved. Since I've arrived, you have completely forgotten about your art. It is an old truth, going back all the way to the Egyptian sculptor Minadir, that the artist cannot die before he has completed his masterpiece. You have been give the gift of creation but you have not been given the power to choose the time and place of your death."

Both observed with melancholy interest the ship which was distancing itself from the shore. It looked like an eggshell on the foamy ocean surface, though it was visibly moving away.

"Whatever moves," thought Fehrat, "succeeds, to a point, in resisting time. Whatever remains still, loses without any resistance."

The fighting around Bihac intensified but the town was still relatively safe (Yudja continued his story from Second World War). We found out about the German and Ustasha losses from the retaliations against the town's Serbs. When they couldn't get revenge up in the mountains, they looked for their blood tribute in town.

Time passed by for me as it does for a bird in a cage. I got used to it, accepting the new pace of life, and it would have been strange not to have the cage surround me. They didn't call me up into the army because it had been noted that I had suffered from stomach typhus and would be unfit for military service for some time to come. Such treatment was fine with me, even though I felt completely healthy.

Father found work with a merchant who had arrived in Bihac with the wave of refugees from Kulen-Vakuf. Most of the time he seemed withdrawn despite all of his attempts to hide this from us. My aunt waged a daily battle for the bare necessities needed to feed us. The more kunas* we had, the more difficult it became to buy flour and cooking oil.

The townsfolk adjusted to life under occupation. The period of peace and seeming security lasted for quite a long time. The first signs of upheaval came during the middle of the second year of the war, somehow in sync with the arrival in Bihac of the first larger Italian units.

The Germans held themselves to be above the rest of the town's inhabitants, probably in accordance with the superior feelings natural to members of the Aryan race. Their only contact with the people came during retaliations and executions and this task they usually left to the Ustashas.

The Italians were something completely different. As soon as they arrived, music filled the streets, which instantly seemed to come alive. The children's pockets were filled with chocolates and the women were given various perfumes. The town's whores were automatically accorded special status, while the respectable families immediately set about fixing their high courtyard gates and locking them up at sunset. Simply put, all of the women now found themselves in danger.

I came into contact with Emina occasionally. We were acquaintances, and when we met Omer was usually around. Omer was increasingly opening up to me and I discovered that he was one of the leading scroungers for the Partisans, supplying them with ammunition and other necessities from the German storage dumps. He considered me a friend but kept me out of his shady dealings. Often he would say: "Never mind…Sooner or later, we will need you. Just you do your job well in the warehouse and gain the trust of the supervisors."

I concluded that soon I would be given a significant assignment and was upset by my sitting-duck role. I had no desire for any assignments and was happiest when I noticed how quickly a day had passed. Simply put, I wanted time to pass me by as fast as possible.

I first met your mother quite by accident. Esma was five or six years younger than me and when I was a young man she was still a girl. Your uncle Ekrem I knew from occasionally seeing him in the town's square but he also was younger and we did not socialize.

That fateful day, the Cherkessians* had come to Bihac. Their unit had moved down the River Una canyon from the city of Priyedor. They rode large, long-legged horses; on their backs were long-barreled rifles; across their chests were belts full of bullets and on their heads were black fur hats. They entered howling and shooting, leaving behind them a trail of horse manure. They were headquartered in the large old school house right by the river. They brought fear with them. A war atmosphere covered the town. Far from the German arrogance and discipline, from the loud music and Don Juan insanity of the Italians, these Cherkessians were true barbarians; aggressive, loud, filthy, unshaven, one hand always on the trigger, the other on the sheath of the sabre. Above all, they were violent sodomites. With their arrival, the number of rapes increased dramatically. Not only were all women in danger but men, especially older boys, were also frequent victims. The plague had come to Bihac.

I was returning home one day from work with Tusek. The day was peaceful and hot.

"Let's stop by at Ivan's and have a drink," suggested Tusek as we approached the house next to the bridge. We entered the garden of the Pavilion, a cosy little café at the river's edge, and headed toward the tables which were situated right next to the water. Behind the café, in the shallow water, a group of children here horsing around. From behind the willow patch, approaching the playing children, emerged a rowboat. Standing in the middle, a young man pushed the boat along with a long pole while in front and behind him sat two girls. Suddenly, from one of the willow trees, two men jumped into the water and began to swim furiously toward the rowboat. We immediately realised that they were Cherkessians. They overturned the boat, grabbed the girls and began to drag them along to the clumps of willows on the shore. The girls were screaming and when the young man attempted to defend them he was met with a shower of blows to the head and soon sank into the water.

As if on command, Tusek and I jumped over the fence and ran through the shallow water toward the willow patch. Tusek threw off his cardigan as he ran and I my shirt before we both dove into the deeper water. As soon as they noticed us, the Cherkessians let go of the girls and rushed toward us. Tusek was an enormous man and the water in which the short Cherkessians were swimming reached up only to his shoulders. When they reached him, he grabbed them by the necks and pushed them under. They threw punches like possessed madmen trying to reach his head but Tusek's arms were too long. He held them under the water while I tried to find the young man. The girls had made it to shore and immediately began shouting: "There is Ekrem! Over there!"

Seeing how he was trying to keep his head above water, I swam toward him. As I pulled him to shore, I noticed that Tusek had already unceremoniously deposited the two Cherkessians in the shallow area. When they finally managed to get to their feet they observed Tusek's hulking figure in disbelief, all the while rubbing their eyes in an effort to regain their composure, before running off as far away from us as they could get.

The young man was your uncle Ekrem, and one of the girls was your mother. From then on, and for years to come, Ekrem and I were great friends.

I adjusted to my life as a refugee just as a man adjusts to living with a shrewish woman. If I had been a woman, the roles would probably have been reversed. We Psetian refugees quickly realised how different we were from the people we now lived among. Though only fifty kilometres separated our mountain highlands from their damp valley, the differences were great. I heard it in their speech, saw it in their customs and, increasingly, in their characters, the direction of their emotions. These people were softer, and wrapped in a fog, emancipated but elastic enough to always be prepared to say to your face "How's it going, friend!" only to show you the middle finger the moment your back was turned, along with the obligatory hiss of *Peasant!* I wasn't overjoyed to come to the conclusion that we had more in common with the Psetian Orthodox Serbs that we did with the Muslims of Bihac. The inhabitants of Bihac obviously felt the same way and would often point out to us that a refugee had to live among them for at least half a century before they would stop considering him a newcomer. This feeling of not belonging awakened within us a melancholy and the hope that we would soon be able to return to our highlands.

With the change in the colour of the River Una's depths, from intense dark green to a more grey green colour, nature was informing all concerned of the transition from scorching summer heat to the long autumn rains. This change was most evident in the early mornings: at the very onset of dawn a haze began to gather above the water's surface. As the days progressed, its tufts began to grow thicker and wider, rising up to meet and embrace the willow trees, creating mystical shapes among the branches. Thereafter, with increasing frequency, from the direction where a couple of hours later the first rays of sun would break through, came the sound of wild geese high above the haze.

With the beginning of autumn there also came news of increasingly bitter fighting up in the mountains. In Bihac, reprisals were once again carried out and the innocent fell victim in front of the walls of the old part of town and from the branches of the trees which lined the streets.

That great changes were about to occur was made clear by two events. Somehow synchronized, hand in hand, came the first Partisan cannon fire from the woods and the illegitimate children. The first shut the mouths of the Ustashas and their sympathisers, who had until now mockingly talked about the bandits up in the woods, dressed in furs and armed with clubs and pitch-forks. The second came as the inevitable after-effect of every war which is waged by men and in which tormenting and raping is just a part of the general mood of moral anarchy.

One morning, from the willow patch below the bridge came news that someone had drowned. When they brought the body to shore, they noticed that it was that of a woman with a noticeably grown stomach. Word spread that the drowned woman was Redzic's widow, whose husband had been killed in front of his blacksmith's shop when the first shells fell on the town just before the Germans entered Bihac. She had tried to hide her stomach behind loose and bulky clothing, but when the child began moving its legs and when Ragib, her father-in-law, had noticed the change in her appearance, she threw herself before him and pleaded:

"Father, they caught me in the woodshed. Two of them held me down while the third one dishonored me. Take care of my son Asim!"

The night swallowed her up and, on the third morning, the water threw her out into the willows under the bridge.

Soon after, illegitimate children began sprouting like popcorn above a grill fire: at first, a couple of isolated instances, but then with increasing regularity and noise. Women gave birth in barns, behind sheds, in willow groves, without midwives present or anyone else to help. Many women died along with their babies, many babies were swallowed up by the Una and taken down its cascades toward the mute canyon. Omer told me how he had discovered that some women who had thrown their babies into the river in the darkness of night wept by the shore, lit candles and left them at the places from where they had thrown their infants. Others also saw the candles at night and passed on the story of how people were seeing things over by the willows, how the souls of those murdered in the reprisals made their way over from the pit graves up on the Garavice Hills to the river's shore and spent each night lighting candles and sobbing.

The climax came one Friday during prayers when the local Imam, in between references to Allah and lecturing, whispered to those in the first rows that an angel had called to him and said that they should all be kneeling for the souls from the river and that soon the water under the bridge would turn bloody red.

The atmosphere of fear was simultaneously increased by stories of the Imam's angel and the more numerous artillery rounds which fell on the town.

One night, while we dined, Omer knocked on the door and said that I had to go with him before the call to evening prayer.

I immediately knew that his visit was connected to Emina and his frequent claim that the time would come when I would be needed. It occurred to me that perhaps it would be better for me to say directly to his face that I simply wanted to be left in peace, that I had no interest in them or their illegal activities and that, for that matter, there was nothing of interest for me in this entire nightmare they called war. However, my father was standing behind me. Now that I think of it, I doubt that I would have had the courage to say anything to Omer even if Father had not been there. Simply, there was no coordination between my thoughts and actions. I would find myself without an ounce of energy or will whenever thought needed to be turned into deed. It was like turning on a light switch, and then watching the current fill up the bulb only to see the filament disintegrate from excess electricity. Darkness remained darkness.

The same thoughts refused to leave me in peace as I sat with Emina under the quince tree in the orchard between her house and the river. Twilight had passed from the water's surface to the orchard and conquered the tree tops while Emina patiently delivered her monologue regarding my thoughts, as if we were Siamese twins.

"Don't be angry if I tell you that I am worried about your spiritual state," she went on, as the torrent of her words mingled with the melody of the millions of drops of water diving into the icy foam below the rapids, which formed a natural watershed since from there on the Una settled down and quietly flowed toward the canyon, where it would again go wild and rush toward the Panonian plains.

"I don't believe that the warehouse is sufficient to quench your thirst for life," she continued. "But perhaps such a thirst does not exist within you. Perhaps you are like the branch which the rushing water has torn from the tree. You are not a branch, Yudja! It is possible to return. We can continue to live on even after being torn away."

"What have I to look forward to?" I murmured, provoking her. "The ones up there ran me off, while down here—with each passing day I notice more revulsion toward us refugees. By tomorrow, it will have turned to hate and soon you will be trying to murder us, just as they did up there. Even you insulted me the first time I laid eyes on you."

The raised tone of my last words she understood to convey my insistence upon an answer to my early offer of love. She turned red and reached for my hand, hesitant as a child attempting to pet a large animal. I had run out of ideas. I felt an overwhelming desire to throw myself into her lap, while she quickly withdrew her hand. She was adeptly moving the strings. I felt ashamed over my growing feebleness.

"They drove you away by force. It would be pathetic if you remain this way for the rest of your life. If you continue to feel yourself to be a refugee, Yudja, after a while such treatment will become preferable to you. If you use it as a defence, an excuse, it will serve merely to cover your weakness. We are all refugees." Her voice became softer, as if coming from somewhere near the rapids. "From the day we are born, we can all cry that we have been driven against our will from our mother's womb. We can all say: I was thrown out…from where I felt best!" This whole earth is ours. If you want to be a refugee, everywhere you will find some guttersnipe who will be more than happy to drive you away."

I sat before Emina as a student sits before a teacher. Secretly, I hoped that she would reveal herself to me as the woman that she was, while she continued trying to convince me that I must not lose hope, that I must stop being so depressed and indifferent.

"Let's walk over to the rapids." She stood up and held out her hand. "I thought that you people from up in the mountains were afraid of water but I was convinced otherwise by the stories I heard of how you rushed into the Una and fought off the Cherkessians."

The night was warm and dark. There were no clouds in the sky, but the light of the stars was distant and weak.

"When those colossal flames up there are so insignificantly small to the human eye, then imagine how we humans must seem to them," I thought to myself as I followed Emina to the increasingly boisterous rapids. That which the darkness hid of the body which walked in front of me, my imagination made up for. Even though I instinctively rebelled against her cheerfulness and optimism, wishing perhaps that the entire world would accept my depression and feelings of rejection, when I was near her the juices of life came back to me.

When I placed my hand on her waist from behind, she twisted away like a deer trying to avoid hunting dogs, instinctively withdrawing the body part closest to their eager jaws. In her twisting there was the attempt to elegantly escape a potentially uneasy situation. But her reaction was lukewarm, not desperate—for us men, an unmistakable signal to make one more lunging attempt. I grabbed hold of her with my other hand as well and glued myself to her back. The trembling of her body did not seem like that of a woman who only moments before had spoken to me of human dignity in such tones of superiority.

Our contact lasted only a few seconds but the warmth and feeling of our blood meeting will remain vivid in my memory till the day I die. The entire length of my body I wound around her. In several places where our bodies met, I began to boil. By her shaking I could tell that she was also enjoying the contact. Gently, she took my hands away from her waist, turned to face me and buried her incisor teeth into my neck. She began kissing me, covering my neck with her lips, when something happened and she bit me again.

"Father!" she whispered. "Father is somewhere near. He went out to catch fish for supper."

Just then, off in the distance, I heard a rattling. The sounds were murmured and differed from the rushing water of the rapids.

She stooped, and waited to feel me behind her.

"What is the point of all this between you and me in a world such as ours? As long as the evil surrounding us exists, love is absurd. Do you want me to end up like all of these women by the river?" She extended her hand in the direction of the unusual rattling noise. "Man's hatred created children which they were forced to throw into the river. Now their only contact with the drowned infants is their weeping…Weeping under the cover of night's darkness so that they won't be discovered and further humiliated."

When I realised what was going on, the rattling became clearer: tens of female cries combined and mixed with the rushing sound of the water. Through the willow branches, I could see the lit candles on the other side of the river.

"What a haunting scene," whispered Emina, as if not wishing to disturb the mothers' contact with their drowned babies. "Can there be a greater crime?" her rough voice accused. "You men have no idea what evil you are able to do to us women. And we…we…we can only weep and light candles. You drive us to murder our new-born…And those who will be born…Your entire minds will think of nothing else but how to invite war and murder our children."

We remained silent for what seemed the longest time. My desire to embrace and hold her disappeared like some blasphemy. Finally, we realised that it was time to return home.

"Our troops will soon attack the town. The two of us must blow up the railroad in three places from Srbljani to Pokoj. That is our assignment." She spoke to me as if talking through a telegraph. "We have to do it, also, because of those women weeping on the other side. Our soldiers would never commit such outrages. Once they are in power, the women will no longer be forced to feed their infants to the rapids."

"I don't know anything about mining a railroad," I pointed out, not meaning to oppose her in any way.

"I know everything that needs to be done. You will carry the load. I will set the explosives."

As the stranglehold of Tito's Partisan units tightened around the Bihac Valley, the food shortage in the town became more desperate. Soon, the only means of communication for the military forces in Bihac with their co-belligerents in other parts of the occupied country was through the air. Wide regions of the Bosnian Krajina, Lika, Banija and Kordun had been liberated by the Partisans.

The population became increasingly hungry. When famine knocked at the doors of the local inhabitants, its fist was hardest and loudest at the homes of the refugee families. People began to cook everything that could be cooked. Flour became a luxury while salt, sugar and oil were just exotic words. Hunger began to rule over the town. There was nothing to be had from the army, and black marketeers were executed like dogs.

Shelling of the town from the surrounding mountains became an everyday event. First the sirens would sound and then the artillery rounds would begin falling upon the centre of town. With the passing of time, the calibre of the cannon steadily increased. The Partisans were returning that which they had taken from the enemy. The ones who paid the highest price for their revenge were the ordinary townspeople. The sirens signaled the beginning of a barrage while the howling of the dogs began soon after the last echo of the explosions had died down.

The howling of the dogs was something else. Such howling could never be heard in times of peace.

There developed a rhythm to the process which preceded the final assault on the town. At dawn, the people would quietly emerge into the streets. Men, women and children, like an enormous river, would mutely make their way to the nearest woods. They would remain there until dusk, when they would return in the same manner, quickening their tempo only if they noticed that their house or barn had been hit. Thus, the number of funerals was drastically brought down, though every evening fewer people would return from the woods. Many made their way higher up into the mountains and joined the Partisan units.

My father and aunt were a part of this unusual human tide which moved toward the forest in the morning and returned back to town in the evening. Zjakic's family followed the same pattern. Emina, Omer and I remained in town throughout. I, naturally, in the warehouse. At first, the dogs also stayed behind. After a barrage, they would rush to each spot where a round had fallen, in search of food. Soon enough, though, they joined the rhythm of the rest of the town's inhabitants. The only ones who remained were the bitches with their pups, and the old and crippled. There would be a full-scale outburst of howling when the dogs returned from the woods and saw the damage done to their lairs. Only at nightfall did it die down. In the daily migration from town to the woods and back there were always casualties; in the fights over scraps of food, and from sticks and stones thrown their way. In all this chaos it was hard to say who had it worse, the dogs or the humans. The only certainty for both was that their greatest problem was the children—their crying and screaming when there was no food to give them; their pleading faces and the parents' efforts to avoid eye contact at all costs.

"I don't know how things are up on the mountains," Father uttered in misery, "but this life as an outcast is the lowest I have ever reached. If only I could detach myself from this back-and-forth insanity between town and the woods, even if it means having to march to hell and back in full army gear. Sometimes the urge comes over me to go out into the street and join in the howling of those cursed dogs."

One afternoon, Emina sent word that she was waiting for me at her father's mill. I found her standing by the enormous water wheel, looking obviously troubled. Ever since her father began spending his days in the woods, the water-mill had been working only at night.

"The German's are using large numbers of troops to keep the railroad tracks to Bosanski Novi safe and working. They are expecting major reinforcements to arrive in Bihac any time now. Tomorrow night, we have to carry out our assignment." She said this, the whole time staring at the water, before begging me to immediately return to the warehouse before anyone noticed us conspiring.

The next evening, I waited for my father and aunt by the front gate. The daily trek to the woods and back had created a waxen look of aimlessness on their faces. I told them that I would not be home that night because I was going fishing with friends.

I'd reached half-way down the street when I turned around—to see old Zjakic and his wife returning to their home. The venerable thatch-covered house, surrounded by a high wooden fence, bore more resemblance to a scorched photograph than an object inside which life had found shelter.

I couldn't hide my surprise when I found Tusek sitting on the long wooden bench under Emina's grape vines. He was also visibly surprised.

"I'm waiting for an experienced saboteur, and along comes this refugee!" He held out his hand toward me while speaking to Emina, who stood behind him. His smile was full of good nature as can be found only in such a giant of a man.

"And you chose this mountain to come with us," I tried to return the jibe. "We'll be discovered before we even start."

We headed out as soon as the dark hat of night covered even the crests of the western mountains. We played the part of three youths going out fishing, with Emina looking like a very gaunt one at that and still awaiting the first whiskers to make an appearance. On our backs we carried fishing haversacks, inside of which was portioned our destructive equipage wrapped in rags. Our poles looked more like spears than willow fishing rods, but the darkness of night helped hide our secret.

First we crossed the corn fields, where we struggled against unavoidable rustling, then the meadows with their thick, uncut grass and finally the soft earth which signaled the close proximity of the river. Emina led us directly to a rowboat hidden in a thick willow patch. Its perfect adaptation to the dark surroundings gave me more reasons to appreciate Emina's qualities. For the first time since I felt her body pressed against my breast, I was overcome by a rushing wave of contentment. Far from having to do with the importance or danger of the mission we were on, this feeling came simply because she was near me. I loved her, even though her habit of always going tit for tat annoyed me.

She sat behind me in the bottom of the rowboat as Tusek rowed quietly. During the entire crossing, she kept her leg rested upon my thigh. Her hot blood, coupled with the trembling and straining of limbs, raged in waves from her groin to her tips and toes. The rhythm of her blood circulating provoked such a sexual tension within me that as I was getting out of the rowboat and on to the sodden shore I felt a warm fluid between my legs. She adjusted my backpack and walked on ahead of Tusek. Emina always succeeded in being so close to me while always being sure to be out of my reach. My mood of contentment quickly turned to silent protest and soon enough I was reproaching myself for this unceasing awkwardness with women. When a vision of my brother Osman appeared in my thoughts, I pinched myself in a sudden rush of rage.

We reached the railroad at the very entrance to the canyon. The night's darkness made mystical the rushing water of the numerous rapids. This was where the river took on speed and through a mass of foam and muffled moans accelerated to its end.

She stopped us below a gravel mound, gave a signal to sit down, and with the manner of an experienced saboteur gave orders.

"Yudja, you follow me. I'll set your charges. Tusek, you'll be over there under the nearest overpass...and both of you, wait until you hear the first explosion before lighting your fuse. We'll meet by the rowboat. Good luck."

The further we went into the canyon, the darker and further off the sky above seemed. Soon, the canyon's brows were unattainably high. Emina was hurrying. We stopped near the next crossing of the railroad tracks over the road. She crouched down, which I understood to mean that I should follow suit.

"You're staying here," she spoke softly, her hand on my knee. "Next time, you will have to set up the explosives all by yourself."

Quickly, under the tracks by the middle of the overpass, we dug holes in the gravel for the sticks. She set about her work like a meticulous science teacher demonstrating an experiment to her students.

"Where are your matches?" she asked while connecting the fuses. "When you hear my explosion, light the fuse and run. Head along the shore. Easy. The most important thing is that we all be at the rowboat by dawn."

She reached with her finger tips for my nose and in no time disappeared down the canyon.

"How wonderful it would be to spend the rest of my life with her," I thought to myself as I tried to listen for any sound which would betray where she had gone. But, I was now left alone with my matches, the explosives under the tracks, the water battling its way through the narrow channel and darkness.

She had left much unsaid. In the end, she didn't mention that after these explosions chaos would reign in the valley where my banishment had forced me to seek asylum. The three explosions we set in the canyon were the signal for a all-out attack by those from the mountains against Bihac's considerable army base.

Emina's explosion deafened the river and like a blitz lit up the rocky canyon. I lit my fuse and ran, but the explosion threw me into some thorny bushes anyway, and sent a mass of gravel flying into the trees and river. As the echo of the explosion returned from somewhere in the belly of the canyon, Tusek's was also heard, but quieter and spread out. I dashed along the river and toward the fields, light as a bird, and only after a few hundred metres did a voice in the back of my mind shout: "What about Emina?" I stopped to wait but her last words began drumming at me: "…light the fuse and run. Head along the riverbank. Easy. The most important thing is that we all be at the rowboat by dawn."

I slowed down and only then did I begin to feel an uncertain fear. The thought came to me that perhaps it would be better not to return to town, that something had happened to Emina and that I would never see her again. The earlier feeling of romantic carelessness which Emina's presence automatically awakened in me was replaced by the fear that things in the valley would never be the same after the mining of the railroad. I had become accustomed to her like a cuckoo's egg in the foreign nest.

I had yet to reach the fields when the first salvos of artillery fire sounded from the mountain passes and descended upon the town. A few moments later, from the valley shot up masses of blazing torch-lights. Human rage and hatred had drowned out the murmuring of the river and with its threatening lights was poking holes into the night's darkness. Increasingly and with growing proximity to the bottom slopes of the surrounding hills came the sounds of rifles and machine-guns, followed by shouts of *Hurrah* emitted from the throats of the thousands of assailants.

All of my thoughts were directed toward the rowboat where we were supposed to meet. I don't remember how long I spent walking along the field by the river until a few well-aimed rays of light pointed out the sought-after tall tree in the thick willow patch. There was no one by the boat.

The bitterest fighting was at the edge of the field. That is where the occupation forces had set up their fortified lines and the first attacking wave of the Partisans was stopped. Just before dawn, the first defence lines were broken from the direction of the canyon. As I noticed Tusek's bulky frame approaching the willow patch, an unusual commotion could be heard coming from town.

He came up to me, squeezed my hand and inquired about Emina. I said that she still hadn't arrived. The commotion was getting nearer. The wrinkles now visible on Tusek's forehead simultaneously announced his concern and dawn's arrival.

The undefined commotion soon turned into the very clear sound of galloping horses. It arrived at virtually the same time on both sides of the river. Horses emerged from the early morning mist and just as quickly disappeared into tufts of fog where their galloping sounds mixed with those of the shouting mass attacking the fortified town. Only then did Tusek loudly realise that the horsemen were Cherkessians and as he pulled me to the safety of the depths of the willow thicket I noticed the riders. They were virtually glued to their mounts, their heads resting against the horses' necks and arms stretched down around the bellies of their mounts. Each of them carried a gun in one hand and a drawn sabre in the other.

The deafening sounds of the horses' hoofs drowned out the whistling racket of rifles and machine-guns coming from the valley. Of all the sounds of war, only the firing of cannons could outdo the noise made by large groups of horses.

The terrifying wave of the Cherkessian cavalry rolled toward the entrance to the canyon, aimed directly at the point where the Partisan units were making their most concentrated attack toward town. For a moment, it seemed as if fighting on the other parts of the battlefield had come to a standstill. The skilful Cherkessian horsemen had surprised the attackers and with their ready sabres massacred the most exposed Partisan lines. Once the guns became silent, they were replaced by the piercing screams of men being hacked to death. When the rifles and machine-guns returned to work, the human sounds were replaced by the whining of wounded horses.

"Good. Our units have consolidated themselves," Tusek concluded with obvious relief. "These Cherkessians must have been sent here by the Devil himself. We're going to have more problems with their battalion than with all of the Germans and Ustashas put together."

Both of us were worried about Emina. We knew that she was familiar with the terrain and that she was capable, but if she'd had the misfortune of finding herself in the jaws of the Cherkessian cavalry, she wouldn't have had a chance. While Tusek whispered to me how she would certainly appear any minute now, for he realised that my worry for Emina was more than just collegial. My imagination turned on me and I couldn't help but think of a young woman's nude body being dragged along the river's shore by a group of Cherkessians.

Soon behind the Cherkessians, with the coming of day, down the field and from the direction of the centre of town there appeared people. At first, individuals with burlap sacks and crude bundles in their hands. Then, families of four and five. Eventually, large groups emerged—men, women, children, horses, cows, sheep—all in a raging race down the field and toward the place where the satanic cavalry had disappeared.

"The town is falling!" I commented on what I was seeing.

"It's falling on the south side," added Tusek. "The plan was to break through on the south-western side, in order to cut off the enemy's escape route. It seems that the Cherkessians managed to wipe out our troops from Podgrmec…"

The wave of people and cattle moved in unison down both sides of the river until sounds of gunfire were once again heard coming from the canyon. The wave began winding toward the north, toward the nearest entry to Huska Miljkovic's "Green Cadres" territory. From the proximity of human voices and the sounds of the cattle, it was clear that a few hundred metres below us, where the river curved sharply toward the northeast, the mass had come to a stop.

My attempts to get a sense of everything going on around us, to get a better picture of why the people had been stopped, was cut short by Tusek as he pointed toward the other side of the river. A woman wearing traditional Muslim trousers was descending the steep bank to the water. By her movements, we knew it was a younger person. It looked as if she was going down to throw in the sizable bundle she carried. She stopped at the very edge of the water. Turning, she scanned up and down the river. Her movements betrayed great fear and uncertainty, the temporary chaos of a mind about to make a great decision. I changed my mind about her intent.

"She is going to throw herself into the river," I whispered, unsure of what, if anything, I should do about it.

"We have to stop her," shouted Tusek, and we both ran toward the rowboat. When we jumped in and pushed off toward her, the woman noticed us, lifted the bundle above her head and threw it as far as she could toward us. She was cursing us, but the striking of our oars against the water drowned out her protests. Grabbing a large branch from nearby, she threw it toward us. When she realised that we were not about to turn back, she began to flee downstream toward the rapids around the bend. We got out of the rowboat on the other side and ran after her. Tusek had a tougher time navigating the riverbank, which was covered with underbrush. Upon reaching the very bend of the river, I saw the woman's clothing disappear into the foaming depths below the rapids. Our waiting for the water to throw her up proved to be unsuccessful.

As we were returning to the rowboat, we came across an old woman. Tired from running and old age, she tried with difficulty to explain that she was searching for her daughter Refika.

"She will drown. I will be so wretched and heartbroken," she wailed to no one in particular.

I was about to tell her that we had not seen her daughter when the woman noticed a piece of clothing which had managed to get tangled up in some collapsed branches by the side of the river. She froze, her eyes darted between the clothing and our eyes, several times. She didn't say anything more, but with her entire being she sent out a condemnation to the whole world. Thereafter, she sat down near the edge of the river, looked to the sky and began whispering something which neither of us could quite make out.

"What does this old woman now have to say to the forces in whose justice she has spent her entire life believing?!" I asked as my glances went from her to Tusek, who had been standing all the while next to the rowboat. By the deep lines on her face, I gathered that she had entered into a dialogue the likes of which she previously never would have believed possible. Honestly, to this day I often think about it; how man can spend his entire life looking on at misfortune and injustice, only to console himself with the thought that "It's just fate," or "God wills it." In fact, aren't we talking here about a slavery which no God has the right to ask of any man?!

At last, the woman stood up, took a stone in her hand, gazed over the water until she noticed her reflection in it and, aiming directly at her own image, broke up the reflection like some explosion.

She was no longer paying any attention to us. It was as if she had forgotten all about our presence and spoke directly to the river:

"Why did you take her with you, water! She wasn't ready for death. She was the happiest child in town. If those monsters dishonoured her, she wasn't to blame. You should have swallowed them up instead. The infant wasn't to blame either. She should have had it and then given it to me. But now, they are both gone."

Unexpectedly, she seized a long stick and began lashing out and striking the water, as if a hated image had appeared upon its surface. She struck and shouted:

"I will scar your face, you fiend! You have planted the seed of death into my daughter. I will disfigure you, so that you may be ashamed of yourself!"

Turning, she looked toward us, opened her eyes wide as if in disbelief and began swinging her stick at us, all the while stepping back closer to the water. Instinctively, we walked toward her, determined not to allow her to fall into the river, when from behind us, from the crest of the steep bank, thundered a threatening command:

"Don't move! Get away from the woman!"

As we turned our heads in the direction from which the command came, down the bank rushed a dozen or so men, each with a gun. The one who had issued the command remained up on the bank, intently following our movements. By their motley uniforms, I quickly realised they were Partisans. We had yet to utter a word in our defence when they grabbed us roughly and began tying our hands.

"It's not them..." the old woman tried to defend us, but the husky moustachioed young man cut her off:

"We know they didn't, mother...But, were it not for our arrival, they would have...They would have strangled you just because of that ring on your finger. Their companions were defeated so they began to rob the people."

Hearing these words, the old woman approached us and her eyes became lightning bolts.

"So, it was you who strangled my Refika. Look at the sweater over there in the water!" She pointed her finger at the piece of clothing caught up in the branches.

"Hold them tight!" shouted the one from the top of the bank, just before leaping in several large steps down to the edge of the river. He stood before us, legs wide apart. Below the bushy eyebrows, his eyes shot forth menacingly. A large, fresh wound below his left ear accentuated his rage.

It didn't take long for us to figure out that we had suddenly found ourselves in great danger. And from none other than the side for whom the previous night all three of us had risked our necks.

"Perhaps Emina's in an even worse situation," I thought to myself and immediately felt a slight tremor in my chest. Throughout my veins a strong warmth began running, the same warmth as always appeared just before I heard my mother's voice. Some force was crawling into me and taking command. I could feel myself losing control over functions of my consciousness and the thick rope which bound my hands began to break apart into hundreds of pieces.

Tusek later told me what happened next. He said that with inexplicable strength I began throwing the soldiers around me into the river and the moustached commander I lifted above my head with the apparent intention of hurling him out to the very depths of the middle. At that moment, another group of soldiers appeared above us, Emina and Osman among them. I reacted to their appearance by throwing the moustached one onto the gravel at my feet. It took a lot of effort to convince their leaders that we were in fact two of the saboteurs who had blown up the railroad tracks.

My absence from reality was interrupted by German warplanes which arrived in several squadrons from the west, machine-gunned the town on their flyby and disappeared behind the mountains. After them came the heavy bombers, which began to shower the town and surrounding valley with tonnes of their destructive cargo. This was proof that the town had fallen into the hands of the insurgents and the occupation forces were seeking vengeance for their first large defeat on the soil of Pavelic's state. The tab paid by the ordinary people was high: more than three hundred dead civilians, more than a hundred destroyed buildings. The Partisans court-martialled and sentenced to death a large number of townsfolk whom they accused of collaborating with the enemy, Omer among them.

Tusek met up with his countrymen from the Zagorye detachments and joined them.

I was reunited with my brother and Emina. Osman was known among the Partisans to be a brave fighter and a skilful politician. He and Father were in favour of my joining the same unit. No one asked me what I thought. The only reason why I didn't object to this idea was that Emina was standing next to me at the time when it was brought up.

It made little difference to me whose army I served in. I just wanted to be close to Emina. While I worked at the warehouse, the most important thing was to avoid mobilisation and not carry the occupier's gun. When I went off to dynamite the railroad, as I lit the fuse and ran toward the river and away from the explosion, I realised that this was also my battle and that I was fighting on the right side. But…after meeting up with them and being bound and nearly tried as a thief and murder, I became ambivalent about everything. I realised that truth is relative and justice depends upon the position from which it is being observed. Perhaps truth and justice could be possible if those values weren't created by people. As things stood, all it took was for some moustached type to wink and a human life no longer counted for anything. It made no difference to which army the moustached soldier belonged. An army is still an army. Blood is the favourite liquid of each and every army. Each army measures its men by the number they have killed.

I was in pain the entire week, even though I wasn't sick. My soul was aching. It seemed that I wasn't capable of accepting such drastic changes, that my intellect spent too much time studying each new occurrence. I was maturing and I wasn't even aware of it. Maturing with an arduous nausea. With intellectual vomiting. That which I had accepted uncompromisingly was pressing up against the recent past. While the town was alive, while in its heart a new state was being created for the Southern Slavs and all the other nationalities living under these skies, I was suffering from a sickness for which no cure existed.

I was wrestling with the problem of my own sense of sovereignty over myself. I was tormented by my sudden membership in a tribe and the unlikelihood of finding individual freedom within this tribe. I knew that I was compromising my individuality, and that with this new membership had ceased to be the same Yudja from the Psetian highlands. My torment was further aggravated by the realisation that I had not been myself for quite some time, that my "I" had been steadily diluted from the day my mother passed away. A duality had been created within me and against my will. While I raced with the garden warblers, climbed up trees to spend time with the sparrows and howled at the full moon during cold winter nights—that was the real me. Ever since the first time I heard my mother's voice after she passed away, and felt the arrival of the strange warmth which came and left my veins, I knew that I was no longer myself. The culmination of these contacts with something which I didn't understand took away Zemka, infected my relations with Emina, and was always strangely present in all of my dealings with my brother. I had no answer for the sudden shifts in my blood temperature, lazily pushing it aside and attributing it to chance and the mysticism of inexplicable occurrences, such as the changing of memories of Mother into spiritual meetings. With each day, I was further from myself.

Eventually, the changes going on in me during the days that followed succeeded in thinning out my "I" so that I was able to ease into acceptance of being a part of the collective interdependence of the tribe, which had before it a far-off guiding star and all around it blood, hunger and immoral behaviour. With good reason was I left breathless at the thought that I would never again return to being the same me, because now I had too much evidence, because once you give up your freedom, the very memory of its surrender will not allow you to return to inner peace. Memories of misfortune, memories of blows, rile the blood and pull you further toward misery. This is especially true when one's character is still maturing. Realising that it was no longer me, that I was a drop which had rolled into the mainstream, I began to hate, and hate has never been an insightful adviser.

I did not see Osman or Emina that entire week. When they appeared together at the door, I wished that I had not seen either him or her.

CHAPTER XI

Yudja could feel life slowly seeping out of him, the way the soft breath of spring winds shrinks banked snow to a dense, wrinkled biscuit. His breath, too, was becoming shorter, quicker, more forced, full of trembling and arrhythmia, but above all he could observe the deterioration of his physical condition by the bulging of the bones to the very surface of his skin. Where powerful male curves once used to dominate, bones and veins were now taking over. The former explosive transmission of commands from the brain to the far corners of the body had become so slow that he could follow their movements and easily stop them merely by exerting a little pressure with his forefinger on the appropriate nerve.

Without the slightest bit of build up, he admitted to himself that he was not sorry. That in fact, he had nothing to be sorry about. There was much in his life that he had left uncompleted but was it really so important for a man to roam around trying to complete everything? There must be some damnation, he thought to himself, that goads us into competing with time. We never stop to think that. time observes us with disinterest, without the slightest inclination to join us at the starting line or beat us to the finish. If man at least knew which dot in the infinite realm of dots which make up the universe was himself and only himself, then it would perhaps all make sense. But, this?…He had nothing to feel sorry about. Even this withering body of his, which was losing strength daily, was beginning to seem like an undeserved penalty, an injustice over which he had no control. What, then, was there to feel sorry over?! Something that could have been, that never was?…Or, something that seemed beautiful, but which passed away long ago?…

Nevertheless, he believed that man has some kind of mission. There is more to him than flesh, lymph and hair...The human mind must have some greater purpose. It soothed him to think that he too was a part of some galactic computer system and that when his assignment in this carcass, which was steadily abandoning him, was complete, he would be sent on some other mission. That is why he, Yudja, now knowing that the end was near, considered all the internal explosions which had rocked his body at various critical points in his life to have been mistakes, or the effects of someone else's interference upon his psyche. Whenever he was in a situation to roar, hiss, or throw his arms and legs in all directions, it had never really been him. Especially not when he could feel barbarism and service to Satan coming forth from this body. Even though he had never been truly attached to any earthly philosophy of life, he was increasingly apt to attribute all his body's explosions to service of Satan, while his soul's accomplishments were credited to God. The fact that he had not been aware of the part his soul played, while mysterious, seemed logical: had the Satanic forces been aware of it, they would have put it to destructive use.

"Are you religious?" Out of the blue came Fehrat's question, in the middle of a conversation regarding the latest news from Bosnia. "When I listen to your stories, I get the feeling that you grew up in Islam or, better yet, in its traditions—but that, in fact, you have your own beliefs, that you are searching for some truth which the human mind has yet to discover."

Fehrat's unexpected inquiry seemed crass to Yudja. With great self-restraint he blocked the wave of anger which threatened to lead to their first confrontation.

"It would be infantile to believe that I must think the same way my father thought. If it were left up to Imam Selman and Vasilije the priest, man's knowledge would end with truths as old as their religions."

"Many people are basically believers but they do not accept the institutions of religion," noted Fehrat, as if speaking to himself. "Sometimes, beliefs can become mixed up in an individual, so that it becomes impossible for him to decide between conflicting institutions."

Yudja jolted from his confrontational pose, raised his face toward the ceiling and then lowered it over the rough marks on the forehead of the wooden creation which his carving knife was reshaping. "If only I could, you Devil, carve your brain as well," the idea repeated itself throughout his head as he stared intently at the wooden forehead, "if only I could smell the nature of this game that you are still playing at my expense…" Instinctively, his glance turned toward Fehrat and, for the first time, Yudja realised that the figurine he was working on eerily resembled the man sitting across from him. The blade cut deep into the upper corners of the wooden forehead as he incised beauty-marks at the places where the little horns had been.

"Perhaps you are right," he answered, calmer than he'd expected. "Perhaps what you say is true. My father never pushed us to pray five times daily or to attend the great prayers at the mosque. We didn't even have to fast, probably because of our mother. But we had to learn the Arabic alphabet and all of the prayers from the Musaf*. We had to wash in the washroom and bathe at the Turkish baths before each Friday. From our mother we retained the cooked cobs of corn and coloured eggs of Easter, and stories of a God who descended to earth to help people but who was in turn crucified by the very same people he had come to help. Now I know why I could never look upon the crowning pavilion of a minaret without at the same time noticing the bell tower of the nearby church."

Father and son fell silent. Their silence was occasionally interrupted by the squealing of the wood as it was being carved away by Yudja's knife. The last few days, since he'd begun to make the trek to the karate club and back, Fehrat was finding it necessary to wrap the stump of his amputated leg in a plum-brandy compress in order to lessen the pain. The wooden prosthesis was hidden under the couch while the remainder of the leg was covered by a blanket, in order spare Yudja's eyes the uncomfortable sight of the very visible symbol of his misfortune.

"I don't think that man is to blame if he doesn't have conventional belief. Everything held to be inviolably sacred is stupid. Just when it begins to burn, light turns into fire. Until then, you analyse its colours…and after that its heat. If I'd had more brains to understand my neighbours' evil intentions before they crippled me, I would still have both hands and legs. But I'm like this…" Fehrat's followed his last words with a quick glance over his deformed limbs.

"It happened to me several times, that I didn't believe," whispered Yudja. "But, I'm steeped in that…The blood running through my veins is mixed…I'm like a goldfinch in a cage, thrown in while he was still an egg. That's where he broke out, began to see, began to sing. He learnt to see what they showed him and sing the songs they expected. These wires all around me have become a habit. And you…You grew up in a time when we thought that all of the cages had been destroyed. You should have felt the evil, but you didn't…"

"I didn't…" admitted Fehrat, turning his hand above the *Le Figaro* newspaper before him.

They thought differently but still came to the same conclusions. Yudja was hurrying through the time of his ancestor, who escaped to Bosnia from Dalmatia and thereby hung the fugitive bell around the necks of all of his descendants. "Exile is in my blood", he reproached himself. His father also didn't take exile as a great blow. But Osman… "Osman stayed behind to defend our home," he admitted and immediately felt a bitter feeling rise from his stomach. "Even though he did it in the service of the Devil, he did not move far from our doorstep…"

Fehrat's thoughts roamed over a cuckoo's damnation: the curse of his illegitimacy that if he has descendants, they will be raised in someone else's nest, that the he/she cuckoos will never have a nest of their own…If only his mother had given birth to him in his father's house.

"The French feel sorry for us even though they are actively encouraging the Chetniks." Fehrat pointed his finger toward the text in the newspapers. "They feel sorry for us only long enough to satisfy their own long-lost proclamations of liberty, yet they encourage the Serbian criminals because their idol, Draza Mihajlovic* went to a French military academy with Charles De Gaulle. They say that the Serbs and the Croats want to enter the third millennium with clean bills. What is to become of the smaller nations over whom they swing their axes? I ask you. This Montigny character in *Le Figaro* thinks that the answer is to seek the protection of stronger powers. Perhaps Mitterrand wants to have a protectorate over Bosnia just as Napoleon did for a short time."

"Stronger…" mumbled Yudja, "The stronger will defend you so that they can either destroy you or push you into a cage where they can ration your food and procreation."

They were startled by a series of siren blasts coming from a vessel in the harbour. The wind was blowing from the direction of the harbour so that the sound seemed much closer than it really was. Yudja's imagination immediately created a picture of an ocean-monster being sent by a great force in front of his window, to yawn and screech like some slowly dying beached whale. He lifted his glance toward Fehrat, to see him scratching with what remained of his left hand the palm of his right and looking into the dark night beyond the narrow window. With a long and painful hoot of its horn, the ship announced again its leaving, as if it had a premonition that it would never again return from the huge ocean spaces to its own port.

"I wonder what Delveta and Alma are doing now?" blurted Yudja through nearly closed lips, sorrow and helplessness evident in his breath. "Did you see? Alma writes that I shouldn't worry, that there are other Bosnians also living there, that she is learning English and will soon be working. She writes that they are now trying to arrange for me to join them in America. And I…I wasn't made for here, let alone for America. Only the strong and the brave have always gone there. If that wasn't the case, then America wouldn't be America. America isn't an old-age home or some hospital for empty stomachs."

Fehrat pulled the blanket higher over his legs and shoved the remainder of his hand deeper under his shirt. Yudja understood the instinctive reaction to signal revolt at his own disabilities, against his "expendable" designation. Trying to patch things up, he quickly added:

"With you it's different. You have a healthy heart. You have your whole life before you…"

His words seemed unreal, as if spoken by a blind man. The usually quiet Fehrat could no longer contain the enormous surge of protest which suddenly welled up within him. Throwing off the blanket from his leg, tearing the hand from under his shirt and extending both deformed limbs before Yudja, he stared cold-bloodedly at the man who now claimed to be his father yet who had been a stranger to him all his life.

"Me?! Like this?!…Is this what you call a healthy heart?!" Still lying on the couch, he began to swing his arms and legs above his head, barely able to keep himself from screaming at the top of his lungs. "When I jumped from my left leg, I could leap like a panther. It was thanks to my left hand that I earned the black belt. And what did they do? They cut off both of them. They did it like they would to a lamb meant for slaughter, not a human being. If only they had slit my throat!" He lowered his limbs and continued in a calmer tone, as if trying to dilute the bitterness which had broken through the dam of his self-control. "No. They left me to live and threw me out into the world to suffer and spend the rest of my life in misery. And do you know who it was that did this? Dmitar's grandson, Damyan! Your blood relative, and perhaps my brother. The one who spoke openly about how your father had saved them from the Ustasha's daggers. The one who went to school with me, received his diplomas and competed with me in the martial arts…The same Damyan who danced the kolo with us, slept in our haystacks…

Swallowing his spit and trying with all his might to regain control of his emotions, he felt an overwhelming sense of embarrassment at having made such a scene before the old man who himself had much to curse and fume about. But, he justified himself simply enough, why should he hide his feelings before the man whom he considered to be his father and whom he had gone out of his way all his life to avoid because the entire town thought of him simply as Yudja's bastard son. Was this not in fact his first opportunity to discover whether he was the descendant of Cain or Abel? This Yudja before him was telling him the story of his life as if he were passing down to him a valuable family inheritance yet at no time had he tried to tell him how he had come about; a result of love or of hatred. He expected the old man, now in the twilight of his life, to try to show himself to be the father that he had never been, but instead he kept on putting Osman before himself. He was overcome by the syndrome of the exile, as if these all-too-frequent Bosnian odysseys were a part of some divine program and not the work of monsters from the past who regularly come to life only to plunge the world around them into their own private underworld of darkness and lies.

"So, it was Damyan…" Yudja's voice was, to Fehrat's surprise, absolutely resigned. "When I heard it, at first I didn't believe it. I never felt them to be family…But he was more ingratiating than the rest of them. A doctor is supposed to heal madmen, make them feel better… but he turned out to be the maddest of all the madmen."

They grew silent again, as if they had just discovered a secret from which both had been trying to flee. Yudja returned to carving his block of linden wood in the area where the figurine's torso was to be while Fehrat threw the blanket back over his wooden prosthesis.

"Still, you have most of your life ahead of you," continued Yudja after a lengthy pause. "Your anger seems like a thirst for vengeance, while I was hoping that you would save our blood by getting married and continuing our line. You are going to be alone, Fehrat!"

"You wouldn't allow me to carry your family name," commented Fehrat as he looked intently at the linden wood in Yudja's lap.

"It happened…" Yudja mumbled awkwardly.

"It happens to all of us. You are the drop of water which is thrown out of the stream but you still manage to return because that's where you belong. I never had that chance," Fehrat whispered.

"I know," Yudja replied, feeling the dryness of his throat.

Again, they were silent. Outside, the city on Canada's west coast was just as silent.

"In any case, you have to continue your story," Fehrat pronounced at last.

"I must," immediately retorted Yudja, and for the first time his voice lacked its previous uncertainty, now replaced by a purposeful tone.

You are more of a stranger to me now than you were before you started, Fehrat thought to himself as he observed the old man from under lowered brows. You want to suck me into your still unresolved relationship with your "evil" brother when in my eyes the two of you have grown into Siamese twins, Cane and Abel both in one body, a common spine and intertwined destinies. Doesn't every man carry within him the Cain and Abel complex? Isn't this obsession with your brother a self-defence mechanism, an attempt to justify yourself, an escape from your own image?

And, Yudja continued with his story.

I said good-bye to my father and aunt in the hope that it would lead to the end of my wandering and that with a rifle in my hand I would gain the right to a homeland I could call my own...As soon as we reached the highlands above the town, the command decided that half the battalion would head down the southern slopes of Grmec while the rest would continue straight along the highland plains and onward toward Pset. This is where I was separated from Osman and Emina. When they ordered that she go with the left wing, the pain in my chest spread to my throat.

As I parted with my brother, things my father once said to me returned:

"Why feel sorry over a parcel of land when before you lie enormous spaces? When you become used to wandering, you will realise that some people are cursed. Those who drove you away will feel the sting of their own curse. Man isn't called upon to judge other men's worth... and he is certainly not authorized to wreak vengeance on other human beings. "

I had the feeling that my brother's eyes could see through mine straight to the centre of my brain where I was weighing the worth of our father's blessing. Realising that I knew what he was up to, he turned away. We parted theatrically, embracing, but both of our hearts were cold and indifferent.

Emina's image remained with me long after she disappeared into the hornbeam forest, twitching my heart.

After their departure I could not help but doubt the wisdom of my decision to follow these people into the mountains and, instead of remaining a passive observer, act on the stage in the role of a stuntman. Perhaps it was also the fact that I had no developed idea of what drove many of those around me to put on the caps with the red stars and follow a vague vision of bliss and equality. To me, when I now think back to those times, the red colour was a symbol of some kind of extremism and a desire to dominate. It represented life hidden somewhere deep within the body and death as it emerges and gushes forth from just-slit veins.

My unit roamed along mountain ranges without hurry or any evident goal. The officers awaited orders from the high command. I got to know the commander during the mandatory daily political lectures. He was the well-known Colonel Dzeran and resembled more a typical professor of literature than a commander celebrated for being a fierce warrior. Only once did he ask me who I was and where I had fought before Bihac. When I stuttered, surprised by the question, his eyes zoomed in on me and he smiled suddenly, shaking his head as if to say it was no longer important.

One of the members of our unit was the Prophet, the prisoner from Kula who dropped the playing cards when he tried to foretell Osman's fortune. Meeting him brought me face to face with the width and breadth of sociological and political alchemy and sorcery which are the secret weapon of all skilled individuals in times of great turbulence. In fact, that is when I confirmed some of my formerly uncertain beliefs that the individual separates from the masses in situations when, for lack of acceptable motives, he successfully enters the realm of the alchemy of the soul.

Several days we spent roaming among the mountain hamlets on the passes behind which lay the unfortunate Psetian highlands. We slept in hay-sheds and barns. Only for the officer corps, select heroes, and women, was there room in the low-built wooden houses, from whose shrub roofs smoke began increasingly to creep out as the frost began to take hold. The peasants feared us and stoically put up with our depletion of their winter food supplies.

The odd German fighter plane would fly over us and the subsequent echo of explosions from the direction of Bihac convinced us that fighting was now taking place there. In our unit the main battle being waged was for our souls.

The Prophet was in charge of ideology for our platoon. He would speak at length several times a day, full of the desire to destroy our individuality and transform us into an ideologically monolithic mass. Masterfully, he brought us into a state somewhere between dream and reality, fighting a battle against our wills and filling us up with his alchemic materials, which shut the entire history of the human race into a hermetically sealed box without any keys, and upon it lit a red fire meant for future generations. I began to fear for myself when I realised that the Prophet was using incorrect formulas and that his symbols were similar to those used in the anathematised times of uniformity and intolerance.

"Isn't man's desire to create a good life for himself and his family the main driving force in social progress and the flagship of civilisation?" I confronted him after one particularly long séance in a woodshed at the bottom of a village.

For the longest time, he observed me as one would a coiled snake, trying to determine whether he should simply avoid and walk around me or if he should crush me with all the strength at his disposal.

"The desire is not the problem but the egotism of such an idea is unacceptable," he responded, trying to uncover the gist of my protest. "If you wish to create just for yourself, then you are taking from others. Men will truly be content only once we all have the same."

I didn't like him and instinctively rejected his theory. In fact, the idea that an intelligent person and an idiot, or a worker and a freeloader, should be rewarded equally seemed stupid to me. This delusion would later become the obsession of the masses, but I always had my reservations about it. I was truly against the exploitation of man by man, but I was not for levelling either…

The Prophet's alchemy had little success in breaking through the wall which I erected between the two of us, but with Dzeran it was more difficult. His speeches increasingly seemed like the stoking of a fire which would not keep us warm for very long and which could spread and join the other forest fires which had been visited upon us with destructive regularity. He spoke boisterously, flitting from idea to idea like a ghost appearing from behind a screen in some hot summer night's dream.

"We must take our strength and morale from our past," he spoke before the soldiers of the unit, yet all that I knew of our past contained little that would give me strength or happiness. It was full of blood and suffering, slavery, humiliation and fratricidal butchery and it would have been far better to simply forget it. Yet, here was Dzeran asking us to return to the past as if the past were a river that does not flow into the present, and as if its waters hadn't flooded our lives long ago.

I began to participate organically in all this whenever he mentioned very far away Battle at Kosovo* as our common symbol and the cradle of our future. I knew much about this symbol and because of it I could barely contain myself from running out of the shed and off toward the icy mountain.

"Upon this six-hundred-year-old battle we have to sharpen our strength and hatred toward the enemy. Our nation has been kept alive by this hatred and by the memories of heroism and you must head along the same path if you wish to gain your liberty." He spoke firmly, keeping his sights focused upon the worm-eaten logs of the shed. When he was silent, the industrious woodworms could be heard.

My agony was interrupted by a lanky soldier whose name I didn't know.

"We must be victorious, Comrade Commandant! And all of us, all together. We must not lose, as our forefathers lost at Kosovo. We must liberate, and not become slaves like they did after Kosovo," thundered the soldier, fully believing that he was continuing the commander's thoughts. He stood up, legs apart, as if our path to happiness started at the crack of his ass.

The colour of the commander's face turned to greyish blue with rosy rings around the nose and ears. The movement of his Adam's apple betrayed his uneasiness and psychological dilemma.

"Singing about the battle of Kosovo our Serbian nation was able to survive," the commander tried to reestablish his concentration. "And now we are all together in the same battle: Serbs, and Croats, Slovenes, Montenegrins and Macedonians. All of our nations." Dzeran's intensity grew as he looked into the far-off distance.

Barking, muffled by the snow, could be heard from the direction of the village.

*You didn't mention everyone...*my brain protested like a cannon but I didn't have the strength, nor the will to say anything. *What about us Bosniaks, what about the Albanians, Jews, Hungarians, Italians...in Yugoslavia that are fighting alongside us?*

The more Dzeran tried to explain, the more I feared that the exodus of my people would be passed down to future generations like a genetic disease and that we would always live with the fear that those around us who are stronger and more numerous might decide to swallow us up and beat us over the head with the drumsticks of the past. If only I could have lain down in a flowery field under the mountain, I would have gladly traded the drumming of Balkan historians for the buzzing sound of the bees.

The political lectures failed to convince me of the strength of the new ideology. I accepted that it wasn't all bad, that in places it did offer hope, that it was close to the elementary postulates of religion, but its interpreters were evidently unequal to the task before them. There was far too much traditional blood flowing in their veins for them to be truly willing or able to accept any form of common happiness. Later, in the postwar years, I was definitively convinced that the same old blood ran in many of them and that the new times were only as good as they were willing to make them. My nation was once again cheated, just as the old rulers had cheated my grandfathers before. This most recent Serbian aggression against Bosnia & Herzegovina and the Croatian reluctance to help the unarmed Bosnian nation confirmed all of the suspicions of my youth.

Fehrat scratched along his severed hand. The problem wasn't the coarsely healed stitches but the severed nerves. As he listened to

Yudja, the sudden urge came to him to move this Balkan story to the ends of the earth, with different climates and mentalities, and thereby to change both the stage and the actors. Nevertheless, his imagination did not have the strength for such a change. There also, he saw flags of war and quickly he returned to the atmosphere of the room. Again his sights rested on the helpless old man clutching the piece of linden wood in his hand. As soon as he closed his eyes to erase the picture before him, countless severed arms and legs would come hurtling toward him.

He no longer heard his father, but his own teeth that chattered in the quiet of this night in the apartment overlooking the sleepy harbour at North Vancouver. The silence was broken by a noise in the apartment building which sounded like something out of one of Schubert's arias.

"I'm not to blame," Yudja's voice cut through Fehrat's images. "I didn't have the courage to face him and say what I felt. But I did tell it all to that long-winded Prophet, who was always standing behind the commander and fretting over our future happiness. He once took me aside from the column as we were marching through ever-deeper snow and, acting like an insulted teacher, told me that we Bosniaks were either Serbs or Croatians of Islamic faith and that it would be the best for all concerned if we rid ourselves of religious chauvinism and returned to our respective tribes as soon as possible.

I looked toward the column that was leaving me behind, disappearing beyond trees and heading in a direction covered with freshly fallen snow. With one hand I seized the Prophet's carbine while with the other I pushed him into the snow and held him by the throat. As I looked into his eyes, they nearly burst out of their sockets from disbelief. I pushed him deeper into the snow and through clenched teeth hissed at him that for him and his kind we were just the sawdust of their history. I knew that we would be thrown before the cattle so that they wouldn't get muddy, or around the fruit trees so that they would bear better fruit.

My words were suffocating him. "We're not from the same tree," I hissed, "and the passing of time hasn't distanced us from anyone.

If things were otherwise, then Karan's Chetniks wouldn't be going around and butchering us like cattle."

"Don't talk like that, someone will hear you..." the Prophet managed to gasp, the fear in his eyes obvious. My grip around his throat tightened.

"The day will come when the sawdust will turn to stone, when brothers such as the likes of you will no longer be able to look down on us like some garbage." Then I took my hands off him as if he were a piece of rotting wood.

He stood up, shook the snow off, rubbed his throat and headed after the column. Some hundred paces later, he turned around and pointed his finger toward the mountain across from us. In an unusually calm tone, he shouted"

"Say it to your brother! He also spoke to me about sawdust..."

Standing there I stared at the Prophet's receding back as he quickly disappeared among the snowdrifts carried down the mountain by the storm. I turned my head toward the grey abyss which hid the Psetian highlands and, somewhere in the frozen outskirts of the town, my father Fehrat's shingled house. Sometimes it seemed like a castle sunk in the midst of chirping sparrows and heavily scented roses and lilies, but then I imagined that Chetnik bastard Karan standing over it like a colossus and trying with all his might to stomp it as deep into the ground as possible, to destroy it to its very foundations and wipe away all trace of it having ever existed. My concentration was broken by sudden rumbling coming from down below, as if hundreds of horses were crossing the field, followed by the whistling of the snowstorm between the fir trees and the slapping of the icy winds against my cheeks.

I had to hurry after the column. All my alternatives were much worse.

We marched for hours. In the snowstorm the differences between day and night became blurred. Three nights we tramped across the mountain and three days we spent glued to the trees like mummies. Only when we came under direct fire from light artillery did we realise that we were being pursued. The column received two direct hits and three men died. Their body parts were scattered among the tree branches. There wasn't enough left of them for us to have reason to bury them.

It was not uncommon to go hours without saying a single word. I could sense an entire army closing in on us—their stomachs full and their clothes dry. The only food that I had on me was what remained of a barley crust—it would be my only food until we received new rations somewhere near mountain Klekovaca, which was far away. We knew that there were people there.

One day, some of our scouts informed us that the enemy had returned to Pset and had left us to face the wrath of the mountain and winter on our own. We headed down the mountain and soon came upon some paths through the snow which connected the nearby villages.

In the middle of the column were the horses which carried the machine-guns, while mules carried the bundles of equipment and crates of munitions. Frozen and starving, we prayed to God for the sight of any, it did not matter whose, houses and barns.

As we descended, the path became more slippery and on both sides of it the snow was above waist height. Both we and the animals walked in single file. Then the horses and the mules began to slip and slide. As they fell, their stomachs echoed like empty caves. Their legs tried to flee to the sides, to escape the slippery, packed snow of the path, but they managed only to collapse into the soft whiteness. The helpless few who remained on the path lay on their stomachs. The sight of it all was both humorous and grotesque. Some strange glow, full of reproach, condemnation and helplessness radiated from their eyes. We tried to pull them out of the snow, get their hooves back onto the packed snow and have them upright. Their legs shook uncontrollably with helplessness and fear and after a few steps they once again tried to flee from the path and fell again in the deep snow by the wayside as if they were felled logs, all the while helplessly looking at us. They didn't even try to free themselves of the icy embrace, preferring to wait for our help to come. The howling of wolves from somewhere high above in the mountain did little to motivate them to stand up and continue the march. When we finally reached farmhouses, the animals foundered next to the haystacks, their full loads still on their backs, and with their last ounces of strength began chewing on the frozen hay.

The sun appeared timidly above the fir trees and coloured the entire mountain ridge crimson. Even the snow turned as red as a live coal. When I was a young boy I had seen the snow turn this red whenever the first rays of the sun surprised it from behind the eastern peaks.

Some fifty wooden houses, and women and children…Not a single man to be see anywhere. It wasn't until the next day that we learnt that they were hiding some feeble old moustachio, so that their male seeds wouldn't die out.

In the houses at the ends of the village we left sentries while we moved in with the villagers, two or three to a house.

The women received us coldly but with understanding. There was sour cabbage, potatoes, bread and a little smoked meat. A little of everything.

Stana was of mature age, a bit hefty and with dark hair and complexion. She wore a leather vest over her thick sweater and a black kerchief covered her head. She asked us where we were from and what family we had. Micha and I couldn't take our eyes off the fireplace above which the kettle was hanging and strained our necks trying to see if the water with the potatoes was boiling yet. Stana brought us a head of sour cabbage and we dove head first into the meal.

"Where are your men?" Micha attempted to draw our taciturn hostess out.

"What do you ask?" Stana turned to face him.

"Men…We didn't see any men in the village, only women and children."

"The devil knows," palely answered the mountain woman. "Same as you, in the woods. Bothering some poor folk, just like you. Those still alive…And the others…" Weakly, she shrugged her shoulders.

As darkness fell we learnt that we would be spending the night in the village. The women could barely hide their hostility to this idea and we didn't insist on them telling us where their men were and in which army. We knew that there were Chetniks in these parts but if they were near, we would have come across some of their tracks. Usually they tended to be isolated and kept close to their homes.

"All of you, be alert!" Ivan, our company commander, advised us as he read out the schedule for guard duty. "Rifles ready and one eye always open."

"What will I do?…The cabbage has given me the runs," Hajro, the lean, moustached machine-gunner, tried to joke.

"Then go sleep with the cows," Droban counselled him and laughed.

"Micha, wait!" Ivan called after my friend and stopped the two of us. "I've heard that the mountain woman you two are lodging with likes to make hen-parties and drink slivovitza*. Be careful, you hear, and don't get fooled. This here village smells of trouble. Sleep in shifts."

As we walked back to the house, I slipped on the icy path. My rifle went skittering some ten metres muzzle-first and became stuck in the snow. Micha couldn't help but laugh and comment:

"What? You too, just like the mules. On your stomach."

At this time, the Prophet was nowhere to be seen. It seemed to me that he chose to be on the other side of the village just to avoid me.

Micha slept till supper. He shook, moved his lanky legs, whistled and blew like a pregnant cow. Sleep would have been a fine thing for me as well, but we were to take turns sleeping, and I needed to clean the snowplug out of my rifle's muzzle and oil the barrel. I did not like carrying a gun, but there was no sense having it blow up in my face.

Stana entered and exited the house from time to time and would look toward us two. For the most part, she remained silent. Her animosity was obvious. But she did prepare a simple meal of potatoes and pickled cabbage for us.

As we sat to eat, there came the sound of gunfire: far off, somewhere in the darkness behind the forest. The wind swept down the mountain in waves and brought with it the reverberation of shots. This became our dinner music.

After supper, Stana declared that she was tired and that wax candles were hard to come by. She went into the room next door and we could hear her dragging something to barricade the door. The two of us exchanged a few remarks at the expense of the mountain woman. It was now my turn to sack out.

My sleep was broken by the pressure of a heavy hand on my shoulder. Micha stood above me, the fireplace behind him outlining his large frame.

"What is it?" I asked.

"What do you mean: What is it? Do you have a nose, if you don't have eyes, or did they fall out?"

Whatever it was, it really did stink, of rotting sour cabbage.

"What is it? Talk! How should I know what stinks?" I protested.

Not answering, Micha walked away and to the other side of the fireplace. When he returned, he looked like a wet ram. He was taking off clothes and mumbling.

When he dried off just before dawn, he told me that he had been sniffing around the house in the dark. In one nook he came upon a huge vat. He didn't tell me what he was hoping to find, nor what was wrong with his own nose, but while kneeling down to feel what was at the bottom, he slipped and fell into the vat.

He cursed the cabbage, and Stana, and the darkness, but begged me:

"Don't say a word of this to anyone. At least until we're far away from this place. You know Ivan and his principles. This fucking brine could cost me my head."

"If the stench doesn't betray you first, I won't say a thing." I couldn't help but laugh at his expense and regret not having been there to watch him struggle to get out of the vat. "Surely you didn't think that Stana was hiding in the brine," I joked, but Micha didn't say a word.

In the morning, we headed out of the village. Sparse flakes of snow were fluttering around, tiny from the cold. The children had not woken yet. The women were standing at the front doors of their houses and looked on as if it mattered little to them if we were leaving sooner or later, this way or that. The main thing was that we were leaving and as far as they were concerned the Devil could have us.

We climbed up the mountain again, through deep snow. It was slow going, but easier than on yesterday's icy path. Plus, we were fed and rested. The horses and mules were also more alive. I noticed that they were greater in number as well, and concluded that every army is the same—unfortunate is the village through which it passes.

We crossed a pass in the mountain range and the village was behind us. The fir and spruce trees patiently held layers of snow upon their outstretched branches. Someone ahead of me in the column was talking about how the people up here were like wolves: wild and dangerous.

"Stay away from them even when they are on your side, not to mention when they are against you!" another voice warned. Instead of further commentary, the only sound to be heard was the heavy breathing of men struggling with their loads and the steep terrain.

Instead of descending into the valley below, we traversed its south slope. The fir trees lined up like people at a meeting: all upright, some standing on their toes to see above the ones in front. On the north side, the trees were pasted with snow. At the valley bottom the snow had covered up the low-lying bushes and they looked like well-hidden bunkers.

At once, as if the sky had broken in half, both we and our mounts were scattered like chaff before a hellish wind. One tumbled down the valley while the other fled among the trees. Above, some fifty metres from us, gunfire swept down like something out of a nightmare. Blood sprinkled all over the snow-white rug while the panic of humans and animals fleeing for cover was drowned out by the banshee chorus of bullets and their echo reverberating to the edges of the deep valley. Screams and panting…Horses and mules huddled whining below us.

Two bullets hit me, one after the other, as I was burrowing deeper into the snow. I aimed at a dark figure up on a tree and saw it fall face first into the snow. The trees around me seemed to collapse on my head, the roots came out untangled like vipers under a March sun, my eyes caught fire, my right temple received two or three blows, and then nothing, darkness.

I couldn't see or hear, while the brain remained obstinate and insanely tried to rewind the reels of memory. I succeeded in realising that something was pulling me out of the blood-soaked valley taking me under the Chetnik dagger. I wanted to believe that it was Osman, or Father, but couldn't remember what they looked like. Memories of Mother came to me. I tried to call to them but my lips were glued shut. As I strained my head as far as it would go, all of the blood in my body seemed to rush to my eyes and—they opened. I recognised the hairy, sweaty face of Karan, the Chetnik leader. I could feel myself being dragged through the valley and sank into the dark night of total unconsciousness.

When I regained my senses, the first thing that I managed to see was a narrow window and several long, thick icicles on the other side of the glass. My entire body itched as if an army of lice and fleas were under the bed-cover with me. On the brick stove tufts of steam rose from the aluminum pot. Again I couldn't feel my feet, just as at the beginning of my exile from Pset. There, I had been with my family in a large convoy of refugees. Now I was in a strange house on a snow-covered mountain.

When I looked upon a hunched old woman in black as she approached me, I realised that I was indeed alive, and assumed that Karan had been merely an apparition in my delirium. However, the old woman soon disabused me of this hope:

"Don't worry, sonny. The worst is over. One wound has healed while the other one is getting better!" She spoke in a motherly tone and held her hand to my forehead.

I managed to push words through my rock-like mouth. "Where am I?"

"With me and Grandpa. Don't worry…Karan left you here with us. We know your uncle Dmitar." As she spoke, she gripped my hand in friendship.

Yudja took a long pause, trying to remember details. His hand wandered through the thinning grey hair scattered over his forehead and across his ears. With the other, he rested the knife on the furrowed fingers of the as yet roughly carved figurine.

"So, it was Karan…" He heard Fehrat's voice as if from somewhere down in the snow-covered valley.

Yudja quickly turned his head at the mention of Karan's name, only to wave it listlessly away with his hand.

"Yes, Karan…He brought an entire unit of Chetniks over to our side and would later go on to gain fame fighting in Herzegovina. They say that he often boasted how he had saved many Muslims from Vakuf and Orasje because, he claimed, if it wasn't for him they would all have been butchered by the enraged guerrillas. As if under his command more than two thousand weren't butchered. Guerrillas…"

"You mean Chetniks," added Fehrat.

"No, I mean guerrillas," answered Yudja, unsuccessfully trying to smile. "These guerrillas helped us win the war. They were rewarded with high positions and for fifty years they planned this latest round of evil."

"What do you think about that plan or those plans? What do you feel about it? Today, why do some 'national fathers' want to create a Great Serbia or Great Croatia? Or, maybe, an independent Bosniak country, doesn't matter how big…Could be a pocket country, but Muslim?" Fehrat provoked his exhausted father with these references to plans that had been publicly noised about for many years.

Yudja rested his tired head upon his chest. He couldn't hear the increased howling of the wind among the tall trees by the apartment building, nor the occasional child's scream coming from the apartment below. Even the pictures from days long gone failed to take any foothold in his brain. But he understood his son's question and struggled to keep speaking.

"You know that better than I but you have your knowledge from books. In those parts of the Balkans, history books are written by victors and they are full of blood in the brain and in the eyes. In our legends…" Yudja choked for a moment on his words "…there are heroes…who are always killers. There is never the fact written that killing creates more and more hatred and, later, more and more killing. And the plans of national leaders? Mostly, they are plans how to conquer, capture and make as much pain as possible to the others. And who ever had profit from somebody's pain? Especially today. Civilization is unified by the media. It will be really unified, without hatred, pain and killing, when human beings, all of us, today and in the future, realise that we all are brothers and sisters, and when we all actively accept a nonkilling way of life. But even now you cannot conceive some idea that the entire world doesn't know about within hours....Plans for a Great Serbia came from somebody's idea that Serbia is wherever Serbs live in the Balkans. Similarly with plans for a Great Croatia. From the beginning, those plans intended to feed their appetites on the territory of Bosnia-Herzegovina. And in Bosnia-Herzegovina there were Bosnians, or Boshnyans, or Bosniaks much earlier than the formation of either Serbia or Croatia. Later, as a part of nationalist strategies in both our brother nations, there evolved the philosophy that all Bosnian Orthodox are Serbs, all Catholics are Croats and Bosnian Muslims are either Serbs, or Croats. Later Bosnia also became a separate nation of Muslims—from the end of last century, Bosniaks." Yudja was explaining these things as though he wanted to be sure, himself, that this is how these things truly were.

"Our brothers-neighbors have the power now to realise those plans by killings, mass graves, genocides," added Fehrat.

"They called our nation Muslim so that they would have someone to teach their young ones to hate. They aligned us with the Turks so that they would have someone to take their revenge against. They helped us build mosques so they could show the West how they were being threatened by Islamic fundamentalism. And this, when most of us know as much about Islam as we do about Orthodoxy and Catholicism. Instead, we urge our children to use computers and learn foreign languages. To make everything even blacker, more cruel, the entire world is tricked by this vile treachery of theirs and allows them to butcher and burn, rape and scatter us to the four corners of this wretched planet that we live on."

The old man was visibly shaken and fighting for breath like a fish taken out of water. You don't need to hit it over the head because soon enough it will die anyway. No difference if it's caught by a fisherman with a valid license or some crazy poacher who fishes where and when he pleases.

"They suppressed the name Bosnian in order to erase our ties to Bosnia, making it easier for them to dismember it," Yudja gasped. "And they defend us like they would an unwanted chick in someone else's nest."

"Here's to him who is defended by the mean streets!" Fehrat extended his healthy leg.

"Are you in pain?" Yudja asked in concern.

"Ah, no…Everything is all right," Fehrat quickly answered and ran his hand over the stump of his severed leg. For some time now he had begun to feel his flesh crawl up the leg and the sawn bones of the shin increasingly stretch the skin.

"And Osman?…" Despite a marked tone of fear in his voice, Fehrat couldn't help but ask.

It was obvious that old Yudja didn't have the strength to continue his story. The whistling of straitened bronchioles in his lungs grew louder. His skin had grown pale, and Fehrat could almost see the blood slow its circulation through his body. But the old Bosniak shook himself and responded to his son's question.

"It wasn't until two years after the war that I saw him again. We met at Father's house. The refugees had returned to their homes and were starting life all over again. And Osman…Osman became a bigwig… Just like Karan," he added quietly. "Later, he got tripped up by the Informbiro* and ended up serving three years on Goli Otok.

"I heard that they ruptured his kidneys while he was in prison. The story was that he had strangled a couple of guards and after that they kept him in chains for two years, just like Bash-Chelik.*" With that, Fehrat quickly drained his memory of all that he knew of Osman.

Yudja reached for the wooden Osman figurine standing on the cupboard and looked directly into its eyes, as if seeking the permission of his work of art to keep speaking.

"The war definitely made strangers of Osman and me. Especially after I heard that he was saying that he was shamed by me because I wasn't a hero…Because I didn't kill anybody in that war. Once he told our father that he would never understand my saying that nobody has a right to kill human beings and there is no special occasion or event which justifies killing," Yudja spoke, and stared intently into the tiny eyes of the carving…

"But the ruptured kidneys didn't kill him. The three years he spent in the political prison on the island Goli Otok he didn't talk about to father or to me. In fact, after he returned he was in very poor physical shape. Many years after his death, one of his fellow inmates told me that for the first year on Goli Otok Osman was very disciplined. He had completed the course in political re-education and was first on the list of those being considered for amnesty. Then something happened. The monotony of prison life was shaken up by a change in Goli Otok's administration. Among the new guards Osman recognised two Chetniks who had exchanged their Chetnik uniforms for Partisan ones at the very end of the war. He began to say openly that the prison was being run by Chetniks. They locked him up in a solitary cell and declared him insane. At night, the other prisoners would regularly hear screams and howling coming from the part of the prison where he was being held. One night he broke through the wall of his cell, managed to make his way undetected to the room where those two were sleeping, and strangled them in their beds. The next day, all bloody and in chains, Osman was led on display from cell to cell. His eyes burned with a strange glow and there was foam coming out of his mouth. Physicians later concluded that he had caught rabies and treated and beat him for two years. In the end, Dmitar's daughter Jelena succeeded in proving that Osman had been right about the two guards and he was released from Goli Otok."

The old man sighed, as if he'd just had a great load taken from his shoulders.

"Jelena had completed art academy in Ljubljana and soon after Osman's return from prison she opened an atelier in Pset. The greater part of the last three years of his life Osman spent with her and alcohol. Despite his sickness, he could still turn on the charm when he felt like it and the looser women in town enjoyed his company."

Fehrat looked at the horn places on the head of the muscular figurine and tried to understand the reasons behind the constant trembling in Yudja's voice. After a short pause, the old man continued, as if wanting to rid himself of Osman and Jelena as quickly as possible:

"He knew that he would soon be dead, so he started coming around to visit Father regularly. One day Jelena left for Banyaluka. She didn't return for some time and Osman came back to live in Father's house. It was as if he wanted to die in the family home. A fever held him for several days. He twisted and turned, and you could hear him having a conversation with Mother, begging her to free him. When he had let out his last breath and the soul had left the body, Father and Auntie were startled to see that half of his face had turned blue while the other half was red...I wasn't surprised.

"After Osman's death," Yudja continued introspectively, "Jelena lived a short time in town. She painted Osman's portrait with some strange glow in the eyes and then left. Later we heard that she had a son, Damyan. Just when the earth was packed into Osman's grave, Father handed me a note with the inscription he intended for the tombstone: "Late Osman, son of Fehrat in both worlds." I didn't ask why because I understood that this was Father's way of silencing his suspicions and easing his soul.

"Father died the following autumn, when the first thunder brought with it the winds and the rains. He left unexpectedly, like a refugee... He didn't even have time to make his peace with anyone."

Fehrat's breathing grew louder, while Yudja's rattling drowned out the soft moan of the wind entering the apartment through the window.

"It doesn't matter," Fehrat declared into the dismal soundscape. "When a man's life ends, it doesn't matter if he leaves loudly or if he steals away quietly in his slippers."

"Oh no, no..." whispered the old man into the blanket that he had drawn over his head. "When you wish your family a good night before going to sleep, you also will sleep lighter."

"Emina?...What happened to her?" enquired Fehrat, trying to free that information also from the old man's enfeebled memory.

Yudja stopped his preparations for sleep and raised his eyes to the carving of the ballerina standing atop the cupboard with a gun in her hand. "I think that she is still alive. Somewhere in Serbia. At the end of the war she married a political commissar and had children." He spoke as if he were scraping the information from the very depths of his soul.

Both of them were being overcome by the night. Yudja turned toward Fehrat and asked:

"You said that they bulldozed through our graveyard, levelled it and built a parking lot on it...?"

He didn't wait for an answer. Drew the blanket over his head as if to hide from Fehrat, and from the whistling of the wind, and from the unfortunate child's weeping which could climb up the stairs at any give moment. Then he whispered:

"Even our graves haven't been left in peace. It is better to die in this foreign land...at least your bones will be left in peace...Oh, my poor father..." the old man wept quietly, "Oh, my dear mother...oh people...oh God...Why?..." he stuttered deeply under the blanket, seeking to hide both himself and the sorrow which was suffocating him.

Fehrat could feel a life being extinguished under that blanket and felt sorry for the old man, just as a blade of grass in a hot field might feel sorry for a cloud which heartlessly moves off over the horizon. Softly he got down onto the floor and on his knees crawled to the window.

The room behind him was dark. Outside, the bare branches were toying with the rays of the street lamps, trying to block them from entering Yudja's window. Fehrat strained his eyes to the brink of pain searching for some signs of life on the other side of the window, and out of his imagination he created cats and dogs and moved them along the pavement and among the thick branches of the trees, convincing himself that he really was hearing barking and meowing. He eventually grew tired of the improvisation and turned toward the dark room. Yudja's mounded shape under the bedclothes seemed to him like a grave without a tombstone, like the grave mound of an unknown refugee under the roof of some foreign house. Shaking off the feeling of powerlessness and protest, he inadvertently shoved the remnant of his severed hand among Yudja's figurines. Immediately, a thorny, burning pain struck him. In the near darkness his hair stood on end as he saw that he stood face to face with the whole melange of them. The grotesque wooden things had come to life and were turning on him the way a brave cat sitting in a tree would turn on a dim-witted dog. Closing his eyes and lowering himself to the floor again, Fehrat crawled back to his sleeping place. Thereafter, he too drew the blanket well over his head and tried to ease the panic of his bewildered brain. Even in his sleep the agony did not subside; instead it changed form and sent down a new wave of terror; familiar faces, deformed and enraged, hounded his dreams mercilessly.

The two of them, Yudja and Fehrat, had many reasons to hold hands tightly and strengthen each other's circulation, but were instead sinking ever deeper each under his own blanket, isolated. Both were painfully aware of this but neither could summon the courage to do anything about it.

The day when they first met under this same roof, they had felt a strange pulsating of the heart and hope that something would happen over time which would bring them closer together, something which would find them walking the same path and overcoming their strained relations through their common tragedy. That night both of them realised that each was hermetically sealed in his own personal pain and out of these two great pains a third happiness could not be built.

As far as Fehrat was concerned, he hadn't expected much to come out of the meeting with the old man. As he was crossing through the mobile hallway which connected the plane with the Canadian ground, his wooden leg skidded on the slippery surface and he was saved from a serious fall only by the quick reflexes of a mature gentleman who caught him firmly under the arm. He looked with compassion upon Fehrat's severed limbs, spread his hand out in a sign of greeting and then quickly distanced himself, just as an amateur actor would leave a scene too quickly.

Fehrat knew full well that compassion had a short shelf life. The desire to die quickly and be done with everything returned to him again but since even this decision isn't placed in man's hands, he remembered that he had come to finish two final jobs, after which it wouldn't matter how much longer he would have to look on various expressions of man's humanity.

Days spent with Yudja were truly tiring. Whenever he considered interrupting the old man, he knew that the silence wouldn't make him any more happy. His father's stories didn't raise hope. At times, Yudja resembled the remains of those Patarenian graves which were to be found on the eastern slopes of the Pset highlands, whose time-worn headstones pulsated with fear of the past.

"Often we are mute when faced with the enigmas of nature," thought Fehrat shortly before sinking into sleep. "Perhaps, though, cuckoo birds leave their eggs in strangers' nests just to avenge themselves against unfaithful parents, whom nature didn't endow with an instinct for a family home.?!"

The next morning, the callous interpreter from the Immigration Centre brought him two bits of information: that the financing for the prosthesis had been approved and that the Serbian camp in Keraterm near Priyedor, in Western Bosnia, had been disbanded.

CHAPTER XII

For three days Yudja was seriously ill. He couldn't tell which part of his body was being attacked. He could feel himself rapidly deteriorating. Nausea had entered him; not the nausea in the stomach which sends you rushing to the lavatory and pounds against your temples, but the one which spreads throughout the blood vessels and brings forth wishes to depart from your own body.

Fehrat didn't insist on knowing what was going on with the old man and, without the slightest wish to contradict, accepted the explanation that this was just a wave of mental fire which would pass when the Moon's force subsided. He wasn't surprised by Yudja's somewhat humorous commentary because he was very close to concluding that his father's philosophy was marked by the colours of the cosmic laws in which man, despite being inflated to great proportions from his own point of view, is only an insignificant speck in the universe.

"There is no use in praying when misfortune comes knocking at your door because we are too minute and unimportant. No one could seriously register our prayers," the old man gloomily concluded.

"And tea? Maybe that would help!" Fehrat joined Yudja on the same wavelength of thought.

"Perhaps, but only the one in the yellow box…" Yudja pointed to the shelf where all the plates and glasses were. "It soothes nervous attacks and cleans the blood of sorrow and depression. The recipe is ours, the ingredients are international: buds from young pine, grape concentrate and apple leaves. Strong enough to lessen the aggression even of madmen."

Fehrat's hand stopped just before it reached the yellow box while he tried to decipher the tone in which the old man had just spoken, but he quickly gave that up. It mattered little to him what was in the box, especially if the old man was trying to convince himself that he was something more than an ordinary human being. He knew that people in dire need of victims were apt to turn men into deities. According to that theory, whole nations could be made into victims for the common good of mankind—regardless of the fact that when Ibrahim took his only son to sacrifice before Allah, Mohammed stopped him and told him that Allah would be satisfied with a well-fattened ram. But, the question "Why again…Why all over again…?" tired him even before the water for the tea began to boil.

He later went to the Centre to see about his prosthesis. The following two days also. Yudja was healing himself with his tea and in conversations with Fehrat choosing his words carefully. He had a premonition of something severe and believed that it would also involve him. He wasn't one of those people who believed that an idea would die if it wasn't said aloud but he also wasn't one to stoically wait for someone else to think of it.

On the third day, they read how the Americans would try to save the dignity of the Western powers and that their air force would soon attack the Serb heavy artillery positions in Bosnia.

"They will if someone pays them. Otherwise…The world's humanity has been transformed into dollars." Fehrat spoke bitterly as he skimmed through the newspaper. "We Bosnians aren't important. It is as if we were from some other planet. If our skin was covered in green dollars, only then would we be important."

Thereafter, he spent a long time at the desk writing. When he was finished, he folded the paper and placed it in the breast pocket of his bulky shirt. He waved to Yudja from the entrance door, as one would to an acquaintance passing by in a car, and headed off carefully down the stairs.

"It's him. The plastic operation might have changed some of his features but I know his movements too well," he thought as he walked and swayed down the tree-lined street. "He's probably changed his name but the voice and the foreigner's unmistakable accent will surely give him away. No matter: even if he wanted to he could never change the trembling in his left leg just prior delivering a blow with his right, or the eagle-like screech just before the blunt blow with the elbow to his opponent's Adam's apple."

Again, for the who-knows-how-manyeth time in the last few days, he subjected himself to re-examining the grounds for this identification of his camp torturer and one-time sporting colleague. Fehrat was stubbornly certain that it was he, the very same fellow who was now the karate trainer in the sports hall next to the soccer field, but he kept returning to the evidence at hand and suspiciously scrutinising it. He did not want to make a mistake. A mistake would be intolerable.

He grew fatigued on the way to the sports hall and sat on a wooden bench situated between two thick maple trees. A leaf landed next to him on the bench; ruddy red, unblemished in appearance, a virtual twin to the one on the Canadian flag.

Perhaps the most fortunate are the countries who have incorporated symbols of nature upon their flags—Canada with its maple leaf, Brazil with its coffee bean—he whispered to the leaf mutely keeping him company. But here fortune and misfortune also kept close company, for his thoughts quickly wandered over to the tall cedar of Lebanon and the six *Lillium candidum* flowers on the white, blood-soaked flag of his own country. Looking up at the tree from which the leaf had fallen, he saw its full enormity; the huge branches nearly bare with only a handful of leaves remaining suspended between earth and sky.

Resonant laughter brought him back to the world of the street. A group of young women neared, completely preoccupied with their own amusement. Swinging their sports bags in the air, dressed in fashionable track suits, they radiated elegance and youth. For a split moment, Fehrat imagined himself in their company, in his favorite warm-ups and most comfortable sneakers. The pleasant daydreaming would have lasted longer if his eyes hadn't become fixated somewhere between his wooden leg and their healthy ones. As they approached, the women noticed him devouring them with his eyes. They slowed their pace and the bright skin of their faces shone above their sweat suits like an array of chrysanthemums above a variegated hedge, all the while their healthy hair swaying about their necks.

He stared at them, not comprehending what he was doing, while they stood before the bench, also surprised. One of them, whose eyes were a sparkling deep blue, opened her mouth to unveil a blinding smile, with the same effect as the wind blowing away the clouds to allow the sun's rays to startle all of nature with its intense light.

He welded his eyes upon her as a weak swimmer helpless in deep water seizes upon a life ring. The vision before him returned him to days of youthful bliss, when he also was proud to show off his youth and vitality in the town streets and eagerly registered all of the approving glances which women threw his way. He wished to retain at least that picture from his life's album, and to run away with it somewhere on the coast of the cold northern Pacific, to a well-hidden cave, far from people and all of their eagerness.

Fehrat suddenly extended his hand toward the young woman, at which she started and instinctively jumped back. The others also saw his severed hand and held their sports bags in front of them as if for protection. Realising that they were frightened by the sight of the remains of his hand, he quickly dropped it to his side. The women also dropped their sports bags to their sides and sized him up searchingly, from his wooden leg to his deformed hand. They turned red, as if in sympathy, and tried to look somewhere in between, their eyes like wet sand.

He didn't understand what the one in the middle said, the one who had smiled at him, but gathered that she was trying to apologise. She realised that she was talking to a foreigner, that he didn't understand a word, and smiled again, as if posing for a photographer, as if wanting to leave her smile as a memory.

It dawned on him that it would be wrong to leave them with this impression of him. Taking his crutch, he got up in front of the young women and handed the red maple leaf to the one in the middle.

"C'est pour toi, mademoiselle," he said, demonstratively bowing in front of them.

Surprised at the words and the gift, the woman took the leaf by the stem, showing it to her friends, and responded respectfully:

"*On à pensé que vous êtes Bosniaque, monsieur. Excusez nous, s'il vous plaît.*"

Taking a few steps back, she looked at him directly, and pointing toward the leaf thanked him again:

"*Merci beaucoup, monsieur. Le cadeau est joli. Bonne journée!*"

They moved away, and Fehrat's heart was left to tremble like a chick thrown out of its nest by a strong gust of wind, and falling into a clear field. Everything before him was new and pleasant, and nowhere near him was there a bush or a rock to be seen.

They recognized my status, he whispered to himself, but my tongue surprised them.

He got up to continue on his way when he noticed a second maple leaf lying there on the bench.

"Leaves have already begun to cover you, my Fehrat. Beauty flees at the sight of you while you hand out worthless gifts in Canada. If only that bastard weren't so near…but I'm forced to look at him one more time…" he said to himself as he walked away from the bench.

In the distance, the timepiece on the Lonsdale Square tower indicated that it was three o'clock. Fehrat neared a large, white church. Though clean, its weather-beaten boards showed that time had taken its toll on the edifice. Next to the church was a playing field covered with artificial grass and behind it the sports hall, which looked like a mushroom of steel and glass sitting there in the green field, surrounded by square-cornered concrete structures.

As he dragged his wooden leg and crutch along the tiled sidewalk in front of the house of worship, he remembered how his elders would say that a Muslim could kneel in an Orthodox church, as long as he wiped away the dust from the floor under him, while in other churches he couldn't kneel even if he dug forty metres down.

"And this is how they repaid our feeling of closeness to them. In return for our respect, they butcher and cripple us…" He spoke aloud, at the same time trying to quicken his pace, turning toward the church as if seeking pardon for his unbecoming train of thought.

There was no one in front of the sports hall, only about ten cars in the parking lot.

He lifted the collar of his jacket, took out of his pocket a green camouflage cap which used to be part of a uniform, pulled it down almost to his eyes, clenched his fist and entered the sports hall. >From behind the closed doors, he could hear the sporadic war-like shouts of people training inside. He slowly climbed up the empty bleachers. In the middle of the hall, in front of the students in their white kimonos, stood he. His yellow kimono was decorated with a black belt and his jet black hair immaculately slicked back.

Fehrat descended slowly to the metal railing which separated the upper bleachers from the lower ones. He wished to confirm his discovery one more time, after which he would report the war criminal to the police. For he was not capable of a fair fight with him, a fight to the death. He had concluded also that the propaganda effect would be greater if the criminal was handed over to the police because an international warrant for his arrest had already been issued.

As he sat down and leaned his wooden crutch against the railing in front of him, he had the feeling that in the space of a split second his presence had registered on the criminal's glance. Soaring up high, the karate master then demonstrated a blow to the head of the practice dummy with his right foot thrown from the knee. The students followed suit and began practicing the move.

In his eyes there remains that same beastly shine, Fehrat thought to himself as he followed the instructor's every move. Yellow kimono didn't waste any time on the ceremonial formality of the eyes, deemed meaningful in karate. Instead of the formal glance which suggests helplessness to the opponent and for a moment paralyses his movement, his eyes flashed a spark of bloodlust. The first time that he displayed this barbarian shine in his eyes was when he had the bound Fehrat brought into a large room in the camp were he was demonstrating his bone-breaking skill upon the already mutilated and exhausted inmates.

Fehrat couldn't stop the stream of images which had obsessed him for days, especially their intertwining with the actual everyday world around him. Suddenly, the sports hall transformed itself into the large camp room. The kimono-clad individuals became the guards, dressed in foul and torn makeshift uniforms. Only Damyan, the first assistant to the camp commander, was wearing light army trousers and a blue sports shirt.

The sports hall in Fehrat's mind was infused with the hard-drumming beat of Eastern melodies, and his imagination increased the frequency of its images like a still-camera turned on automatic. The criminal was throwing the inmates, one by one, to the filthy floor, lifting them and, before they could regain consciousness, demonstrating upon them his skill in unleashing a flurry of punches, each harder then the last. When he was done, the lifeless bodies were dragged to a corner of the room and thrown on a stack with others.

Somewhere through the drumming of the music in the sports hall, Fehrat heard the sound of screams from the camp holding room, the shrieks of women being taken away to be raped, the quiet calls of male and female voices inquiring about family members, the whistling and hissing of the drunk guards…

Fragments of his clash with the criminal came back to him like cars passing by on the highway; that hated one's failed attempts to deal a fatal blow to Fehrat's larynx with his elbow and then his heel, and the one decisive strike with the flat palm of his own hand against the criminal's chest, which sent him foaming to the floor. The remaining Chetniks quickly rushed Fehrat, again bound him, dragged him to the medical room, gave him an injection and then, darkness…He remembered that the next thing he saw was clouded by pain in his hand and leg. They had severed half of his limbs. Before his eyes appeared the criminal, an enormous figure who shoved under his nose the greying remains of his fist, and hissed:

"Death would have been too easy. You are going to live, champion!"

His ears noted a change in the musical rhythm and his eyes focused on the sports hall. Below, the students were practicing their jumps, kicks and flexibility against invisible opponents. The yellow kimono wandered among them, offering brief advice or criticism.

"It *is* him", whispered Fehrat to himself. "Aziz was right when he told me in Zagreb that Damyan had fled to Canada. After all of the atrocities and the plunder, it makes sense that he would now want to settle down. Instinct has brought me to him…as my wishes brought me to Yudja."

Momentarily off guard, he realised that there was no yellow kimono in sight in the sports hall. In a panic, he looked everywhere for the easily distinguished figure. As he strained his neck muscles in vain, an unmistakable gust of cold air from behind turned his blood to ice.

"You again, my adversary," observed a whisper behind his ear.

No such scene existed in Fehrat's script. He decided to remain calm.

"What in the world would make you want to follow me here? Fate… You would have been better off if you had wrapped yourself around a poisonous snake!"

He paused to allow Fehrat an opportunity to speak, but. Fehrat remained silent.

"Or…maybe you came to thank me for saving your other hand and leg? If it wasn't for me, you would have been without all of them."

Fehrat slowed his breathing to a minimum and his eyes wandered around the sports hall. There was no one else in the bleachers, while on the floor the students continued their exercises.

"Perhaps I'm mistaken, sir? Perhaps you are not that Muslim cripple, Fehrat?"

He had changed his tone and now pretended he was speaking to an over-sensitive child.

"Because, if you are, I am prepared to buy you all of the necessary prostheses so that you can move around like a man in this great big world of ours."

Fehrat's head jerked back slightly and he began to flex the fingers on his healthy hand.

"Let me see who you are!" the criminal demanded sarcastically while he grabbed Fehrat's head and abruptly twisted it around.

Their eyes met, glued to one another. Fehrat summoned every ounce of strength to remain calm. He acted disinterested, just as he had prior to delivering the lightning blow with the flat of his palm to the chest.

Damyan became playful. Squeezing Fehrat's head with his sweaty hands, he whispered into his ear:

"Don't ask me to tell you what happened to your mother. Topina and I gave her a decent burial. I was worried if we didn't bury her, those filthy animals would rape her corpse or the starving dogs would tear her to bits…"

Fehrat's muscles tightened like the strings on a guitar. He tried to pretend he didn't hear what he'd just heard but the biceps of his right arm were expanding and his head was uncontrollably heating up.

"So…aren't you going to thank me?" the fiend hissed schizophrenically and the students in the sports hall immediately stopped to see what was going on up in the bleachers.

Thereafter, everything developed contrary to Fehrat's plans. His right hand shot back, caught Damyan by the neck and flung him on top of the concrete wall in front of him. But Damyan was prepared. Quickly regaining his concentration, his left leg firmly planted, he delivered a powerful blow with the right one against Fehrat's chest, mowing him down like a blade of grass and sending him sprawling between the wall and first row of chairs.

The students on the floor, finally realising that their instructor was involved in a full-contact fight, ran toward the two.

Damyan refused to allow Fehrat to get up from the concrete surface. Jumping high, he landed with his right heel striking directly against Fehrat's chest, the left heel immediately followed suit. Leaning against the wall, looking down at the helpless man on the floor, his students watching in frozen shock, Damyan leapt into horizontal flight and quickly jolted his feet forward in time to bury them in his victim's chest like a Peruvian fighting cock when he strikes out with his spurs against an opponent. In a moment, a split second of exploding pain, Fehrat flung like arrows the remains of his left hand and left leg toward the criminal's chest. Again and again he did this. And then nothing…A frightful silence followed…broken bones in both bodies, a deathly rattle, both men twitching to free themselves from the other's fighting embrace…and, slowly, both did.

When the students separated them, they saw that the old suture scars on their instructor's face had burst and blood was slowly tricking out of his mouth in rhythm with the slowing beat of his heart.

"I had no choice…" Damyan forced the words out through the foam and blood in his mouth. "They found out that I'm Osman's bastard… Bastard of that horned Devil…"

The words died with Damyan.

Those nearest to the two men lying on the cold cement noticed Damyan's futile attempts to stretch his hand closer to Fehrat. Nevertheless, they remained near to one another yet at the same time so far that all the humanity of earthly civilizations could never bring them together. Civilizations of wars, killings…Humanity on the border of lethal hatred…

Damyan's heels had broken most of Fehrat's ribs and shattered both lobes of the lungs. Several times, Fehrat tried to say something by motioning with his eyes toward the dead trainer but it was evident that death had already begun to rule over his own body.

The frightened students immediately called for an ambulance and the police. For them, the confrontation, despite all of its drama, was devoid of a human element. But after that fighting they called it "the Balkan hug".

Two policemen came to get Yudja and from all that they said to him he understood that he had to go with them because something had just happened to a man with a missing arm and leg.

In the sports hall, along with the karate students, were people from emergency services and, of course media reporters. Yudja also immediately noticed the repulsive interpreter from the Immigration Centre. As soon as she spotted him, she walked over and explained to him that she had already told the people present that the man without the hand and leg was a Bosnian Muslim and that he had come to Canada in order to receive the necessary rehabilitation treatment.

Yudja remained silent and tried to comprehend what had happened. Glumly holding on to the chair next to the dead Fehrat, he looked down, eyes wide open, waiting for the dead man to tell him how he came to be that way.

All eyes were turned inquisitively toward Yudja. Only the photographers were doing their job.

Leaning over Fehrat, Yudja threw a glance toward the man lying dead nearer the wall. Reaching to wipe the blood from Fehrat's mouth and nose, he was stopped by the hand of a policeman who said something that Yudja did not care to understand. Everything was becoming clearer. He was looking into Fehrat's disbelieving eyes and through them issued a reproach for having placed him in this situation. He was then pained by the thought that Fehrat had come to North Vancouver because of the other dead man and he, Yudja, had only served as a smoke-screen. As he lifted his head toward the policeman, the interpreter tried to help:

"The gentleman would like to know…" she began, but Yudja stopped her with his outstretched hand and turned toward the policeman and spoke in understandable French:

"I do not understand this woman. She does not speak a language that I understand."

Stopping long enough for the policeman to gather his concentration, he inquired, "Do you understand me?"

"Yes. I know some French," accepted the policeman and in turn inquired, "Do you know these two men, sir?"

"Yes…" quietly answered the old man, his glance returning toward Fehrat. After a lengthy pause, taking a deep breath, he continued: "This one I know quite well and that one I don't know personally but I am quite certain I know which tribe he belongs to. May I take a look?" he asked, pointing down toward Fehrat's lifeless body.

The policeman was surprised, but approved the request with a simple nod of his head.

Yudja opened Fehrat's coat and out of the shirt pocket took some papers. One contained writing on both sides. He read slowly. His breathing grew faster and then, with a shaking hand, he began rubbing his eyes. He read the note several times, lifting his head toward the high steel rafters of the sports hall only to bring it back down again. Each time he came to the same conclusion—that between him and the one to whom he had been pouring out his heart existed an immobile metal construction. Handing the paper to the policeman, he declared, as if speaking before a grand jury:

"This is an indictment against that one over there. Now I know both of them well."

Walking over to Fehrat's other side, he lifted the dead man's mutilated limbs.

"That one lying over there did this to him while he was a prisoner in the Serbian concentration camp near Priyedor, in Bosnia…On the piece of paper are listed these and other charges against your karate trainer."

Yudja paused long enough to observe Damyan's sprawled corpse. Even though death had already given him various shades of blue and yellow, he could recognize in him Dmitar's wide, rounded nose and split cleft of the chin…For a moment, it seemed to him that Damyan's face also had many of Osman's features, but by force of will he freed himself of any such ideas.

"Yes…And you welcomed this man to your country; him and his money, money stolen from those he murdered, tortured, humiliated… You offered him a hiding place and what's more, employed him as a karate trainer, so he could demonstrate daily how he beat to death helpless inmates in some God-forsaken place most of you have never heard of until now, in Bosnia…"

He spoke slow and grammatically incorrect French but the policeman and most of the media present understood him well enough.

Pointing toward a second paper, he said: "This is for me."

Quietly, like a man communicating with an object of his faith, Yudja whispered:

"You could have asked me," speaking directly to dead Fehrat's corpse, "I would have told you…I meant to suggest it myself…But you didn't give me enough time." The old man stuttered as he spoke, staring directly into Fehrat's wide-open pupils.

"May I look again?…" He turned toward the policeman and pointed at the dead man in front of him.

Tears trickled down the time-worn lines on his face and his entire body radiated a sorrow which was searching for solitude and answers to his most intimate questions.

The policemen approved the request, nodding their heads and shrugging their shoulders.

Yudja unbuttoned Fehrat's shirt, pulled his pants down past the hips and searched along the left, then right, sides. From his temples down a nervous twitch began to spread which kept rhythm with his pulsating blood. Simultaneously his eyes were struck by a wave of heat, the intensity of which burned in his eyeballs like a western sky just before sunset.

"He too, like Osman, has a mark on his left hip," he whispered, gasping for air. "Here also that Devil has made his mark…He has taken him from me also!"

Quickly scanning around the faces gathered near him, around the sports hall and the audience in the spectator seats which was conspicuously absent, Yudja's eyes eventually focused upon the dead war criminal. He seemed to be resting in peace. After pulling Fehrat's pants back up and tidying his shirt, Yudja stood up and responded to the questioning stares in a rough, proud voice, as if he had just retrieved it somewhere out of times long gone and almost forgotten:

"Let each rock return to its boulder, each ash to its dust!"

The cameras were filming and the journalists were writing.

"According to the Bosnian horoscope, which our elders preserved from their ancient ancestors and passed down from mouth to mouth, this one here was born under the sign of the stone and served others so they could bring down fruit from the trees…And that one over there was born under the sign of ash, which brings fire with it from the distant past and burns whenever the wheat is brought in and the storehouses are full. Those with the sign of the stone are thrown through history like cuckoo birds bouncing from nest to nest. As soon as they are hatched and are wearing their feathers, others begin to peck away at them, as though they didn't even belong to the bird family."

"What is the name of this one which you say is yours?" asked the policeman, on whom Yudja just now noticed an unusually long nose and a large mole just above the left side of his lip.

"What is his name…?" The question drummed through Yudja's head as if it had just been shouted down a long, empty hallway. For some time now he had been trying to think of a way to suggest to Fehrat that he accept his family name and thus correct the injustice which had been done to the two of them, but now the policeman's question cut through his chest like a sharp knife. Something in him burst like a watery bladder and an icy liquid spread throughout his body.

"Now it would be an empty victory. A victory in honor of my ego" he thought to himself as he looked at Fehrat's greying face. "No…One gesture cannot make up for all the misfortune and injustice I've caused him throughout his life…"

"Fehrat…" he said slowly, turning his head toward the policeman and the others gathered around. "He is Fehrat Bosniak…Same given name as my Father…May both of them have an easier time in the next world than they had in this one!"

After Fehrat's death, Yudja crawled even deeper under his blanket and with greater energy tried to convince himself that he needed to dig his head so deep that eventually he might come across an opening through which he would be able, without waiting for Allah's judgment, to escape this world. Several times he was almost certain that he could see an opening somewhere in the foggy distance, but each time some magnetic force pulled him back. Whenever he came out from under the blanket, he handled each figurine, one by one, and carved new features on each. Thus, for who knows which time, they changed shape and meaning. The figurine of the ghastly colossus, like the Patarenian markings at the corners of the Psetian highland, the one with the screaming scars in the corners of his forehead, remained unfinished.

Fehrat was buried several days later in the city cemetery. Yudja, in accordance with the custom of the day, threw a handful of dirt on the casket before it was lowered. All the expenses were paid by the Immigration Centre with money that was originally approved for Fehrat's prostheses.

That same day, the karate trainer was also buried.

"Both have gone to God so that he may weigh them on the scales of truth and divine justice," Yudja said to himself as he walked out through the large iron cemetery gate.

The sun shone upon the city which would be Fehrat's final resting place but its rays were cold. That night, the ocean rose up against the coast and lashed out against the containers waiting for their ships in the harbour.

Yudja was woken up the next morning by the sound of sparrows from the other side of the window.

"Just like at home," the old man thought to himself as his head emerged from under the blanket. "Storms at night, followed by singing sparrows in the morning."

The next couple of days Yudja was tormented by a pain which had taken hold of his chest. He lost sight of time and the only things which shared those four walls and the ceiling with him were the wooden figurines and Fehrat's note. He looked at the carvings and read the paper and it began to seem to him like this was in fact his entire life, full of painful incompletions, beginnings with endings under someone else's direction, questions which seemed like strange answers, like the audacity of a man to enter the space between birth and death. Fehrat's question in the note, it was becoming clear, wasn't directed at him. It was an enigma taken from the core of life and each individual would interpret it with a great deal of personal bias.

Time no longer meant anything to him. Space neither. Everything was there, in the room. Like falling into quicksand, the less you resist, the longer you will last.

When he heard the knock on the door, fear immediately rushed at him. He felt wounded that they were so senselessly disturbing him. He opened the door in time to see the building manager's back as she walked down the stairs. On the floor he found a letter. It was from Alma, from America.

Yudja was overcome by a desire to free himself of the walls which surrounded him, painted with deafening pain. He wished to read the letter somewhere where life could still be felt. He got dressed and went out with the unopened letter in his pocket.

On the same slope where Yudja and Fehrat once sat and talked, the ocean was tirelessly pounding against the shore. Several seagulls circled overhead, waiting for the water to retreat and leave the odd fish stranded along the jagged coast.

Yudja resisted the heavy winds and felt a physical release, like before, when he was young and his father and mother sat together at the dinning table and each in their own way prayed for the happiness of their two sons. It seemed he could catch the scent of ripe peaches through the slightly opened window and, miraculously, nothing changed the instant that he realised that since that day an entire human era had elapsed.

His feeling of comfort increased when he read that Alma had met a good man from Bosnia and that they would be married when Yudja joined them. The letter also contained a form which he needed to take to the American consulate, so that he could receive the necessary papers to enter the country.

"Now America...," he whispered quietly, and a new wave of comfort entered his body. "Happiness must be there if my Alma calls me...Delveta...Perhaps we will all meet there and start a new life?... Perhaps my fields are there...and that sweet-smelling peach tree which took over the entire house each autumn? At least I should leave these memories...Maybe I will find instead the world without killing, and sweet scents of my youth..."

He felt comfort spread needling along his body and the picture of the open ocean was beginning to melt before his eyes. He didn't feel the blow like a headbutt into the wrinkles of the thick arteries, nor notice the crude odour which spread under his core.

ENDNOTES

BOSNIAKS—Bosnians, mostly Muslims, under that name from last decade of 20th century. Their ancestors (before then Bosnian Kingdom was occupied by Ottoman Empery in the middle of 15th century) were Bosnians, Christians, mostly Bosnian Bogumils, or Patarens. That Christian sect was across centuries attacked and terrorised by neighboring Catholic and Orthodox armies. That was one of reasons why they mostly accepted Islam under Turkish oppression.

BOSNIAN SERBS—They are Bosnian citizens, mostly Orthodox Christians.

BOSNIAN CROATS—They are Bosnian citizens, mostly Catholic Christians.

CHETNIKS—were Serbian nationalist and monarchist paramilitary organisations from the first half of the 20th century, formed as a Serbian resistance against the Ottoman Empire 1n 1904. In the Second World War they collaborated with Hitler-Mussolini occupational armies and satellite governments on the territory of Yugoslavia. Chetniks were partner in the pattern of terror and counter terror against Croats, Muslims and Partisans and their supporters. In the last Balkan wars in Bosnia and Croatia Chetniks were monstrous killers and genocide executors.

BOSHNYO—insulting name for Bosnian Muslims.

GOLI OTOK (Barren Island)—Throughout World War I, Austria-Hungary sent Russian prisoners of war from Eastern front to Goli Otok. From 1949 to 1956 that was top secret prison and labor camp created from Yugoslav authorities. During Informbiro period in Yugoslavia it was used to incarcerate political prisoners, known or alleged Stalinists or sympathisers of Soviet Union.

VLAH—insulting name for Bosnian Serbs, remain after Turkish occupation.

Turk (Turtchin)—insulting name for Bosnian Muslims, remain after Turkish occupation.

BATTLE OF KOSOVO—took place between 1389 between the army led by Serbian Prince Lazar Hrebljanovic and the invading army of the Ottoman Empire under the leadership of Sultan Murat I. After that battle Ottoman Empire occupied Serbia.

BASH CHELIK—folk story about bad prince and good hero.

TUDJMAN, MILOSEVIC, IZETBEGOVIC—leaders of Croatia, Serbia and Bosnia-Herzegovina responsible for secret arrangements about division of Bosnia-Herzegovina and for war in that central Yugoslavian republic (1992-1995).

GIMNASIUM—high schools on the territory of former Yugoslavia without specialisation. When you finish it, you can chose every single specialisation on universities.

MOMCILO DJUJIC—Lieder of Chetniks during the Second World War in parts of Croatia with mostly Serb population.

FINISH KALEVALA—The Kalevala is a 19th century work of epic poetry compiled by Elias Lonnrot from Finish and Karelian oral folklore and mythology. It regarded as the national epic of Finland and is one of the most significant works of Finish literature.

BOGUMILS (Patarens)—Christian sect in Balkans, especially in todays Bulgaria, Macedonia, Dalmatia, Bosnia-Herzegovina, Italy, France and England (11th to 15th century). They were rejecting the ecclesiastical hierarchy, and their primary political tendencies were resistance to the state and Churches authorities. They didn't have churches, priests, cross and they preferring to perform rituals outdoors. On Balkans the sect disappeared in 15th century under attacks of Ottoman Empire and Islam.

KUNA—Croatian currency established 1994, after disintegration of Yugoslavia and creation Republic Croatia. Before that time, Kuna was official currency of Ustasha's Independent State of Croatia (1941-1945).

The GUSLE—is a single stringed musical instrument traditionally used in the Dinarides region of the Balkans.

BEG (The Bey)—In Ottoman Empire the title "Bey" came to be applied to subordinate military and administrative officers. Bey has also been used as an aristocratic title in various Turkish states, even in Bosnia.

USTASHA—Ustasha—Croatian Revolutionary Movement was established 1933 as a Croatian Fascist movement. Its ideology was a blend of Nazism and Croatian nationalism. Before World War II, Ustasha's movement functioned as a terrorist organisation, but in 1941 they were appointed the rule a part of Axis-occupied Yugoslavia as the Independent State of Croatia. Ustashas are responsible for terror and holocaust in that Nazi satellite state over Serbs, Jews and Gipsies.

BLACK FRIDEY—In central parts of Balkans that means the day when everybody is going to be punished for bad works in a life.

SDS—Serbian Democratic Party in Bosnia-Herzegovina formed 1989 by Radovan Karadzic, accused for war crimes and genocide against Bosniaks and Croats, led Bosnian Serbs into the biggest crime and holocaust in Europe after Second World War.

SLIVOVITZA—Plum brandy in Balkan countries.

NDH—Independent State of Croatia during Second World War.

MUSAF—Muslim's prayer book.

ZAGORAC—Inhabitant of North-Western part of Croatia.

BERGE-ISTRA—one of the biggest cargo ships in the world, built in Croatian shipyard Uljanik in the port city Pula 1972, for Norwegian company Sig. Bergesen, exploded and went to the bottom of the Pacific ocean with secret cause of tragedy. Four years later the other, similar one, Berge-Vanga, disappeared on the same way.

CHERKESSIANS—Inhabitants of Russian Cherkessian Republic on Kavkas region.

DRAZA MIHAILOVIC—Dragoljub "Draza" Mihailovic was a Yugoslav Serbian general during Second World War. As a royalist, right after Hitler's occupation of Yugoslavia, 1941, he organised bands of guerrillas known as the Chetniks against the occupation forces. Later, his movement lost right way and its groups started to collaborate or established "modus vivendi" with Axis powers. They committed many ethnic massacres in the nationalistic role and collaboration with fascists. Draza Mihailovic was tried and convicted of high treason and war crimes by the authorities of Tito's Yugoslavia and executed by firing squad 1946.